QUEEN OF BLOOD AND STARDUST

KAITLYN SWANSON

First Editon March 2024

Ebook ISBN: 979-8-9894941-0-1
Paperback ISBN: ISBN: 979-8-9894941-2-5

Edited by Caitlin Lengerich
Cover by Moonpress Design | *www.moonpress.co*
Map by Lindsey Staton (@honeyy.fae)

kaitlynswansonbooks.com

To the writers who think they're not good
enough to write that book.
I did it.
You can too.

A NOTE TO READERS

This book contains content that may be sensitive to some readers. Please read through the following content warnings before reading.

This book contains themes of death, grief, loss of a parent, loss of a sibling, alcohol use, talk of substance abuse, mention of suicidal thoughts, attempted sexual assault, blood, gore, violence, explicit sexual content, and vulgar language.

Lethenia

Abode Mountains

Aqua Court

Star Court

Lunar Court

Twilight Court

Mystic Court

Blood Court

Court of Embers

Alethens

Salacia

Janara

Cel Nox

Verbial

Arcadia

Seer

Thyrinian

Ignis Mountains

PRONUNCIATION GUIDE

Characters and Creatures

Alvise (Al-vez-aye)
Arlo Rossi (are-lo Ross-e)
Astria (As-tree-uh)
Bram Adair (Br-am Ah-dare)
Caio (Kay-oh)
Caterina Ambrose (Cat-er-een-uh Am-br-oh-z)
Cecelia (Suh-seel-lee-uh)
Declan Hale (Dec-lin H-ale)
Elena Adair (E-lain-uh Ah-dare)
Este Rossi (Es-tee Ross-e)
Enric (En-rick)
Gulia (jule-e-uh)
Hecate (Hec-caught-ay)
Hellhound (Hel H-ow-nd)
Kahle (Kay-l)
Kara Adair (Car-ah Ah-dare)
Lennox Adair (Len-nex Ah-dare)
Lorenzo Rossi (Lore-en-zo Ross-e)
Loris Driscoll (Lor-es Dr-is-cull)

Luciana Ambrose (Loos-see-an-uh Am-br-oh-z)
Luka Rossi (Luke-uh Ross-e)
Mara Rossi (Mare-uh Rosse-e)
Nico Elsher (Nee-ko El-sh-er)
Nol Adair (N-ole Ah-dare)
Odin (Oh-din)
Olexa (Oh-lex-uh)
Quade (Ashford) Rossi (Qu-ay-d A-sh-f-or-d Ross-e)
Wampus Cat: (Wom-pus Cat)
Zola (Zole-uh)

Places
Continent of Lethenia
7 Courts and their Capitol Cities

Lethenia (Leh-then-ee-uh)
    Star Court: Alethens (Ah-leh-thee-ens)
    Blood Court: Cel Nox (Sell-nox)
    Twilight Court: Verbial (Verb-al)
    Lunar Court: Janara (Jan-are-uh)
    Mystic Court: Arcadia (Arc-ay-de-uh)
    Aqua Court: Salacia (Sa-lay-see-uh)
    Court of Embers: Thyrinian (Thigh-rin-e-in)
    Abode Mountians: (Ah-bo-dee)

PROLOGUE

No one tells you what it sounds like when you kill someone.

They will teach you all the ways to kill, but until you've done it, nothing will prepare you for the sound your dagger makes as it pierces flesh and bone—the distinctive crack of bone and squelch of blood as you remove your weapon from your victim.

No amount of training prepares you for that moment.

This moment.

Warm blood dripped down my fingers as the male stumbled back, his pale, veiny hand removing my dagger from his stomach and tossing it to the side. The clang of the dagger landing on the floor cleaved through the silence of my bedchamber.

"You little bitch," the male snarled, revealing two elongated canines.

No. Not canines.

Fangs.

A vampire.

My heart raced. I didn't know where he came from, but I did know one thing: he wanted me dead. That much was clear when I woke to him sneaking into my room. I'd never been more grateful my father made me sleep with a dagger under my pillow. I used the element of surprise, and my years of training, to my advantage, shoving my dagger into his side before he realized I was awake. But my advantage was gone. I had to be quick, quicker than a vampire with its enhanced speed.

The vampire reached for me but I ducked out of his reach, sliding off my bed and under his outstretched arms. I lunged for my sword in the corner of my chambers—my hand closing around the pommel as I was yanked back. A frustrated scream tore from my throat as the vampire pulled me firmly against him. *Damn vampire speed.* I thrashed violently in his arms, trying to find purchase as he pinned my hands to my sides, rendering my magic useless. The warm blood from his wound soaked into the thin fabric of my nightgown with every movement causing the fabric to stick to my skin.

If only I could thrust my elbow into his injured side. But the way he held my arms made it difficult to move my arms at all.

I attempted to twist out of his hold, still gripping my sword in the hand pinned to my side.

"Now, be a good little princess and drop the sword before I sink my fangs into that pretty little neck of yours and drain every last drop of blood from your body."

His words turned my blood cold, knowing he would most likely drink from me whether I cooperated or not.

"Not a chance," I ground out. This was not how I was going to die.

I attempted to wriggle my arms loose again and he made good on his threat.

A scream of agony tore from my throat as his fangs pierced the side of my neck. My sword fell to the ground as blinding hot pain ripped through me. I continued to thrash in his arms as he drained the blood from my body. My fight growing weaker with every swallow—my consciousness waning.

No amount of training could prepare me for *this*.

This was it.

This was how I was going to die.

No. Tears pricked at the corners of my eyes, my vision blurring.

And then I was falling. I landed in a heap on the floor—mind swimming, darkness swirling in my vision at the loss of blood. I heard fighting coming from somewhere in the room, but I couldn't make sense of anything. I blinked rapidly, trying to clear the fog from my brain. I closed my eyes and took several deep breaths—feeling the warmth of my magic as it worked through my body—my strength and consciousness returning with every breath.

When I opened my eyes everything was clear again. The vampire who attacked me was laying in a pool of blood on the floor next to me—his lifeless eyes staring back at me.

I swallowed a scream as I scrambled away from him, fumbling for my sword.

Where had it landed?

My magic rushed back into my fingertips begging to be let out as a cloaked figure stepped out from the shadows.

"Lennox! It's me." Relief washed over me at the familiar calming voice.

"Olexa?"

"Yes, Princess, it's me." My nursemaid removed her hood as she stepped into the light. Her dark hair was pulled back at the nape of her neck, with several pieces falling loose around her face. She kneeled next to me, gently placing a russet hand on my shoulder, before surveying the wound where the vampire had bit me, her dark brows furrowed as she took it in. The wound had not yet healed itself as my body's natural healing abilities were focused on replenishing the extreme blood loss.

"Are you okay?" she asked.

No, I was not okay, but I needed to be. I needed to figure out what in the Goddess's name was going on.

She placed two fingers on the wound as she murmured under her breath, and her magic rushed through my body. When she removed her fingers I moved my hand to my neck to find the wound completely healed, only smooth, healed skin remained.

"You're a witch," I whispered. She only nodded as she stood and offered her hand to me. I took it and followed her as she guided me to sit on the bed next to her.

"Olexa, what's going on?"

"We don't have much time my dear, I need you to listen to me—I need you to trust me." Her gray eyes shone with fear as she clasped her hands in mine. "You need to go. You need to find Kara, and you need to get to the safe room. *Now*. You don't have much time." The panic rose inside me at her words, while my magic climbed to the surface of my shaking hands.

There must be more vampires in the palace.

"What about Mother, Father? What about Nol? What about everyone else?" I gripped her hands tighter, I couldn't go hide and leave them behind. "If there are more vampires we need to go and help."

I stood, making my way to where my sword lay discarded on the floor next to the dead vampire.

"Lennox, you need to listen to me. I fear it may be too late for them."

I froze, flames threatening to spill from my fingertips. My magic was harder to control when my emotions ran high, it responded to my emotions like a wave, cresting and crashing in the blink of an eye. I took a deep breath, balling my hands into fists as I willed my flames back to me.

"It might be too late for them, but it's not too late for you and Kara."

I turned slowly to face Olexa—her face was leached of all color.

"What do you mean it's too late for them?" The words felt like lead as they left my mouth.

"It may be too late for them, but it's not too late for you and Kara. If you leave now and get her to safety, you will survive. I have seen it."

"You've seen it? Wait, you're a Seer?" My head swam at the realization. My nursemaid, who had taken care of me and my siblings our entire lives, was a witch *and* a Seer.

"Yes, but I do not have time to explain, you need to go. *Now!*" Olexa pleaded, pulling me towards the closet in the corner of my room. "Or it will be too late for you as well." The lantern lit up her dark face as she turned to me once again, I could see the fear in her eyes—begging me to head to her instructions.

"I don't understand." The words caught in my throat. How could I leave my parents and Nol? It went against everything I had ever been taught. I was supposed to be a fighter, not a coward who hid from monsters and let others fight my battles for me.

Olexa held my face in her hands as she continued to speak. "I know you don't, my dear, but please listen to me. Please trust me at this moment. It will all make sense later."

And I did trust her—Olexa, the female who cared deeply for my siblings and me all our lives, loving and caring for us as her own. I had no reason *not* to trust her.

"If you do not go now, there is only darkness in the future. No light. *You* are the light. The future depends on you, Lennox." Her words were a plea, but nothing she was saying made any sense. The panic started to take over my body, so I squeezed my eyes shut, taking several breaths to steady myself.

"Please," Olexa pleaded.

I nodded. "Okay, yes, I'll go."

I didn't trust many people, but I trusted Olexa. There was something much bigger going on, but all I could do right now was heed her warning and make sure Kara was safe.

Her arms were suddenly around me, enveloping me in a hug. I wrapped my arms around her as she squeezed me tight. "Serving you and your family has been one of my life's greatest treasures," she whispered into my ear before pulling back and holding my face in her hands. "I love you, Lennox."

"I love you too, Olexa." Tears glistened in her eyes and I felt them pooling in my own. This felt like a goodbye; I could only pray to the Goddess it wasn't.

"Tell your sister I love her too."

"I will."

"Now go, My Queen," she said as she opened the closet door and pushed me inside.

"Wait, my sword." I rushed back through the room and picked up Minerva before grabbing my sheath from where it lay discarded in the corner. Olexa watched me in silence, tears streaming down her face as I made my way back to the closet, with Minerva now sheathed at my side. Screams rang out in the distance as I entered the closet, and Olexa sucked in a breath at the sound.

"Quickly now, Lennox. Get Kara to the safe room as fast as you can."

Before I could respond she closed the door and I was bathed in darkness.

☪

"Kara, get up," I whispered as I shook my younger sister lightly.

"Len? What's going on, what are you doing here?" she mumbled as she sat up and rubbed the sleep from her eyes.

"I don't have time to explain, I'll tell you everything later, but we need to go—*now*." I pulled back the sheets and grabbed her arm—her eyes widened as she took me in. I'm sure I looked ridiculous standing in her bedroom in a nightgown with a sword sheathed at my side.

"Lennox, what happened? Are you okay?" It was because of the panic in her voice that I remembered I was covered in blood.

"I'm fine, it's not my blood." Not most of it anyway. Her eyes widened further, and she opened her mouth to speak, but I interrupted her.

"I'll explain on the way, but we have to go to the safe room —*now*."

Kara nodded, she knew as well as I did that the safe room was a last resort. Kara was smart, more trusting than I, and didn't ask any more questions as she grabbed her dagger from beneath her pillow and followed me towards her closet. Once we were both inside I closed the door and willed a small ball of fire into my palm as Kara and I felt around the walls of the closet for the hidden panel that would open to the safe room.

Every room in the palace had a door leading to the safe room, only a few members of the staff knew about them outside our immediate family. I only hoped we'd find the rest of our family waiting for us once we got there.

My hands found the sunken panel and I elbowed Kara to get her attention. We both placed our hands on the panel and a tingling sensation made its way through my palm and up my arm as a dim orb of yellow light illuminated around our palms before we heard a sharp *click*. The wall shifted in front of us revealing a door.

We slipped inside the passage and quickly sealed the door behind us before wandering the hallways, the only light was the small ball of fire in my palm until we made it to the door to the main room of the safe room.

We placed our hands on the door, the magic recognizing us once again, opening to reveal the main room. With the flick of my fingers, I lit the room—the empty bulbs around the room now dancing with my flames, illuminating the room in a dim light. I scanned the tables and couches, my chest deflating at the sight of the empty space

Olexa said it might be too late for Mother, Father, and Nol, but I wasn't going to believe that so quickly—they could still make it here. Olexa had to have gone to warn them next, we just needed to give them more time. I willed my anxious thoughts to still as Kara and I collapsed onto the couch.

"Now will you please tell me what's happening?" Kara

asked, looking at me, there was fear in her emerald eyes that matched my own. I pulled a blanket over us and wrapped my arm around her, pulling her close as I told her everything Olexa had told me.

"I don't know what's going on, but it's not good. Even my magic is on alert," I admitted.

"Mine too," she added.

We sat in silence, her head on my shoulder as we stared at the door, willing it to open and for our parents and Nol to walk through it.

A gasp slipped from my lips as white light burst from my chest—my back arching off the couch as magic ripped through me. I clutched a hand to my chest, a burning sensation ripping through my skin where the light was emulating from. It felt like magic—a burst of power far greater than I had ever experienced. The sensation worked its way through my body, from the tips of my toes to my fingertips until it shifted, no longer like a burning flame, but cleansing. The unfamiliar magic continued to rush through my body, melding with my own until the two became one.

"What's happening? Len? Lennox? Are you okay?" Kara asked, her voice shaking as she stood from the couch. "You're glowing."

I looked at my hands, white light was emulating from my entire body now. A light wind whipped around my head blowing my hair around my face.

"What's going on?" Kara asked, the fear in her voice was clear and I could sense her magic threatening to make an appearance.

"I don't know." I panted, trying to catch my breath as the flow of power stopped. I felt a sense of peace wash over me— the magic brimming at my fingertips felt stronger.

I looked to find Kara staring at me wide-eyed.

"You have a crown." The words were hardly a whisper.

I reached up and took the crown from my head. It was a

delicate silver crown with a blush undertone, its shape was made up of lines that looked like flowers, flames, tiny cresting waves, and swirls of wind intertwined between delicate twigs. Tiny stars were placed throughout, each with different colored gems adorning them.

It was beautiful and vaguely familiar.

A crown representing the four elements and the seven courts. The pieces of the puzzle started clicking together. Stories in ancient textbooks flooded the forefront of my mind.

An excess flow of magic.

White light emulating from the heir.

A crown made of the elements the new monarch wields.

No.

No. No. *No.*

Fear seized my body, squeezing my heart until it threatened to burst.

"Kara. I—" The words stuck in my throat. I'd only ever read about this event in books—heard the stories of the transfer of power from centuries ago.

It couldn't be.

"Kara, does what happened sound like The Dunami?"

I saw the moment my words registered in Kara's mind. Her face paled as she blinked at me, tears rolling down her cheeks. I held back a sob as the crown in my hands shook violently. *My crown.*

If what I experienced *was* The Dunami it meant I was now the High Queen of Lethenia and all power from the previous ruler had been transferred over to me.

But if I was now the High Queen, that meant my father, my mother, and my brother were all dead.

1

LENNOX

Two Years Later

The clang of steel rang in my ears as I blocked Enric's blow, forcing him to take a step back. He gritted his teeth and lunged for me again. I waited a second, letting him get close, before I raised my sword and blocked his next advance. He stumbled back, tripping over his own feet. My sword, Minerva, glowed in satisfaction at the blow—my magic swirling inside my blade.

"Again," I barked. "This time make sure your stance is strong before you strike." I planted my feet and he copied the movement, frustration and determination written on his face.

"Again." He took two steps forward and hesitated, his eyes flashed to my left side before he struck. I blocked the blow easily, letting him land the next blow before counter-striking, allowing our blades to dance for several beats.

I turned slightly at the sound of the door opening, finding Kara walking into the training center. *Why in the Goddess is she here?* I turned my attention back to Enric, disarming him with two swift moves. His sword fell to the floor with a clang.

"You're getting sloppy, Enric." I nodded towards Kara. "I'll find you later to debrief about today's session. In the meantime, keep practicing your positions; you still have to think before you strike. You need those positions to be muscle memory."

He nodded and bowed slightly. "Thank you, Your Majesty."

I smiled tightly at his use of my formal title. He moved to put his sword back on the rack, bowing to Kara before exiting the training facility.

I wiped the sweat from my brow with the back of my sleeve as I sipped the water from my canteen. Kara remained silent, an incredulous look on her face as she assessed me.

"What?" I pressed. My sister shook her head, a smile creeping up her face.

"I don't know whether to berate Enric for letting you beat him so easily, or you for going so hard on the youngling."

"He's not a kid, Kara. He's a soldier in the Royal Guard." I winced. *A sixteen-year-old kid in the Royal Guard.* The majority of Alethens forces were killed in the vampire attack two years ago. Replenishing the Guard has been a hard task—many don't want to risk their lives after the vampire attack. The ones that are willing, like Enric, are too young to know what they're getting themselves into. Which is why I spend an hour, three times a week, training him.

Once he becomes sufficient enough I'll take on another student. Though Captain Kahle would have a fit if he knew what I was doing, but I was queen, and my word ruled all. It was the Captain of the Royal Guard's own fault for not letting me help train the guards in the first place.

"*The Royal Guard is no place for the queen,*" he argued.

He said the same thing when I was an eighteen-year-old princess entering the Guard, but I didn't let him get away with it then.

I had bigger battles to wage now. My career as a Royal Guard ended the moment the crown of High Queen was thrust upon my head.

"What are you doing here anyway?" I asked Kara, drawing myself out of my thoughts.

"I'm here to train of course." She flipped her cropped, honey hair dramatically over her shoulder. I lifted my eyebrows in silent question. My sister was a trained warrior, just as I was, but she didn't enjoy training as frequently as I did. She'd much rather occupy her time with one of her many hobbies.

"Sure," I remarked, "and I'm going to go and garden after this."

Kara snorted as she eyed the daggers I'd left on the table earlier. "I'd pay a thousand coins to see you get down and dirty in a garden, Len."

I twisted my lips at the thought. My mother had loved to garden, I had tried to help her on several occasions and hated it more and more every time. Anything I tried to grow always ended up dead, leaving me frustrated and incinerating the dead plant to ashes.

"Tell me why you're really here, Kara." She perched herself on the edge of the table and picked up a dagger, twirling it between her fingers as she spoke.

"Alvise is looking for you. I volunteered to come find you."

I groaned. "You didn't tell him where I was, did you?" Alvise, my royal advisor, would not be pleased to find out I was coming out here and training every morning. He was another person who thought it was *un-queenly of me* to train. My parents thought it was important for my siblings and I to be trained as warriors, my father wanted us to be well-rounded heirs. I started training five days a week when I was eight years old.

No one ever said a word about me training as I grew up, but now that I was High Queen they found it highly inappropriate for the queen to train as a warrior. An unmarried, High Queen who also knew how to wield a sword? *How scandalous.* I rolled my eyes at the thought.

"You'll never find a suitor that way," is what Guilia told me when she recommended I stop training. Which was why I now trained

in the morning, in secret, to avoid the pestering. They couldn't force me to stop, and I wasn't about to give up the one thing that kept me grounded to placate my advisors, but I quickly grew tired of the argument and decided to keep it my little secret instead. I preferred it this way, no one could bother me if they didn't know where I was.

"Of course not, I'd never give up your secret, you know that. But it is only a matter of time until they figure out where you go every morning. No amount of cloaking spells can keep your secret forever." She waved the dagger at me. "Especially with you training the younglings." Kara slipped off the table and turned towards the target, twirling the dagger in her fingers once again. "If Captain Kahle finds out he'll come for your head."

"He could try, but even *he* knows I'm twice the fighter he is." *Which is part of the reason he despises me.*

I moved to stand next to Kara at the targets. Although my sister didn't choose to train as often as I did, she was still incredibly skilled with a multitude of weapons, and hand-to-hand combat. I made her train with me two afternoons a week to keep up with her skills.

"Do you know what he wants?"

She shrugged. "They have something to talk to you about." She stood and took her position at the target.

"What is it they want to talk about?"

"I don't know. I didn't ask questions." She threw the dagger, and I watched as it pierced the center of the target. She turned towards me, a smug grin on her face. "See, I don't need to train for two hours every morning to keep up with my skills."

I scoffed. "You know as well as I do that you could not touch a dagger for two years and still hit a target dead center, Father made sure of it." My heart clenched at the mention of our father. Kara's smile widened, her green eyes sparkling. Funny how they were the same eyes as mine, but mine hadn't sparkled like that in years.

"How much time do we have before they start looking for me?" I asked as I took position again.

"I'm not sure."

I flung my dagger, hitting right outside the center. I cursed under my breath. "Enough time for you to shoot some arrows with me?"

Kara's eyes lit up at the mention of arrows. "There's always time for archery, Len. You know that."

☾

The council was seated around the table in the War Room when I arrived. It hadn't been used as an actual War Room in centuries, but it was the largest meeting place in the palace. Detailed maps of Lethenia and each of the seven courts lined the walls, along with a massive map of the entire continent of Lethenia.

A large oval table sat in the center of the room, taking up the majority of the space. The flecks of silver in the onyx stone shimmered in the sunlight gleaming in from the wall of windows at the far end of the room. Guilia and Alvise, my royal advisors, were seated at the head of the table on either side of the empty chair left for me. The other eight council members filled in the remaining seats.

I took my seat and the room remained silent as they waited for me to begin the session.

"Anyone care to explain the reason for this impromptu meeting?"

The council looked at one another, mumbling under their breath, causing a sense of dread to course through my system.

It was Alvise who worked up the courage to speak. "Your Majesty, we have received word from the Blood Court."

My stomach tightened at the mention of the Blood Court. Ties between our courts had been strained since the vampires breached our walls two years ago. The vampires' enhanced speed and strength made them the perfect assassins. After slaughtering my parents and brother they proceeded to drain the blood of any staff member they came across before the Royal Guard finally arrived.

The two vampires that were captured admitted to being hired for the job by someone in the Blood Court. The *who* remains a mystery to this day. Alethens—*stars*—the entire continent of Lethenia's relationship with the Blood Court has been strained since. The people didn't take their king and queen being murdered well. *Rightfully so.*

"They would like to revisit the marriage agreement."

My gaze snapped to Alvsie. *The marriage agreement.* Before he was killed, my brother Nol was engaged to a duchess in the Blood Court. The High Fae mostly reside in the Star Court and are viewed as the purest form of Fae—the Goddess Astria's prized creation. All other forms of Fae were her attempts at creating the High Fae. High Fae possess elemental magic like the rest of the Fae, but appear mortal. The only difference is the pointed tips of their ears. The Fae first created by the Goddess possessed different shifting abilities, along with their elemental magic. She created sirens, dragons, wyvern, harpies, and wolves among many other types of Fae. Vampires were once High Fae but were cursed by the Goddess herself to crave blood and depend on it to survive.

According to the stories, all of Lethenia has been hesitant of the vampires since their creation. Their craving for blood keeps most Fae at bay and causes the vampires to isolate themselves in their territory.

My father had been wanting to smooth tensions between our courts since the moment the crown of High King was placed on his head. An arranged marriage between my brother and a vampire seemed like the perfect solution. We would combine the Star Court and Blood Court in marriage, which meant a vampire would be the High Queen of Lethenia one day. We hoped that it would create a better future for us all. It surprised me when my father first brought it up, even more so when Nol quickly agreed, but who was I to argue?

With Nol's unexpected death, the marriage agreement remained unfilled. But the signed agreement between our courts resided in my father's desk, haunting me every day.

The king of the Blood Court had allowed us, had allowed *me*, time after the murders to get things sorted, before revisiting the marriage agreement.

It appeared our grace period had ended.

I squirmed in my seat. I couldn't marry a vampire, not after what they had done to my family. My stomach twisted painfully, and my breathing grew rapid as my magic rushed to my fingertips. I could not lose my composure in front of the council—I could not show them weakness. I forced myself to unclench my fists, my nails leaving angry, red marks on my palms.

Breathe, my Sitara. Breath. My mother's voice echoed in my mind. *Picture a happy memory. Call your magic back into yourself as you picture that memory, channel those joyous feelings.*

I had always had a hard time controlling my magic when my emotions ran high. After I had unintentionally lashed out with my magic too many times my mother started teaching me mind-stilling techniques. These days I didn't always have to picture a happy place to calm my emotions, recalling my mother's voice and words was sometimes all I needed. She had always exuded such a calming presence, Kara took after her, and I, our father.

"Your Majesty, what do you think?"

I shook my thoughts from my mother, already finding myself gaining control over my body again with her soothing voice echoing in my head. I looked up to find the entire council staring at me. Waiting for a response to a question I didn't hear.

"I'm sorry, can you repeat that."

"They would like to propose an alternative to the marriage agreement." Relief washed over me, and the tension in my shoulders lightened immediately. An alternative agreement. I wouldn't have to be forced into a marriage with a monster.

"What does this alternative argument include?"

Alvise swallowed. "They have not come up with one yet"

"What do you mean they haven't come up with an agreement yet?"

Alvise scratched at the skin behind his ear. "That's part of their proposal. King Arlo would like to send a representative from their court to come and stay here while the two of you work together to come to an agreement."

Murmurs rang out around the table.

"A vampire, here in our court? You won't seriously allow that, Your Majesty?" one of the males interjected.

Alivise continued, "I know it is not ideal, but it will be the easiest way to come to an agreement with the Blood Court."

I had to agree with my advisor, the last thing I wanted was a vampire living in my home, but it was better than the alternative.

"The options as I see it are, we allow a vampire into our court for a short period of time, or I marry a vampire, tying him to our court permanently. Is the choice not clear?" I kept my voice steady as I talked, even though my emotions were running high. I tucked my shaking hands under my thighs where no one could see them.

My thoughts instantly went to Kara. I would do anything to protect her. Allowing a vampire in our home went against every protective instinct in my body. I hated everything about this plan. Not only would a vampire be allowed into my court, but I would have to work closely with the monster, for however long it took to come to an agreement.

Every fiber of my being was screaming at me to refuse the proposal, but this wasn't just about me. This was about my people as well—the people of all of Lethenia. I wasn't going to let Kara, or myself, marry a vampire without putting up a fight.

So I picked the lesser of two evils: I wouldn't have to marry a monster, I'd just have to work with one.

"Tell the Blood Court that I agree to their proposal."

I hoped I wasn't making a deadly mistake.

A mistake that could cost more lives than it would save.

The golden spires of the Star Court's palace became visible as we crested the hill leading to our final descent into Alethens, the capital city of the Star Court. The palace stuck out among the dotting of small buildings clustered around the main dwelling. Spring was in full bloom in Alethens, and the land was green with leaves and tiny buds forming on the trees at the top of the hill.

We were scheduled to arrive at the palace gates late this afternoon. I was looking forward to a proper shower, a real meal, and most of all, an actual bed. I loved traveling, but it wore on me. There are few cities between my home in Cel Nox, the capital of the Blood Court, and Alethens, forcing us to camp more often than not over the past two weeks.

But most of all, I was looking forward to meeting the High Queen.

Lennox Adair, High Queen of Lethenia. The youngest High Queen our continent has ever seen. She was twenty-five years old, a year younger than I, and yet she ruled over the entire continent of Lethenia, and its seven courts.

It wasn't common to have such a young ruler, especially as High Queen. Most heirs took over power when the current monarch chose to step down as they got older. Although Fae can live close to two hundred years old, most opt to rule early in their lives, and step back when they reach the later half of their life span. Never had there been a twenty-three-year-old High Queen until the power was shifted to the princess upon her parents' deaths.

Their murders, by a group of vampires.

My stomach twisted. *My own people.*

There was a large possibility I wouldn't leave the Star Court alive. The High Queen's court has made it clear in the past two years how unwelcome we were in their home. But if I did make it out of the Star Court alive, I would find myself the newly crowned king of the Blood Court. One final test from my grandfather: get what I needed from the Star Court and I would finally get my crown, and out from under his thumb.

$$ \mathbb{C}^{\cdot} $$

We bypassed the main road through Alethens and rode around the city, entering the castle grounds from the North, opting not to parade a group of vampires through the city.

Once inside the gates I dismounted my mare, Zola, and was guided inside the palace. My own Captain of the Royal Guard, Declan, fell into step beside me, his dark wings tucked in tight.

I strode through the double wooden doors leading into the palace expecting to find the High Queen there to greet us, but finding the hall empty instead.

Light streamed in from the curved wall of windows at the center of the empty foyer. A golden winding staircase cut through the center of the windows. A large crystal chandelier hung from the top of the stairway, and the natural light from the windows reflected fractures of light throughout the room from the tiny gems. The space was grand and opulent, everything you would expect from the palace of the High Queen.

"Where is everyone?" I murmured. I had visited many

palaces and never once had I walked into one and found the grand hall empty. Usually, Fae were rushing around, eager to greet me, to make sure my every need was met.

No one dared to anger a vampire.

Not that I expected a warm welcome from the Star Court, but I had expected some form of welcome. I am a prince for fucks sake. That still held some weight, vampire-hating court or not.

"Strange isn't it," Declan mused from beside me. Footsteps sounded in the hall to the right and we turned as a male rushed towards us out of a golden-arched hallway.

The male wore a blue suit that stretched tight over his stomach. The royal crest, a large star surrounded by a circle of smaller stars, adorned the lapel of his jacket, embroidered in gold and silver thread.

"My apologies, Your Highness," the male stammered. He bowed and quickly rose, sweat flying from where it beaded on his balding head. "I am Alvise, your Royal Majesties, royal advisor to her Majesty, the High Queen." A note of frustration crept into his voice. "Your Majesty was supposed to be here to greet you, I don't know what happened." He looked around the room as if the queen might be hiding somewhere in the hall.

"It's no problem," I assured him. Anything to get him to stop sweating. "I'm sure the High Queen has many duties to attend to and one has taken longer than anticipated."

The male's face pinched for a second before he forced a smile. "Thank you for understanding, Your Highness. I'm sure she will be here any minute." He didn't sound convinced by his own words, but I smiled anyway and nodded towards Declan.

"Why don't you take the head of my Royal Guard, Captain Hale, and introduce him to the Captain of your guard while I wait here for the queen?"

He nodded. "Yes, of course, Prince Rossi. If you'd like I can set you up in the sitting room."

"I assure you, I am fine waiting here. Thank you."

Alvise finally turned to leave, guiding Declan out the hallway he entered through. Declan turned and gave me a half-hearted shrug as he followed the male.

Once they were gone I surveyed the room again, wandering towards the windows, finding they looked out into an extensive garden. At the sound of boots clicking on the staircase, I turned my gaze upward to find the High Queen of Lethenia descending the stairs.

Her red gown flowed behind her as she descended the stairs towards me. With every step, the slit in her dress parted, revealing the lightly tanned skin of her leg and the three daggers strapped to it. My eyes roamed up the lean, muscular slope of her body before landing on her face.

She was stunning.

I had come across many females in my travels across Lethenia, but none of them compared to the beauty of Lennox Adair. I bent into a slight bow as she reached the final stair. When I rose I found her gaze locked on mine. Her eyes were a shade of green so deep they were almost black—I was drawn into their depths. I should have looked away—not that I could have if I wanted to—but she was staring right back.

"You must be the High Queen." I offered her my hand. "I am Prince Luka Rossi, Heir to the Blood Court." Her green eyes narrowed as she stared at my outstretched hand before finally taking it in her own.

"Lennox Adair."

I brought her hand to my lips, pressing a kiss to the back of it. "It's an honor to finally meet you, Your Majesty." The second my fingers loosened around her hand she wrenched it back to her side.

"I can't say I return the sentiment."

I chuckled. Her honesty was refreshing; I grew tired of fake pleasantries long ago. "I can't say I don't blame you." Her eyes widened at my admission before she opened her mouth and closed it again, shaking her head slightly.

"I'm supposed to give you a tour of the palace and show you to your room." The tight smile on her lips didn't come close to meeting her eyes.

"A personal tour from the queen herself." I put my hand to my heart. "What an honor." She raised an eyebrow as she continued to glare at me, those dark eyes evaluating my every word and movement.

"Trust me it wasn't my idea." She started walking towards one of the arched doorways. "Shall we?" She turned, walking backward as she flung her arms out dramatically, a fake smile plastered on her face. "This is the grand foyer." She turned back around and continued, not waiting to see if I followed.

I used my enhanced speed to catch up, falling into step beside her. The walls were all the same white as the foyer, with the same golden accents, and the white marbled floors continued down the hallway as well. Whoever decorated this place took the whole *Golden Star Court* thing literally.

"How did the High Queen end up as my tour guide anyway?"

"I drew the short straw."

I huffed out a laugh and I swear I saw the corner of her mouth turn up slightly.

"But still, you're the queen, you have the last say." From what little I knew about her I had a hard time believing she frequently did things she didn't want to.

"Let's just say there are bigger battles worth fighting than being your tour guide. Besides, my royal advisors thought it would be a great idea to have my smiling face be the first thing you saw when you arrived."

"And clearly they knew you'd charm me with your sunny disposition."

She let out a breath of air, which I assumed would be the closest thing to a laugh I'd get out of her.

"Or maybe they knew I'd scare you off."

"You'll learn quickly that I don't scare easily, My Queen."

Her nose wrinkled. "Don't call me *My Queen*."

"Sorry, High Queen," I countered.

"Don't call me that either."

"Your Highness?"

"No," she said through gritted teeth.

"Your Majesty?"

"No."

Now I was starting to get annoyed. "My lady?"

"No."

I swear there was more contempt behind that *no*. "I'm running out of ideas here, Sweetheart."

She whirled on me, her nostrils flaring as she pressed a finger into my chest. "I am not your *Sweetheart*," she sneered. Flecks of gold—*of magic*—now danced in the depths of her green eyes. I crossed my arms as I met her gaze.

"Then tell me what I should call you."

"Maybe you shouldn't talk to me at all and you won't have to worry about what to call me." She removed her finger from my chest and took a step back. As if she needed to distance herself from me before she did something she would regret.

I clenched my jaw. "Are you seriously not going to tell me what to call you? You *do* remember why I'm here don't you?" I took a step towards her and she took another step back. "We're supposed to work together? It would be pretty inconvenient working together and not knowing what to call you."

I watched as she clenched and unclenched her fists, her hand hovering over where I knew daggers sat on her thigh, fingers twitching over the blades. This was going to be a much bigger problem than I had anticipated.

"Fine, I guess you can call me Lennox."

"You guess?"

"Yes, *I guess*. I usually only let my friends call me Lennox, and we are not friends, nor will we ever be friends. But, for convenience sake only, you can call me Lennox."

As much as I wanted to dive into the *we will never be friends* comment she didn't give me the chance before she turned and started back down the hallway.

"The ballroom is here." She gestured to the open doorway, not stopping as we passed by.

"In case you were wondering, you can call me Luka."

"I wasn't."

"The kitchen is this way, the garden is out back there."

"Thank you for that riveting information. Without it, I would have never guessed it was the garden." I shoved my hands in my pockets. "I heard you were a decent queen, but your tour guide skills can use some work," I mumbled under my breath. Lennox stopped abruptly and I almost ran into the back of her before she whirled on me.

"I didn't have a choice in being your tour guide. Just like I didn't have a choice in being queen since vampires, like yourself, decided to make that choice for me too. So my apologies if my tour guide skills are lacking, I have much more important things to worry about than being a proper host. Like making sure the vampire staying in my home doesn't kill anyone."

I remained frozen in place as her words rolled through me, hitting their intended mark. She turned and continued down the hallway. Fuck. This was *way* worse than I thought.

What did I get myself into?

I sped to catch back up to her, stopping in her path. "Do you really think I'm here to kill your people?"

Even though she was a few inches shorter than me she managed to tilt her chin up and look down her nose at me. "I'm not saying it's not a possibility."

"I am not here to kill anyone." Not intentionally at least. If there was a threat to my life I wouldn't go down without a fight, but I wasn't like those vampires who came here with the intention to slaughter innocent Fae.

"Only time will tell, Bloodsucker." She tried to move around me, but I moved faster, placing a hand on her shoulder to stop her. Her lips curled as she looked at where my hand touched her skin before shrugging out of my hold.

"Bloodsucker, huh? We're doing nicknames then? I thought only *friends* had nicknames. Change your mind already, Sweetheart?" I couldn't help the smirk that curved on my lips.

Lennox on the other hand was not amused. All I got was another steely glare. "Can we get on with the tour now? Or do you have more nonsense you'd like to spew?"

"Oh I've got plenty more nonsense, Sweetheart, but I'll save the rest for later." I winked as I gestured for her to continue. "After you, Sweetheart."

We continued through the palace—Lennox pointed out various rooms and their uses, and I kept my mouth shut. I delighted in pushing her buttons, but I had to remind myself that we needed to find some way to work together, amicably. Pushing her too far, too quickly wouldn't be the way to do that.

Every room Lennox showed me was as extravagant as the next—all decorated in shades of white and gold. We made our way around the main floor and ended back in the foyer where we ascended the spiral staircase to the second level. There were three libraries in the palace, each grander than the next, lined with books dating back to the creation of Lethenia, according to Lennox.

I couldn't wait to explore the extensive libraries.

The palace was grand and opulent, but it also felt comforting. Homey. Soft. *Welcome*. Like an actual home. Such a stark contrast from my home in the Blood Court.

Lennox finally stopped at the end of a long hallway on the third floor. "This is your room." She gestured to the large wooden door. "A member of the staff can get you anything you need, and they will bring you dinner in your room tonight. We will have our first meeting tomorrow morning. Someone will bring you the details later tonight." Before I could say anything in return she turned on her heels and was walking back down the hallway.

"Thank you," I called after her, but she gave no indication that she had heard me as she continued. I shook my head as I turned the gold-plated door knob. She hated me already, that much was clear. But I couldn't say the same.

Lennox Adair intrigued me in more ways than one.

My room was decently sized, smaller than my room at the palace in Cel Nox, but larger than I would expect to be given to a so-called enemy visitor. The far wall held two large windows and a set of glass doors leading out onto a small balcony over-looking the back garden. The sunlight filtering through them lit the bedchamber where a large, four-poster bed sat in the middle of the left side of the room; and a makeshift living space with a small couch, a chair, and a coffee table sat in the opposite corner. There was a small desk, along with a large armoire in the room as well, and off to the right, there was a door, which I assumed, led to the bathing chamber.

I laid back on the bed, basking in the softness of the mattress beneath me and I closed my eyes as I relaxed—a nap sounded perfect right now. After almost two weeks of traveling and my tour with Lennox, I was exhausted.

A knock sounded at my door jostling me from my thoughts and my looming nap. I groaned as I scrubbed my hands over my face. "Come in," I called out, not bothering to sit up from the bed.

The door creaked open and a set of heavy footsteps entered my bedchamber. I opened an eye to find Declan scanning my room, wings spread wide as he looked for potential threats.

"You shouldn't allow anyone into your room considering how much this court despises vampires," Declan scolded.

"But that's why I brought you with me, my protector always looking out for me." I gave him a sarcastic smile.

"I'm serious, Luka, you're not safe here. You need to be on alert at all times."

I glanced over at Declan as he reappeared from the bathing chamber, his hulking figure taking up the entire door frame. He had a point, even if I desperately wanted to ignore it. We were a far cry from the comforts of Cel Nox. There I was the celebrated prince, here I was the enemy.

"I promise I'll do better in the future, Captain Hale."

He grunted in approval. "What is the High Queen like?" Declan asked as he opened the glass doors, peaking out to the balcony.

"She's different from what I anticipated," I said, sitting up.

"Different how?" Declan tucked in his wings behind him as he sat in one of the chairs in the makeshift living area.

"She's not how I expected the High Queen to act." I replayed my tour with Lennox in my mind, trying to figure out the right words to describe her. "She's . . . feisty." Although the word didn't fully encapsulate Lennox Adair. I had a feeling there was a lot more to discover underneath her steely exterior.

"Feisty, huh?" Declan took in the information—filing it away for later. "How so?"

"She didn't take any of my shit that's for sure. She dished it right back."

"It's about time someone besides Nico and I put you in your place."

I huffed a laugh.

"Sounds like your type," Declan added.

I scoffed. Lennox Adair might be my type, but I doubted she'd ever look at me with anything but hate in her eyes.

Declan leaned forward placing his forearms on his knees. "Don't tell me you're already turning your eyes to the queen?"

"Of course not. I simply enjoyed getting on her nerves. If we're going to have to work together I might as well get some amusement out of it." I waved a hand at Declan and his constant need to analyze every situation. "You'll see what I'm talking about when you meet her."

Declan leaned back in his chair. "I look forward to it."

"She does hate me, that much is clear. Working together is going to be a disaster." I placed my face in my hands.

"Maybe you should try turning on some of your Prince Luka charm."

"Trust me, I tried. She's immune." Declan laughed—a rarity from him—and a small smile creeped up his face.

"Seriously, it made her hate me more."

Declan shook his head. "Sounds to me like you might have finally met your match."

3

LENNOX

I awoke with a gasp, fighting to get enough oxygen to my lungs. My magic was brimming at my fingertips, threatening to spill out as I exhaled my next breath. The sky was still dark outside my windows, the glow of the moon illuminated my bedchamber. Sweat coated my body—my hair and nightgown clinging to me.

I expelled a bit of my magic, bringing a flame to my fingertips and lighting the lamp at my bedside. The bulb bathed the room in a dim light and my eye caught a spot of black on the bed. I brought the sheet closer to the light to inspect it. There was a hole the size of a fist in the white fabric and the fabric was singed with black around the hole. I had cast magic in my sleep. *Fuck.* I must have been fisting the fabric hard enough it caused my magic to flare. I hadn't cast magic in my sleep in years. Not since the months directly *After*.

I guessed it had everything to do with the vampire down the hall. Goddess above, I needed to get myself under control. I cannot let Luka Rossi get under my skin. I had tried hard to keep myself in check yesterday, but the moment he gave me the opportunity I struck, my emotions running rampant like a stampede of wild beasts that could not be contained. Determined to trample everything in their path—including the vampire prince.

I pushed the singed sheet aside and headed for the bathing chamber; there was no way I was going back to sleep now. I used my water and fire magic to fill the bathtub with scalding water, and once it was full I slipped in, leaving my sweat-coated nightgown in a pool on the floor. My magic was still tumultuous inside me, so I drew it to my fingers, expelling it in small flames to keep the bathwater warm. I summoned water too, using it in combination with air to make a whirlpool of sorts—already feeling the edge wear off.

Every Fae held claim to at least one form of elemental magic: air, water, fire, or earth. No one knows for sure how each Fae claims the elements they hold, there is only speculation that when you start to develop your magic you claim the elements that call the strongest to you. The age at which Fae develop their magic is different for everyone, but it typically starts around the age of ten and ends by seventeen. We are taught how to feel a connection to the earth and the elements. How to focus on our connection to the earth with the hopes that one day one of the elements respond to your call. We spend hours sitting by lakes, surrounded by trees or fires in hopes an element will find its way to you.

The first element to respond to you is typically your strongest element. I claimed my flames shortly after I turned seven. I was sitting by a small fire, when the flames started wrapping themselves around my body until my entire body was engulfed in them. They didn't burn me, but they were absorbed into my body. The warming sensation of the flames intertwined with the very fiber of my being like they had belonged there all along, waiting to find their way back home.

By the time I was eleven, I had claimed all four elements—the first Fae to do so in centuries. Only a few know of my extensive power: my parents, siblings, my aunt, and cousin. A secret to keep me safe, my father claimed. My father didn't even want my aunt to know, but my mother argued she'd be able to help advance my training with the knowledge.

I am the most powerful Fae to grace Lethenia in years.

The arrival of a vampire prince should not be bothering me this much.

I needed a new plan, I had not factored in the effect being in the presence of a vampire would have on me. I had to keep my emotions in check—I couldn't let him see my weakness.

As I soaked in the tub I let my mind wander towards Luka. The thought of being in a room alone with him caused a chill to run through my body despite the scalding water surrounding me. I wanted him out of Alethens as quickly as possible. I know we are supposed to demonstrate to our people that there is peace between our two courts, but part of me wondered what my people thought about me inviting a vampire into our home. My parents had been working their entire lives towards true peace within all of the courts in Lethenia. Peace is something I've wanted too. But still, I was conflicted. Why should I want peace with the Fae who wanted my family dead?

But it wasn't just about me—nothing was ever just about me anymore. I had to think for my court, for the entire continent. Every decision I make has a cost.

The cost of working with Luka Rossi was still to be determined.

☾

Hours later I stood in front of the mirror in my bathing chamber, staring at my reflection. I wanted nothing more than the mirror to open up and swallow me whole so I didn't have to meet with the prince. I didn't want to spend time with the prick, but what choice did I have? The quicker we figured out a solution, the quicker he would be gone.

Unfortunately, I still hadn't figured out the best way to go about dealing with him. Any other queen might have tried to butter him up with compliments and trinkets—perhaps even flirt with him.

The old Lennox could have easily pulled off flirting with the prince. The Lennox who had loving parents and a wise older brother and had never experienced tragedy. The Lennox who was second in line for the throne. The Lennox who's eyes were filled with joy, not sorrow. The Lennox who was spontaneous and carefree. The Lennox who used to laugh and smile.

But that Lennox didn't exist anymore.

No matter how hard I tried to bring her back. *That* Lennox was smashed into a million little pieces like a glass vase dropped onto a marble floor—the pieces scattered and broken, never to be put back together the way they were before. The parts that were slowly being put back together were raw and ragged; if you touched a piece the wrong way it would pierce your flesh, leaving you bleeding and wounded.

That Lennox shattered the second the power of High Queen shifted to her. She died alongside her parents and Nol.

The eyes staring back at me through the mirror were glassy and I quickly blinked the tears away. *This* Lennox couldn't afford to show any weakness.

I took one final, steadying breath and turned from the mirror.

4

LENNOX

The belt of knives strapped to my thigh bounced as I descended the staircase to the main floor of the palace. My unbound hair flowed behind me as my boots clacked on the marble stairs. I'd opted for black leather pants with a white, long-sleeved blouse, and a black, leather corset was fastened over the blouse. The outfit was intentional. Today, I wasn't the queen in a pretty dress, I was a warrior ready for battle.

A battle of words and wills with the vampire prince.

When I arrived in my office, the Blood Prince was lounging in a chair, leafing through a book from the stack towering on the table next to him. *How long had he been in here waiting for me?* The room wasn't large, it was meant to be a comfortable meeting space—an intimate space—rather than the war room where bigger meetings took place. The office used to be my father's, and seeing the prince in his space soured my stomach, but I didn't want to meet anywhere else.

My father's—*my*—office, made me feel safe and secure. It reminded me of the many hours I sat in the chairs reading, or listening, to him while he worked. I'd ask him questions, and if he didn't know the answer he'd research it and come back to me days or weeks later with the answer. My chest tightened at the thought of the hours spent here with my father. How many times had I fallen asleep in one of these chairs, only for him to carry me to bed in his arms?

I didn't want Luka in this space, but I hoped that being surrounded by my father's memory would help guide me—give me the strength I needed to deal with the vampire prince.

Luka had yet to notice my arrival, so I took the opportunity to look at him. I had stolen glances yesterday, but I never got to fully take him in. His dark hair was cut shorter on the sides and left longer on the top. It was swept up and out of his face, although a loose strand had fallen across his forehead. His frame made the large chair appear small as he sprawled carelessly, legs spread wide, as he flipped through the book. The sleeves of his white shirt were rolled up, revealing his corded forearms; while the top few buttons of his shirt were left undone, revealing the dark lines of a tattoo peaking over his shoulders and curving around the sides of his neck—the dark ink a stark contrast to his ivory skin.

I licked my lips. As much as I hated to admit it, the prick might just be the most stunning male I'd ever laid eyes on. In any other circumstance, I might have found myself gravitating towards him. But he was a vampire, the heir to the Blood Court.

The prince finally noticed my arrival, glancing at me and closing the book before placing it on top of the stack.

"Good morning," I said with as much cheer as I could muster, and I forced my lips into a tight smile as he brushed the loose strand of hair out of his face.

"Good morning, Sweetheart."

My fake smile quickly turned to a scowl. "I told you to stop calling me that." So much for my plan to be nice. I leveled my shoulders and tried again. "Please, call me Lennox," I fixed a smile back on my face.

"I don't know, I quite like the look on your face when I call you, Sweetheart"—the sides of his mouth quirked up— "think I might keep doing it."

I moved past him to the desk at the far end of the room, letting out a deep breath through my nose as I sat. I should have never let him know it annoyed me, that was my first mistake. Did I learn nothing from having siblings? I had let my composure crack while I was giving him the tour, now I had to pay the price.

The old leather of the chair groaned under my weight as I sat behind the giant wooden desk, my fathers' deep woodsy scent wrapping around me.

"Let's get started, shall we?"

Luka took a seat in one of the chairs in front of the desk. "In a rush to get me back home, Sweetheart?"

"Why would you ever think that?" I asked sweetly, once again forcing an innocent smile to my lips. Luka leaned forward, that lock of dark hair falling across his forehead once again. My heart stopped as he pinned me with his blue eyes. Goddess above *those eyes*. They reminded me of the surface of the lake on a summer day—sparkling and alluring. It took a physical effort to look away from those piercing eyes.

"Your more than pleasant attitude towards me this morning makes me think you had a change of heart and want me to stay here as long as possible."

"What does the Blood Court want?" I all but sneered. If this is the way he wanted to play then this is how we would play.

"There she is." Those blue eyes gleamed. "Your acting skills could use some improvement, Sweetheart."

I let my scowl deepen as I watched him lean back in his chair, crossing his arms over his chest. His muscular arms strained against the white fabric of his shirt. I hated that he could see right through me. I was wrong to think being sweet to him would work. He was a vampire after all. They were known for being cruel and calculating. Why did I think the sweet and innocent act would work on him?

"What does the Blood Court want?" I asked again through gritted teeth.

"Depends on what you have to offer."

An irritated laugh tumbled from my lips. "Really, this is the way you want to play this?"

He stood and leaned over the desk, bracing his hands on the wooden surface. "This isn't a game to me, Lennox."

I kept my gaze locked on his. Refusing to give into whatever power play he was trying here. I tried to stay out in front of him, to control the situation, but he was still two steps ahead of me. I was at his mercy, whether I liked it or not, and while I could essentially give him whatever he wanted, I had no idea what that was. What did a bunch of bloodthirsty vampires want?

Blood?

Goddess, I hoped not. That's the one thing I couldn't give them.

"When your father first proposed the idea of your brother marrying a female from the Blood Court, the hope was the deal would help ease the tension between, not only the Blood Court and the Star Court, but the Blood Court and all of Lethenia. To see the Blood Court and the Star Court working together willingly and binding them to one another in marriage would show the entire continent that we were allies, not enemies. The vampires were to be respected, not just feared."

"I'm aware of the original deal, what's your point?"

He leaned further over the desk. "My point is, my grandfather, *the king*, is insistent that whatever deal we come to, must emit the same results an arranged marriage would. Something that would redeem vampires in the eyes of the rest of Lethenia."

I clenched my hands into fists under the desk in an attempt not to wrap them around his neck instead. "How in the Stars are we going to manage to achieve that without a marriage involved?"

The panic started to rise within me, but I didn't let my gaze move from where it was locked with his. I refused to show him this bothered me. The only reason I agreed to work with him was to avoid an arranged marriage to a vampire. I had already given up too much of myself in becoming queen. I wasn't prepared to give up my choice in who I married.

I forced myself to breathe as I continued to hold the prince's stare. The silence between us grew with each passing second. Finally, he tore his gaze from mine, fixing it on the desk between us instead.

"I don't know."

My stomach dropped at his admission. I watched as he stood from where he leaned against the desk and turned away from me.

"What do you mean you don't know?"

"I mean I don't know. I don't have any ideas." A muscle ticked in his jaw.

"You're joking."

He turned to face me again as he rubbed a hand across the back of his neck. "My grandfather didn't send me with a proposal, he wanted to see what you might come up with." His hands fell to his sides as he looked at me. I blinked at him, the silence continuing between us.

"I'm guessing you don't have any ideas?" His eyes searched mine.

I shook my head. "I was under the impression you were coming here with an idea already in mind." I expected him to be here a week at most. But what I didn't expect was for us both to come empty-handed. These negotiations could take weeks without him coming to the table with a proposition in mind.

I watched the prince out of the corner of my eye as he shook his head before straightening and turning his attention back to me. "You don't have anything to offer? Not even an idea?"

I clenched my fists on the desk. It was *his* job to come in here knowing what his court wanted, not mine. *His* court was the one who demanded this meeting in the first place. My job was to give in to his demands—to make this deal and be done with it as quickly as possible. Which *he* was making impossible. Not me.

"You want to know why I don't have any ideas?" The words started tumbling out of me like lava spilling from an erupting volcano, hot and fast. Unstoppable. I stood and stalked towards him where he stood by the bookshelf. "If it were up to me, my court wouldn't be making any kind of deal with the Blood Court. I'm perfectly content icing out vampires and letting them be viewed as the villains for the rest of time. But because my brother was killed before he had the chance to marry his vampire bride, I'm stuck here, trying to soothe your court's hurt feelings over being the least favored court."

The prince flinched—my words hitting their intended mark.

But I wanted more. I wanted blood. His people had caused me pain and I wanted him to hurt like I hurt. My hand closed around one of the daggers at my side.

"You forget this is already a done deal, *Sweetheart.* Either we work together, or you, or your sister, marry a vampire."

"Don't. Call. Me. Sweetheart." My hand closed tighter around the hilt of my dagger, its grooves biting into the skin of my palm. I focused on the sensation of the pain—it was only a fraction of the pain I felt every day since I lost my parents and Nol. "I'm the High Queen, I don't have to do anything I don't want to do."

"But that's not true is it?" He took a step towards me. "Do you want to be known as a queen who doesn't honor deals?"

"Better than being known as a murderer," I spat. He growled in return, revealing two sharp fangs. I stepped back instinctively, pulling my dagger from my side. The prince's eyes flicked to the glinting steel.

"Would it make you feel better to stab me? To slice this dagger across my neck? To drive the steel into my heart?"

Yes. That's exactly what I wanted. I wanted nothing more than to see him dead; to see him hurt and bleeding on the floor like my people, *my family*, were at the hands of vampires.

"Would watching the blood drain from my body, and the life leave my eyes, on the floor of this office soothe the ache you feel?" My eyebrows furrowed. "If it would, then by all means, have at me." He stood back a step, holding his arms out, offering himself to me.

When I didn't make a move he continued, "You have every right to feel anger towards the vampires who attacked the palace. And I am truly sorry for their actions and your loss." His face softened. "But you cannot let the actions of a select group of vampires impact the way you treat an entire population of people. No matter how angry or hurt you may be." He stepped back and let out a deep sigh.

"I came here thinking we'd have a real chance of making peace between our people. What you're showing me now is you're not willing to work with me. Why don't you come find me when you are?" I didn't move as he brushed past me, the door closing quietly behind him as I remained rooted in place.

Was he right? Was I treating him unfairly? Was I letting my anger and grief cloud my judgment? I had been living in these feelings for such a long time it was hard to tell.

Was this what my parents would have wanted? Is this how they would have treated the heir to the Blood Court? *No.* My parents were a beloved king and queen for many reasons, their compassion being one of them. And *I* have been so concerned about making the vampires pay for what they did to my family —*to me*—that I forgot the pillars of our kingdom that my parents had instilled in us from a young age.

It had always been my instinct to reach for my sword first— ask for forgiveness later. But I couldn't do that anymore. I was High Queen now, not a member of the Royal Guard.

My mother would have been disappointed in my actions today. Luka Rossi didn't deserve my wrath—he did nothing wrong. Again, I had let my anger and grief take over my actions.

What would my parents have done in my situation?

How many times over the past two years did I ask myself the same question? How many times had I wished I could walk into my father's office and ask for his guidance on how to rule his kingdom?

Grief washed over me like a wave. If I wasn't already sitting I would have buckled under the pressure. Tears threatened to spill from my eyes.

This is why I never let myself think of them. I took that grief and shoved it back into the box that I kept it in, and locked it up tight. I took a deep breath and asked myself again, what would my parents do? What would Nol have done?

They would have been devastated, but they wouldn't have held a grudge toward the Blood Court. They wouldn't have blamed an entire population of Fae for the actions of a few. They would have worked night and day with the Blood Court to find peace between our courts—between all of Lethenia. They wouldn't have let this unrest, this *hate*, fester like an infected wound as I had these past two years. It's why my father had proposed the arranged marriage in the first place.

I don't know how long I sat there with my face in my hands, contemplating what I needed to do. Sometime later, a knock on the door startled me. I sat up and removed my hands from my face.

"Come in."

"Your Majesty"—Guilia slipped through the open door—"the Duke and Duchess are here. They are waiting in the Council Room when you're ready."

"Thank you, I'll be there in a moment."

She ducked back out of the room and I took a steadying breath and stood from the desk. The Blood Prince's words were still playing on a loop in my mind.

I didn't know how we were going to come up with a bargain that would satisfy the Blood King, but I did know one thing: Luka Rossi was right.

5

LUKA

Two days passed and I had yet to hear a word from the queen.

I bid my time in the libraries, scanning the multitude of volumes while waiting for any word from the queen.

Did I screw up the one chance. I had to prove to my grandfather I was ready to be king?

I refused to let her steal this opportunity from me. I just needed to give her more space before I jumped back into trying to get into her good graces.

I shouldn't have spoken to her the way I did, but it was a risk I needed to take. Her hatred for vampires was worse than I anticipated. There was no way we would be able to work together if we couldn't get past our differences. Every word I told her was true, but as we spoke, I could see the anger and grief in her eyes—the fear.

Feelings I was all too familiar with.

I shook my head at the thought and took a large inhale of the cool morning air—relishing the sting in my chest as I exited the palace and made my way through the extensive garden. With Lennox ignoring me the last two days, Declan and I had spent time exploring the palace, but the garden was one of the places I hadn't wandered into yet.

The garden wrapped around the back of the palace, arranged similarly to a rectangular maze, with a fountain at the center, surrounded by several small tables, chairs, and benches. I let myself wander through the garden, letting the twists and turns of the maze guide me until it spit me out on the opposite side. Beyond the garden were rolling hills and planes, and the snow-capped tips of the Abode mountains were visible in the distance. At the bottom of the hill was the entrance to a forest. The trees were thick and dense, which didn't allow for me to see far beyond them. I'd have to look at a map later and see what lay on the other side, but I didn't dare enter it alone. I had heard enough bedtime stories as a child to think twice about entering an unknown forest.

I started to turn around to make my way back when the hairs on the back of my neck stood up. My magic stirred at my fingertips.

Magic.

I stretched out my senses, reaching for the source, only to run into a barrier. Someone had placed a cloaking spell on the forest. What could they possibly be hiding back here? I pushed through the magic as it pulled and pricked against my skin, causing a shiver to wrack my body. I shrugged off the uncomfortable feeling—like being squeezed into a too tight jacket—before the sensation lifted as I made it through the invisible barrier. I continued until I came to a clearing, where a depleted brick building appeared. The sun was starting to shine through the trees on the crumbling brown bricks, bathing half of the decrepit building in light. The sunlight illuminated the ivy crawling between every crack and crevice—covering the entirety of the flat roof.

I should turn around. Every instinct told me to run; to come back when I wasn't alone. But some other instinct, buried deep inside, urged me to continue forward.

I needed to know what was in this building.

I approached the heavy wooden door. The same imprint of

magic I felt in the forest lingered on the door as well, mixed with another. When I placed my hand on the door it swung open easily. I created a shield of air to silence any sounds I'd make and entered the building. The outside of the building may have looked old and rundown, but the inside was anything but. It appeared to be some kind of training facility. I had been to training centers in almost every court in Lethenia, but I'd never come across one as extensive as this one.

Rows upon rows of weapons lined gray brick walls. Daggers, swords, staffs, bows, scythes, axes, any weapon you could dream of training with, were in this room. *Declan would be in heaven here.* On either side of the door sat two large training rings, while the space in the middle of the facility hosted weights, boxing bags, and various other training supplies.

At the far end of the building sat five targets, each separated by a wire fence about a foot high. A female stood at one of the targets, notching an arrow in a bow. As I drew closer, I recognized the figure.

High Queen Lennox Adair was wearing leathers that clung to every dip and curve of her toned, muscular body. Her blonde hair was bound at the nape of her neck and fell down her back in loose waves.

She knocked an arrow and another and another—every one hitting true.

"Do you ever miss?" I asked, removing the shield around me.

Loose hairs whipped around her face as she turned to face me, the string of her bow pulled taught, ready to let the arrow fly. *Maybe I shouldn't have let my shield down yet.*

But I saw the moment she recognized me, and she hesitated a second before lowering her bow to her side.

"No." She pushed a stray hair from her face with the back of her arm.

"Noted. I'll make sure to never go up against you with a bow then."

She smirked. "See, you do have some wits about you, Bloodsucker."

"You were in the Royal Guard, weren't you, before you became queen?"

Lennox nodded, placing the bow back on the rack. "I've been training as a warrior since I was old enough to hold a sword. The Guard was a natural choice, once I was old enough." She swept her fingers over the daggers lining the table. "I've always been better at working out my problems through steel rather than using my words."

"From what I've experienced, your tongue might be as sharp as your sword."

Her eyes shifted from deep green to a slightly lighter shade as her gaze flicked to me, the left side of her mouth kicking up an inch. "You have no idea what my tongue is capable of."

Her lips clamped shut as soon as the words left her mouth. She looked as surprised by her words as I was. Where was the female I had encountered two days ago? The one fueled by rage and grief? The female who couldn't look me in the eyes without a look of disgust crossing her features? Now she was—what in the Stars *was* she doing? Was she *joking* with me? Lennox opened her mouth like she was going to say something before clamping it shut again and looking back at the daggers in front of us.

"Maybe one day I'll find out?" I winked at her, watching with pleasure as the tips of her pointed ears turned pink.

Her head tilted as she took me in, eyes roaming over my body. "In your dreams, Bloodsucker."

And dream I will.

She palmed a dagger. "How did you find me out here anyway?"

"I was exploring the garden and I wandered into the forest when I sensed the magic from the cloaking spell and curiosity got the better of me."

She blinked at me, and all previous amusement vanished. "You could move through the cloaking spell?"

I nodded. "It wasn't easy, that's for sure."

Lennox chewed at her bottom lip. "*Interesting.*"

Cloaking spells were an intricate form of magic. From what I've read, the magic picks and chooses who can make it through the cloaking, besides those whose signatures are initially woven into the spells. Not that I was well educated on witch magic. Maybe there was a hole in the spell. Or it was old and the magic was starting to fade.

"Why do you have a cloaking spell over this place anyway?"

She twirled the dagger between her fingers. "I don't want any of the staff to find me. My royal advisors find it appalling that I want to continue to train now that I'm queen. And they believe my people will say the same."

"You are the queen, you know. You make the rules."

"I'm aware," she deadpanned, "but sometimes it's easier to hide things than deal with the judgment. They judge me enough as it is. Or they'd use it as a bargaining chip—tell me I can continue to train if I add something else to my plate." My eyes flicked to her lips and she sucked on her bottom lip.

"Everyone likes to underestimate me. I've learned to pick and choose my battles when it comes to being queen."

That's something I was all too familiar with. My grandfather and uncle were not easy males to please. Which is why getting what I needed from Lennox was vital. Who knew what hoops they would make me jump through if I failed at this task?

"Would you like a tour?" Lennox's voice rang through the silence, surprising me with her offer. I expected her to yell at me, force me to leave, threaten me for being here—and invading her time and space—but instead, here she was, having a civil conversation with me. Instead of kicking me out, she was offering me a tour. I felt like she was trying. Maybe my words had had an impact after all. Had I managed to slip into a small crack in her defenses?

I nodded. "I'd love that, thank you."

She gave me a small, tight-lipped smile.

I waved my hand out in front of us. "After you, Sweetheart."

Lennox showed me around the facility. Telling me the story of how it came to be—letting me get to know a small part of her. The building used to be the stables when the palace was first built. When the new stables were built, this building was abandoned until her father decided to transform it into a private training facility for his children.

The silence stretched between us as we stood in front of one of the many walls of weapons. I pretended to study the fine details on the handle of the dagger in front of me, but I felt like I had overstayed my welcome. Not that I was welcome in the first place since I invited myself in, but—semantics.

"Thanks for the tour," I said as I turned to leave.

"Wait." Lennox reached out, catching my wrist. I stared at where her skin met mine. Her touch felt like a bolt of lightning pulsing through my body. I couldn't help the sting that rippled through me when she pulled her hand back, like she'd been burned by that lightning.

"I'm sorry." The words tumbled from her lips quickly, like if she didn't get them out all in one breath she wouldn't at all. "I'm sorry about what I said the other day." She crossed her arms over her chest, looking at the wall of weapons as she continued. "You were right. It's not fair for me to take out my anger on the entire vampire population"—she took a deep breath—"on *you*, because of the actions of a few vampires."

I was stunned by her apology. I had the feeling Lennox Adair didn't do much apologizing.

"I do want peace, I want nothing more than to continue with the legacy my parents started. I think—" She shook her head and let out another long breath.

When she finally turned and looked at me, I could see the sincerity in her eyes. "I want to work with you. Ultimately, we both want the same thing. For the sake of Lethenia, I will try my best to put aside my less-than-ideal feelings about vampires while we are working together."

"Does this mean you're going to act all sweet and nice towards me?" I gave her a knowing smirk.

She scoffed. "Of course not, I will tolerate your presence and nothing more. Don't push it, Bloodsucker."

I smiled, beside myself at her admission. This was good, this unspoken truce between the two of us; I could work with this. It would take time, but one day, I would make Lennox Adair more than tolerate me. I turned again to leave, not wanting to push my luck any further, only for Lennox to stop me again.

"But there is one thing I need from you." She moved quickly as I turned back around, the only warning was the faint whistle in the air before a sharp pain radiated from my leg. I let out a groan as I looked to find one of Lennox's daggers protruding from my thigh. Lennox stood, arms crossed over her chest, a wicked smile on her face as I clutched my wounded leg.

"What the fuck?" I gritted as I pulled the dagger from my thigh. I let it fall to the ground with a clang, my blood splattering the floor beside it.

"I decided killing you wouldn't make me feel better, but I thought stabbing you might. Turns out I was right."

"You violent creature." I couldn't keep the amusement from my voice. I should be angry at her for stabbing me. I should be reaching for my weapons, but instead, I found myself amused. She waved a hand towards me dismissively.

"You'll be fine. I'll call you a healer once we're back inside, and I made sure not to hit anything vital. You'll be fine in a day."

"I appreciate you being so considerate about where you chose to stab me."

"Don't get used to it, Bloodsucker."

"Wouldn't dream of it, Sweetheart."

6

LUKA

The next night Declan and I were invited to dinner with Lennox and her sister. I hadn't seen Lennox since she deposited me with the healer after stabbing me. But the note I received from her regarding dinner was seen as an official peace offering—the mark of a new beginning to our political arrangement.

When Declan and I arrived in the formal dining room, Lennox and her sister were already waiting for us. I had yet to meet the princess, but the resemblance between the two was clear—they were two sides of the same coin.

Lennox wore a dark blue gown—the cut, simple and elegant—with a slit that went up her thigh, once again revealing the daggers sheathed there. Half of her hair was pulled back, accentuating her long jaw and high cheekbones. Her sister wore a simple pink gown; the fabric hugged her generous curves, and her hair, the same golden color as her sister's, was cut so it dusted her shoulders. Declan and I bowed as we approached the pair before rising to address them fully.

"Prince Luka, this is my sister, Kara."

I took her hand in mine. "It is a pleasure to meet you, Princess Kara." I placed a kiss on the back of her hand before letting it go. Her cheeks turned the color of her dress as I did.

"Please, call me Kara."

I smiled and nodded before turning to Lennox, who stood holding her hands firmly behind her back. I smirked and dipped my head at her. "It is a pleasure to see you again, Your Majesty."

Her jaw clenched. "As I told you earlier, please call me Lennox."

"Of course, how could I forget? It's a pleasure to see you again, *Lennox*." I loved the way her name felt on my tongue.

"Who's your friend?" Kara interjected, releasing my attention from her sister. Both females stared at the male beside me, I couldn't blame them. Even I could admit Declan's appearance was captivating. It wasn't every day you came across a half-shifted harpy.

"This is Captain Declan Hale." I placed a hand on his shoulder, causing his black, feathered wings to rustle behind him as he stood firmly in place. "He is the captain of my Royal Guard, and my best friend."

"It's a pleasure to meet you, Your Majesties."

"And you as well, but please, call me Lennox."

Declan only nodded.

"Please be seated," Lennox said, gesturing an arm towards the table, before bypassing the head of the table to sit next to her sister, while Declan and I sat directly across from the pair. Plates of meat, potatoes, and various vegetables were placed in front of us—the smell of fresh spices filling my nose. We all took our time scooping copious amounts of food onto our plates, and Kara drove the conversation as we ate, asking us about our travels. Kara made it sound like the sisters rarely traveled outside of their court, which I found strange considering how much their father traveled while he was still alive.

I let my gaze land on Lennox as Kara carried on. Her eyes were trained on her younger sister like she was inspecting every piece of food she brought to her mouth. I noted the casual grace she sat with. Her back was straight in her chair, but she still appeared to be at ease, while her gaze drifted from her sister to roam around the room. I watched as her eyes tracked the guards at the door and roamed to the windows. Her gaze didn't waver as her eyes met mine.

I speared a tender piece of lamb and brought it to my mouth. I scoured my brain for a topic of conversation that wouldn't result in disaster. I wanted to maintain the peace Lennox and I had come to yesterday, but I had to admit, it was boring placating her. I enjoyed riling her. However, perhaps at the dinner table, in front of others, while still navigating our new-found peace agreement, was not the time.

"Your Highness?" Kara asked, pulling me out of my lingering thoughts.

"Please, call me Luka."

"Luka, can I ask you a question?"

"It would be my honor, my lady."

Color bloomed over her cheeks again as I spoke.

Such a different reaction than what her sister had towards me.

"I don't mean to be intrusive, but how did Captain Hale end up in your Royal Guard? It's just that it's rare for Fae to work in a different court than their home court, I was curious how this relationship occurred."

I smiled and looked at Declan, finding him smiling right back at me. I guess smiling would be a stretch. The left side of his mouth was slightly turned up, as much of a smile you could get out of Dec in this situation. But Kara had a point, it was extremely rare for Fae to leave their courts for other courts. Even more rare if they ended up in high-ranking positions.

"That is a long story."

"We've got time," Lennox added, surprising me with her interest. Declan nodded, giving me his approval to continue.

"Growing up, my father let me travel with him when he visited other courts." He always thought travel was the best way to learn than simply from books. I loved the trips I got to take with my father. Many Fae don't get the opportunity to see all Lethenia has to offer, I'm grateful I've had the opportunity. "When I was in the Lunar Court, I met a young wolf who was the son of the Lunar Court Emissary. He was a wild thing, still is." I chuckled to myself as I thought of Nico.

"We became friends right away. Our families started coordinating trips to other courts at the same time. According to them, it's never too early to start forming political friendships, even if we were only seven years old. Several years later we started hearing rumblings about a winged youngling in the Twilight Court's Royal Guard who was predicted to be the next great warrior. The rumors sparked both of our parent's interest, so we traveled to the Twilight Court when the first opportunity presented itself."

"As it turned out the rumors about this winged youngling were exaggerated. He was a phenomenon to look at, but his fighting skills were some of the worst I had ever seen."

I watched Lennox as she leaned back in her chair, crossing her arms over her chest. Her eyes roamed between Declan and myself.

"After watching him struggle for long enough I wandered over to him and asked if I could give him some pointers."

"And I told him to go fuck off," Declan grumbled.

"And I ignored you and asked if I could train with you."

"Which I also ignored."

"So I told him if he was going to pretend to be Lethenia's next great warrior he was going to need all the help he could get." I didn't know it at the time, but my words had been a trigger for Declan.

"Declan decided to ignore me instead of giving into my request, and since I don't like being ignored I knocked him on his ass with a swift punch to the gut." A huff of breath came from Lennox. "We've been friends ever since." I looked over at Declan. His face remained stoic, but his eyes glimmered in silent gratitude. Even though we never talk about it, I know how much that day changed his life. I don't like to think what would have happened to him if Nico and I hadn't taken him under our wing all those years ago—if we hadn't shown him that there was a place for him in the world out from underneath his father's thumb.

"You're kidding." Lennox shook her head. "You told him to fuck off, he doesn't listen, but punches you and you still become friends with him instead of killing him?"

"In my defense, I did punch him back," Declan added.

"A knife to the leg would have been much more efficient in getting your point across," Lennox remarked as she took a sip of her wine. She was something else, wasn't she? I shook my head. *Now is not the time, Luka.* Declan raised a brow at me. I ignored him and continued.

"We didn't become friends right away. I forced him to meet Nico later and trail along with us for the rest of the trip. I thought he needed some cheering up, and I wasn't going to leave him alone until I got a smile out of him."

"So, I take it you were successful?" Kara asked, glancing between me and the giant harpy beside me. "In getting a smile out of him?"

"Of course. It just took a couple years." I shoved Declan slightly and Kara smiled, her eyes fixed solely on Declan, almost like she was waiting to see even a hint of a smile from him. She likely wouldn't get one, not anytime soon anyway. Declan kept his emotions locked up tighter than anyone I'd ever met. Years ago he would have never accepted this dinner invitation. It made me proud to see him sitting here and interacting with others with ease.

"Wait, who's Nico?" Lennox asked.

"He's the annoying wolf pup, Luka mentioned before."

"He wanted to come too, but one of us had to stay back." I shrugged, taking a drink of my wine. "Nico drew the short straw. He threw a fit about it for a week. Claimed it was more important for him as my emissary to accompany me than Declan."

Lennox raised an eyebrow. "I would be inclined to agree if you weren't going into the heart of enemy territory."

"So, you're saying the decision was the right one?"

She raised her glass and held it towards me in a mimicked toast. "Only time will tell, Bloodsucker," she said before bringing the glass to her lips. I raised my glass in return before taking a sip myself.

"But that's not the real reason why I'm here," Declan added, sitting back in his chair.

"You're right, Captain Hale."

The sisters shared a look between them before glancing back at us in silent question. Sometimes I wondered if Declan delighted in watching people squirm because of how he grew up. Either way, now that he brought this up there was no turning back.

"The real reason why Declan is here is so I can feed from him."

7

LENNOX

The blood drained from Kara's face as the words fell from Luka's lips. Her fork clanged loudly on the table. "I think I lost my appetite," she murmured under her breath.

I looked over at the vampire prince to find the prick smirking at me. *Smirking.* I'd like nothing more than to smack the look off his face. "You truly are a bloodsucker then."

"Your nickname rings true, Sweetheart."

Anger rolled through me at the use of the nickname, but I kept my face expressionless.

"Did you forget vampires need to feed?" His eyes locked with mine—an ocean of deep impenetrable blue staring back at me. How had I let it slip my mind that vampires needed blood to survive? It was their curse from the Goddess after all.

"No, I've just assumed all of their victims were unwilling participants." *Like I was.* A tremor ripped through my body at the memory of the blinding pain from the vampire's bite. I had never been more helpless than I was when that vampire was draining the blood from my body. Luka's eyes softened as he studied me. He opened his mouth to speak, but I continued before he could get a word out. I turned my attention to the giant, half-shifted harpy sitting next to him.

"How sweet of you to come along as his own personal blood bag, Captain Hale. How loyal of you." It wasn't the smartest idea to provoke the captain of the Blood Court's Royal Guard, but how could a male like him let a vampire willingly feed from him? It couldn't have been by force. Captain Hale was one of the most intimidating males I had ever seen.

If the scar running across his left eye wasn't enough to make me want to hold my tongue, then the large black wings protruding from his back should be. I had never seen a half-shifted harpy before. I never knew harpies, or any shifting Fae, could only shift halfway. As if he knew I was talking about him, his feathery wings shifted as his golden gaze slid to me.

"It is my honor to serve my prince." His cool voice cut through the silence and I shook my head, draining the rest of the wine from my glass.

"Unbelievable," I muttered under my breath. I understood a willingness to serve, but wasn't there a line? I wondered what he did to convince Declan to participate in the first place.

"Would you rather I find someone *here* to feed from, Sweetheart?"

Rage bloomed in my chest at the thought as I formed my hands into fists on top of the table. Frost coated the cloth under my hands.

"That's what I thought," he said with a smug smile. "Since I figured you wouldn't be willing to offer anyone from your court —or yourself—as my source I figured I better bring back up."

I glared at the male in front of me—taking several deep breaths as I tried to keep my magic under control.

I opened my mouth, a retort posed on my lips, when Kara placed a hand on my leg. "Len, relax, it's fine," she whispered. I stared at her, bewildered at her calmness at the conversation at hand.

"I think it's considerate of you to bring your own blood source. We, and our people, appreciate it." When Kara spoke like that she reminded me of our mother—calm and graceful even under pressure. Never one to offend or anger anyone. Always the peacekeeper.

I took a deep breath, trying to channel as much of Kara and my mother as I could as I addressed the prince and his captain again. "Yes, thank you for being so considerate, Your Highness."

"Of course, I wouldn't want to make you uncomfortable, would I, Sweetheart." I gave him a tight-lipped smile, bringing my glass to my lips only to discover it was empty. It was for the best, I needed this dinner to be done before I did something unbecoming of a queen.

8

LENNOX

The morning breeze whipped the loose strands of hair across my face as I made my way through the trees toward the training center. I slept better last night than I had since Luka's arrival earlier this week. As much as I hated to admit it, I assumed it had everything to do with the truce between myself and the vampire prince.

I meant what I told Luka, I wanted peace between our courts. It was an idea that had been buried under layers of grief and anger. His words pulled back some of the layers and reminded me what my parents goal had been in the first place. It was never a task that could be completed overnight, they had been working toward peace for years. And I threatened to destroy all of their work with one conversation with the vampire heir. My mother had always preached forgiveness. She was soft and kind-hearted, traits synonymous with her people. While my father was hot-headed—his temper evened out by my mother. They made the best combination, bringing out the best in one another. They were both passionate about wanting the best for their people.

I was more like my father—I always have been. But there was never anyone who could smooth my jagged edges. My siblings tried, but it never worked. They didn't understand what I needed. None of my short-lived relationships were able to either. But my actions back then had little to no consequences. I could act out and be brash. I could hold a grudge and speak my mind. That all ended the moment the crown was placed on my head. My actions were no longer just a drop in the bucket, they were a tsunami breaching the shore, affecting everyone in their path.

I would need to channel more of my mother while I was working with Luka. I needed this relationship to work if I wanted to avoid an arranged marriage.

I passed through the last of the trees in the grove, the tension in my shoulders easing as the training center came into view. My relief was only temporary and I cursed at the sight of a familiar vampire.

Luka stood, arms crossed over his chest, leaning against the building with one leg propped on the wall. The light breeze blew his dark locks across his forehead. I swear his sapphire eyes glimmered even from a distance. What in the Stars was he doing here? My attempt at being nice and showing him the training facility the other day seemed to please him. *And ease some of my guilt for treating him terribly.* But why was he here now? We weren't due to meet again until this afternoon.

"Good morning, Sweetheart." He pushed off of the wall and strolled towards me. There was a casual confidence about him. Like he knew he was going to get what he wanted before he even asked.

"What are you doing here?" I crossed my arms as he stopped in front of me.

"I'm here to train, why else?" My eyes roamed over him, taking in how his training leathers displayed his sculpted muscles.

"I didn't say you could train here." When my eyes made their way back to his face I found him smirking at me.

"I know, but you dangled this beautiful facility in front of me and it's all I could think about."

I knew being nice would come back to bite me in the ass.

"There is a training facility in the palace you can use." I tried to brush past him but he was quicker, moving to block my path again.

"I don't want to use that one, I want to use this one"—he hiked his thumb over his shoulder, pointing at the facility—"with you."

"Why in the Stars would you want to train with me?"

He shrugged his shoulders. "From what I saw the other day, your skills are impressive. I figure we can both learn from each other."

He had a point, *I was pretty impressive*. And he hadn't even seen me wield a sword.

"Please, Lennox. We don't even have to talk to each other. You can ignore me the entire time." I looked to find those blue eyes blinking at me like a wounded animal. I sighed. I always was a sucker for animals.

"Fine." I might very well regret this decision, but I had to admit I didn't hate the idea of having someone to train with. My sessions with the younglings did nothing to improve my training. I could use a new opponent. I had been training with Kara for so long that we both knew each other's every move. And since Captain Kahle refused to let me train with the guard, it made Luka my best option. I made a move towards the door again and this time Luka let me pass. A wide smile plastered on his face.

"But if you touch my sword, you're out, Bloodsucker."

☾

After that first morning, Luka showed up every day to train with me. At first, I was taken aback by the intrusion. I liked my time training alone. But we had been training together for three weeks now and as the days went on I had to admit, it was nice to have someone there with me. Even if we hardly interacted. At the end of each session, we sparred in the ring. Each day we chose a different weapon. Some days it was daggers, others, swords or staffs, and sometimes it was hand-to-hand combat. For the first time since I was in the Royal Guard, I could feel my skills growing and improving. He even helped me during my sessions with Enric, who was improving at a much greater rate now with the help of the two of us. I'd be ready to start on a new youngling soon.

After training, we'd each go our separate ways to clean up, eat breakfast, and attend to whatever duties we needed to before meeting back in my office for the afternoon where we bounced ideas back and forth for the bargain. Although, we had yet to come up with something Luka thought would satisfy his grandfather.

Even with Luka and I training in the morning, I still upheld my afternoon training sessions with Kara three days a week. Luka and Declan had wandered upon us one day and had started training with us as well. I was hesitant at first, but I had to admit I appreciated being able to train with others. Especially since Declan was Captain of the Blood Court Royal Guard. He immediately dismissed our training guard and deemed himself our new trainer. I argued against him at first, but quickly gave in once I saw him at work. He's only a few years older than I, but he demonstrated more skills than any other guard I'd ever encountered. He started teaching me and Kara techniques from all of the different courts. He even broke down the strengths and weaknesses of each court's fighting style, including my own. Luka had shown me a little of this in our training sessions, but Declan was a much better teacher and his depth of knowledge on different fighting styles was extensive. It was fascinating to watch how the harpy came alive while he was teaching us.

In the few short weeks he'd been teaching us I could already tell I was improving. Declan's lessons brought attention to where my training had been lacking. I was able to practice different techniques and face new opponents who fought differently than any other opponent I'd ever faced. The only Fae I'd ever fought had been from the Star Court, except for the vampire two years ago.

But what might have been my favorite part of each training session, was watching Declan fight. Not only had I never seen a half-shifted harpy, but I had never witnessed a half-shifted harpy *fight*. It was one of the most magnificent spectacles I had ever witnessed.

The first day we trained together, Kara and I watched Declan and Luka spar for what felt like hours. Luka, with his twin blades, and Declan with a single sword he kept sheathed down his back, right between his wings. You would have thought Declan's wings would have been a weakness. That an opponent would be quick to try and strike them, or they would throw Declan off balance. They did none of those things. They were an extension of his body. His wings were a weapon in and of themselves. They moved in perfect synchrony with Declan's movements—shifted with every move of his blade. Watching him fight left me and Kara in awe and breathless. I couldn't stop my eyes from wandering toward Luka too. He wielded his twin blades like they were an extension of his own body. Every move was executed with deadly precision, and I couldn't tear my eyes from the veins that pulsed in his forearms, or the muscles that shifted in his back as he executed each strike. Watching the two friends duel was like watching a dance.

A hot, sweaty dance I would gladly watch every day.

This morning I arrived at the training facility before Luka, which I almost always did, but he was always soon to follow. I didn't wait for him as I started my warm-up routine. But after a half hour of warming up, Luka still hadn't arrived. *Maybe he slept in*. Or maybe something else came up.

A better offer.

Something more important than training this morning. The

thought sent an unfamiliar pang through my chest, but I shook off the feeling. Luka had no obligation to train with me. We never even made a plan. It just happened. He might have changed his mind and decided to train later in the day without me.

I've been training by myself for two years. I didn't need him here. Even if I didn't exactly mind his presence. It was better this way. I have my own space again.

I moved to one of the targets, daggers in hand and strapped to my thighs. I needed to get this build-up of energy out of me. Anything to shake away these feelings plaguing me. So, I took my stance and threw dagger after dagger until there were no more left. My chest heaved as I stared at the target.

I summoned a dagger of ice to my palm. The cold stung my fingertips as I aimed and the ice shattered as it hit the target. My flames tingled at the tips of my fingers as my power rose to the surface alongside my emotions.

I closed my eyes and took a steadying breath. What if something happened to him? *It's fine. He's fine. He just chose not to come. Something must have come up. You don't need him here.*

My eyes flew open at the sound of the door opening behind me. I whirled, reaching for a weapon as magic danced in my palms. I stilled as my eyes landed on Luka walking through the door towards me.

There was no reason for me to feel relief at his arrival. He didn't owe me anything—including showing up to training each morning, but that's what I felt . . . relief.

"Hey," he said as he approached the edge of the platform. I swung my legs over the wall and sat with my legs dangling beneath me.

"Hi."

"I'm sorry I'm late." He ran a hand through his hair, the pieces already falling every which way like he had been running his hands through it all morning.

"I was on my way out here when I was stopped by Alvise;

my grandfather sent word to me." It was then I noticed the letter in his hand. The red seal of the Blood Court, already broken.

"What did he say?" Luka ran his hand through his hair again. I swallowed.

"He's disappointed we haven't made any progress yet. That *I* haven't been able to make progress."

"Did he say anything else?" I asked hopefully. If only King Arlo would give us an idea of something that might satisfy him, it would make this process pick up. Luka rubbed at the back of his neck, I had never seen him this agitated before. His typical calm confidence was nowhere to be found.

"I'll spare you the details, but in short, he said I can do better."

I nodded. "I see."

We sat in silence. The only sound was my legs kicking anxiously against the wall—the thud reverberating through the empty facility. I studied Luka as he sat on the edge of the platform beside me. His arm brushed against mine as he took a deep breath before he finally spoke.

"Coming here and working with you—coming up with this deal—it's a test for me. A test set by my grandfather to see if I'm ready to be king."

His admission should have surprised me, but it didn't. It was common in many courts for the reigning monarch to put their heirs to the test before they received the crown. Especially when they were as young as Luka and I. If anything, it helped put the court's mind at ease.

"I bet you were hoping I'd be a lot easier to work with, huh?" I swung my foot and knocked it against his.

"That would have made things a lot easier, but nowhere near as fun." A hint of amusement lined his voice now as he knocked his leg against mine.

"Being king isn't an easy job, it's only fitting that the task fits the reward."

"You have a point." I kicked him one more time before jumping off the ledge to stand in front of him. I couldn't take his somber attitude right now. If I continued to let him talk like this it would rub off on me, and the last thing I needed was both of us in a spiral.

"C'mon Bloodsucker, let's save the sulking for later. You're already late, let's get to training and then we can get to work on figuring out a deal that will make you king."

"Wait, Lennox." Luka grabbed my arm, pulling me back towards him. "There's one more thing."

"What?" I put my hands on my hips as I waited for him to continue.

"I lied."

Dread settled low in my stomach. "What do you mean you lied?" I kept my voice as calm as possible.

"Well, I didn't lie, my grandfather technically did."

"Get on with it, Bloodsucker."

"Fine, fine." He ran his fingers through his hair. "My grandfather isn't looking for a trade agreement, he's looking for a book."

"A book? What do you mean he's looking for a book?"

"He and my uncle are looking for the Goddess's original spell book and he sent me here to find it."

My brows furrowed. "I've never heard of such a thing."

"Neither had I until shortly before I left to come here. My grandfather is under the impression you have it here, in the palace somewhere. That's why he sent me here. To either convince you to give it to me, or to find it for myself."

"Are you telling me you've been snooping around the palace?"

"No! No, Lennox I swear, I've only been in the libraries."

"And why should I believe you?"

"I'm telling you about the book, aren't I? Isn't that reason enough for you to trust me?"

I considered his words. This could be a ploy to get me to

give him the book. Not that I had any clue what book he was talking about.

"My grandfather made me swear I wouldn't tell you. He doesn't want you to know he wants the book. I'm risking my crown to tell you, Lennox. Think about it, if we work together to find this book, we both get what we want. I get my crown, you get me out of your hair and you escape an arranged marriage." I hated to admit it, but he had a point. "I've been spending my spare time combing through the books in the library, but I haven't made any progress. Think of how much quicker it would go if both of us were looking for this book."

I rolled his words over in my mind. "What's so important about this book anyway?"

Luka swallowed. "According to my grandfather, the book contains the cure to vampirism." My legs threatened to give out from beneath me.

"A cure to vampirism? How is that possible?" I breathed as a weight settled over my chest.

Luka shrugged. "I don't know. I don't know where or how my grandfather came across this information, but he's under the impression that when the Goddess created vampires, she also created a way to reverse her spell and turn them back into High Fae. He thinks that information is in this book."

A cure to vampirism.

Imagine a world without vampires. A world where we wouldn't have to worry about having life drained from us at the hands of a monster with a lust for blood. Why was King Arlo adamant about finding the book? Perhaps vampires didn't enjoy having to drink blood to sustain their livelihood as much as I thought.

A book . . . all we had to do was find this book and our problems would be solved.

"Okay."

Luka looked at me, a crease formed between his brows.

"Let's find this book, Bloodsucker."

9

LENNOX

"I heard you're throwing a ball in my honor, Sweetheart!" Luka called across the training center. I placed my bow back on the shelf and wiped the sweat off my brow with the back of my arm before turning to Luka, finding him with a smirk on his lips. Every time he smirked at me I wanted nothing more than to wipe it off. With a slap, a punch, or . . . something. Those smirks irked a part deep inside me.

"Where did you hear that nonsense?"

His smirk widened. I swear he knew how much those smirks aggravated me. "From Guilia, who insisted I share my preference for the color scheme."

I rolled my eyes. "The Star Court is throwing you a ball. Not me. Apparently, it is blasphemy you've been here this long and I have yet to throw a ball in your honor." Luka had been here almost two months and we were still no closer to finding the book. We spent all of our free time over the past weeks searching every inch of the palace for the book, with no luck. It didn't help that we had no idea what kind of book we were looking for. We spent hours in the library, researching, trying to find any mention of Astria's original spell book—or any kind of book associated with the Goddess, or a cure to vampirism. We had yet to find anything useful. If anything, the ball might offer a good reprieve from our search, if only for a day.

"I have to say, I'm excited to see how Alethens' balls compare to the celebrations in Cel Nox." That Stars damned smirk still resided on his lips as he spoke. "Promise me you'll save me a dance, Sweetheart?"

I rolled my eyes again—at both the idea of dancing with him, and the obnoxious nickname he continued to use.

"Only if you stop talking and let me continue on with my training, you prick."

Luka smiled broadly. "Sounds like a deal, Sweetheart."

☪

The palace has been buzzing with activity all week in preparation for the ball tonight. Everyone was excited, excluding me.

I used to love balls. I loved the music and dancing, I still do. But now, without my parents and brother by my side, the events felt empty and lifeless. Like a necessary task I needed to float through to check off my to-do list.

Growing up, after attending to our formal duties during a ball, Nol, Kara, and I used to get up to all kinds of mischief. When I was twelve we started daring each other to make the balls more entertaining. The dares started simple with things like: see who could sneak the most dessert and eat them without puking, dance with someone we had our eye on, or someone we despised. But slowly they became sneakier. Such as daring one another to steal a pin of a duke's lapel. Kiss one of the visiting lords. Or we'd escape the ball altogether. We'd load our plates with food, steal bottles of wine, and hide out in the garden until dawn.

We had always thought we were sneaky, that our parents had no idea. But our mother revealed to us one year that she and our father had caught onto our antics years ago. From then on she would sometimes give us a dare of her own. Or distract Olexa so we could sneak off.

But other times, we simply danced. We would dance all night until our feet couldn't hold us anymore—until our bodies gave out. We'd limp to bed and fall asleep the minute our heads hit the pillow. Sometimes all of us tumbled into the same bed, in whoever's room was closest, insisting we were too tired to make it on our own.

My heart clenched at the thought of waking up sandwiched between my two siblings. Remembering how Nol's dark hair would fall over his face, making him look younger as he slept.

But tonight would be different. There would be no sneaking off. There would be no dares. Only my duty as High Queen.

But Kara was trying to get me to see it differently. Trying to make new memories. Part of that being picking out the perfect dress. Something I could get excited about. I never underestimated the power of a good dress, and Kara knew that. I took pride in my appearance, as I always had. I liked the way clothes could make me feel. I felt as strong and powerful in this gown, as I did in my fighting leathers. It was the extra boost of confidence I needed going into tonight's ball.

I stared at myself in the mirror. Kara had helped me pick out a dress made of black silk with a high neckline. The back, or lack thereof, was my favorite part. The fabric dipped as low as possible without revealing my ass, and silver chains, adorned with small jewels, covered my exposed skin.

Kara spent the better part of an hour intricately pinning up my hair, leaving my exposed back on display with only a few loose pieces left out to frame my face. On top of my head, I wore a silver crown, adorned with black and red jewels.

A smile lit up her face as she took me in. "Wow, Len, you look stunning." She took my hands in hers and spun me around. "Everyone at the ball will be drooling over you." Her green eyes glimmered as a small laugh slipped from my lips.

"I bet Luka will lose his mind when he lays his eyes on you."

I laughed again. The idea of Luka looking at me in any other way than as a puzzle meant to be solved was preposterous.

"Don't laugh, you know it's true. I've seen the way he looks at you when we're training."

I gave her an incredulous look. "And what does he look at me like?"

"Like he'd love nothing more than to rip your clothes off."

"Kara!" I gaped at her, slapping her lightly on the arm.

"What?" She shrugged. "You can't tell me you haven't wondered what he looks like underneath those leathers. I know I have." She wiggled her eyebrows, and I rolled my eyes in response.

I *had* wondered what he hid under those leathers, not that I would ever admit it, even to my sister. I blamed it on the lack of Fae in my bed as of late. That was it. Nothing more.

"What about you?" I asked, quickly changing the subject to her. It had been a long while since Kara had spoken to me about a male or female she had an interest in. "I've seen the way you can't keep your eyes off of Declan."

A blush crept up her cheeks. "I just like admiring the way he looks. The same as you do with Luka, nothing more."

I took the hint and dropped the subject. If I didn't want her to push me any further, I wouldn't push her either.

"Anyway,"—I looked at myself in the mirror once again—"I'm not thrilled about having all eyes on me tonight." Growing up I had never minded attention, I could hide in the background if I wanted to. I had a choice if I was seen or not.

I no longer had that option.

Everywhere I went all eyes were on me. Everyone wanted a glimpse of the High Queen of Lethenia. "I'd much rather blend into the shadows."

Kara wrapped her arms around my waist, placing her chin on my shoulder as she stood behind me. "Len, you were never made to hide in the shadows." She gave me a slight squeeze as I met her eyes in the mirror, giving her a small smile.

"What would I do without you, Kara?" I squeezed her hands resting around my waist.

"I honestly don't know and the thought scares me."

I laughed, a real laugh.

Sometimes I forget what it feels like to laugh. To have fun and not worry about everyone else. To not stand under the crippling weight of grief, even if it was only for a few minutes laughing with my sister. I rarely laughed these days. *Genuinely* laughed. When I did it was usually because of Kara. She's the only thing that kept me tethered to this world when the ground crumbled out from underneath me—from us, two years ago.

I stared at our reflections in the mirror. It baffled me sometimes how we could look similar, yet so different. We shared the same heart-shaped face, narrow nose, and full lips. But that was where the similarities stopped. If I was the star in the dark sky, she was the shimmering sun.

Kara wore a gown the color of golden honey, a shade lighter than our matching golden hair. The shimmering material fell in a pool around her feet. The fabric was embroidered with flowers, stars, and suns in golden thread. Her shoulder-length hair was loosely curled and she wore no adornments besides a pair of yellow, teardrop-shaped jewels in her ears. The smattering of freckles across her nose was more visible now from her time spent in the summer sun.

I moved out of my sister's embrace and went to my dresser, picking up the crown I had requested from the vault this afternoon, and brought it over to Kara. Her mouth widened in surprise.

"Lennox, is that what I think it is?"

I placed the crown gently on her head. "It is."

Tears glistened in her eyes.

"It suits you." I stepped back and took in the crown on her head. It was a simple gold crown with a blush undertone. Delicate, golden vines with flowers wove their way around the base.

The rounded spires held various sizes and shapes of diamonds. It was simple and elegant. So utterly Kara.

It was our mother's favorite crown.

"I miss her." The words came out a whisper so soft I almost missed them.

"Me too." I pulled my sister into a hug. Tears threatened to spill down my face as emotion, thick and heavy, clogged my throat. This was another reason why I now hated balls, it brought back this well of emotion I spent every day trying to outrun. With Kara, it was harder to shut those emotions down. She was the only person who knew what it felt like to lose what we had lost. Although she handled her grief much better than I did. Kara embraced it—charged forward through it. While I chose to push it away and hide from it, hoping one day it would all disappear.

I hugged my sister tighter, letting her live in this swell of emotions for a minute longer while I locked mine back down. Pushing them back into the box in my mind and locking it up tight. There was no room for emotions tonight. Tonight I needed to be High Queen Lennox Adair. So I allowed myself one last moment before I locked the box up completely.

"I love you, Kara."

She wrapped her arms around me tighter. "I love you too, Len."

I stepped back and surveyed my sister—my strong, beautiful sister. "Until the stars turn to dust," I repeated the words our mother had whispered to us every night as she tucked us into bed.

Kara smiled. "Until the stars turn to dust."

10

LUKA

Heads turned in our direction as Declan and I entered the ballroom. I was used to the attention being on me, but this felt different. The energy surrounding us was mixed. I could sense it, my magic was on alert, swirling and pushing against the surface of my skin.

By the looks on the Fae's faces, some were happy to see me, while others were wary or outright appalled. But could I blame them? In their minds I was the enemy in the same way Lennox viewed me when I arrived. I tried my best to tune out their whispers—I had no interest in hearing what they thought of me. The only High Fae's opinion that mattered was the High Queen herself. And wondering what she thought was taking all of my time and energy. In the months since I'd arrived, I felt like I started to make headway with Lennox and I wondered if she realized what she was doing. Little by little, in each of our interactions I could feel her warming up to me. She no longer shut down conversations immediately, sometimes we even dined together or spent time outside of training or our research together.

A servant carrying a tray filled with glasses of sparkling wine passed us, I snatched two glasses off the tray as she passed, handing one to Declan. He accepted it with a nod, before continuing his surveillance of the ballroom.

Banquet tables, filled with a wide assortment of food lined both sides of the room. The far right wall was lined with floor-to-ceiling windows looking out into the garden, where orbs of lights lined the darkened path. Two thrones, made of swirled gold and white marble sat on a raised dais at the far end of the room. A large gold star, representing the Star Court, sat directly in the center of the headrest. The symbols of the magical elements were etched into the marble on either side of the star, and all were etched in gold. Whirls and swirls for air, a cresting wave for water, three snow-capped mountains for earth, and burning flames for fire.

Silence fell over the ballroom as everyone's attention turned to the grand staircase at the front of the room. A royal guard stood at the top of the small balcony, by a set of closed double doors. Once the crowd had quieted, the male opened the door and Kara appeared and descended the stairs. Her golden gown flowed behind her, a small smile poised on her lips. The simple crown adoring her head glimmered in the light of the ballroom. I looked at Declan beside me out of the corner of my eye, but his gaze was set fully on Kara, as if he was watching every step her slippered feet took on the marbled stairs.

My focus moved from Declan to the guard at the top of the stairs again as he spoke, his voice booming through the room. "Your Royal Majesty, High Queen Lennox Adair." My heart stopped as Lennox appeared at the top of the stairs.

She was breathtaking.

I watched as the throng of people parted to allow their queen through, heads bowed as she passed.

My eyes tracked her every movement through the crowd. When she passed me, my gaze snagged on the back of her dress. Sparkling jewels caught in the light as they covered the bare skin of her back. *Fuck.* I rubbed at the back of my neck.

Someone handed Lennox a glass of wine as she reached the

dais, and she surveyed the crowd for a second before signaling everyone to rise. Her eyes found mine where I stood in the crowd, and stayed locked with mine for several seconds before she continued her perusal.

"Thank you all for coming tonight. It is the Star Court's honor to have the Prince of the Blood Court, Heir to the Throne, Luka Rossi, visiting our court." She gestured to where I was standing, a ring of murmurs breaking out around the room as she did. "Tonight we celebrate and honor him, and the Blood Court. We look forward to a fruitful alliance between our two courts."

This was the first time I had truly seen her play the part of the queen. But I knew her well enough now that I could see behind the mask of her words. I could see behind the fake smile, she pasted on her face as the words flowed from her blood-red lips. I had to admit, the role of queen suited her. Although, I much preferred the fiery side of Lennox.

Lennox raised her glass. "To Prince Luka and the Blood Court." Her gaze landed back on mine, and I lifted my glass in salute. The room cheered around us, but Lennox and I remained fixed on one another. I threw her a wink, and she brought her glass to her lips, hiding her growing smirk before turning back to the crowd.

"Let the celebration begin," Lennox commanded and the crowd dispersed. Some moved towards the banquet tables, while others began dancing as the musicians started playing again. I watched as Kara leaned over and whispered something in her sister's ear that made Lennox's lips twitch upward for a split second. The sisters squeezed hands before Kara stepped back and made her way into the crowd of Fae, leaving Lennox to man her throne, alone.

I scanned the room.

Most of the Fae were engaged in conversations with one another, and many glanced at the queen as they murmured to themselves before quickly looking away. I wondered how often the court got to see their High Queen.

I turned my gaze from the crowd and found myself fixed on Lennox again. She sat alone on her throne, legs crossed and arms firmly against the armrests on either side, her crown glimmering in the light. She was the picture of elegant power. I felt like if I looked at her too long I'd get sucked into her orbit and never be able to find my way out of it.

She surveyed the room with a flat expression. Not angry, but not happy either. I didn't know her well enough to discern what the expression meant, but it didn't look like she was enjoying herself.

Time ticked by slowly. It appeared everyone wanted to have an audience with me and I was pulled into mundane conversations every three steps. I was so bored talking to a Duke that I considered plucking my eyes out for some slight amusement. I might not have been in everyone's favor, but it didn't stop them from wanting to catch the ear of the heir to the Blood Court. I hated political conversations at balls.

In the Blood Court, balls were not a place for political gain. They were for fun. A place to let loose with no regard. A place for royals to give in to their deepest desires. This was a far cry from a Blood Court celebration. In Cel Nox, the walls of the palace's ballroom were stained with debauchery. I was hardly ever alone at a Blood Court celebration. Males and females were vying for my attention all night long. It was something I enjoyed, it was what I had grown up knowing. But seeing the stark difference between the Blood Court and the Star Court was unsettling.

Lennox and Kara engaging in Blood Court celebrations would be a sight to see. Kara might die of embarrassment, but Lennox . . .I had no idea if Lennox would balk or bask in the celebrations. I had to admit I was curious to find out.

"How is the gem harvest looking this year?" The Lord, whose name I had already forgotten, asked. I put on my most charming smile and I drew my attention back to our conversation.

"When I left it was looking pretty promising."

The Ignis mountains that bordered the Blood Court and the Court of Embers were hosts to Lethenia's largest gem mines, and the Blood Court's largest source of income. If anything was made with gems in Lethenia, odds were they came from the Blood Court. The Court of Embers had no interest in the gem trade, they made their profits helping with the mining process before passing everything off to the Blood Court. Everyone was looking to get into our trade routes, which had been tightly locked down for centuries.

"That's great to hear," the male said, taking another sip of his drink. I tuned him out again as he continued to drone on about trading, my gaze again wandering towards the throne at the front of the room.

Throughout every conversation I engaged in I found myself looking towards her, perched on her throne. She had yet to move from her spot. Fae came up and engaged her in conversations, but she remained on the dais assessing everyone around her. I kept wracking my brain, trying to find an excuse to go and talk to her. Why? I wasn't sure. But I was growing tired of dull conversations and conversations with Lennox were never dull. She was full of fire and I wanted nothing more than to stoke it —cause a flame to rise. I delighted in seeing the fire in her eyes.

I could ask her to dance—no one had yet, or at least she hadn't accepted any dances. She might very well reject me, but it was worth a shot. Something deep inside me urged me to move forward through the people to offer my arm to her. It was my duty as the guest of honor to offer her the first dance, right?

Why I was desperate for scraps of Lennox's attention was a problem for another day.

Having made my decision, I discarded my empty glass on a table and I started making my way through the crowd towards Lennox. As I reached the dais I watched as another male took her hand, placing a kiss to it before leading her to the dance floor.

A growl threatened to slip from my throat as the male placed his hand on her back. Something about the sight of another male touching her stirred something inside me. An urge to claim her. Although, I knew she wasn't mine—she never would be mine—she *wasn't* his. Whoever *he* was.

I was so focused on Lennox and the male's hand on her exposed back that I didn't notice Kara appear at my side until she spoke.

"Enjoying your ball?" she asked as she sipped from her drink, handing me a glass as well.

I plastered a smile on my face, momentarily shoving down the swell of emotions festering inside of me. "Of course, it's wonderful." We stood in silence for a moment before I lost my restraint. "Who's that?" I asked, although I don't know why. It was none of my business who Lennox danced with.

"Lord Loris Driscoll. He's one of the many here who are hoping to have my sister's hand." She took another sip of her wine as she nodded to the crowd around us.

"Her hand in marriage?" Not that there would have been another hand she was talking about, but I needed to hear the confirmation.

Kara nodded. "Lennox doesn't invite suitors to the palace, or accept any of their invitations. Any time there is a ball where they can get a moment with her they take the opportunity to try and persuade her."

Rage burned inside me. Or was that jealousy? The idea of other Fae vying for Lennox's attention stirred something vile inside me. Something dangerous and unfamiliar. The urge to claim her as mine coursed through me again. *I* was the male who fought for her attention. That was *our* game.

I knew what it was like, I was the heir to my own court. I had males and females vying for my hand at any given opportunity. But the idea of them treating Lennox like a prize . . . that pissed me off. I refused to watch her dance with anyone else. Stars be damned, Lennox Adair was *mine*, and mine alone, until I left her court.

"And Lennox let's it happen?" I all but gritted out.

Kara scoffed. "She doesn't have much of a choice. It's not like she can decline every dance offered to her." I looked to Lennox, where she moved on the dance floor with the lord. Her posture was stiff, her hands placed strategically on the lord's frame, a tight smile planted on her lips. "She used to love balls before she was queen."

My eyes didn't stray from Lennox as Kara spoke. "Sometimes I wish I could whisk her out of here like we used to."

I glanced at Kara out of the corner of my eye. "What do you mean?"

"When we were younger, when a ball was particularly boring, Lennox, Nol, and I used to sneak bottles of wine out to the garden. We'd wind up drunk and pass out in the hedges."

It was hard to picture *that* Lennox in my mind—someone carefree. It didn't match up with the rigid queen before me, or the defensive female I spent my days with. Maybe that's where her spark stemmed from, the old version of herself.

"We lost a lot that night, two years ago." Kara's voice was hardly a whisper. If it weren't for my enhanced hearing I wouldn't have been able to hear her over the voices of the crowd. "But sometimes I feel like I lost Lennox too. Neither of us will ever be the same as we were before . . . but Lennox, she lost more than I did. Sometimes I miss the person she was before."

"Grief changes people." *Didn't I know that.* "Lennox will never fully be the person she was *Before* . . . no one ever is."

Kara only nodded as she continued to survey her sister on the dance floor.

"Give her time. Give her time to forge a new version of herself. One that will merge with the new."

Kara looked at me, her green eyes, a mirror to Lennox's,

glistening. "Anyway," Kara said, her voice rising an octave as she blinked her eyes furiously. "You should do me a favor and ask my sister to dance."

"You think that's a good idea?"

A cat-like grin spread over her face." I think she'd love nothing more. It is a ball in your honor after all. She owes you that much."

I drained the rest of my glass and placed it on a tray as it passed. "I underestimated you, *Princess Kara.*"

A laugh bubbled from her lips. I bowed to her dramatically before making my way through the crowd to Lennox, Kara still smiling after me.

I saw the moment Lennox realized what I was doing. Her eyes widened before she looked around anxiously.

"Excuse me, may I cut in?" I tapped the lord on the shoulder. He turned, a deep scowl painted on his face, but his expression changed to pleasant in a matter of seconds when he recognized who I was.

"Oh course, Your Highness." He stumbled, bowing and stepping backward.

The fake smile Lennox had pasted on her face faltered for a second as she took a moment to scowl at me.

"My Queen." I bowed slightly. "May I have this dance?" I held out my hand to her. She rolled her eyes before hesitantly placing her hand in mine.

"I don't have much of a choice do I?" she muttered under her breath.

"No, you don't, Sweetheart."

11

LENNOX

I jumped as Luka placed his hand on the small of my back. The feel of his cool, calloused palm against my bare skin sent a jolt of electricity up my spine. He pulled my body towards him and I let him, his cool, fresh scent invading my senses as he overtook the space in front of me. I silently cursed as I placed my hand on his shoulder and he joined our other hands together before leading me around the dance floor.

I let myself look at him, really look at him, for the first time, all night, as he led me in a dance. His dark suit was embroidered with silver and red thread, and was fitted perfectly to his muscular frame. His dark hair was tamed back from his face with some kind of product, keeping it in place for once. His blue eyes glimmered in the light of the ballroom.

I hated how handsome he was.

I watched as every male and female took turns sneaking glances at him throughout the night. But was I any different?

I missed a step, and Luka chuckled lightly as he caught me, his breath warm against my skin.

"Kara tells me you have a whole line of suitors bidding for a moment of your time tonight."

I tilted my head back to meet his gaze. "And here I was having a pleasant time until you had to remind me."

His eyes glimmered. "Did you just admit to having a pleasant time with me?"

"Don't test me, Bloodsucker."

He pulled me closer, my waist now pressed against him as he moved us, causing heat to spread through my body at the contact. "Do you have any interest in any of them?" Something changed in his gaze, an emotion flickering across his face I couldn't place.

"No. Not if I have any say in it." I felt Luka's body relax slightly under my hands.

"What do you mean?"

"There is no law in the Star Court that a king or queen must be married to rule, so I don't plan on marrying for the sake of an alliance. I'd rather remain unmarried than have an arranged marriage."

He spun us in a circle, his eyes never leaving mine. "Interesting. So that's why you're trying so hard to get along with me." I nodded as we continued to move around the floor. I weighed my words, deciding how much I wanted to share with the vampire prince. Maybe it was the wine loosening my tongue, or the need for a genuine conversation tonight. I refused to admit there was something about Luka that made me want to open up to him. He'd be gone soon anyway, there was no harm in indulging him in this conversation.

"I hope, one day, if I do marry, it will be for love." I couldn't look at Luka as I spoke, instead I looked over his shoulder at the room of Fae dancing around us. "I have had little control over my life in the past few years. Any, if all, choices given to me have already been made for me, or I have to consider the consequences the choice would have. It's never just about me. It's about my sister, my court, and all of Lethenia. I rarely get to choose something selfishly. I'd like to think someday I can make the selfish decision to marry for love. That I can find my mate."

Luka remained silent as he continued to move us around the dance floor, waiting for me to continue.

"My parents were mates." True loves, equals, a perfect match in every way—a gift given by the Goddess and the Stars to a rare and select amount of Fae as they saw fit. "Their love for one another was evident whenever you saw them together. You could feel the intensity of the mating bond flickering between them. When you are raised around love like that you can't help but hope you find something similar someday for yourself. That's why I want to avoid an arranged marriage."

When I finally looked back at Luka I found him staring at me with intensity.

"I hope you get to make that choice, Lennox, I really do."

I blinked at him—once, twice, three times.

His grandfather was holding an arranged marriage over my head and yet Luka was telling me he hoped I got to choose love. That I could one day find my mate? Every time I thought I was starting to figure him out, he threw me for a loop. I mentally shook my head, willing those dizzying thoughts to scatter, and instead turned my attention back to Luka. I didn't want to talk about myself anymore. Or even think about myself.

"What about you?" I cocked my head as I looked at him. "Do you have anyone waiting for you back in Cel Nox?" My stomach dipped at the thought, but I ignored it as he chuckled softly.

"No, there isn't anyone waiting for me."

"Well then, has anyone here caught your eye tonight?" I looked around the room, looking for someone he could be interested in. They were here in plenty tonight, he'd have lots to choose from if he desired. When I turned back to Luka he was looking at me with such intensity I felt I might burn. I shivered and sucked in a breath as he leaned in close, his lips dusting the shell of my ear. Goosebumps rose over my body at his warm breath on my ear.

"The only one who has caught my eye since I've been in Alethens is you, Lennox Adair."

I swallowed, my breathing unsteady as he pulled back. He still looked at me with that burning intensity.

"Don't look surprised, Sweetheart."

Somehow we were still dancing, my body on autopilot as he continued to move me around the dance floor while I tried and failed to process what was happening. My body suddenly became conscious of every place we touched.

His thumb brushing over the back of my hand that was intertwined with his.

His hand splayed possessively on my hip as he held me to him.

The tips of his fingers resting on the bare skin of my back.

"Every male and female in this room has their eyes on you, including me."

The song ended, and I took a step back, attempting to move out of his hold only to have him pull me back in. I looked at him, confused, as he continued to hold me to him. I wanted to pull out of his embrace, but I wasn't sure I'd be able to without making a scene. The last thing I needed was the court talking about me pushing Luka away when we were supposed to be allies.

"Can you pretend, for a moment, that you trust me?" His face was pleading, but there was something else there too. A mischievous glimmer in his eyes. I could almost hear him silently taunting me. *I dare you to trust me, Sweetheart.*

I didn't trust Luka. But I was curious what he had up his sleeve. I gave a slight nod of my head, my words evading me. The grin that spread over Luka's face was devastating. It spread all the way to those dazzling eyes. My stomach did a little flip at the sight of that smile.

Luka finally let go of me only to hold out his arm instead. "Right this way, My Queen."

I reluctantly looped my arm through his and followed as he

led me through the crowd toward the banquet tables where Declan was standing. His wings were tucked in tight as Fae moved around him. His black hair was down tonight, falling in loose waves at his shoulders. He stood out amongst the Fae in the room, not only because of his wings jutting out behind him, but also because his broad shoulders and stony expression caused Fae to stumble out of his way as they passed. The stories of the half-shifted harpy preceded him.

Luka let go of my arm and I watched as he whispered something into Declan's ear. Declan nodded and glanced at me as Luka continued to speak.

What in the Stars is he up to?

Luka patted Declan on the shoulder before turning back to me.

"C'mon." He grabbed my hand and pulled me along, giving me no option but to follow him. As we passed one of the banquet tables he grabbed a bottle of wine, quickly stashing it inside his jacket.

"What are you doing?" I hissed, but he only grinned as he glanced around the room, still holding onto my hand as he guided me.

"You'll see."

I let out an irritated sigh.

"You're pretending to trust me, remember?"

"Then stop making me regret it so quickly, Bloodsucker."

He smiled at me over his shoulder as he continued pulling me along.

When we made it to the far edge of the ballroom, Luka pulled us through the glass doors that entered into the garden. Realizing where we were going I stopped, but Luka tried to pull me along, not acknowledging my resistance.

"I can't leave the ball."

"Yes, you can."

"No, I can't, did you forget I'm the queen?"

"I could never forget that, Sweetheart." He flashed me one

of his devastating smiles. "If it makes you feel better, I told Declan if anyone asks about your whereabouts he is to say you are with me, attending to an important, queenly duty."

I cursed under my breath before letting him continue to lead me.

I was curious, that's all. I had been bored to tears sitting on the throne alone, and he was the guest of honor, after all. I would indulge him this once.

We wove our way through the garden until we came out the other side. Luka led me out farther, until finally stopping on the top of the hill. You could no longer hear the ball behind us, and the lights lining the garden didn't reach out this far. The moon and the stars were the only light.

Luka plopped down on the grass and uncorked the bottle of wine before taking a swig and offering the bottle to me.

I stared at him. "Why did you bring me out here?"

"Sit down and try to relax and I might tell you."

I huffed a breath and reluctantly sat in the grass next to him, my dress pooling around me. He held out the wine bottle again and this time I took it, taking a long swig from the bottle before passing it back to Luka.

"I was talking to Kara earlier and she mentioned you used to love balls before you became queen."

I kept my gaze straight ahead, but out of the corner of my eye, I saw Luka watching me.

"She wished she could whisk you away. I thought I'd take it upon myself." He took another swig from the bottle. "You can either thank or blame Kara later."

A noise adjacent to a laugh sounded in my throat. I held out my hand for the bottle, taking another sip. Stars damned, my sister—constantly trying to ease tensions between everyone.

"What else did Kara tell you?" I asked, taking another drink of wine before handing it back to him.

"She said you used to sneak out and get drunk." He took another sip from the bottle.

"We also used to dare one another." A small smile crept up Luka's face. I felt mine start to do the same, the wine already taking effect. "It started innocently, like who could eat the most cookies. But as they got older they got riskier."

"Riskier how?" he asked.

"One of us would distract a guest while the other stole something from them."

Luka let out a laugh. "You're kidding?"

"Nope, one time I stole three coins out of a Duke's pocket while Nol distracted him in conversation."

"Lennox Adair, you sly thing. I never expected the High Queen to have been such a rule breaker."

I scoffed, as he passed the bottle back to me. "You don't even know half of it. I was the rule breaker—the risk taker. I pushed the boundaries constantly. I drove my brother, Nol, crazy; he felt like he was responsible for me. When he caught wind of whatever trouble I was up to, he'd lecture me and when I still wouldn't listen he'd come with me." I smiled softly at the memories. "He'd piss and moan the entire time, but no matter how many times I told him to leave me and let me do it on my own, he never did. Even when I'd get caught. He never tried to place blame on me to avoid punishment. Even when it was all my doing, he never tried to evade punishment. He always stayed by my side."

Until he didn't. Because he left me. Grief so sharp, like a knife stabbing through my chest, hit me suddenly. My chest tightened painfully—my breathing became shallow. *This*, this crippling, all-consuming feeling, *this* is why I rarely let myself think of him.

"He sounds like a great brother."

I blinked back the dampness threatening to clog my sight. "He was." We sat in silence as I took several deep breaths. Luka moved, reclining on the grass, interlocking his hands behind his head like a pillow.

"I don't have any siblings, but I had a cousin."

I blinked, not taking my eyes off him as he continued to stare at the sky above us.

"Her name was Este. She was the closest thing I had to a sibling. We spent a lot of time together growing up. She was my only friend until Nico."

I continued to watch him as he spoke.

"When she was fourteen and I was ten she disappeared."

The breath left my lungs.

"She and her friend went out into the woods beyond the palace, they did all the time, but one day they never came back."

I didn't dare move as he continued. "We searched for them for weeks, months. But never found any traces of them. Still haven't to this day."

"I'm sorry." The words felt like sandpaper in my throat. I couldn't imagine losing someone and not knowing what happened to them. Not knowing if they were dead or alive. It made me thankful I at least knew what had happened to my family.

I moved so I was laying beside him, the grass tickling the bare skin of my back as I looked up at the stars. When was the last time I had looked at the stars?

"What was she like? Your cousin?"

"She was . . . she was complicated." Silence stretched between us as he chose his next words. "Her mother died when she was young, which led to my uncle being overprotective of her. She was kind and caring, but she was also reckless. My uncle had no idea the trouble she got into behind his back. Her disappearance changed him. He hasn't been the same since."

Grief hung thick and heavy between us—both his and my own. Luka shuffled beside me, his arm moving into the space between us. I flinched as the back of his hand brushed against mine. He moved it away before gently placing it back against mine. The contact was light—I could hardly feel it—and a long-forgotten part of me yearned to grasp his hand in mine. To let my fingers dance over his skin. It had been a long time since I'd touched another like that. Since I had wanted to for more than a night of distraction.

"The stars don't look like this in Cel Nox." His words broke through the silence and I closed my eyes, willing those thoughts to scatter. When I opened them again I rolled to the side, moving my hand away from his and creating a pillow under my head as I looked at him. His gaze stayed firmly on the sky above us. "I don't know why."

I said nothing as I continued to stare at him. I took in the hard line of his jaw. His full bottom lip. The way his dark hair appeared to gobble up the moonlight. He must have felt me staring at him. He turned to look at me, a smirk playing on his lips, but he didn't say anything as he turned on his side and faced me.

"So, Lennox, what ball tradition do you want to partake in tonight? Is sneaking off enough or do we need to take a step further?" I rolled my eyes as he continued.

"We could go back and find an unwilling Fae to harass." I felt a smile creeping up my lips as he continued, "Or I could go find something stronger than wine and get you filthy drunk."

My smile fell, I recovered quickly, but not quick enough.

A crease formed between Luka's brows. "What is it?"

"It's nothing." I turned away, forcing myself to look at the stars and not the male staring at me.

"It's not nothing," he pressed. I continued to ignore him as he sat and scrubbed his hand through his hair, messing up his perfectly tamed locks. "I didn't mean to upset you." His voice was strained. "I just . . . I thought we were having a good time and I said something to fuck it up."

"It's not you . . ." I drifted off. How could I explain to him it wasn't him, it was me and my demons that haunted me? My head was light from all the wine, blurring lines in my mind that shouldn't be crossed. I had already given Luka so much tonight —I shouldn't give him anymore. I had already shown him too much of myself. But the dejected look on his face—I wanted to get rid of that look.

"I don't drink like that anymore."

Luka turned and looked at me over his shoulder. I tore my gaze away from him and looked back at the stars. If I was going to share this I couldn't look at him while I did.

"*After* . . . two years ago I was in a dark place." I closed my eyes and shuttered at the memory. The months after their deaths were dark. I only remembered a small handful of the memories. "I put on my mask of queen during the day and did what I had to do, it was the distraction I needed during the day. But at night . . ." I squeezed my eyes shut and I heard Luka rustle beside me. When I opened my eyes he was laying next to me again, staring at the sky.

"At night there was nothing to distract me. After a while I couldn't take it anymore. I couldn't sit and wallow in my grief every night. Instead I altered my appearance and would go into town and drink until I couldn't see straight. Sometimes I'd fall asleep in the tavern." I didn't remember much that happened those nights—only the walk to town and waking up early in the morning with my face stuck to the bar. But when I drank there were never any nightmares. "Or I'd wake up in a stranger's bed." I swallowed the lump in my throat. I never cared about any of the Fae I bedded during those months. I used them as a distraction and I hated myself for it.

"Kara eventually caught wind of what I was doing." The look on her face when she found me in the tavern that night is scorched into my memories forever. "If it wasn't for Kara, I might still be living my life that way." Luka remained silent beside me, but I could feel his eyes on me. His hand found mine in the grass between us and he took it in his, giving it a light squeeze. His thumb rubbed gently over my skin.

"I only drink in moderation now. I never want to do that to Kara again. I never want to go back to that dark place." I focused on the feeling of his hand in mine, the motion of his thumb, and not the swell of emotions that threatened to over-flow inside of me. I focused on the feeling of Luka's skin on mine as I wrangled my emotions back into the box I kept them in and locked them back up tight.

"Okay, your turn." I took a deep breath. "I overshared, now you go." A light chuckle left his mouth as he looked back at the night sky.

"I already shared about my cousin, we're even now."

"Fine, but you better promise never to breathe a word of anything that transpired tonight to anyone."

"What would happen if I did?" Mischief danced in his eyes. "Would you stab me again?"

"We'd start there, the rest would be a surprise."

"Such a vicious creature."

I said nothing, but smiled as I stared at the stars—I swore several of them glimmered. And I couldn't help but notice the warmth that had spread throughout my body as we lay in the grass, despite the chill of the night. A long-forgotten feeling started clawing its way back to the surface through the dust and rubble that was my heart.

I would never say it out loud to anyone, but I silently thanked Kara for tonight.

12

LENNOX

Luka and I continued laying under the stars, chatting idly for over an hour. When I finally told him I should get back to the ball, he didn't refuse. He offered me his hand and pulled me to standing before escorting me back inside. Neither of us said anything, but he didn't let go of my hand as he led me back through the garden.

The second the sounds from the ballroom hit my ears the light feeling I had from our excursion dissipated. I straightened my shoulders and schooled my face back into its resting place of mild indifference.

When we reached the doorway Luka turned to me, he opened his mouth to speak but was interrupted.

"Your Majesty. I've been looking for you."

I turned to find Alvise rushing towards me.

I resisted a scowl. I was about to dismiss him when Luka squeezed my hand, giving me a wry smile before releasing my hand and disappearing into the crowd.

After my conversation with the duke Alvise had introduced me to, I made my way back to the dais. As I sat on my throne and scanned the room I told myself I was looking for Kara, but I also found my gaze searching for a certain blue-eyed vampire. Disappointment flooded my system at my inability to spot either one of them. I didn't want to sit here alone anymore. I didn't want to have any more political conversations, or dance with anyone else vying for my hand.

I was tired. So tired of sitting here. Of being forced to put on this act.

It was lonely here on this throne alone.

It was late into the evening now, and I felt like I had spent enough time presiding over everyone so I excused myself and made my way back to my bedchamber.

I was exhausted. I wanted nothing more than to drop face first into my bed and never attend another ball. The hours spent with Luka under the stars seemed far away.

As I entered the corridor to my room the hairs on the back of my neck rose. My magic stirred inside me—my fingertips tingled as it rose to the surface.

Someone was following me.

I paused. Heavy footsteps sounded down the hall. Whoever it was wasn't making an effort to be quiet. I continued walking, making sure to keep my footsteps light, but quickening my pace.

"Your Majesty," a voice rang from behind me. I cringed before turning to find the lord that I had danced with earlier, making his way towards me.

"Yes, my Lord?"

His name had been familiar, although I failed to remember it now. I assumed his name crossed my desk on several occasions in proposals for my hand that I promptly discarded. He hadn't been forward to say as much during our short dance, but he had skirted around the subject, offering me an abundance of platitudes in the process. He spent the entire time trying to charm me, failing to realize his attempts were in vain.

"Please, call me Loris."

I offered him a tight smile. Right, Loris Driscoll, he was the Lord of one of the cities on the outskirts of Alethens. "Loris, is there something I can assist you with?"

"I was hurt when I noticed you slipping off without saying goodbye." He invaded the space in front of me. "I was hoping to earn some more of your time."

I could smell the alcohol on his breath as he continued to move in closer.

"I'm afraid I couldn't stop and wish every guest a good night." His light auburn hair was bound in a knot at the nape of his neck, but several pieces had slipped loose and hung around his face.

"You had plenty of time for the vampire prince tonight."

My stomach tightened at the mention of Luka.

Lord Driscoll took another step closer, leaving little space between us now. He ran his finger up and down my arm as his eyes roamed over my body. I balled my hands into fists in an effort not to slap his hand away. I wanted nothing more than to turn on my heels and ignore his pursuit, but I couldn't risk damaging our political relationship, his territory provided a majority of the produce in Alethens. But if he continued to touch me I might not be able to restrain myself.

"I was hoping you would be looking for me. That *I* made an impression on you."

I took a step back, my back meeting the wall. "If you'll excuse me I should go." I attempted to duck out of the space he had trapped me in, but he caught me by the wrist, pulling me back to him.

"Not so fast, Your Majesty."

I tried to wrestle out of his hold, but the grip on my wrist tightened, quickly turning painful as his fingers dug into my arm. My magic swirled violently inside me, my swell of power pushing against my skin. If I unclenched my fist I worried it would shoot out involuntarily.

Lord Driscoll leaned in closer, licking his lips. "I am not done with you yet, Your Majesty."

A snarky remark threatened to spill from my lips, but I held it back, biting my tongue hard enough to taste blood. I couldn't let my anger take control of this situation. I needed to nullify it as best as I could. Even though I wanted nothing more than to send my dagger through his heart.

My magic sang in response. *Not yet.*

"Let me go or you will regret it."

His free hand started moving down my body. My fingers curled around one of the daggers sheathed at my thigh. I gritted my teeth. "This is your last chance. Let. Me. Go."

He leaned in close, I recoiled as his lips brushed my ear.

"C'mon Your Majesty, it's time you let loose. You looked wound up on that throne all night." His hand fisted in my gown and it severed the last tether of my restraint. I pulled my dagger from its sheath as I kneed him in the groin. He doubled over in pain, but not before I twisted, smashing my elbow into his nose. The sound of his bones cracking echoed in the hallway, mingling with his groans as he stumbled back grasping his nose.

He swore as blood gushed from his nose, staining his white shirt. "You little bitch." He stumbled towards me, eyes blazing as he tried to grab me again. With a flick of my wrist vines started growing around him, wrapping around his legs until they reached his arms, pinning them to his sides.

He stared at the vines ensnaring him—trying and failing to break them. I pushed him against the wall, my dagger at his throat, as I willed ice to freeze the vines to the wall, keeping him in place.

"If you ever try to touch me, or anyone on my continent again, I will tear out you fucking throat." I snarled as I pushed my dagger into his skin, drawing blood that dripped down his neck in a slow, steady stream. "You will leave Alethens immediately and if I ever see, or hear, of you again I won't hesitate to kill you." In one simple move I could push my dagger harder into the delicate skin of his neck and watch as the blood drained from his body.

Instead I took a breath, steadying myself. I couldn't kill him, not yet at least. It would be much more satisfactory if I killed him for disobeying my orders, if he dared. I took another breath and once I was sure I wouldn't stab him I stepped back removing my dagger from his throat and wiping his blood off on the fabric of his jacket.

"I hope you learned your lesson, my Lord," I told him sweetly as I sheathed my dagger and turned, starting back down the hallway.

"Wait, you're going to leave me like this?"

I looked over my shoulder at the male as he struggled against my ice encased restraints. Blood continued to gush from his broken nose.

"I'll leave it to you to explain to whoever comes across your sorry ass what got you into this position." I smirked at him over my shoulder.

"You can't do that, you can't leave me here!" he shouted after me.

"And you can't touch a female when they say no. Seems like a fitting punishment to me!" I yelled back at him as I continued my way to my bedchamber.

13

LUKA

My head pounded.

I attempted to open my eyes, but shut them immediately at the bright sun shining through the windows. *Fuck.* How much did I have to drink last night? Too much apparently. As Fae, with as much power that I had, it was rare that a night of drinking would impact me the next morning. The only time it did was when I overindulged. And by the pounding in my head, I had *severely* overindulged last night. I scrubbed my hand over my face as I tried to recall the events of last night.

Flashes of me dancing with Lennox, the way my hand had felt on the bare skin of her back filtered through my mind. My hand in hers as we snuck out of the ball. Talking and drinking under the stars. I don't know what had come over me last night to make me act the way I did, but I didn't regret it.

I didn't stay after we returned. I couldn't stand the thought of watching her dance with others as the night continued. I found Declan instead and we came back to my room with a bottle of something, or perhaps *several* bottles of something. What transpired after that was fuzzy.

It was well past dawn, the latest I had slept in ages. But it was Sunday, I hadn't missed training this morning with Lennox, we were all planning to train together this afternoon. That gave me plenty of time to mend the pounding in my head, otherwise Lennox would wipe the training room floor with me. And she'd relish it.

☪

By the time I arrived at the training facility that afternoon my head was no longer pounding and I felt relatively back to normal. Well enough to put up a good fight against Lennox.

We were focusing on hand-to-hand combat today, Lennox had chosen to forego wearing her leathers, opting for a pair of leather pants with a black long-sleeved blouse with a black leather corset over it.

I tracked her every move as she walked across the training room, admiring the way her leather pants hugged her perfectly rounded ass.

"My face is up here, asshole," she called out over her shoulder.

"I was admiring the view."

Her cheeks heated, but she didn't look away.

I walked past her, urging my thoughts to clear as I climbed up on the mat. "Let's see what you've got for me today, Sweetheart."

Her eyes gleamed at the challenge as she rose onto the mat, rolling up her sleeves as she did. "I've been looking forward to kicking your ass all day, Bloodsucker."

She gave no warning before she pounced, attempting a blow to my left side, but I blocked the move with my forearms.

"You've got to admit, it's a nice ass though." I tried and failed a blow to her side as she ducked under my fist. She bounced back and forth on her toes.

"I've seen better." She shrugged before pouncing again.

I blocked her incoming blow, using my speed to my advantage and grasping her wrist in my hand. I smirked and she growled in return. As she twisted to get out of my grasp my gaze landed on the dark marks on her wrist, right above where I was grasping her. Several dark circles. *Bruises.* But not bruises from training. Those looked like fingerprints, like someone had grabbed her. My blood heated.

Lennox stilled, her arm going limp in my grasp as she noticed my distraction. I flicked my eyes to hers. "Who did this to you?"

Her brows furrowed for a second before her gaze flicked to the wrist I was still holding. She sucked in a breath before yanking her arm out of my grasp. She stared at me with wide eyes, her chest heaving, but she remained silent.

"Lennox." I took a step towards her. "Who did that to you?" My magic pushed and pulsed against my skin in time with my rising emotions.

"It's nothing." She turned and started to walk away from me, but I used my speed to appear right in front of her. "Prick." She crossed her arms and glared at me.

"It's not nothing. Someone hurt you." My voice felt rough as it left my throat. The thought of someone touching her set a fire inside me. The thought of someone touching her and hurting her . . . I would kill the piece of shit. She remained silent, unaware of the storm raging inside me. How was she so calm?

"Tell me who it was."

"Why do you care?" Confusion clouded her features, her eyes turning a shade of mossy green I had yet to see before. I took another step towards her and she didn't make a move to evade me this time.

"Because whoever dared to lay a finger on you without your permission deserves to have their head removed from their body and I want to make sure that happens." I stepped even closer, our chests brushing against each other. I felt every heaving breath she took as she tilted her head back to meet my gaze. "And not only did the bastard dare to touch you, but he hurt you. I intend on cutting off every finger he bruised you with."

One side of Lennox's lip tilted up, her eyes gleaming at the threat. "Although I appreciate the sentiment, I already took care of it."

I blinked at her as she took a step back from me, breaking our contact. "Took care of it, how?"

"I heard she left him tied up and bloody in the hallway for the guards to find," Declan called from behind me. I hadn't even noticed him arrive.

A smirk crossed Lennox's face at his words. *Goddess above.* "You left him tied up and bloody?" I couldn't stop the smile from spreading on my face.

She nodded. "He tried to touch me and I told him if he continued to try he'd regret it. He didn't listen so I broke his nose and told him if he ever touched another female without permission on my continent I'd rip out his throat."

"Well, shit, remind me to never get on her bad side," Declan mumbled.

Her ability to fight off his advances was impressive. She should be proud of herself. But the smile on her face didn't meet her eyes. She rolled down her sleeves, the bruises now covered, her hand rubbing over the spot repeatedly

Her shoulders caved in slightly and there were dark circles under her eyes that I hadn't noticed when she first walked in. She suddenly didn't look as strong as she was playing out to be.

It clicked then.

"This has happened before, hasn't it?" I asked gently.

Lennox whipped her head in my direction, eyes going wide before quickly looking at her feet, kicking at a discarded dagger. *Fuck.* No wonder she was adept at handling him.

I moved forward and placed my hand gently on her elbow. "Lennox."

She took several breaths before speaking. "It hasn't happened since I've become queen." She swallowed. "But—" She opened and closed her mouth several times.

"You don't have to say anything more."

Her shoulders sunk further in. The movement felt like a dagger to the heart. I gently pulled her into me, wrapping my arms around her torso. She was stiff in my arms, but I didn't let go.

"I'm sorry that happened to you."

She sucked in a sharp breath. I was about to let go when she relaxed into me, wrapping her arms around my middle and squeezing. We stood there, holding each other for several minutes. I felt every shuddering breath she took, every erratic beat of her heart. I held her until her breathing stilled and her heartbeat steadied, beating in time with mine.

14

LENNOX

I don't know how long I stayed in Luka's embrace. It could have been minutes, seconds, or hours. Time seemed to stand still in his arms. His warmth, the feel of his large body enveloping mine, it provided a sense of calm within the storm that was my mind—my life. A calm that I had not felt in years. Since *Before*.

I took in his cool, fresh scent as my head laid against his chest. I timed my breath with the steady beat of his heart. And when I finally felt myself steady, and my magic had retreated back to resting peacefully inside me, I started to move out of his embrace. As I stepped back, a tear slipped free from my eye, I moved to wipe it away before Luka could see it, but he was faster. He stopped my hand, using his free hand to wipe away the tear with the pad of his thumb. His calloused finger was rough as it brushed against my cheek. His hand remained on my face, his fingers gently cupping my cheek.

"They don't deserve your tears, Lennox." His voice was rough as he spoke, thick with emotion. I tilted my chin to look at him. His eyes were a dark shade of blue, like the early night sky. Silver embers of magic swirled in his iris' like stars themselves.

"The people who have tried to hurt you, the people who *have* hurt you, they deserve to die a slow, painful death for ever laying a finger on you. If it were up to me I would kill them right here and now. And I'd delight in killing them for hurting you, Lennox."

The threat should have scared me, but it didn't. The idea was comforting. It made me feel safe. "You are strong, beautiful, and powerful. Don't ever forget that."

Every thought emptied from my head at his words.

But he was right. Last night had rattled me, more than I had let myself admit. I had never told anyone besides my mother about the many times males had tried to take advantage of me when I was younger.

The first time it happened I was terrified. A duke far older than me had cornered me and tried to slip his hand up my skirt. Every action I had learned in training fell from my mind in those first moments. I froze, incapable of even trying to defend myself. But then my instincts kicked in. I kicked him in the groin and ran right into my mother. I could hardly choke out the words before I collapsed into sobs in her arms. I laid with my head in her lap as she stroked my hair until my sobs finally subsided. When I was finally ready to talk, she listened. I had never seen my mother as angry as she was that day. At first I thought she was angry with me for letting that happen, but she quickly reassured me that she wasn't upset with me, but upset with the duke who thought he could treat me as such. She told me instances like this had happened before, and that there would be a consequence for his actions. I begged her not to breathe another word of it to anyone, it wasn't that I was afraid of him getting what he deserved. No, it was because I was embarrassed that I had let that happen to me.

If something like this could happen to me, a princess, someone with training, one of the most powerful Fae in all of Lethenia, what about Fae that didn't have my background? I thought about all of the Fae in the palace—of my sister. The idea of someone trying to touch them was enough to make me want to empty my stomach. But at the same time, anger stirred violently inside me. I hated the idea that some Fae thought that they could take whatever they wanted from others without consequence. That was the first time I had ever thought about killing and delighted in the fact.

After my mother comforted me I went straight to the training facility. I was determined to make myself stronger. I was determined to learn how to take down anyone who was double my size. I studied the most efficient ways to take down an opponent without a weapon—how to get out of holds. I practiced more than sword fighting and hand-to-hand combat. I practiced how to protect myself, not only against opponents, but against threats. I started teaching Kara as well. She never asked any questions, and she went as long as I showed her the most sensitive places to strike. Teaching Kara helped ease some of my anxieties, but not all of them.

The next time a male tried to touch me, I broke his nose. I didn't intend to inflict such an injury, but I couldn't stop the rage that coursed through me at his unwelcome touch. I was sure he would go to my father, but he never did. Or if he did, nothing ever came of it. With the next male I kept my control, I elbowed him in the gut before threatening him with my dagger to his throat. None of the males I attacked for trying to touch me ever went to my father. There was never a consequence for my actions. After a while, the attempts became few and far between.

I had assumed that, when I became queen, that would stop any male from ever attempting to touch me again. I was the High Queen. The most powerful female, the most powerful Fae, in all of Lethenia. But last night proved that not to be true. They still saw me as weak. As someone they could control. Someone they could manipulate. If they continued to underestimate me, well, I'd have to remind them who their Queen was.

I am Lennox Adair, High Queen of Lethenia.

I do not bow to anyone.

I do not yield.

I do not cower.

I will not be manipulated.

I will not be made to feel weak.

I am strong and powerful and I will crush anyone who dares to underestimate me again.

I looked at Luka, as he eyed me curiously. This male had infuriated me more than not since he arrived, but he has never made me feel the way those males made me feel. I didn't have the words to express the thoughts jumbled in a tangled web in my head. So I offered him the only words I could come up with.

"Thank you."

The words felt insignificant after everything he had said to me, but that was all I could manage right now.

Luka's eyebrows raised and a slow smile crept up his face. "Those are two words I never thought I'd hear from your lips."

I shoved him lightly. "Don't expect to hear them again, Bloodsucker."

His smile widened as he brushed past me and picked two swords off the shelf behind me.

I eyed him questionably as he handed me one. "I thought we were practicing hand-to-hand combat today?"

"I thought some swordplay might help you sort through all those thoughts and emotions bottled up in that pretty little head of yours." Swordplay was exactly what I needed right now. I needed to get lost in the movements of my sword and my body. When I was one with my sword, everything around me disappeared. It was the practice I went to in a crisis. How Luka knew that was another thing I didn't want to consider right now. So I shoved that thought into the box with all of the rest of my scrambled thoughts to be dealt with later, and I took my stance in front of Luka, a slight smile playing on my lips.

The first clash of steel sent vibrations through my body at the force—the sound ringing through my ears. I couldn't stop the smile from creeping up my lips as I retreated and readied to swing again and lose myself in the dance of battle.

Hours later, my body ached at the strain from meeting Luka

blow for blow. Sweat dripped down my face and back, my shirt clinging to my skin. I wiped the sweat from my face with the back of my arm as I placed the sword back on the rack.

A long forgotten part of myself ached to ask him to stay with me. Wanted to spend more time with him.

No. I quickly shut that thought down. I've already let him in too much. I couldn't give him more. I needed space. *That's* what I needed from Luka.

$$\mathsf{C}$$

As I laid in bed that night, a different kind of nightmare kept sleep at bay. The ones that had plagued me *Before.* I tossed and turned—sleep evading me—until a familiar voice ran through my head.

They don't deserve your tears.

You are strong, beautiful, and powerful. Don't ever forget that.

I thought of how it felt to have Luka's arms wrapped around me. Of the feeling and sense of calm and comfort.

I thought of the way he looked at me until finally I found myself drifting towards sleep.

15

LENNOX

I spent the next two weeks avoiding Luka as much as I could, which was proving to be explicitly hard. We still trained together every morning, but I made it my mission to keep any conversation to a minimum. Offering nothing more than a courtesy *good morning* and *goodbye.*

Our afternoons made it harder to avoid conversation. Any time I could, I took meetings instead of helping Luka search for the book. Whenever we did end up together Luka tried time and time again to move the conversation away from our task at hand, but I continued to steer it back, refusing to stray from our goal. I pretended to be engrossed in my search—in scanning the words on a page for any clue about the book to pay any attention to him. I expected him to give up after a couple of days, but everyday he continued to try to engage me in conversations.

To get to know me.

I couldn't have that. He already knew too much.

Luka did nothing wrong, but I was still sorting through all of my thoughts and feelings from the night of the ball, and the day after.

Luka had been nice to me, had comforted me, and I didn't know how to process that. When he first arrived every interaction between us had left me seething and wanting to knock him on his ass. After we moved past that we were cordial. We got along. Everything was fine. But after the ball I realized he had worked his way into my life more than I intended to let him to and I couldn't allow that. I didn't have the capacity to let any more people in. So I needed to distance myself from him. Avoidance was the clear and easiest way to do that.

I no longer wanted to punch him in the face because I hated him. No, now I wanted to punch him for being so Stars damned nice to me. Luka was supposed to be my enemy, so why was he acting like the furthest thing from my enemy? I had been hoping that distancing myself from him would help me gain clarity about the situation, but if anything it was making me more confused. What was he trying to do? Why was he being nice all of the sudden? He shouldn't be comforting me, complimenting me, or worrying about my well-being. I was utterly confused. I laid in bed every night trying to figure out what game he was playing, because he had to be playing some kind of game.

My spiraling thoughts were interrupted by a knock on the door. I opened it to find Luka standing in the hallway. Of course he was here. Why *wouldn't* he be at my door?

"Can I help you, Bloodsucker?"

"You've been avoiding me." He tried to make his way into my room, but I blocked him, placing my hand on the door frame.

"No, I'm not."

"Then let me in." He leaned against the door frame, crossing his arms as he stared at me defiantly.

"Just because I don't want to let you in doesn't mean I'm avoiding you."

His face told me he didn't believe a word that came out of my mouth.

"I'm busy." I squared my shoulders, tilting my chin up slightly.

Luka cocked a brow. "What, Your Majesty, is keeping you so

busy that you can't spare me a couple minutes of your time?" I opened my mouth, but quickly shut it again.

"Too busy brushing your hair?"

I narrowed my eyes. "More likely I'm planning your murder."

He laughed. "That I'm sure of, but you wouldn't hide those plans from me."

"I would if I wanted to catch you by surprise." Another laugh left his mouth.

"Or do you have someone in there that you're hiding from me?" The urge to punch him in the face grew stronger and stronger by the minute.

"Who I may, or may not have, in here is none of your concern."

Luka pushed himself off the door frame and closed in on me.

There was only a millimeter of space between us now. I tilted my head to look at him, his blue eyes darkening to appear almost black. "You see, Lennox, it is my concern." My brows furrowed. Luka pushed past me into the room using his vampire speed to his advantage.

I cursed at him as I whirled, rage filling me as my magic rose to the surface. I seethed at the sight of him lying lazily on my bed staring at me with a wolfish smile.

"Fucking prick!" I snarled.

"There she is."

I blinked at him, confusion dulling my rage for a moment.

"I much prefer you being angry at me than whatever you were feeling towards me to make you ignore me for two weeks." He stood from the bed as I blinked at him.

The bastard had been baiting me.

"I missed your rage, Sweetheart."

I stalked towards him. My so-called missing rage was fully boiling again, I didn't care if he had baited me. If he was giving me an excuse to stab him I'd take it.

"Are you sure about that, because my rage is about to cause you a world of pain." I landed a swift blow to his gut. A groan of pain left his lips as he doubled over. I turned my back on him as he clutched his stomach, moving towards the door so he could see his way out. A slight breeze was the only warning before Luka descended on me. My back landed against the wall, causing the air to rush out of my lungs.

Luka crushed his body against mine, pinning me to the wall. I tried to push him off of me, but he gripped my wrists, pinning them to the wall above my head. His body pressed against every inch of mine. Each point of contact sent a buzz through my body.

"Now don't try to get any ideas, Sweetheart. I'm not going to hurt you."

I bared my teeth, but the bastard only smiled wider. "Why would I believe that? You have me pinned to the fucking wall." I could feel every inch of him against me. My breath came in heavy pants as anger continued to course through me causing my magic to thrash violently inside me. If he didn't let go of me soon I wouldn't be able to stop my magic from bursting from my fingertips.

He leaned in closer, his lips brushing the shell of my ear. "Most females would be begging me to pin them to a wall."

I raised my leg in an attempt to kick him, but he only pressed his body further into mine, further restricting my movement. He pressed in closer, his warm breath skidding across the expanse of my neck.

"I bet one day, you will be too." His lips dusted over my ear sending an involuntary shiver through my body. Again I tried, and failed, to get out from under him. Why did he have to be so Stars damned strong? If only I had my dagger on me. I eyed where my weapon lay discarded on the side table. Without a weapon, and using his weight against me, I was powerless, and his grip on my wrists kept my magic at bay. He knew my weaknesses after all these weeks of training together and I mentally berated myself for letting myself get into this position in the first place. I was helpless against him. Luka must have noticed my defeat, he moved back a bit, allowing space to meet my eyes.

"I'm serious, I'm not trying to hurt you. I was only trying to get your attention. You've been avoiding me for two weeks. The only way I figured I could get you to talk or interact with me is if I made you angry at me."

I wanted to wipe the smug look at his face. Because, *fuck* he was right. I hated that he was right. All of my anger towards him pushed my confusion aside in the blink of an eye.

"Now, if I let you go, will you promise to stop trying to kill me so we can have a conversation?"

I sighed. "I make no promises, Bloodsucker. But I'll try my best." My answer seemed to satisfy him, and he stepped back, my body instantly cold from the lack of contact. I balled my hands into fists as I followed him to the sitting area, sitting on the couch across from him as I worked to pull my magic back into its resting place.

He picked up the book on the coffee table and started flipping through it. I sent a burst of air towards him, knocking the book from his hands and taking the edge off of my magic. The book fell to the floor with a thud behind him.

"Speak, Bloodsucker, or I won't hesitate to punch you again."

He shook his head, causing a lock of dark hair to fall across his forehead. "Now, before I tell you my plan, I want you to agree to listen to what I have to say before you say no."

He leaned forward, resting his hands on his knees. But I could see the tension lining his shoulders and face—his eyes. Was he nervous? What in the Stars did he have to say to me that made him nervous? My stomach dropped. Nothing good could possibly come from this conversation.

"Fine," I conceded, my curiosity winning out over my dread. Luka ran his fingers through his hair as he searched for his words, his fingers leaving strands falling every which way.

"I want us to spend time together today. Just the two of us."

I couldn't stop the laugh that burst out of me at his words. "Why would we do that?"

"Because two weeks ago we had a pleasant time together at the ball. And the next day I—we—" He stopped, weighing his words. I glared at him, daring him to put a label on what occurred in the training facility the day after the ball. A moment of weakness on my part, that's what I had chalked it up to.

"We—we had a moment."

I let out a snort at his choice of words. Me essentially crying in his arms while he hugged me and said encouraging things was *a moment* that's for sure.

Luka ran his hand through his hair again. "Then you avoided me for two weeks. I won't make you tell me why you decided to avoid me, but I know it has something to do with the events of those two days. Something that happened between the two of us spooked you."

I tried to interject, but Luka continued, "So you started avoiding me, because you were too scared to confront me about whatever set you off."

I felt my defenses rising. "I was not scared to confront you."

Luka's gaze was unwavering. "Then tell me why you're avoiding me."

I clamped my lips together. No way was I letting him into my thoughts. He already knew too much.

"That's what I thought, Sweetheart." He sat back, crossing one leg over the other. "Therefore, I think we need to spend time together. Just the two of us. Not training, not looking for the book, but spending time together. Getting to know one another. It will give us a chance to establish a common ground between us." I still couldn't believe the words that were coming out of his mouth.

"You think us spending time together is a good idea?" I let out a bitter laugh. "Ten minutes ago I was trying to kill you. Or at least seriously maim you."

"That's exactly why we need to do this." My brows furrowed. "If we spend time together we might become friends, and you won't try to kill me every time I try to have a conversation with you."

"Friends. You want to be friends." I shook my head.

"Yes." He was serious. He truly wanted to be my friend.

"Why in the Stars would you want to be friends with me?" I asked, exasperated.

"Lennox, who wouldn't want to be friends with you? You are the most exquisite creature I've ever met. I want nothing more than to see what's underneath that violent exterior."

Exquisite creature. What the fuck was that supposed to mean? Did he truthfully want to get to know me? Or this was all a part of a game I didn't know we were playing? But I had to admit, I was curious about him. I hadn't exactly hated the time we spent together. Maybe he had a point. If we became friends maybe I wouldn't spend two weeks analyzing his actions when he was nice to me.

"Please Lennox, give me a chance." Something about the way he said my name—*Lennox*—undid me slightly. And the pleading look in his eyes. That look appealed to something deep inside me. This meant something to him, and a long forgotten part of me wanted to do this for him.

"Fine." I huffed. "But I can't guarantee that getting to know you will make me want to stab you any less."

The smile that spread across Luka's face was enough to freeze the breath in my lungs. It almost made me want to smile back at him. *Almost.*

"I'd be disappointed if it did." He rose from his chair, crossed the sitting area, and he stretched out his hand to me. I let him help me from the couch, but he didn't let go of my hand as he pulled me towards the door. It was me who finally removed my hand from his so I could strap my daggers to my thigh before following him out into the hall.

I followed Luka through the hallway, neither of us saying a word until we arrived at the stables.

"Where are we going?" I asked as two stable hands brought out our horses, already saddled and ready.

"I don't know," Luka admitted. I gave him a questioning look as I stroked Odin's dark mane. "I was hoping you could take me to one of your favorite places considering this is *your* court not mine."

"Do you make all your friends plan the outings you invite them to?" I placed my foot in the stirrup and hauled myself up and over onto the saddle.

"Only the ones that admit to wanting to stab me on a daily basis." Luka smirked over his shoulder at me as he mounted his own horse.

"Please tell me you have other friends who want to stab you?"

He laughed as he fisted the reins in his hand. "Hate to let you down, but you're the one and only."

"There goes my fan club idea."

He laughed again and the sound worked its way through the fractured remains of my soul, threatening to upheave that darkened part of me and rile it awake. Any other time I would have urged that fractured piece back into the deep dark depths of my being, but right now, I decided I'd let it stay. I'd let an orb of light into the darkness.

Luka and I rode in silence as I led him to my favorite place. Part of me was hesitant to show him the lake. It was a place that meant a lot to me, to my family. But I could see that he was trying with me. For him, or for his court, I wasn't sure, but the least I could do was put in some effort in return.

"Here we are," I told him as we exited the trees and the shimmering lake appeared before us. The lake wasn't huge, you could see the outline of the forest on the other side. Where we stood was shaded by a couple towering trees on one side, but vacant on the other side if you preferred to bathe in the sun. Wildflowers ran along the sides of the lake until they met the forest on the other side. And the tops of the Abode Mountains peaked out from behind the towering trees of the forest.

"It's beautiful." Luka breathed. I only nodded in confirmation. It had been a long time since I'd visited the lake. We tied the horses to a tree and Luka pulled a blanket out from his saddle bag and laid it on the grass at the edge of the lake. I sat next to him as we took in the beauty of the lake—the rustling of the tall grass and the trees the only sounds. It was Luka who finally spoke, breaking our spell of silence.

"Why is this place your favorite?"

"I used to come here all the time when I was younger . . . with my family." The words left my mouth before I could think better of it. "We'd make a whole day of it. Either our whole family, or Kara, Nol, and I would sneak down here for the afternoon. My best memories are here at this lake."

I thought of those scalding summer days when Kara, Nol, and I couldn't dismount our horses fast enough as we ripped off our clothes, discarding them in the grass as we ran to the lake, squealing with joy as we ran into the water. We'd stay in the water for hours, only coming out to eat a quick snack before returning, while our parents lounged on the grassy edge, smiling as they watched over us. Occasionally, on particularly hot days, they would join us in the water.

As we got older we didn't spend as much time in the lake, but we still visited often. My siblings and I would lounge on the edge, basking in the sun. Sometimes we all sat in silence while we read or worked on other projects, enjoying time spent together. Other days we'd talk for hours about anything and everything. Events from our childhoods, our hopes and dreams for the future, whoever we had our eyes on at the time.

When was the last time I had spent a day relaxing, having

fun? Not worrying about anything? Days like those were frequent growing up.

"Will you tell me about them—about your family?" Luka's question jarred me from my memories. I twirled the ends of my hair between my fingers as I considered his question. I rarely talked about my family. I rarely let myself *think* about them. When was the last time someone asked me about my family? When was the last time I had let myself talk freely about them?

"You don't have to if you don't want to," he added softly. "I know it can be hard to talk about them. I don't know if you remember, but I lost my parents too."

It all came back to me, the death of the future king of the Blood Court, and several years later, the future queen. Leaving Luka as the sole heir at nineteen, nearly the same age as Kara when our parents were killed.

"I know everyone grieves differently, but for me, talking about them helps."

I had never talked to someone else who had lost their parents. No one besides Kara, and we rarely spoke candidly about our loss. Whether that was because of me or her I'm not sure.

"No, it's just—" I took a breath and hid my shaking hands under my thighs. "I never talk about them."

"Not to be an ass, but that's a shame." Even with his preface the words struck like a blow to the chest, ratting the lid of the box locked up in my chest. "The way I see it, when you lose someone important in your life you should talk about them any chance you get. It helps keep their memory alive." I turned over his words in my head. What good was I doing by not talking about my family? Both of my parents had shared with us about their families throughout our lives, why couldn't I do the same? Was I further disappointing them by refusing to share who they were? Part of me wanted to open up to Luka, to talk about my family.

But the other part of me feared that if I opened up that part of me I might not ever be able to close it again.

I didn't know if that would be a good thing or a bad thing.

16

LUKA

I tried not to stare at Lennox as she took in my words. Maybe they were too harsh, but I recognized the look on her face, in her eyes, when I asked about her family. A look that I saw in the mirror more times than I could count.

"Does it ever get better? This feeling—"

I looked at her out of the corner of my eye. She was staring out at the lake as she fisted the grass at her sides.

"Grief?"

She nodded as she continued to stare out at the water.

"No, not really. It lessens as time goes on, but I don't know if it will ever truly go away. I imagine the only way it will ever go away is if you stop missing the people you lost."

It had been almost ten years since I lost my father, seven since I lost my mother, and I still missed them every day. But now, when I think of them, I try to think of times when we were happy, instead of about how much I miss them. Or who my mother turned into after my father died.

"I was still grieving my father when my mother died. His death changed my mother." She was already the harder of the two, when he died so did the soft sides of her that he brought out. "After my father died my mother left."

"What do you mean she left?"

I shrugged. "She left. I think I saw her four times in the three years after my father died." The shaky foundation I was standing on crumbled beneath me when my mother left. It took me a long time to crawl back from that destruction.

"The last time I saw her I asked her why she left, why she never stayed for more than a few days. She said there was nothing left for her in Cel Nox." I'll never forget that moment—the crippling pain that seared through my chest. "Even though my mother didn't die for another few months after that, she died to me that day." Lennox remained silent besides me as I continued, "It never made much sense to me back then, and I still don't understand it completely now. Part of me thinks I was blind growing up—I only saw what I wanted to see. I thought my mother loved me. Although I knew it was never in the same way my father loved me."

I thought of the way my fathers eyes lit up when he saw me. How my mothers never did. My father took me everywhere. Taught me everything. Spent every moment with me that he could, but still I craved those moments with my mother—those scraps of attention. I clung to the small moments with her. The kisses goodnight. The occasional bedtime stories. What son didn't want to be loved by his mother? When my father died I thought I missed my mother because she left. I didn't realize until much later that I missed her because my father was no longer around to fill in the gaps that she left throughout my entire life.

I was almost jealous of Lennox losing her parents at the same time. She only had to experience the deadly blow once. But grief and loss aren't something that you can compare.

"I try not to think about my family if I can help it. It hurts too much. If I think about them for too long sometimes I feel like my body will be crushed underneath the weight of their loss."

I nodded, not daring to interrupt her in fear that she'd stop.

"I never got time to grieve for them, you know?" She picked at a blade of grass and ran it between her fingers. "Do you know how I found out my family was dead?"

I shook my head. There had been whispers throughout the years, but no one knew what was truth and what was rumor.

"I felt the power of High Queen transfer to me through the Dunami when Kara and I were hiding during the attack. The only reason that the power would have transferred to me was if all three of them were dead. I hoped and prayed that it wasn't truly the Dunami that I experienced. But Kara and I sat in that safe room, for who knows how long, until it was finally safe—*safe*. Ha." Her laugh was bitter, laced with contempt. "Safe to come out to find our parents, our brother, and half of the palace dead."

Fuck. I had heard rumors about that night, but never the actual story.

"I got about two minutes to process the fact that my family was dead. I didn't even have a chance to shed a tear or comfort my sister before I was whisked away to fulfill my queenly duties. Because, not only had I lost my parents, but Lethenia had lost their rulers. I was comforting my sister *and* the continent, making sure our forces were in place to protect from another attack. Planning my official coronation. I had all of these duties to attend to and I never got the opportunity to stop and grieve that I had lost my family. Kara was all that I had left. I spent whatever free time I had with her. Comforting her. Being strong for her. Being strong for my people."

"But you had no one there to comfort you. To be strong for you." *Goddess above.* When my parents died my only responsibilities were to be the grieving son at their burials. A grieving heir. After my dad died I spent the next two weeks drunk. But Lennox . . . Lennox had to be queen. *Fucking High Queen.*

A tear slipped down her cheek and she quickly wiped it away with the back of her hand. It was incomprehensible how someone could withstand all of that and still come out on the other side. How much of her persona was an act? Was she this strong? Or was it all a facade to hide the crumbled person inside? Either way, I admired her. She stepped up when she had to, even if she didn't want to.

"How are you still standing?"

"Honestly, I don't know." She let out a bitter laugh, blinking back the wetness in her eyes. "Kara, I suppose. She tries to take care of me now. But I can't blame her for not taking care of me at the time. She was only nineteen." She paused. "If it weren't for Kara, I—I'd—"

A strange look that I couldn't place crossed her face. But as soon as it appeared it was gone. She squared her shoulders.

"So that's why I won't let myself think about my family. Because I have yet to deal with the mountain of grief that I've been shoving down for two years and I'm afraid that if I let it out I'll never recover."

I took her chin in my hand gently and turned her face toward me. Glassy green eyes stared back at me as I brushed my thumb across her jaw.

"That's not true. I've only known you for a short time but I know that you are one of the strongest people I have ever met. Even stronger now knowing what you told me. You have withstood the unimaginable. I believe that there is nothing that you can't survive, Lennox Adair." I tucked a stray hair behind her ear. "You are a survivor."

She kept my gaze for only a moment before looking away, staring back at the lake.

"Thank you, for saying all that. And for listening to me." Her fingers tangled in the grass again. "I'm not sure what came over me and made me feel like I should share all of that with you."

"That's what friends are for," I bumped my shoulder lightly into hers.

She let out a small laugh before silence fell between us again. I watched as she continued to caress the grass beneath her fingers. After a while she stopped, curving her fingers in an upward motion. Pink, blue, and white flowers with small circular petals grew up from the ground around her hand. She stopped the motion and formed her hand into a fist as the flowers picked themselves from the ground. She continued to manipulate the flowers and their stems until she had a tightly woven bracelet— the small flowers adoring it like charms. She directed her magic to tie it around her wrist before starting the process over, making another bracelet identical to the first. I watched as she effortlessly used her magic. When the second bracelet was done she held it out to me.

"Guess we better make it official with a friendship bracelet."

I couldn't stop the laugh that boomed out of me. I didn't miss the twinkle in Lennox's eyes at the sound.

"Pretty impressive." I held out my wrist as she directed her magic again to fasten the bracelet around my wrist.

"It's nothing. Kara and I used to make them all the time when we were younger."

"Well, I feel honored to have been let into an Adair sister tradition." I ran my finger along the bracelet, admiring the intricate woven pattern. I had never tried to use my magic to create something intricate like a bracelet. I bet if I tried it would be a sad attempt at a bracelet and Lennox would laugh in my face. Part of me wanted to try to see if it would indeed make her laugh.

"What elements do you have?"

"Fire, Water, and Earth," I told her as I summoned each of my elements in the palm of my hand before closing my fist and summoning my magic back into myself.

"What about you?"

"Water, Air, Earth, and Fire."

Four elements. She has all *four* elements. "You can't be serious."

I watched as she wielded all four of her elements into existence in her palm. "Goddess above. That's unheard of. How did I not know this?"

"No one knows." She made the fire on her finger tips dance higher as she spoke. "My parents thought it would be safest for me if we kept my fourth element a secret. And considering that my family was murdered, that was probably the right decision."

I couldn't remember the last time a Fae wielded all four elements. *Centuries?* The wealth of her power was unimaginable. Power like that scared Fae. Her parents were smart to hide her power. Holding three elements was plenty to brag about in the first place. Younglings started claiming elements around the age of thirteen. By the time you turned sixteen your powers solidified and you started looking for professions that suited you elements. It was common for most Fae to hold one or two elements.

Three was common in pure bloodlines. Four was unheard of.

Leave it to Lennox Adair to be the most powerful Fae to grace Lethenia in centuries.

17

LENNOX

Three weeks had passed since the afternoon Luka and I spent at the lake. Things were better between us now that we were so-called *friends*.

We had still made no progress on finding the book. We had searched every inch of the place twice with no luck. The libraries were doing us no favors either. We had scanned each of the books in the palace library and found no pertinent information. Now, we were carefully making our way through the collection again. We spent several hours every afternoon reading and sharing any information that might be even slightly relevant to what we were searching for. Carefully combing through any edition that mentioned the Goddess. Earlier this week I had sent a letter to the library in Alethens, asking the Scrolls to send over any books that talked about the Goddess Astria from their collection.

The books had finally arrived this morning.

I had taken my lunch outside and was eating while I dove into the first book the Scroll had sent over. A warm breeze blew my hair around my face. I had left it unbound and loose down my back today.

Summer was finally upon us—the sun was warm on my bare skin.

I was engrossed in a story about how the Goddess had created the dragons and wyvern that now resided in the Court of Embers, when a large shadow blocked the sunlight behind me. I turned to find Luka strolling towards me.

He was wearing dark pants that clung to his muscular thighs. The sleeves of his white shirt were rolled up to showcase his muscled forearms. I tracked him as he took the seat across from me, placing a letter on the table between us. I frowned, his usually sunny disposition was nowhere to be found. An expression I had only seen him wear on a couple occasions plastered on his face. His hair was messed up as if he had been running his fingers through it. What little joy I had over this weather vanished when I realized what his disposition meant.

He had bad news.

I glanced at the paper he placed between us. The red seal of the Blood Court was already broken on the envelope.

"Your grandfather sent more good news I'm assuming?" Luka raked his hand through his hair as he let out a shaky breath.

"My grandfather is making plans for war, Lennox."

My heart stilled. *War.*

There hadn't been a war in Lethenia in centuries. The last war was decades after the courts were developed, deemed the Solar War. It all started when the Twilight Court tried to take over part of the Lunar Courts land. There was no High King and Queen, each court ruled on their own. It had worked that way until it didn't. No one could agree on who should get the land, so war broke out. Courts chose sides, and many Fae were lost as the war waged on for close to a year until the Twilight Court came out victorious. After the war, in an effort to maintain peace amongst the continent, the roles of High King and Queen were created. Lethenia has remained in relative peace ever since.

He couldn't be serious. No good outcome could come from war.

"That's ridiculous." I casually brushed my hair over my shoulder.

"I wasn't supposed to tell you, but he wants me to send intel back. He wants Declan to send details about your forces and allies, any potential weakness he sees. He said that perhaps the only way to find the book is to come and find it himself by taking over Alethens."

I almost choked on my tea. I set my cup back on the table, careful to hide my shaking hands.

"He has no grounds to wage a war against me and my court." I crossed one leg over the other. "And the fact that he's planning war is enough to be considered treason. All of this over a Goddess forsaken book?" My hand slammed on the table, harder than I anticipated, rattling the dishes. Luka remained silent as his words rang in my mind. War. *War.* We were talking about an actual threat of war.

"No one will side with him." My voice came out weaker than I intended.

"Are you sure about that?"

I wanted to throttle him for knowing what I was thinking. My anger and distress started rising inside me. My magic felt it too—it warmed at my fingertips. I let a small amount in the form of a wisp of air out under the table. Afraid that if I didn't let some of it out it would work its way out in my fit of emotions. Luka's eyes flicked under the table before looking back at me curiously. I slipped my hands underneath my thighs.

Luka sat forward, resting his elbows on the table. "Think about it, Lennox. Your parents are the ones who established relationships with the other courts, not you. They all like you enough, but they don't know you, not really. They don't have a political relationship with you. You have their sympathy no doubt, but their support? That isn't a guarantee."

His words hit like a blow. Each one precise enough to fully

knock me out. I swallowed the lump in my throat. He was right. My parents had great relationships with the courts. My father made a point to visit them frequently and entertain them whenever they visited Alethens. I had met most of the other kings and queens at some point, but that was as Lennox the Princess, second in line to the throne. I was nothing but a child. I was introduced and swiftly sent away while the adults talked. In the two years since I had become queen what had I done to maintain those relationships? *Nothing*. They sent condolences after my family's passing and we corresponded over trade agreements and other matters of need. They sent me their quarterly updates. But would that be enough to side with me in a war?

How did I appear to them? Was I simply the queen who accidentally inherited her throne? The poor girl who was thrust into a role the moment after her parents were murdered? They didn't know me. As a person or as a queen. They only knew *of* me.

I had no idea what was whispered among the courts about me. Would they blindly follow a young, inexperienced queen into war? I had been busy tending to the other parts of my role and keeping my grief contained that I neglected those relationships. But war had never been in the picture. But now that it was, I was ill prepared.

Any royal adviser that could have guided me were murdered alongside my family. I was left to swim against the rip tide by myself. Guilia and Alvise were not my parents' main advisors, they were far down on the totem pole, that's why they had survived that night. They were not privy to the ins and outs of my parents' political relationships.

"I know that if my grandfather wages war, the Twilight Court will join him. And there is a good possibility the Lunar Court will too. My grandfather has a strong relationship with both courts."

I remained silent. What was there for me to say? He was right. How did he know so much about these political alliances and yet I knew nothing? Shouldn't the High Queen know of alliances between her courts? Should I be questioning where the Fae's loyalty lied? I knew with my ties to the Mystic Court they would side with me, but the rest of the courts? I wanted to throttle him for how calm and rational he was acting.

Luka continued speaking, despite my continued silence. "All of the largest armies in Lethenia lay within the Blood Court and The Twilight Court." I knew that. Everyone knew that. And the Twilight and Lunar Courts were the largest suppliers of weapons in Lethenia.

Luka raked his hands through his hair, the first sign of emotion from him since he started talking. "What kind of forces do you have here?"

None. What small forces that still remained after the attack were not ready for battle. My thoughts immediately went to Enric, and all of the other younglings in the Royal Guard. My stomach twisted at the thought of asking them to fight in a war for me.

Not only did I not have allies, but I didn't have an army. Only the small number of forces that patrolled the palace. Alethens had never been a court to host an army. That was on the Blood Court and the Twilight Court. The vampires and shifting Fae from the Twilight and Lunar courts made perfect warriors. Declan was a perfect example of that. His Twilight Court heritage shined when he held a weapon. The dragons in the Court of Embers kept to themselves in their land at the southernmost tip of Lethenia. They would be lethal in a battle, but convincing them to join would be a feat in itselves. As for the Aquatic Court . . . their shifting abilities kept them water born, the sirens and other creatures could use their Goddess blessed abilities in the water, but on land they possessed the same abilities as any High Fae. We'd be severely outmatched going up against the wolves and all of the land shifting Fae that resided in the Twilight and Lunar Court.

Never did I think Lethenia's army would be used against my

own court and we'd be left to fend for ourselves. Would I have to start training civilians? Force them to sign up to fight in a war of my doing? My stomach rolled at the thought of subjecting my innocent people to that fate. Of bringing war to their doorstep. I had to protect them. I would protect them. I would do whatever I had to to protect them.

I refused to lose anyone else.

18

LUKA

I stared at Lennox as she stared at the flowering bushes surrounding us. She had yet to say a single word since I told her about my grandfather's plans. I could see the conflict in her eyes. Death and loss scared her more than anything. Although war was a threat, it wasn't an empty one. I knew what my grandfather was capable of, what lengths he would go to get what he wanted, to get this Goddess-forsaken secret book.

What he would get out of war against Lennox, I didn't know.

"I know my grandfather and uncle. They will try to sway anyone who will listen to them, to turn against you. They will spin you as the young, unmarried, inexperienced queen." I flinched at my own words. They might have been true, but not in the way that my grandfather would use them. I saw those traits as Lennox's strengths, my grandfather saw them as her weaknesses. I had no doubt he could convince others to believe them too. He wanted to scare her into submission. But he didn't know Lennox like I did. Lennox wouldn't scare easily, she would not be manipulated, and she would not back down without a fight. He wanted to light a fire under her.

Little did he know that she was living breathing flames.

"I'm not saying this to make you feel threatened. War is the last thing I want. I'm telling you this because you deserve to know this. So that you can be prepared. I want to help you."

"You want to help me?" She all but spat the words. "How are you going to help me, Luka? Hold the gate open while your grandfather and his army march on my people?" She stood, her chair scraping on the bricks.

"Lennox, I—"

She twisted, pointing her finger at me. "Don't you dare say my name."

I flinched.

I had seen Lennox, angry, but never like this. Her eyes churned, the green no longer a welcoming soft green, but vicious green so dark it was almost black.

"You came in here trying to convince me that you wanted to help me, that you wanted to be my friend. And then—" She laughed, the sound cold and bitter. "And then you come here and tell me that you want to help me because your grandfather, who's throne you are getting ready to inherit, is plotting to wage a war against me and my people." Her magic was swelling to a dangerous height, the embers of it flickering in her eyes. She was on the brink of losing control. She opened and closed her fists rapidly. I had to figure out some way to calm her down before she spiraled.

I stood, reaching for her. "Lennox."

She ripped her arm out of my reach. "Don't fucking touch me." The look on her face was enough to make me take two steps back. She uncurled her first as she swung her arm, a shard of ice flung from her palm, slicing through the skin on my arm.

I hissed, placing a hand over the cut, wincing in pain at the contact. It wasn't deep—the ice skimmed the surface of my skin and would heal easily. So much for my attempt at trying to calm Lennox. But I'd rather her take out her anger on me, to hurt me, than anyone else.

I looked up from my bleeding arm to find Lennox starting at

me, mouth agape. She looked at her hand and my bleeding arm. All traces of her rage were gone as panic took over instead.

"Lennox, it's okay, I'm okay. It's only a little cut."

Her hands shook as she stared at them. I slowly took a step towards her. When she didn't move I continued until I stood in front of her. I carefully took her shaking hands in mine.

"Lennox, look at me."

She closed her eyes and took a shaky breath.

"I need to see your eyes."

Slowly she opened them, tilting her chin to look at me. Her green eyes were wide and glassy, back to a shade of mossy green.

"I'm okay. I know you didn't mean to hurt me. You were upset, and rightfully so. It was my fault. I shouldn't have tried to touch you."

She closed her eyes again.

"Lennox, I need you to look at me when I'm talking to you." She opened her eyes and I continued, "War is the last thing I want. I do want to help you, if you'll let me. I want us to keep working together. I know you are a good queen. I've seen it. But there is still a lot for you to learn. I want to help you in any way that I can. I need you to trust me."

I'd get on my knees and beg if that's what it took to convince her. I didn't want war. Nothing good ever came out of war. Worst of all, I feared that if it did come to war, Lennox wouldn't come out on top. That scared me more than anything. I continued to stare into her green eyes, urging her to believe me —to see the truth in my words. Lennox looked to where I still held her hands. The blood from my cut, now dried and crusted onto her hand as well. She ran her thumb over the dried blood on my palm before removing her hands from mine and taking a step back.

"I'm sorry that I hurt you."

I let out a sigh of relief.

"But I don't trust you."

The flutter of hope that had sprung in my chest shriveled and died as soon as it had grown. I don't know why I thought I could persuade her. I thought I had given her more than enough reasons over the past months to believe me. To place even a kernel of trust in me. But I guess not.

Lennox turned without another word and walked away.

19

LENNOX

It was early, earlier than usual as I headed to the training facility, the gardens were still plagued with dark shadows. I tossed and turned all night thinking about my conversation with Luka yesterday. About how I had lost control of my magic and hurt him.

Every time I closed my eyes I saw my shard of ice piercing his skin—the blood dripping down his arm. Blood that *I* drew. I kept turning over every word he said. I wanted to believe that he was telling the truth—that he wanted to help me. When I thought about it, he'd never given me a reason not to trust him. Still, I tore myself away from him and the pleading look in his eyes. It was that look that I saw every time I closed my eyes. The hurt in them.

I couldn't trust him, even if I wanted to. Through it all, he was a vampire. He answered to his grandfather. He was going to be the Blood King. I couldn't ever trust him.

When I finally did manage sleep, nightmares plagued my dreams. But this time it was me, killing the innocent people around me, striking out with my magic.

Sleep was pointless, the dreams and thoughts wouldn't stop. I needed to fight. To move by body. To lose myself in the movements of my blade instead of my incessant thoughts and night-mares. That's how I found myself weaving my way through the garden at this hour.

My senses were still out of balance from my disturbing dreams, I woke with my magic drumming at my fingertips. I tried to shake away the strange feeling, but my magic refused to recede.

I swore I could hear footsteps behind me. I strained my ears trying to hear more, but heard nothing. My magic pulsed inside me, pushing at the tips of my fingers—it sensed something was off. I wiggled my fingers in response, igniting my magic by letting out a small puff of air—ready to attack if needed. My senses were rarely wrong.

Someone was out here

I couldn't see them or hear them. But I could sense them.

On cue, a hooded figure appeared in my periphery, emerging from behind a hedge.

Their face was cast in shadows as they spoke, "Good morning, Your Majesty." The male's voice sneered. "A female like you shouldn't be out here all alone at a time like this, should they?" I watched his every moment as he slowly made his way towards me, his footsteps light on the stones.

"You never know who might be lurking in the shadows."

I turned towards the second voice, this one female, as she emerged from the shadows. I reached for my dagger strapped at my side, the only weapon I had on me.

"That won't do you any good, Your Majesty," the male hissed, baring his fangs.

My stomach lurched.

Vampires. Why were they here? Where did they come from? How did they get past the guards at the gate? I swallowed the lump in my throat. *The guards were most likely dead.*

"We will make sure to make it hurt before we drain every last drop of blood from your body, *My Queen.*"

"Or maybe we should make her watch while we kill the

princess." My blood ran cold. *Kara.* My eyes flicked to where her window sat, overlooking the garden. Her room was still dark. *Good.* But that didn't mean she was safe. They could come after me, but I would not let them touch Kara. Visions from nightmares flashed in my mind. Nightmare after nightmare of being forced to watch my sister die. I refused to let that nightmare become a reality. I had to get to her.

I moved before they could pounce.

I ran down the path as quickly as possible.

"The little queen thinks she can out run us." The male laughed, the sound sending a shiver down my spine.

"I do enjoy a good hunt before my meal," the female chided. Neither one of them started after me right away, that I could hear. They thought I'd be easy to catch with their enhanced speed. But I was no damsel in distress.

I was Lennox Adair. I would not go down without a fight.

I used my earth magic to crumble the ground behind me as I ran. Hoping it would give me more of a head start. But the move was sloppy, I hadn't ever practiced manipulating the earth behind me while running. If I survived this I'd make sure to add it to the list of things to practice with Luka. I had been hoping to create a hole for them to fall into, but I only managed to crumble the path to make it harder to run after me.

I ran until I came to the edge of the garden on the far side of the palace. I turned and hid behind one of the hedges. What would be the best way out of here without being seen? I could skirt around the edge of the garden, to the servants door, but there was a large, open area where they would easily spot me. Or I could try and make my way back through the maze to the main door.

"Where are you, you little bitch." The female's voice was too close for comfort. I steadied my breathing as much as I could, hoping she couldn't hear my stuttering breaths.

"Come out, come out wherever you are." The female's footsteps grew closer.

"You can't hide from us forever." The male's voice came from farther away.

My heartbeat clamored in my chest. I took a steading breath and palmed my dagger, flexing my fingertips—bringing my magic to the surface. I was going to show those bastards who they were dealing with. No one threatened Lennox Adair and made it out unscathed.

As the female passed me I created vines, stretching them out towards her and causing her to stumble. I manipulated my vines, directing them to climb up her legs until they bound them together. She tripped, a curse falling from her lips as she hit the cobblestones. My vines continued, wrapping around her arms, sealing them to her sides as I sat on her chest and pressed my dagger to her neck.

"Tell me who you are, and why you're trying to kill me," I demanded. My voice was raw and rugged. Desperate. Not the voice of a calm queen, but of a killer. I dug my dagger deeper into her throat, breaking skin. Red blood dripped down the side of her neck and onto the stones. I knew with her strength my vines wouldn't hold long, and her friend would find us soon, but I wanted answers. *I needed answers.*

"I don't answer to you, High Fae scum."

I rammed my knee into her side, she swore as she thrashed underneath me. I dug my dagger harder into her throat, blood now gushing from the wound.

"Don't think I won't kill you. Tell me who sent you, or I will slit your throat and go ask your friend instead."

She hissed and bared her fangs and I sneered right back.

The whoosh of air was the only warning before I was thrown off the vampire in a burst of speed. I hit the ground with a violent thud, the blow knocking the wind out of me and sending my dagger falling from my hand at the impact. I groaned as the other vampire landed on top of me and attempted to secure my wrists. With my open palm I threw a wave of water at his face before throwing out my fist. I connected with his jaw with a sickening crack. Blood sprayed from his mouth, splattering across my face. The vampire swore as he stumbled back and I kicked out my legs. I didn't see where they connected, I only felt the impact as I rolled out from underneath him.

I stood, scrambling to find where my dagger had landed in the dim light. I'd feel much better if I had my sword, but I had magic. The handle of my dagger glimmered in the dim light, I reached for it before turning back towards my opponents.

I eyed the two vampires, marking my target. I palmed my dagger and threw it, aiming for the female's chest. She anticipated my throw and moved, but not fast enough. My dagger missed her heart, embedding itself in her shoulder instead. I didn't wait to see her react before I turned and ran.

I only made it a few feet before I collided with a wall. No, not a wall. The male vampire.

"Told you you couldn't run from me." He grasped my palms in his hands, pinning them together, rendering my magic useless as he held me against him. The female vampire reappeared, my dagger in her hand. Her blood stained her shirt from my dagger, the wound already healing along with the one on her throat.

"That hurt. I think I should return the favor, don't you think, brother?" She smiled wickedly.

The female moved until she was right in front of me. I tried to get out of her companion's grasp, but he was too strong. He still held my wrists, keeping me unable to cast any magic. *Fuck, fuck, fuck.* I kicked out again, colliding with the female's legs. She swore, hissing before planting my dagger in my shoulder, exactly where I had hit her. I screamed as blinding pain radiated from the wound.

I bit down on my cheek to stifle my screams as the female slowly removed my dagger from my shoulder. I felt every movement as the dagger inched from my body. When it was finally out I watched in horror as the female brought the dagger to her mouth, her tongue darting out to lick my blood from the steel. My stomach lurched.

"Mmm, delicious." She smiled, her teeth stained red with my blood. "Would you like a taste brother?"

"I'll wait for the main course, it will taste much sweeter coming straight from the vein."

Pain seized my limbs.

"Suit yourself." She shrugged before sheathing my dagger at her side. *My dagger.* I'd kill her for that. She pulled out a vile from her pocket. In the dimly lit garden, I couldn't tell what it was. She removed the cover with her teeth, spitting it on the ground. She stepped until she was directly in front of me—until I was sandwiched between the two vampires. I tried to squirm out of their reach, to free one of my hands, but it only made the vampire's grip tighten, and the wound in my shoulder scream louder in pain.

"Be a dear and open now, won't you."

My brows furrowed, but the female pried open my mouth and poured the contents of the vile down my throat. I tried to spit out the liquid, but the vampire was quicker. She held my mouth closed with an iron grip. I was sure to have bruises. Although bruises were the least of my worries, I needed to make it out of here alive.

"Swallow," she commanded. The liquid burned as it slid down my throat. The vampire, having seen me swallow, released her hand from my mouth. I bared my teeth at her and spat.

She wiped my spit from her face with the back of her arm as she reached for my dagger again, raising it between the two of us.

"I'll enjoy killing you, you little bitch." She sneered as she slid the dagger into my side. I screamed in agony. If I wasn't being held by the other vampire my legs would have given out beneath me as pain seared through my body.

She removed the dagger from my side and brought it to her mouth. I watched as she licked my blood from the blade once again. "Mmmm, you taste like a dream. I wouldn't mind keeping you for my own personal blood bag." The male holding me laughed, the sound grating against my skin.

With every bit of strength I had left, I kicked out my legs, hitting the female square in the chest. She stumbled back, my dagger falling from her hands with a clang as it landed on the cobblestones. I wrenched back my arm and elbowed the vampire holding me in the nose, my shoulder screaming in the process. *It should have been healing by now.* The male let go of my arms to press a hand to his ruined nose as he yelled out in pain. I used my free hand to cast a circle of fire around him, enclosing him, making it an even fight between me and the female. I drew my dagger back to me with the flick of my palm.

I pressed my hand to my side, praying to the Goddess that my wounds would heal quickly. The blood seeping through my leathers wasn't a good sign. It wasn't healing, neither was my shoulder. Was my magic already depleted? But how? I hadn't used that much magic. I willed fire to my fingertips, a smile grew on my lips as the flame appeared.

But as quickly as it appeared it extinguished like a candle in the wind. Odd. It had never done that before. I tried to summon the flame again, but nothing. I tried to summon water instead, but still nothing. I wiggled my fingers, willing my magic to come to the surface, but I felt—nothing.

I felt nothing.

I couldn't feel my magic.

Every Fae's magic had a limit, if you used too much too quickly and didn't give yourself time to replenish it, your magic would run out. I had emptied my reserves before, but I'd always been able to feel my magic inside me. Something was wrong, very very wrong.

"I see my little concoction worked." The female grinned like a wolf as the pieces clicked into place. Whatever was in that vile she shoved down my throat had diluted my magic. Snuffed out every last drop. I swallowed.

I had no magic, only a dagger, and wounds that weren't healing.

I tried the best I could to push aside the pain. I took a deep breath as I palmed my dagger. I could do this. I could make it out of her alive and back to Kara. I had to. I couldn't leave her alone.

I threw my dagger at my attacker, but damn her vampire speed, she caught it. I swore under my breath. Watching as she aimed it back at me. One second she was aiming her dagger at me, the next she was in a heap on the ground, someone else on top of her.

I took my opportunity to escape. I stumbled as I ran through the garden. Tripping over my feet as I winced against the pain in my side. It still wasn't healing and my vision was growing fuzzy at the edges.

"Lennox!" a familiar voice called to me. I tried to see who it was, but my vision was blurred. I stumbled and two strong arms caught me, wrapping around me.

"Lennox, are you okay?" I shut my eyes and took a deep breath, leaning into the strong chest of whoever had come to my rescue. I focused on the throbbing pain in my side. I inhaled, the scent of cool morning rain invading my senses. I knew that sent. When I opened my eyes Luka was standing beside me, holding me against him.

"Lennox. Are you okay? What the fuck happened?"

Luka. Luka was here. Why was he here?

"Two vampires, they attacked me. They were trying to kill me." The words came out in pants. The pain in my side and shoulder thrummed like a drum. Each word, each breath, enhanced the pain.

Luka looked around. "You said there were two? Where's the other one?"

"I trapped him in a ring of fire."

A smile spread across Luka's face. "That's my girl."

My girl? I was not Luka's girl.

I was about to tell him such when my legs finally gave out. Luka swore, but his arms caught me as he lowered me gently to the ground. "Are you hurt?"

I nodded, or I tried to. The pain was almost too much now. Luka's eyes roamed over my body until his gaze snagged on my hands pressed solidly to my side. He placed his hands over mine, moving them away from the wound.

He swore under his breath. "It's going to be okay." He lifted me into his arms. I groaned as he moved me and he swore again. "Hold on Lennox, I'm going to get you help. Hold on."

My hair whipped around me as he broke into a run and then I was being placed on something soft. Luka swept the hair away from my face, and I swore his hand lingered to cup my cheek.

"You're going to be okay, I promise." He moved over me and placed a kiss on my forehead. "I won't let anything happen to you."

That was the last thing I remembered before I let the darkness sweep me away.

20

LENNOX

I couldn't remember the last time I woke to the sun streaming through the windows this brightly. I rubbed at my eyes as I sat, wincing at the dull pain radiating from my side. I was in my room, but I couldn't remember how I got here. I continued to look around as I scrubbed at my eyes—everything slowly coming back into focus.

In the corner, by the window, Luka slept, sprawled out in a chair. His arm was propped on the arm of the chair, his head placed in his hand. His hair was unruly—his dark locks falling across his face.

Luka.

Luka was here.

I shifted to sit up fully, why in the Goddess's name was Luka in my room? A memory pierced the back of my mind. It all came back to me in a rush.

Vampires.

I was attacked by vampires.

I was stabbed. My hand went to where my wounds had been at my shoulder and side. I lifted the fabric of my nightgown to find light pink skin where the gashes had been. I rubbed my fingers over the newly healed skin. A fresh scar had already formed. I let my gaze wander over to Luka sleeping in the chair. Another memory drifting to the surface.

Luka had helped me. My brow furrowed. Why did he help me?

Luka shuffled in the chair, drawing my attention back to him. I watched as his eyes fluttered open, immediately landing on me.

"You're awake." His voice was thick with sleep as he rubbed his hand over his face.

All I could manage was a nod. I was still confused as to why he was in my room. Was he here to finish what the other vampires had started? But why was I still alive? Wouldn't he have killed me while I was sleeping? Why was he still here?

Luka stood, I tensed, fisting my hands in the sheets. The mattress dipped as he sat next to me.

"How are you feeling?" He placed a hand on my leg.

"Okay, I guess." I stared at his hand on my leg. The touch was comforting, something I had become unaccustomed to over the past two years.

"Good." He gave me a small smile as he removed his hand from my leg and ran it through his hair instead.

"What happened? How long have I been out?" I drew my tangled hair over my shoulder.

"You were attacked."

"I remember that part. Bitch stabbed me with my own dagger."

Luka's laugh rumbled through the room. I cursed under my breath at the memory of watching her pierce my flesh with my own Stars damned blade.

"But you still fought them off."

I had, against all odds.

His smile widened. "To answer your other question, you've been out for a day."

A day. I had been out for a whole day.

Luka, either having not noticed or choosing to ignore my

growing anxiety, continued talking. "You weren't healing because they had drugged you with Oleander."

Oleander. Fuck. Oleander was a plant often used to dilute magic. Its growth was restricted to the general population of Lethenia. It's used sparingly in small doses to restrain Fae when needed, typically only if they are a danger to others. It's only supposed to be used in small doses. For it to stall my magic as deeply as it did, and as quickly—my stomach lurched.

"I figured as much. I couldn't even feel my magic." I shuttered as I recalled the utter dread as I reached inside myself finding a hollow empty space where my magic should have been. Anxiety coiled in my gut. Did my magic return? I reached for it now, for the pulsing warmth of my magic that wound itself around the fiber of my being.

Hello. It whispered to me as it wrapped around me like a lover's caress. I let out a shuddering breath. It was still in me. I still had my magic.

I raised my palm, wiggling my fingers. Tiny balls of flames formed at my fingertips.

Luka smiled. "I took you to the healer. She attended to your wound and gave you a sleeping draft along with a drug to counteract the effects of the Oleander. She thought it best you sleep through the healing process since she couldn't heal your wound any quicker until your magic returned."

I had never been more grateful to have a healer residing at the palace. All Fae possessed quick healing abilities, but healers were witches who could access greater healing capabilities to heal large wounds at a quicker rate. They rarely resided outside the Mystic Court and were a coveted commodity when you could find one.

"And you—you helped me? You brought me to the healer, and you helped me with the vampires. You were there." I still couldn't wrap my head around why he was there. Was he working with the vampires? Is that how he knew where I was? But why didn't he let them finish the job? Or do it for them?

Luka eyed me curiously. "I was. I killed the vampire who was about to throw your dagger back at you."

"You killed her?"

"I did. Is that a problem?" A crease formed in between his brows.

"No. of course not." I twisted my hair around my fingers. "She deserved to die. I just—I didn't expect you'd kill another vampire."

His eyebrows rose as he took in my words. "She was trying to kill you. Of course I was going to kill her, vampire or not."

We sat in silence as I contemplated his words. "But I'm supposed to be your enemy. You're my enemy. You're not supposed to protect me against your own people." I didn't mean to say the words out loud. None of this made sense. He must not have been working with the vampires if he killed one of them.

"Am I your enemy, Lennox? Because you're not mine. Did you forget that already?" Irritation leaked into his voice. I looked at the hand he placed on my thigh. "You've never been my enemy, Lennox." Sincerity shone in his eyes. The same sincerity I had ignored days ago when he asked me to trust him and I refused.

"I don't understand." I had been cruel to him days ago. I had said things I regretted. I had lashed out and fucking stabbed him with an ice dagger, and yet he was still here. He had helped me. He had saved me. And he was still asking me to trust him when I had done nothing to deserve his trust.

"Just because some of our people don't like one another doesn't automatically make us enemies. We've been over this Lennox." He liked throwing that in my face, didn't he?

"I know, but—"

"No buts. I have no reason to have you as my enemy Lennox. You may assume you have reasons against me, but think about it, what have I ever done against you? Not my people. Me. You can't judge me for the acts of my people. I am not the vampire who is after you. Despite what you might believe, I don't want you dead."

Luka stood and paced in front of the window. Again, running his hands through his hair. "If I wanted you dead, Lennox, you would be dead."

Hadn't I thought those thoughts moments ago? Wasn't he confirming everything I had been thinking? Why did I still have a hard time believing him?

"I don't know what to say."

He sighed. "You don't have to say anything, Lennox, I just want you to at least try to stop seeing me as your enemy. I could have left you for dead yesterday, but I didn't."

"I know. I—" I truly didn't know how to respond. The argument we'd been having since the moment he arrived was finally coming to a head. I had to accept Luka was not here to hurt me. He wasn't here to kill me. He wanted to work with me. He wanted to help me. He wanted to be my friend. He had demonstrated to me time and time again and every time I shot him down. I spewed words of hatred in his direction for no good reason, but to protect myself. But maybe it was time I stopped. I could try, couldn't I? I looked up from my hands, looking to Luka instead as he continued to pace. "I'm sorry."

He froze at my apology.

"Thank you, for helping me."

He let out a breath. "You don't have to thank me, Lennox. I'm never going to let anything happen to you."

A memory lost in the back of my mind, in the haze of the pain, made its way back to me. *Luka, caressing my face, promising me he'd never let anything happen to me, promising I'd be okay. Pressing a kiss to my forehead.* I had no idea what to do with this memory, or any of Luka's words from this conversation.

"Where's Kara?" I couldn't talk about this anymore.

"She's been here. I made her go to breakfast a little bit ago."

I let out a sigh of relief. My sister was safe.

"What happened to the other vampire, the one you didn't kill?"

"You mean the one you encircled in a ring of fire?" Luka smirked. "He's in the dungeon, I figured you'd want to talk to him and decide what to do with him. Although it took everything in me not to go and kill him myself for what he did to you." Anger flashed across his features.

"It was only a stab."

He scoffed. "*Only* a stab? Lennox, I'd kill anyone who dared touch a single hair on your pretty little head without your permission, or did you forget that?" His gaze was challenging. Even though he had spoken those words to me before, they ignited something inside me. A shattered fragment of my heart trembled.

"I don't need you to protect me."

"Oh, I'm keenly aware of that after yesterday, Sweetheart. But it's not going to prevent me from trying." Part of me hated the idea that he wanted to protect me, but another part, a part of me that had been stagnant for a long time, stirred at the idea. I was the one who looked out for others. Protecting my people, my sister, and myself. No one ever seemed to be looking out for me unless they were bound to by duty.

"Why were you in the garden? How did you find me?" If he wasn't there to aid the other vampires, then how did he know I was there?

"I was awake and I could hear fighting, I started making my way outside to see what was going on. I didn't know who it was, but—" He paused, his body eerily still. The only movement was the muscle that ticked in his jaw. "But I heard you scream." He didn't need to say anything more. The way he said the words, like they hurt coming out of his mouth, how tense his body remained—I didn't want to think about why Luka cared if I lived or died. Or how hearing me scream made him feel. Instead, I stood from the bed and headed toward the bathing chamber. I couldn't entertain where this conversation was going anymore.

"Where are you going?" Luka called after me.

"I believe I have a traitor to question. Care to join me?" I asked, glancing over my shoulder at him.

A wicked grin spread across his face. "It would be my pleasure."

21

LUKA

Droplets from my damp hair glided down my neck as I made my way back to Lennox's room. I scrubbed at my eyes in an effort to keep myself alert, but my exhaustion was catching up with me.

I hadn't slept well while Lennox had been out. Every time I closed my eyes I saw her laying on the ground in the garden, blood spilling from her wound. I felt her warm blood on my hands. I was too anxious to sleep—worried if her wound would heal, if she would wake up. Worried if the drug would have any side effects. Anxious her magic wouldn't come back.

When those thoughts weren't plaguing my mind, I was mulling over what might have happened if I hadn't come to her aid when I did. Would she have been able to continue to hold her own against those bastards with her wounds and no magic? I wanted to believe she would have, but a sinking feeling in the pit of my stomach told me there was a possibility she might not have made it out of that garden alive.

Then those worries turned to anger. Anger towards the bastards who came here and tried to kill her. Why were they here? Who sent them? Why were they trying to kill her? I asked myself those questions over and over again until my head hurt. I was so lost in my head while sitting by Lennox's bedside waiting for her to wake up that Declan had to remind me to eat. He even brought me meals periodically that I only picked at. But at least I wasn't alone. Kara sat by my side. She appeared to be as distressed as I was, but we didn't speak. Not since I had first explained to her what had happened.

Declan checked in on the two of us and updated us on what was happening outside of the confines of Lennox's room. He was working closely with the Royal Guard trying to discover any other potential assassins and tightening security throughout Alethens.

The healer, Cecilia, came in periodically to check in on Lennox, continuing to update us on her progress and reassure us she would wake. None of which calmed me, or Kara, until she finally did wake up.

I had never felt such relief as when I awoke to those green eyes staring at me. Which is why it stung more than it should have when Lennox questioned my intentions *again*. I could see how conflicted she was, and it was so Stars damned frustrating. What more could I possibly do to prove to her that she could trust me? Saving her from her imminent death wasn't enough apparently.

Lennox Adair had more walls built up around her than the Blood Court palace and I was determined to break down each and every one of them until I got to the center. This morning it felt like I cracked another small fissure in that wall.

She had been grateful for my assistance. She thanked me. She didn't kick me out of her room. And she invited me to come with to interrogate the bastard. For that I was grateful. I had no doubt she could hold her own against the prisoner, but it would put me at ease to be by her side.

When I reached Lennox's door I knocked lightly. Her voice rang out softly from inside, inviting me in. I pushed open the door to find Lennox lacing her boots on the bench at the end of her bed. She was dressed in her fighting leathers, her hair pulled back into a braid she threw over her shoulder as she stood.

"Are we going to a fight I'm unaware of?" I was now questioning my simple attire of black pants and shirt.

"I don't want to get blood on a good dress."

"I like the way you think, Lennox Adair."

She tried to bite back a smile but it slipped through anyways. "You ready?"

She reached for her sword where it rested by the door, her array of daggers already sheathed at her side. She slid her sword into place before nodding at me.

"Let's go, Bloodsucker. I'm hungry for some revenge."

☾

I followed Lennox through the halls of the palace. We passed the throne room and continued down the hallway until we reached a dead end. I watched as Lennox skated her hand along the wall until she found the hidden knob. She pressed her thumb against the knob and a hiss of magic sounded as Lennox pressed her hand firmer into the wall. There was a distinct click before the wall shifted to reveal a hidden door.

She pushed the panel in and the door opened, revealing a dark hallway made of stones, and unlit torches lined the dim hallways. With a flick of her fingers, the torches lit one by one, illuminating the passageway. I followed Lennox down the hallway several feet until we came to a staircase. We continued our decline under the palace until we finally came to the bottom. Lennox nodded to the guard at the end of the staircase. He remained silent as he unlocked and opened the iron door leading to the dungeon. A shiver ran down my spine at the sound of the door locking behind us.

We continued down the hallway until we came to another door.

"My Queen," the guard regarded Lennox as he bowed, ignoring me. "What can I help you with?"

"We are here to see the vampire who attacked me."

The male paled. "I would advise against that, Your Majesty. He is extremely dangerous and we wouldn't want any harm to come to you."

Lennox smiled politely, but I knew she was seething inside at his words. "I appreciate your concern Caio, but I assure you I am more than capable of handling myself."

I smirked. I liked seeing Lennox pretend like this—acting polite and calm. If it were me talking to her like this, she would be threatening and insulting me. Most likely with a dagger to my throat.

"If it makes you feel any better, my companion, Prince Luka"—Lennox stiffened as she gestured to me—"will be accompanying me. I will not be alone."

The guard's expression was still unsure, but he nodded. "As you wish, Your Majesty." Caio unlocked the door before leading us down another hallway. Cells lined each side of the hallway, but from what I could tell, they all remained empty. The guard stopped in front of a cell at the end of the dark hallway, unlocking the door, but keeping it closed. He turned and faced Lennox and I, an anxious expression darkening his features.

"He is restrained, but please, yell if you are in need of assistance I will be right outside."

Lennox nodded. "Thank you."

Caio opened the door hesitantly and Lennox stepped in without a second thought and I followed in after her. The door clambered shut behind us.

The cell was small, and was made up of stone on all sides with a shallow ceiling, making me feel the need to duck or risk hitting my head. The cell was mostly empty except a small bed made of hay with a blanket sat in the far corner, and a bucket on the opposite side.

On the floor, next to the makeshift cot sat the vampire—his

wrists encased in iron chains, buzzing with magic I could sense even from a distance. *Enchanted chains.*

I shouldn't be surprised to find the High Queen in possession of enchanted chains, but they were a rare commodity. They could be used by any Fae, but only witches possessed the magic to create them. With them, the vampire's magical abilities were nullified. Both his vampire abilities, and any elemental powers he claimed, were restricted with those cuffs on his wrist.

"Back again, traitor." The male sneered.

Lennox turned and looked at me, a puzzled expression on her face.

I shrugged. "Who do you think brought the piece of shit down here?" I told her. "And I may or may not have roughed him up a bit." I crossed my arms as I observed the bastard again. His left eye was swollen shut from where I had punched him. It had taken all of my restraint not to beat him to a pulp, but I figured it wasn't my blow to take.

"What do you mean by roughing him up a bit?" Lennox looked both confused and slightly amused at my admission.

"He cut off two of my fingers!" the vampire protested. Raising his cuffed hands in the air.

Lennox's head swiveled back to me, her braid wiping behind her. "You cut off his fingers?"

I shrugged. "Just one from each hand. Seemed like proper punishment for laying a finger on you."

One side of her lips hitched up an inch.

"Now every time you see your missing appendages you'll remember to keep your hands to yourself. Isn't that right?" I walked towards the vampire, kicking his booted foot.

"Fuck you," he said, spitting at me. I used my speed to avoid it, instead wrapping my hand around the male's throat.

"Now that's not a nice way to speak to your prince." I let go of his throat and moved to stand next to Lennox who was still smirking.

"Your turn, Sweetheart." She nodded and stepped towards the male.

"Tell us why you're here."

"I'll never answer you."

Lennox squatted in front of the male, looking at him eye to eye. "I'll give you one more chance to give me the answers I want before I make you regret it. Your prince may have cut off your fingers, but I can assure you I will do much worse."

Lennox had threatened me more times than I could count, and I had a feeling half of them were empty threats, but seeing her like this stirred something inside me.

"In your dreams, whore," he spat. I was ready to pounce on him, but Lennox made it there first. The male screamed out in pain as Lennox slammed her dagger into his thigh.

"I'm going to give you one last chance." She moved the dagger around in his leg. "Why. Are. You. Here." With each word she dug the dagger in deeper. The vampire screamed in agony at every thrust of the blade.

"I was hired to kill you," the male panted out between cries. Lennox removed the dagger from his leg.

"That wasn't so hard was it?" She used the male's shirt to clean the blood off her blade. This was a side of Lennox I hadn't seen before.

I wanted to see more.

"Now." She stood, twirling the dagger in her fingers. "Who hired you?"

"I don't know." Lennox's dagger whirled through the air, planting itself in the male's other thigh. He screamed.

"Try again."

"Okay, okay, I'll tell you." The vampire looked between Lennox and the dagger still embedded in his thigh, but Lennox stared at the male and raised a single brow expectantly.

"We were sent by our Master. We don't know his true identity. They want you and your sister dead. I didn't ask any questions. I only wanted the money."

Lennox removed her dagger. "Prince Luka, do you have any questions?"

"I think you covered it, My Queen." She nodded before unsheathing her sword.

Fuck.

"You've outlived your usefulness," she told the vampire as she swung her sword in front of her, I didn't miss the wicked gleam in her eyes as she did. The male's eyes widened, he opened his mouth to speak, but nothing came out. Lennox's hand was fisted at her side, she was using some form of magic to keep him from talking. Most likely filling his lungs with air or water to silence his screams and pleas for mercy.

I watched as she slid the blade across his neck without hesitation in a slow precise motion. Blood leached from the wound, gushing down his neck and staining his clothes. "That was for thinking you could kill me."

Blood spurted from the male's lips as he tried again to speak. Lennox placed the tip of her sword at his heart. "This"—she slid the tip of her sword in an inch—"is for my family."

The male's mouth opened in a silent scream as Lennox slid her sword through his chest. She twisted the blade before removing it and using his clothes to clean off his blood as he slumped lifeless against the bale of hay. His dull eyes stared back at me as Lennox re-sheathed her sword before turning to face me.

"Looks like you didn't need me at all, Your Majesty."

Her expression was flat, emotionless. That of a killer.

She tried to move past me, but I stopped her. "Lennox, wait." I grabbed her arm. She turned and faced me, eyes narrowed. "Are you okay?"

Her face softened, but she remained silent. I stepped into her space, my voice shifting to a whisper as my chest brushed against hers.

"Have you ever killed anyone before?"

She hesitated for a moment before nodding. "I have, but not

like this." She looked at her feet. "Do you think it was the wrong choice?"

I shook my head. "That's not my decision to make, Lennox." I placed my thumb under her chin, tilting it up, forcing her to look at me.

"If killing him is what felt right to you, I support you. He was your prisoner, he tried to kill you, and he committed treason, you had every right to kill him. I just want to know if you're okay. I know the taint killing someone can make on you." I brushed my thumb across her cheek.

Lennox let out a shaky breath, but didn't tug out of my grip. "I don't regret it," she admitted. "I've never killed someone who couldn't fight back." She chewed on her bottom lip. "But I couldn't rest well knowing he was alive in this castle. I could have asked someone else to do it, but I felt like I needed to do it myself."

"Okay." I released her chin and her eyes searched mine for any trace of regret.

"Let me be clear, if you didn't kill him I would have killed him myself. Honestly, I'm a little jealous you got to have all the fun."

She smiled slightly. "Next time, I'll make sure to include you more." She shoved my shoulder lightly.

"Sounds like a deal, Sweetheart."

"You're not upset I killed one of your people?"

I glanced over Lennox's shoulder to the body slumped against the hay. "How many times do I need to remind you, Lennox Adair? I will not hesitate to kill anyone who dares lay a finger on you before you believe me?"

Lennox remained silent as she twirled the end of her braid between her fingers. "Need I remind you I killed the other vampire?"

Silence stretched between us as we stared at one another.

"You aren't my enemy are you?" Lennox said finally.

"No, Lennox, I'm not." *I'm the farthest thing from it.*

She brought her bottom lip between her teeth and nodded. I watched her as she took a deep breath and turned from me and moved until she was kneeling by the male's motionless body. I stood behind her and watched in silence as she slipped the enchanted cuffs from his wrists. As she moved the iron over his right wrist, my gaze caught on the black mark bearing the inside. I moved to kneel beside Lennox, careful to avoid the blood pooling at our feet.

The marking tugged at the back of my mind. I squinted in the orange light of the torch as it illuminated the marking on the male's wrist as I pulled it closer towards me. Three interlocking circles in a horizontal line with a triangle through the middle were etched onto the male's wrist in dark ink.

My stomach dropped.

The mark of the Vanir.

22

LUKA

"Tell the guards to burn the body!" Lennox called out as she walked into the hallway. I followed silently behind her until we had passed both guards and made it to the top of the stairs.

I blinked at the blinding sunlight as we exited the hidden passage.

"Lennox, wait."

She turned, tapping her foot as she waited for me to continue.

"We need to go and talk somewhere." I lowered my voice. "In private."

Her brow furrowed, but she agreed and I followed her to her room.

"Can you put a shield of air around us? I want to make sure we're not overheard."

She nodded. Within a few moments, I could feel the pocket of air forming around us as Lennox's magic filled the room. I surveyed the giant invisible bubble encasing us, poking at it with my finger.

"Nice job, Sweetheart."

Lennox crossed her arms and glared at me. "Will you tell me

what is going on? Or do I need to stab you to get information too?"

I smiled, despite the pit in my stomach.

"When you removed the cuffs from the vampire I noticed a mark on his arm."

"What kind of mark?" Lennox pressed.

I let out a shuddering breath before continuing. "There was a mark on his wrist, a mark I recognized." I reached for a piece of parchment on her desk, sketching the mark on the paper for her to see. "It is a symbol of an ancient vampire rebel group, the Vanir. The group formed shortly after the Solar War, after the High King and Queen were instated."

A crease formed between Lennox's brows.

"They were against having a High King and Queen ruling over everyone. They especially hated having the High King and Queen come from the Star Court, and for being High Fae. They claimed vampires were the superior Fae and should have been chosen for the position."

It's been a decade-long debate between different groups of Fae.

Who was the superior Fae?

In reality, all Fae are equal, they all derived from the same group of humans. Some Fae will argue shifting Fae came from animals, claiming that's where their shifting abilities derived from, but that's not true. When the Goddess Astria fell from the sky, she landed in Lethenia. Some claim she was a star who fell from the sky. When she descended on our continent there were only humans on the land. Stories claimed her magic worked differently here and in her experimentation she started using her magic on the humans, creating the different types of Fae, and gifting them all different abilities.

Stories claim the High Fae were her perfected species—the most like humans, but with enhanced magical abilities. If any species of Fae is lesser, it would be considered the vampires. According to the legends, Astria fell in love with a High Fae, and they had a torrid love affair before they left her. Legends claim Astria's lover was married and had a family at home they had to return to. Astria was upset when she found out, and she wanted revenge, so she cursed her lover and their entire family. They still had their High Fae abilities, but they would now crave blood and need it to survive. No one knows where Astria went afterward, but she disappeared for years until she finally returned to the sky. Everyone lived in relative peace as the courts were formed, with the Fae gravitating towards living with Fae with similar abilities as their own as they figured out how to use their newfound magic—thus the courts were created.

"After the Solar War, when the High King and Queen were established, the Vanir created their group as well, making it well known they intended on establishing themselves as High King and Queen instead of the High Fae. The Vanir set out to go against, not simply the High King and Queen, but their own king and queen as well for going along with the creation of the roles of High King and Queen. They held secret rallies and meetings to get other vampires on their side. Eventually, the Vanir were big enough that they started implementing attacks. It started off small, they killed random Fae, leaving their mark at the scene somewhere.

"As Fae started to catch on, they got scared and the Vanir charged on, using their fear to their advantage. They started burning villages and establishments and found a way to place blame on the king and queen of the Blood Court, claiming they were not willing to protect them. They tried to claim they were for the people, when in actuality all they wanted was power, not real change—not at the end anyways. The king and queen tried to keep them contained, tried to extinguish them, but they came back every time. Then, after years of creating unrest they tried to assassinate the king and queen in an attempt to take over the Blood Court, and eventually the Star Court."

"What happened?" Lennox's voice was hardly a whisper.

"Their attempt was unsuccessful. The Vanir who tried to

infiltrate the castle were captured and used to lure out the rest of the rebels. They were all publicly killed for their crimes as an example of what would happen if anyone tried to go against the king and queen again. There were still attacks afterwards, but they got smaller and smaller. Each Vanir captured was publicly executed until the attacks stopped completely."

Lennox uncrossed her arms and let out a breath. "But it wasn't truly over, was it?"

I shook my head, a headache forming at the base of my skull. "No. Last year we started getting reports that a form of the Vanir was starting up again. The same symbol from thousands of years ago started appearing in the same way it did when it originated."

Lennox trembled slightly. "Why have I never heard of the Vanir until now?"

"Its history is well documented in the Blood Court, but the information was never spread." I shook my head. "I'm sure it was due to the pridefulness of vampires. They didn't want the other courts to know how easily they were almost usurped."

Lennox nodded. "And now? Why haven't I heard any reports from your grandfather now? This is something I should have been notified about."

"My grandfather has his best spies on it, he's determined to get it under control before it can become anything. Again, I'm sure his secrecy is largely due to pride."

I ran my fingers through my hair. "But anyone captured killed themselves before we could question them for information. We never knew what their intention was this time, but—"

"But you believe they are coming after me." Lennox's hands shook as she moved to sit in one of the chairs in the sitting area, placing her trembling hands under her thighs. I nodded.

"Why?"

"I'm assuming they're trying to get your crown."

"Would that work though? Could they take my throne if I was dead?"

I nodded, swallowing the lump in my throat. "There is an old Fae rule stating if there are no remaining heirs and a king or queen is killed by another Fae, that Fae may take their throne." I could see the panic rising in Lennox, gold swirls of magic churning violently in her eyes.

"How do you know that?"

"It was uncovered when the Vanir came around the first time by a Blood Court Seer. But it's a well guarded secret." *Most likely Lethenia's deadliest secret.* If it got out and everyone knew you could kill a king or queen and get their throne—I shuddered. I had only found out last year, when the Vanir had resurfaced. My grandfather felt it was necessary I know, as the heir to his throne.

Lennox stood and paced the small area we occupied. I watched as she wore a path on the rug before she stopped abruptly. She faced me, all blood drained from her face. "Do you think it was the Vanir who killed my family?" she whispered, like she was afraid to speak the words out loud.

I had never considered it, but—

"It would make sense wouldn't it."

Another piece of the puzzle slid into place. The answer to a question we had all been asking ourselves for the past two years.

"They intended to kill your entire family and take the throne." I met Lennox's gaze.

"But they couldn't find Kara and I." She swallowed.

"So now they're back to finish what they started."

23

LENNOX

I felt like my entire world tilted on its axis. After years of wondering why someone had set out to kill my family, I finally had an answer. I had thought I'd feel relief when I figured out why they had been murdered. I assumed it would be like a weight being lifted off my shoulders to have finally solved this mystery.

But it didn't feel like that.

Not at all.

Instead, it felt like I was running from a boulder as it chased me down a mountain. I knew who killed my family, but I had no way of finding them, stopping them. A ancient vampire rebel group for fucks sake. *The Vanir.* As if I didn't already have enough on my plate, now I had to worry about the resurfaced Vanir who wanted to kill my sister and I, and take over my throne.

Kara. The air whooshed out of my lungs. Having someone out for my head I could deal with, but knowing there was an entire group of Fae conspiring on how to kill my sister . . . . If there was anything in my stomach I would have emptied it right here at Luka's feet.

"We have to do something." The words came out in a rasp and I looked up, finding Luka resting with his head in his hands.

"I know." He sat up and looked at me, rubbing his hands over his face. "But I don't think there is much we can do."

A retort was on the tip of my tongue. It was in my nature to lash out at him, at everyone, but I stopped myself. He was right. What could we do? We had no idea how to find the Vanir. How many of them are there? What else would they set out to do? They were no longer contained to the Blood Court, they were here, in my home, amongst my people.

"I will send word to my grandfather, and we will fill in Declan so he can tighten security. I'm sure he will want to get a group together to search for any remaining Vanir in Alethens." He ran his fingers through his hair. "But besides that there isn't much we can do but be on high alert."

I nodded, crossing my arms over my chest. Luka stood and walked until he was occupying the space in front of me. I tiled my chin to find him looking at me with a soft expression on his face. So different from any of the other ways I'd seen him look at me.

"You've been through a lot in the last couple days." He brushed a lock of my hair behind my ear, and his fingers lingered on my skin causing my heartbeat to quicken. "You should take some time to rest."

"I've rested enough, I have duties to attend to."

His hand moved from my face, down my neck, leaving a trail of heat everywhere he touched. "Your duties can wait." He toyed with the end of my braid between his fingers. "Please, Lennox." My name was a plea on his lips. "Listen to me just this once."

I thought about waking to him at my bedside—the way he gripped my chin and asked me if I was okay after killing that vampire. I thought of those faded memories after I was attacked. Of Luka kissing my forehead and telling me he wouldn't let anything happen to me. *Luka cared for me.* All he was asking was that I rest. It wasn't a hard command to follow, yet every fiber of my being screamed to fight against commands from others. But when it came to Luka, the way he said my name, the way he looked at me. Right now, just this once, I could give into him.

"Okay," I conceded and his shoulders relaxed as he let out a sigh.

He let my braid fall back against my chest as he closed his eyes. "Thank you," he whispered.

His lips dusted lightly across my forehead, sending a shiver down my spine. I opened my eyes, and Luka looked like he was going to say something, but instead he turned and left me gaping at the space he had occupied.

☾

Fulfilling Luka's request after he left, left me alone with no idea how to occupy my time. Exhaustion wore at my bones, the toll of the last couple days catching up with me. So I decided on a nap and I slept through the afternoon. When I woke, I found Kara dozing next to me.

We spent the rest of the evening together, but I didn't tell her about what Luka and I discovered about the Vanir—I didn't want to worry her with that right now. I'd tell her when the time was right. Instead, I told her the details of my attack and she told me how worried she had been, and how Luka had never left my side while I was asleep. I filed that piece of information away with all of the other things Luka had done that baffled me.

We spent the rest of the evening lounging around, reading and napping. Kara had dinner brought to my room so we could eat in bed. I fell asleep early, and Kara snuggled up next to me. But my sister sleeping beside me didn't keep me from tossing and turning all night. I kept turning over the information Luka had revealed to me about the Vanir, trying to figure out a plan. I couldn't sit here and bide my time. I had to do something. I had to figure out what that something was.

When I rose from bed the next morning I had a plan.

I just had to persuade Luka to go along with it.

24

LUKA

I sat in an armchair in Lennox's office, waiting for her to arrive. She had sent me a note this morning to meet her here after lunch. She had been tight-lipped at training this morning, but I didn't try to pressure her to talk to me. She had been through a lot in the last couple days.

After I left her room yesterday—relieved she agreed to my request to rest—I found Declan straight away. I filled him in on everything Lennox and I had discovered, and he took off immediately to meet with the Royal Guard. He had sent a small group out to the city this morning to see if they could find any signs of the Vanir.

I hoped they'd find nothing—that the two vampires had traveled here alone. It would help to ease my mind that Lennox was safe for the time being. Although I wouldn't be relieved until all threats where the Vanir were concerned were extinguished.

I had composed a letter, briefly outlining our findings to my grandfather, but I was careful to not reveal much in the letter, lest it get into the wrong hands. It made me feel better to do these few small tasks, considering there wasn't much else we could do for the time being.

I was flipping through the book mindlessly when Lennox

finally arrived. When she sat down in the chair across from me a slight smile graced her face. I eyed her carefully, unsure of her actions. She crossed her legs and examined her fingernails. There was a different air about her today. She didn't bother to look up from her nails when she finally spoke.

"I have an idea."

"What?" I asked, swinging my legs over the edge of the chair to fully face her. She was still looking at her nails as though the answer to our problem lay within her cuticles.

"So impatient," she chastised, clicking her tongue. "If you ask nicely, I might let you in on my plans."

I sighed, leaning back in my chair. Her defiance made me want to pin her to the wall until she finally released the information she was keeping from me. A growl threatened to slip from my lips at the thought.

"Your Majesty, won't you please grace me with your magnificent plans," I said with as much adoration as I could muster.

"Well . . ." She smiled, uncrossing her legs and sitting up straight. "I suppose I can tell you, since you asked nicely."

"I'm honored, My Queen." I placed my hand dramatically over my chest—she bit her lip to stifle a laugh. This must be one hell of a plan to get her in such high spirits. *Color me intrigued.*

"I have a solution that could solve all of our problems."

I raised an eyebrow. "All of our problems?"

She nodded. "Yes, all of our problems. One being finding the mysterious all-important book your grandfather wants, the other being the Vanir who want to kill me and my sister, and take our throne."

"I am familiar with our current issues."

She rolled her eyes. "If you don't want to hear my plan . . ." she trailed off.

"What do you have in mind, My Queen?"

A smug smile played on her lips. "I think we need a Seer."

"A Seer?" I sat up in my chair. "And where will we be able to find a Seer?" Seer's were hard to come by. Their gifts to see into, and predict, the future were highly coveted, but shamed by many Fae. They worried they would anger the Goddess Astria by looking in their future. Most Seer's lived in secret—only revealing their true identity to those they trusted the most. Often, if they were caught they were either killed by those who were afraid of their powers, or abused by those who wanted their powers.

"I have an idea as to where we might find one."

How in the Stars did Lennox know where to find a Seer? Has she had one here the whole time?

"Do you care to enlighten me, Sweetheart?"

"So impatient this morning," she said, shaking her head.

"Please continue, your Royal Majesty." I sighed.

"The night my family was murdered, Kara's and I's lives were spared because our nursemaid, Olexa, was a Seer. She had a vision that told her Kara and I needed to get to the safe room before it was too late for us too."

I had assumed her nursemaid had died along with most of the staff, but maybe she was still alive, living secretly somewhere in Alethens. But, if she was able to see an event before it happened—she was a powerful Seer indeed. Most Seers had to look to see a vision—they had an end goal in mind.

"Unfortunately, she did not survive the night. But I have a suspicion of where she came from—where she may have family or friends willing to help us."

If we could get to a Seer, that could solve many of our problems. They could tell us where to find the Vanir—predict where they might strike next. They might even be able to tell us where to find the book. I had to give it to Lennox, this was a fan-fuck-ing-tastic plan.

"We will need to travel to the Mystic Court."

I whipped my head in Lennox's direction. "The Mystic Court?" I couldn't stop the laugh that escaped me. "You can't be serious?"

Lennox narrowed her eyes. "I am serious. Do you have any

other ideas as to where we can find a Seer? Because I sure don't."

I agreed a Seer was a good idea, but traveling to the Mystic court? That was insane. No one traveled to the Mystic Court unless you were invited. That in itself was a death wish. From what I had heard, witches were not friendly creatures. Legend claimed they had spelled the boundary around their court to kill anyone from the inside out if they entered without permission. I didn't know if that was true or not, but I wasn't eager to find out.

"No, I don't have a better idea, but you surely can't be stupid enough to want to travel to the Mystic Court uninvited. Do you think it's a good idea for you, the High Queen, and me, the vampire prince, to travel to the Mystic Court right now? It would be a miracle if we survived the trip under normal circumstances, but now? The Vanir are out there actively trying to kill you"

"Oh come on, princeling. We go in disguise." She waved her hand dismissively as if this was simply a trip into the city center. "We can alter our appearances. It will be fine. And besides, if I'm not in the palace, and no one knows where I am, they can't try to murder me."

She had a point, but I still didn't like it. There were still too many risks.

"There is still a chance they could discover where you are."

Lennox shrugged. "If they do, we fight them off." She spoke as though she almost didn't die a few days ago.

"What are you going to do if they don't let you over the border?"

"Did you forget I'm the High Queen? They will have to let me in."

"Okay . . . if we manage to make it to the Mystic Court in one piece, what makes you think the witches will be willing to help you?"

Something flashed on Lennox's face, but she quickly

schooled her expression back. "I think they will be more than willing to help us when they realize who we are."

I braced my elbows on my knees and put my head in my hands. I couldn't believe we were having this conversation. "Doubtful," I mumbled to myself. I had no reason to believe the witches would jump at the chance to help either of us, even if Lennox was their High Queen, the Mystic Court played by their own rules.

A vicious smile played on Lennox's lips. "You're not scared of a few witches are you, Bloodsucker?"

I sat straight in my chair. "I am not scared of witches."

"Sure sounds like you are." She stood and walked until stood over me, one hand braced on either side of my chair. I meet her gaze, her hair falling on either side of her face in a sheet of sand colored waves.

She tilted her head as she assessed me, strands of hair falling across her face with the movement. "Poor little Bloodsucker is afraid of a couple witches."

A slight growl escaped me as she placed a hand on my chest and pushed herself up, turning to walk back to her own chair.

I stood and hooked an arm around her waist and pulled her back against me. A gasp left her lips, but before she could wriggle out of my grasp I spun us, pressing her against the wall. I pressed my body against hers to keep her pinned in place. She mumbled a string of curses under her breath as I tipped her chin to force her to look at me.

"Let me set something straight with you, Lennox."

She swallowed as she stared at me, chest heaving, and defiance clear in the dark emerald of her eyes.

"I am not afraid of a witch. What I *am* afraid of is someone catching wind that the precious High Queen has left her court and seeing it as an opportunity to finish the job they set out to complete a few short days ago. Do you not remember being attacked and stabbed by a couple vampires? That there is an active threat on your life?"

She remained silent as she continued to meet my gaze.

"What I am afraid of is something happening to *you*, Lennox."

She sucked in a breath, her eyes softening for a second before hardening again.

"You can't expect me to sit around here doing nothing because someone is trying to kill me. You know me better than that," she bit out.

She was right, I did know her better than that. Which is exactly why I didn't want to do this. She would go to whatever ends necessary to protect her sister and her people, even if it meant putting herself in harm's way.

"I know. But there are people that need you. Your people need you, Lennox. Kara needs you." *I need you.* I don't know when the statement had become true, but it had. "I won't let anything happen to you." I had spoken those same words to her as the life threatened to leave her eyes, and I intended to keep my promise.

"I don't need protecting."

"Trust me, Lennox, I know. I've seen you wield a sword, but that doesn't mean I won't fear for your life."

I could see her churning my words over in her head. Fuck, even *I* didn't know why I said the things I did. But it was true. The idea of something happening to her stirred something deep in my gut. There were killers out there looking for the opportunity to kill Lennox and her sister, and we had no way of knowing when, or how, they would strike next.

Her silence continued, and I brushed my thumb over her cheek, my calloused finger rough over her smooth skin.

"Lennox, remember you are my friend, I care about you. Caring about you means I don't want you to get hurt. I am justified in that fear, but I will not prevent us from going on this journey if this is what you believe we need to do. I will support you. But I need you to understand my concerns."

She brought her bottom lip between her teeth.

"You might think your life is expendable, but it's not. There are people who care about you—who depend on you. If we do this you have to promise me you won't put your life at risk."

"This is our best option." Her words contained little fight this time. "I can't make any promises, but I will try my best not to get myself killed."

I nodded before finally moving away, the space where her body was pressed against mine instantly turning cold. I knew that was the best I was going to get from Lennox. She cared too much about others and not enough about herself, but I would do everything I could to keep her safe. Even if it meant putting my own life at risk to save hers. The thought should have scared me, but it didn't.

Something deep inside me told me Lennox Adair was someone worth risking my life for.

25

LENNOX

I studied Kara as I set my fork on my plate. Her cropped hair blew lightly around her face where she sat across from me. She looked carefree—a picture of grace with her blush pink gown and the garden surrounding her.

"Luka and I are going to travel to the Mystic Court next week." The words tumbled out quickly, preventing me from taking them back. Kara quirked a brow as she chewed.

"To do what?"

"We're going to find a Seer. We're hoping they could give us some insight into where to find the book." *And tell us how to take down the rebel vampire group that killed our family, and now wants to kill us both.*

I still wasn't ready to burden Kara with that yet.

"That's a great idea, why didn't we think of it sooner?" Kara continued to eat the fruit on her plate. She was reacting better than I anticipated. "When do we leave?"

We. There it was. "You're not going anywhere, Kar." Her fork froze halfway to her mouth. "I need you to stay here and watch over the court while I'm gone." Her face twisted as her fork clanked on the plate loudly.

"That's bullshit. That's not the real reason you don't want me to come with you and you know it."

Fuck.

"I don't understand what you mean?" I hated how easily the lie slipped off my tongue.

Kara's nostrils flared. "I'm not a child that needs protecting, Lennox. I'm more than capable of taking care of myself."

I reared back her words. "I know——"

Kara held up her hand, cutting me off. "No you don't." Her gaze was unwavering as she continued, "You and I are a lot more alike than you'd think, Lennox. You think after I spent those first few months crying in your arms I was magically all better? That I all of a sudden got over our parents and brother being murdered and moved on with life?" Her words felt like a physical blow as they fell from her lips.

Where was this coming from?

"You hide your grief well, but not as well as me, Lennox."

Had I missed that much when it came to my sister?

"What do you mean?" The words felt like gravel in my throat.

"You did such a good job taking care of me those first few months, taking care of everyone—it took me a long time to realize there wasn't anyone taking care of you."

Her face softened. "I pretended I was okay, so I didn't have to burden you with my grief anymore and you could start processing your own."

"Kara, I—"

She held up her hand again. "I'm not done yet." This was a side of Kara I hardly ever saw. I tended to forget it existed. Usually she was agreeable, easygoing, never daring to cause a stir. On the rare occurrences her fire appeared, it was enough to rival my own.

"We both lost a lot that night." She took a shuddering breath as she fiddled with her napkin. "What kept me going those first few months was that I still had you. But the worst part is—" She closed her eyes and took a deep breath. "The worst part is sometimes I feel like I lost you that night too."

A cascade of emotions strong and swift poured over me, stealing the breath from my lungs. My already shattered heart broke further.

How could I have caused so much pain to my sister and not even notice?

"I can never expect you to be the same person you were before, I know I'm not, but I feel like you let everything that made you happy go. You stopped caring for yourself. There are a lot of things I did *Before* that don't make me happy anymore. But there are still activities I find joy in. Some are old, and some are new. Sometimes it feels like a betrayal to move on and be happy without them, but . . . Lennox, you know they would be upset if we sat in our grief and refused to ever move on. They'd want me, they'd want both of us, to keep living the life they couldn't."

"You're a shell of the person you used to be." Kara smiled, bright and unabandoned as she shook her head. "Lennox, you used to be the most magnetic person to be around. People were drawn to you. Now . . . now they fear you, and not in the good way they used to before you were queen."

Had I turned so far away from the person I used to be that even my sister didn't recognize me anymore? But Kara should understand better than anyone that I could never return to the person I was before.

Didn't she realize I was utterly and completely shattered inside?

"I see how much you love and care for me. You are constantly looking out for me and I love that about you. I know you would do anything for me. *Anything.* And I hope you know I would do anything for you."

I did know that. My siblings and I had always had that kind of bond. We would do anything for one another.

"But sometimes I think you forget this relationship goes both ways. You get wrapped up in being concerned about protecting me and worrying about me, but who is worrying about you? Who is protecting *you*? I try, but you won't let me! Do you know how hard that is? You refuse to let anyone take care of you and it is so Goddess damned infuriating, Lennox." Her chest was heaving now as she spoke. Her eyes were full of fire, but rimmed in tears.

"You're concerned about losing me, but have you ever thought what it would do to me if I lost you?"

The pressure in my chest turned painful.

"I'd be left completely alone, forced to inherit a title I never wanted. I think you might be a little familiar with how that might feel."

The screech of her chair was the only sound in the garden. Even the breeze had stopped ruffling the leaves in the trees as if it too left with my sister.

I didn't dare move as I watched Kara walk away, not once glancing back. I watched her until she disappeared into the palace, but I didn't move. I was focused on replaying every word we had spoken, wondering how I had screwed up so monumentally, that I didn't hear the footsteps that walked up behind me.

26

LUKA

Lennox jumped as I gently placed my hand on her shoulder.

"Hey," I said as I took a seat in the chair next to her.

"Hi." She gave me a weak smile that didn't meet her eyes.

Declan and I had been walking through the garden when we overheard the sisters arguing. We didn't mean to eavesdrop, but Kara's voice was loud—it was hard to ignore. When Kara came storming past us, angry tears falling down her face, Declan and I only glanced at one another before he went after Kara, and I came to find Lennox.

"Are you okay?"

"Yes." I knew she wasn't. I'd seen Lennox go head-to-head with almost everyone, except Kara. She protected her as if her life depended on it. Yes, they bantered and had small disagreements, but if anyone dared to look at Kara wrong in Lennox's presence they were lucky if they left without injury, or their pride deeply damaged.

"Don't lie to me. Remember, we're friends now." I knocked my shoulder against hers. I was hoping the sentiment might result in a tiny smile, but it failed. Not a hint of amusement crossed her features.

"Fine, I'm not okay. Is that what you wanted to hear?" Her voice was laced with disdain.

"Yes."

The glare she gave me was pure Lennox. "You're infuriating," she snarled.

"I try my best just for you, Sweetheart."

Still no reaction, not even a flicker.

"Why don't you want Kara to come to the Mystic Court?"

She remained silent for several minutes before she finally let out a long breath. "You remember that whole grand speech you gave me about not wanting something to happen to me?"

"It was one hell of a speech if I do say so myself."

"Yeah, well that's how I feel about my sister, but a million times over."

I didn't say anything, willing her to continue.

"Kara is all I have left. She is all I have. If something were to happen to her—" She shook her head as a shutter worked its way down her spine. "I would never recover." Her voice wobbled slightly. "I know—I know I wouldn't." She swallowed. "I couldn't. I can't lose her."

"You can't live in fear, Lennox." I placed my hand over hers where it rested on her lap and gave it a squeeze.

"I know, and I try not to, but it's so fucking hard when I consider everything we've lost. And I know I'm a terrible sister for asking her to stay behind because if I was in her position I would be kicking and screaming to be included too. That's how we were raised. I hate myself for trying to take away the choice from her, but sometimes the fear of losing her consumes me and I can't . . . I can't think rationally." Sorrow and anger rang through her voice as her chest rose and fell violently.

"Have you tried explaining this to her?"

"You heard how well that went."

"No, I mean, truly explain it to her. From what it sounded like you both have been experiencing similar emotions, but you've been hiding it from one another. You both need to take some time to calm down before you talk it out."

Lennox let out a deep sign. "You might be onto something."

I smiled as we fell into silence. I surveyed the garden around us, keeping an eye on Lennox out of the corner of my eye.

"I'm not very good at expressing my emotions."

I chuckled lightly at her confession. "Really? I'd never noticed."

Finally, a smile cracked through her stony features. I smiled back at her.

"Thank you." She squeezed my hand.

We sat in silence and both of us watched as the clouds rolled over the grassy plains. Her hand still rested in mine, but she made no move for me to remove it as I made idle strokes on her palm as we sat.

"For the record, you have me too, Lennox."

She didn't say anything, but her breath hitched, I felt the slight quickening of her pulse. She closed her eyes for several seconds before opening them again, still staring out at the plains. Her reaction, or lack thereof, made me want to take the words back. I shouldn't have said that. But I also knew she needed to hear those words. To know someone else cared about her. That someone would still be here for her if something were to happen to Kara.

I was about to open my mouth and explain myself out of what I said when I felt her squeeze my hand. It took everything in me not to whip my head in her direction, to assess her expression. But I restrained myself, keeping my gaze in front of me as she linked our fingers together before placing them back in her lap.

27

LENNOX

I laid in bed and stared at the ceiling—trying and failing to fall asleep. After Luka talked me down, we trained again. Letting my feelings out by using a sword was my best and favorite coping mechanism. It might be my only coping mechanism, but it was effective and that's all that mattered.

I had intended to smooth things over with Kara during dinner, but when I found the kitchen empty, the staff informed me she had taken her dinner in her room. She still wasn't ready to talk to me about our fight.

Our stupid fucking fight.

I wanted to go to her room—to apologize and explain to her what was going through my mind, but knowing my sister, she needed time. Time and space to think before she was ready to have it out. It killed me, fighting with her, and knowing she was mad at me. I could care less what anyone else thought of me, but with Kara—I couldn't help feeling like I had disappointed her. That thought alone kept me from sleep.

I turned on my side and looked out the window at the moon in the night sky. Maybe I should pray to the Goddess for guidance and forgiveness. I had never been a spiritual person, not like my mother was—she regularly gave offerings to the Goddess in exchange for asking for anything from a good night's sleep to good health when someone she knew was ill. I had often joined her growing up, but since her death, I had a hard time being thankful to a Goddess who would take my family from me. She'd curse me for the thought alone, but hadn't I already been cursed enough? It sure felt like it.

I reached for the dagger under my pillow at the sound of my door creaking open, and looked over my shoulder to find Kara slipping into my room. I released my dagger as she silently made her way over to my bed and slipped under the covers. She snuggled in close, laying her arm over me and squeezing.

"I'm sorry," she whispered into the moonlit room.

"No, I'm sorry, Kara. You have nothing to be sorry for." I rolled to my other side, facing my sister as she laid with her hand under her cheek. Even in the darkness, I could see her eyes were puffy and red. I had caused her so much pain today.

Not only today. How many nights had she spent crying and hiding it from me over the last two years? There used to be a time when Kara would come to me anytime something happened. I was the person she came to every time someone broke her heart growing up—If someone said something that upset her. We told each other everything. But she wasn't the only one who had stopped. When had I stopped going to her as well and kept it all to myself instead?

"I should have never tried to take your choice away from you. I—I get terrified of the idea of losing you, Kara. And that fear took over me and I'm sorry."

"I know. I'm sorry I reacted the way I did."

So many words were left unsaid. They clung to the space around us like smoke.

"You should come with us if you want."

Several beats of silence stretched between us.

"Okay."

I let myself smile slightly. There was more I needed to tell her. so much more to explain. Starting with what Luka and I had discovered about the Vanir. But that could wait until tomorrow. This moment right here with my sister was more important.

"I love you, Kara," I whispered into the darkness.

"I love you too, Len."

"Until the stars turn to dust."

"Until the stars turn to dust."

28

LUKA

Declan and I sat in the main sitting room off of the grand hall discussing the arrangements we'd need to make before we left on our trip next week. I had only seen Lennox briefly in the days following her fight with Kara. We talked long enough for her to relay that Kara would be joining us before she had to run off to a meeting. She had plenty of arrangements to make herself before she could leave Alethens.

After much debate it was decided Declan would join us too. I thought it might be a good idea for him to stay back and keep an eye on everything in Alethens while Lennox and I were gone, but he disagreed. He argued it was his duty to protect me, therefore he would not let me travel without him. I couldn't argue against his commitment to his position.

And he threatened to tell my grandfather I was traveling out of Alethens, which I did not want relayed to him until after our trip.

So it was decided at the end of the week; Kara, Declan, Lennox, and I would head to the Mystic Court. We would bring no additional guards. Declan claimed it would be easier to travel discreetly with a smaller party. Lennox and I both agreed with his assessment, although her advisors did not. If it was up to them, Lennox would not be leaving the Star Court at all. It was ultimately decided she would leave discreetly. It would not be advertised that she was leaving Alethens. If the matter needed to be addressed, it would be revealed she was traveling to another court for political reasons. Which wasn't a complete lie, but the less people who knew where Lennox and Kara were, the better.

Declan and I were discussing what supplies we would need when Alvise interrupted us. "Your Highness." The male stood in the doorway looking more nervous than normal, sweat already beading on his brows. I swear the male sweat more than any Fae I'd ever met.

"Yes," I ground out.

"You have a visitor."

A visitor? I looked at Declan, who gave me no indication he knew who it could be either. I hadn't exactly made any friends since I arrived here.

"Who is it?" Declan asked, sitting straighter in his chair, tucking his wings in tight.

"A, Sir Nico."

I couldn't stop the laugh from bursting from my chest. Alvises' face turned bright red at my reaction, sweat now dripping down his round face. Declan shook his head.

"Right, send him in."

"Oh c'mon, brother." A familiar voice rang out from behind. "I thought you'd be more excited to see me."

I couldn't believe my eyes as Nico stepped into the room— arms spread wide and a shit eating grin plastered on his face. I let out a laugh of disbelief this time as I jumped from my seat and rushed to him, wrapping my arms around the wolf. He returned the hug before releasing me and pulling a begrudging Declan into a hug while I stared at him in disbelief.

"Now do you care to explain what in Astria's tits you're doing here?" We moved back to the sitting area and Nico sat, resting his ankle over his opposite knee.

"I missed you assholes, so I thought I'd pay you a visit."

"You're supposed to be watching over things at the Blood Court," Declan argued.

Nico waved a hand dismissively towards Declan.

"They'll be fine without me for a few weeks."

Declan looked displeased at Nico's casual dismissiveness, while I for one was happy to have both of my best friends in the same room again. Before Declan and I had left to come to Alethens, the longest the three of us had been apart in the last five years was only a few weeks.

Declan was my reliable, level headed friend. Loyal to a fault. Whereas Nico was everything Declan wasn't—reckless, impulsive, and loud. But he was loyal and trustworthy, too. He was my oldest friend after all.

Declan leaned forward, resting his elbows on his knees. "Tell us why you're here, Nico."

The wolf sighed. "Fine. You always have to be such a buzzkill, Dec."

I smiled at my two friends, years of friendship allowed us to slip back seamlessly into our roles. Declan and Nico bickered back and forth most of the time—their polar opposite personalities clashing at every corner. But I knew deep down how much they cared for each other.

"Your Uncle Lorenzo sent me to check in on your progress."

I groaned. "Of course he did."

Nico's face was serious now. "Your grandfather is willing to be patient, but you know Lorenzo . . ."

I did know my uncle. And now I questioned whose idea it was to send the letter a couple of weeks ago with talks of war.

"He wanted to check on you himself."

What could Lorenzo possibly gain from coming here?

"Your grandfather was against the idea, but Lorenzo fought hard. He was trying to claim you wouldn't be able to get it done."

"And he thought he'd be able to?" I scoffed. There was a reason I was the heir to the throne and not my uncle. He was impulsive, arrogant, and easy to anger. All qualities my grandfather claimed were not suitable for a king. Which angered my uncle even more.

"Lorenzo would try anything at this point to convince your grandfather he's better suited for the crown."

I couldn't count how many times my uncle bad-mouthed me to my grandfather—in front of me, and in private. I had ears everywhere, I knew what he was saying about me. When my grandfather chose me to travel to the Star Court, my uncle threw the fit of all fits. It was rather pathetic if I do say so myself.

My uncle is the oldest of my grandfather's children. My mother was his younger sister. It shocked everyone, but also no one, when my grandfather chose my mother to inherit the throne over my uncle. My uncle was quiet and studious—well versed when it came to politics, but he couldn't wield a sword to save his life. In my grandfather's eyes it made my mother more suitable for the crown. After my mother was declared heir, everyone said Lorenzo changed. He became temperamental, even more so when his daughter disappeared, but he never gave up on trying to prove to my grandfather he deserved the crown.

Which made the blow even bigger when my grandfather declared me heir after my parents died. Lorenzo was already cold towards me before, but now he rarely looked at me without destain in his eyes. He wanted to come with me to Alethens. He jumped at any chance to prove his worth, hoping my grandfather might change his mind before the crown was placed on my head.

"I volunteered to come instead. I told him I'd come and stay for a while before reporting back. Your grandfather thought it was a wonderful idea." Nico's eyes lit up. "He told me as much while he patted me on the back while your uncle tried to not rip my head off." I chuckled. I could see the scene all too clearly in my head.

"Well, thank you. The last thing I need right now is my uncle here."

Nico smirked. "And why is that? What trouble have you gotten yourself into, Luka?"

Declan and I exchanged a knowing look before we proceeded to fill Nico in on everything that had transpired since we arrived several months ago. Starting with Lennox hating me and ending with our realization about the Vanir and their attack last week.

"Well, Goddess be fucked." Nico shook his head and sat back in his chair. "While I've been keeping an eye on things for you in the Blood Court, you've been here having all kinds of adventures." Nico leaned forward, a mischievous gleam in his eyes. "But what I want to know is what is the High Queen like? From the sounds of it, the two of you are pretty close."

"I wouldn't say we're close." We weren't. I cared about Lennox, but we weren't close. I watched as Declan gave Nico a look, a small smirk playing on his lips. "What?"

Declan shook his head.

"Tell me what you're thinking before I break your fucking nose," I ground out.

Nico clapped in excitement. "Fuck, I missed you two."

I ignored his glee, still focusing on Declan.

"Tell me."

"Fine." He gave in. "All I'm going to say is there is a fine line between love and hate."

"What the fuck is that supposed to mean?"

Declan opened his mouth to respond, but quickly closed it, his gaze traveling behind me. I looked over my shoulder to find Lennox herself standing in the doorway.

"There you are, I was looking for you." She brushed her braid over her shoulder as she walked into the sitting room. She had on her signature leather pants and a matching black blouse, with the top three buttons undone, exposing the tanned skin of her chest. She had opted to forego the corset today and instead to tucked the fabric of the shirt into the band of her pants. Nico's eyes gleamed as he took her in, I felt a growl crawling up my throat at his open perusal of her body.

"Well, well, well, if it isn't the Royal Majesty herself."

Lennox turned towards Nico, surprise flickered on her face for a brief second. Nico stood, bowing slightly and holding out his hand. Lennox placed her hand in his without hesitation.

"And who are you?" she asked, arching a brow.

Nico brought her hand to his lips and placed a kiss on the back of it. My knuckles turned white with how hard I was gripping the arms of the chair.

"Nico Elsher, emissary to the Blood Court." Nico released her hand.

"And why, may I ask, are you here, in my palace?"

A grin spread across Nico's face. Sometimes I hated how easily charming others came to him. The way he radiated charisma.

"I'm here to see my best friends of course." He nodded in my direction. Lennox's eyes flicked to me for a second before turning back to Nico.

"You're *that* Nico?"

"So you've heard of me?"

Lennox's lip quirked up. I watched Nico as he hung onto her every word—waiting for her to continue. But she only shrugged before turning in my direction. I watched Nico's face fall slightly, he didn't often get rejected and he didn't take it lightly. Part of me was delighted at her dismissal of my friend.

"I got everything arranged with the council for our trip." She tucked a stray hair behind her ear. "We're on track to leave by the end of the week." I nodded.

"Declan and I were ironing out some final details."

She nodded. "Well, I'll leave you to it then." She turned to walk back out the door, but stopped halfway there. She stood unmoving with her back to us until she finally turned back around, letting out a long sigh.

"Gulia will scold me if I don't invite our guest to a proper dinner."

A wide grin broke out on Nico's face. Lennox put on her best fake smile, one I knew all too well. I used to think it was real, but now I noticed the way it didn't meet her eyes, how she never showed her teeth.

"We will all gather for dinner in the dining room at seven."

"It would be my honor, Your Majesty."

"I will see you all later." She turned and walked back out the door without another word. As soon as she was out of earshot Nico let out a low howl as he rubbed his hands together.

"She's something isn't she."

I said nothing as I stared out the window. I gripped the arms of the chair in an effort to keep myself from punching Nico for the way he looked at Lennox.

"I can see why you're entranced with her, brother." My head snapped in his direction. "C'mon, I saw the way you looked at her when she walked in. You've got it bad." He smiled smugly.

"I do not," I argued. "I can admire the way she looks without taking her to bed." Lennox is my friend, my political ally. That's all.

"Keep lying to yourself, brother." He poured us each a drink from the decanter on the table between us. I downed the amber liquid in two swallows. Relishing the burn as it went down. Where was this coming from? I understood it coming from Nico because that was Nico. But from Declan? He had seen what it had been like between Lennox and I over the past months. I couldn't help it if there was attraction between us, that was natural. It was Fae instinct. But there was nothing remotely romantic between the two of us.

We were just friends.

29

LENNOX

I arrived in the dining room to find everyone else had already arrived. Kara, Luka, Declan, and Nico were all gathered at the far end of the room, drinks already in hand. No one had noticed my arrival, so I took the opportunity and remained in the doorway observing them.

My gaze fell to Nico first. I was taken aback by his striking features when I met him this afternoon. His silver hair fell to his chin in loose waves—it shone bright against the dark pallor of his skin. His silver hair, with his ice blue eyes, were a stunning combination. It was hard to tear my eyes from his striking features. Nico was good looking in an interesting way, whereas Luka was handsome in a more typical fashion with his dark hair and sapphire eyes.

My gaze lingered on where Luka stood. His dark locks were tamed tonight, styled back from his face, emphasizing his strong jaw. He wore black fitted pants and a black button-up shirt that stretched across his shoulders. The top two buttons of his shirt were left undone, drawing my eyes to his tanned chest and the tattoos peaking over his shoulders. Luka's eyes lit up as he laughed at something Nico said. If I was closer I'm sure I could see the crinkles that formed at the corners of his eyes when he laughed a real laugh.

I turned my attention back to Lukas silver-haired friend. He commanded the large room, even from where I stood. It felt as if everyone was orbiting around him. His aura was different from that of Declan and Luka. Nico was boisterous and charismatic—I could see how others could be easily drawn to him. Declan was quiet and reserved—serious at all times. And Luka, well, Luka was Luka. Infuriating and kind. It got harder and harder to dislike him as the days went on. No matter how hard I tried to deny it, I had come to enjoy his presence. Not that I'd ever tell him such.

It was as if he knew I was thinking about him, his gaze traveled to where I stood. A half smile grew on his full lips. I remained in the doorway as he made his way to me. He picked up two glasses off of a tray from a server, handing one to me when he arrived at my side.

"You finally decided to grace us with your presence, huh?" He remarked as I took a sip of the wine, it's bright fruity taste blooming over my taste buds.

"It appears so." I took another sip. "Although it looks like you were all getting along swimmingly without me."

"You would think, but I thought the conversation lacked an heir of violence."

I rolled my eyes and hid my smile behind my glass.

"I don't know about them, but I like living on the edge, never knowing if what I say is going to amuse you or make you want to stab me."

"Or both," I added.

Luka chuckled and I couldn't hold back the small laugh that escaped from my lips. I liked that I could let loose around Luka, I didn't feel the need to put on an act around him, and I didn't have to hold back. He liked the rough edges of my personality, never once did he try to smooth them, instead he encouraged me. He breathed air into my fire, instead of stifling it.

"Lennox!" Kara's voice rang through the dining room as she spotted me, making her way towards where Luka and I stood.

I drained the rest of the wine from my glass as Kara approached. "Let's eat," I declared. "I don't know about you, but I'm starved."

We all sat at the table—Declan at the head with Kara to his left and I next to her. Luka sat directly across from me with Nico at his side. The conversation stilled as the staff brought out the meal. Plates of various meats, vegetables, and potatoes filled the table.

"So, Sir Nico, I never asked, why are you here?" I speared a piece of meat on my fork and brought it to my mouth.

"Please, call me Nico, titles are reserved for the Crown Prince over there." He jutted a thumb towards Luka.

"Okay, *Nico*, why are you here in the Star Court?"

He took a sip from his glass before speaking. "Just checking in on my brothers here, making sure they're not getting into too much trouble without me."

"And he missed us too much," Luka added, shoving Nico's shoulder with his own.

"What can I say, it's a wolf thing, we miss our pack." Nico shrugged. "And I figured Luka here was getting tired of drinking harpy blood."

Luka shook his head, ignoring the remark.

"Luka, can I ask you a personal question?" Kara inquired.

"Sure."

"Do different Fae's blood taste different?" Luka's eyebrows rose as did mine.

"Curious little princess aren't you," Nico purred.

Kara shrugged, the tips of her pointed ears growing pink, but she didn't cower. "I'm simply curious, we don't have many vampires around here."

Luka chewed, seeming to consider Kara's question. I had to admit I was curious to hear the answer myself. I had studied about the different types of Fae growing up, but there was only so much information a book could detail.

"Every Fae tastes different—vampire, harpy, wolf, etcetera, they all have a distinct taste." He waved his hand. "And every vampire has a preference of the kind of blood they prefer. I don't tend to lean towards a species of Fae, instead I find that Fae with more power taste better."

Fae with more power taste better. Like a Fae with all four elements? Did that mean he wondered what I tasted like? Did he crave my blood?

Luka glanced at me for a moment before turning his attention back to Kara. "I've also found that blood can taste different based on the circumstances it's taken."

Kara's brow furrowed. "What do you mean, based on the circumstances?"

"He means that blood tastes even sweeter when he's fucking whoever he's drinking from." Nico's words echoed in the silent dining room.

My cheeks burned as I pressed my lips into a thin line. Did he truthfully drink from his partners while he fucked them? What would that even look like? I squirmed in my seat. What would it feel like to have his fangs scrape along my neck while he moved inside me? I clenched my thighs together. Or did he bite his partners in other places?

"I'm going to go and get some more wine," I said before rushing from the room as casually as I could. When I entered the kitchen I braced my hands on the large wooden island. Trying and failing to steady my breaths and cool my heated skin as the door opened behind me.

I knew who it was before the scent of cool morning rain invaded my senses.

"What's the matter, Sweetheart? The conversation too unsettling for you?"

I turned, my back resting against the countertop as I faced him.

"Were you wondering if I had thought about biting you?"

My breath hitched as his gaze flicked to my neck. He took another step towards me.

"I'd be lying if I said the thought never crossed my mind, Sweetheart."

He was talking about biting me. *Biting me for fucks sake.* He took another step forward, forcing me to lift my chin to meet his gaze.

"I'd love nothing more than to know what you taste like," he admitted, his voice low.

The thought of his fangs scrapping over my neck should have terrified me, instead it heated my veins. My neck tilted involuntarily. I wondered if he thought about tasting other parts of me. He braced his hands on the counter, caging me in.

"I'll never let you bite me." The words came out weak. I didn't even believe them myself.

"We'll see about that, Sweetheart." The smile he threw me was dripping with arrogance. "I bet one day you'll be begging me to bite you."

His words snapped me from my haze—the cloud of lust clearing. I would never beg him for anything. What was I doing? Why was I even entertaining this conversation? Luka was a vampire. *A vampire.* Why was I letting him have this effect on me? Maybe it was because it has been so long since I'd been with anyone. Why did I have such a hard time maintaining space between us? We were inching closer and closer to a line I had no interest in crossing.

"I have no intention of ever letting you near me. I don't have a thing for vampires. Wolves on the other hand—" I let my hand linger on his chest, tracing the lines of his muscles through his shirt. "If Nico is looking for something to do while he's here, you should send him my way."

Luka scowled as I patted his cheek and placed a kiss there before I slipped out from under his arms.

I had no desire to pursue anything with Nico, but maybe it would be worth it to slip into his bed. Maybe it would quench my lingering desire that my fingers did little to satisfy these days.

I grabbed a bottle of wine from the counter before looking back at Luka over my shoulder. He had yet to move from the spot I left him.

"You coming, Bloodsucker?" I called and he grumbled something that I couldn't discern before he turned and followed me out the room.

30

LENNOX

The night before we left for the Mystic Court I tossed and turned, my mind running through all of our plans and preparations, trying to ensure that we were not missing a critical detail.

My royal council was not pleased at my departure, but they agreed to handle things while I was away. They didn't know the true intentions behind my travel, they only thought I was going to visit another court for political reasons. Which was partly true.

It would take about a week and a half to arrive at the border of the Mystic Court. How much time we'd spend there was unknown. It all depended on if we were able to find a coven who was willing to help us locate a Seer.

To get to the Mystic Court we'd have to travel though the Lunar Court.

At dinner the other night Nico had argued his way into coming with us; claiming he could ensure our travel through the Lunar Court would go smoothly. It was his home court after all. I had to admit it would be helpful since I didn't have much communication with the Lunar Court on my end, and I'm sure Nico would offer plenty of entertainment during our travels as well.

We had packed everything the night before, planning to leave as soon as the sun started rising. When I arrived at the stables the three males were already waiting.

I greeted Odin as we waited for Kara, scratching him lightly behind the ears. Odin had been my horse since I entered the Royal Guard at eighteen. He was a trained war horse. It had been a huge disagreement between me and Captain Kahle when I insisted Odin be released as my personal steed when I became queen. He argued I had no right to stake a claim on his best war horse. I only laughed at him and informed him the reason Odin was one of the best horses in the cavalry was because I trained him to be.

Not that Captain Kahle would ever admit that. He never wanted me to be a part of the Royal Guard in the first place. He argued it would be a distraction to have a princess in their midst. He did everything he could to prevent me from succeeding. Including giving me the meekest horse he could find. It took me months to train Odin to run towards a fight instead of away from it. But I never gave up on him. Odin and I built a relationship over the years—one few horses and riders ever did. I wasn't going to let him go under any circumstances. Captain Kahle could add me claiming Odin as my own to the long list of grievances he held against me.

"Are we all ready?" Declan called out. We all nodded in approval before Declan urged his steed forward and we all followed behind. None of us spoke as we traveled, and the light from the sun was starting to creep into the trees surrounding the palace grounds. Since it was early we decided to go straight through Alethens, rather than around the city.

A few Fae littered the streets—up early with the sun getting their shops ready for the day, but the rest of the city was quiet. I had never seen it as such. It was usually bustling with Fae—music, chatter, and children playing filling the streets. How long would it be until I was able to experience that again? My chest ached at the thought. I would make it back from this journey. I had to. I had promised Luka and Kara I would do my best. I also had to make it back for my people.

My people, they needed me too.

☪

We quickly settled into a routine as we made our way through Lethenia. Stopping only for lunch and a quick rest before continuing on until after dark. We stuck towards the border of the Lunar Court to avoid being seen by anyone.

Each night when we set up camp. We worked together to create a barrier around our camp—a shield of sorts, made up of air. It kept our sounds and smoke from our fire in our bubble, protecting us from the outside world and warning us of any potential unwanted visitors. With the shield in place we could all sleep without someone needing to keep watch. If the shield was compromised, whoever's magic was used that night to create the shield would be warned by their magic to the intrusion.

Once our camp was set up and we had eaten dinner, we all trained for an hour, much to Kara's disappointment. I made sure to remind her it was her decision to come with therefore she forfeited any right to deny training with us. Every evening she grumbled as she trained alongside us. As soon as her hour was up she dropped whatever weapon was in her hand and went off to bed. Depending on the day, or how tired we were, sometimes Luka, Declan, Nico, and I trained for longer. Only stopping once we were exhausted enough that I fell asleep the minute my head hit the pillow.

As we rode I found myself tracking the dark lines of the tattoos that peaked out from the top of Luka's leathers. After traveling so many days I had resorted to studying Luka as we rode. Anything to keep me awake on Odin I guess.

I turned my attention back to the ink on his tanned neck. I itched to know what they looked like as they continued underneath his clothes.

His hand fisted the reins and the other rested lazily on the pommel of the saddle. He rode with such causal ease. His strong thighs gripped the horse, keeping him steady as the sun shone through the dark waves of his hair, making it appear a shade lighter. I wondered what it would feel like to wrap my fingers through the dark strands.

A twig snapped in the trees beside me, and I shook my head, snapping out of my thoughts. What was wrong with me? He was my ally, nothing more, and he never would be. *He's a vampire,* I reminded myself. I could not bed a vampire, no matter how much my body might think it desired him. He was a male, that was all. *An exceptionally good looking male who I'm sure could satisfy the growing need between my thighs.*

My gaze flicked to his hand holding the reins. Those long fingers—*for fucks sake Lennox.* Was I that starved for sex? It had to be the boredom setting in. We had been traveling for twelve days now. We should be closing in on the border to the Mystic Court any day now. It was just the travel going to my brain. Too many days of my eyes fixed on his back. I needed something else to focus my attention on besides Luka. But I couldn't help myself sometimes. I felt drawn to him, like a magnetic pull I couldn't deny.

I felt my magic stir inside me, it felt a pull to Luka too apparently. I fisted my hands in an attempt to lock it back down, but it refused—rising right back up to the surface. The hairs on the back of my neck tingled and I sat straighter as Odins's ears perked to attention. I strained my ears. Was there something out there?

My magic surged to life at my fingertips. *Not yet,* I told it.

"Luka," I whispered and he looked over his shoulder in my direction. I waved a hand to signal him to come closer, he slowed his mare to meet the pace of Odin.

"Did you hear something?" My magic continued to churn violently at the surface, poking and pressing against my skin. There had to be something out there for it to react this strongly.

The look on my face must have said enough. Luka got Declan and Nico's attention and I, Kara's. I still couldn't see anything, though. The sun was low in the sky, making it difficult to see farther into the dense forest around us.

There was rustling in the trees and I moved my hand to Minerva at my side—releasing it from its sheath with one smooth motion. My magic sang to the feel of my sword in my hand. I felt it making its way down the blade, wrapping itself around it like a warm embrace. The metal glowed as my magic buried itself in the blade, connecting us together. My eyes scanned the trees once again, looking for a sign of anything. These were Lunar woods, anything could be out here.

I sensed movement out of the corner of my eye. "Luka," I whispered, tilting my head towards the movement. "There's something—"

Kara's scream pierced through the woods as a giant beast leapt from the trees, cutting off the words in my throat. The beast was massive, the size of Odin, with inky black scales covering its body. Its eyes were completely white, a jarring contrast to the blackness of its body. Two thick fangs protruded from its massive jaws. They had to be almost two feet long. *The amount of damage they could cause . . .*

A Hellhound. A fucking Hellhound had found us. Up until now I wasn't sure if they existed or if they were only a myth told to keep younglings from wandering into the forest alone.

The Hellhound let out an ear piercing shriek as it snapped its jaws and leapt out of the trees towards Luka. The beast met Luka's blade as he jumped from his horse. Black blood oozed from the side of the hound's neck as the blade made its mark. It howled, but quickly recovered, bounding towards Luka again. I leapt from Odin and ran to Luka's side, only for three more Hellhounds to emerge from the woods.

Real. Hellhounds were fucking real.

"Fuck," Luka muttered. I spared one last glance at him as he turned to face the Hellhound circling him.

"You got that one?" I asked. He nodded, his eyes never leaving the creature.

"Go, make 'em bleed, Sweetheart." He winked over his shoulder before turning back to the Hellhound.

I took off running towards one of the other Hellhounds. Kara jumped off her horse behind me, her footsteps loud on the ground as she followed me. The other two hounds bounded towards Nico and Declan. Declan stood ready, with his blade in his hand, his black wings out and ready to fight. I watched, out of the corner of my eye, as the Hellhounds bounded towards the males. Nico took off running towards the creature, but before the warning could leave my mouth a flash of white blinded me. I blinked against the light to find a massive, silver wolf charging towards the Hellhound, a howl tore through the woods as the wolf rammed into the beast.

Nico's wolf form was magnificent. His coat was the same silver as his hair, and his form was bigger than any horse I'd ever seen. I stole one last glance towards him to see him rip into the side of one of the hound's neck, his ice blue eyes meeting mine as black blood dripped from his jaws.

I turned from the wolf to find a Hellhound rushing towards where Kara and I stood.

"Aim for its feet," I told her. "Maybe we can disable it by cutting off its legs."

My sister nodded as she took her stance next to me, palming her daggers. "I'll distract it first."

Before I could argue she threw a dagger towards the Hellhound. The first one embedded itself in its back, the second and third in its neck and between its eyes. The creature let out another shriek—the sound making my head pound as the sound rattled my bones.

I bolted towards the creature, swinging Minerva towards its front legs. A crack sounded as the sword hit bone, the impact reverberating through my body. I grimaced as I pulled back, and the hound turned towards me.

Its bones were too thick, cutting off his legs wouldn't work.

Another one of Kara's daggers whistled through the air, landing in the Hellhounds' back. He moved towards her, his long tail whipping behind it, I fell to the ground as the barbed appendage skimmed over me, my body groaning from the impact.

Its tail.

I stood and ran after the Hellhound as it pursued my sister where she stood, sword in hand, a dangerous smile on her face. She may hate training, but my sister loved a fight as much as I did. It was in our blood.

I approached the hound from behind and took my sword to its tail. Minerva cut through the flesh easily this time—warm, black blood splattering me in the process. I wiped the blood from my face with the back of my arm as its shriek pierced the air.

From somewhere behind me, Luka let out a cry of agony. Panic surged through me as I turned trying to find him.

"Lennox!" Kara shrieked. "Watch out!" I turned back around to find the Hellhound bounding towards me. It snapped its jaws, those long fangs aiming for my flesh, as green liquid oozed from the fangs. *Poison.* I ducked and slid underneath the creature. Thrusting my sword up into its chest where I lay beneath it. Thick, black blood rained down on me, but I continued to push my blade in further, my body screaming at the sheer force of the action.

The hound moved, trying to figure out where I was. I gritted my teeth as I used a burst of air to push it back before letting a ball of fire explode from my palm. The beast erupted into flames, crying out as the fire consumed him.

I turned and ran towards where the others continued to fight in the clearing. Nico was still ripping into one of the Hellhounds, black blood staining his silver coat as he spat out the remains. Declan's blade squelched as he removed it from the beast before driving it back in again with brutal force.

But Luka.

Where was Luka?

His groan rang out, turning my attention to the right. I took off running—finding Luka lying on the forest floor, one of the hounds on top of him. Between him and the creature were his swords, the only things keeping the Hellhound from descending on him as he snapped his jaws at Luka. Luka groaned as he kicked at the hound, failing to move him.

I slammed a ball of air at the Hellhound, the force pushing the creature from Luka before I turned the beast into ashes like its companion. My chest heaved as I watched the Hellhound dissolve into nothing but ashes on the forest floor. Luka stood, sheathing his swords and wiping the black blood from his face.

"Thanks." He panted. "Are you okay?"

I nodded. "Are you?" I asked, my eyes roaming over his body.

He smiled. "I am because of you, Sweetheart."

I shook my head, of course he would be smiling after being attacked by a Hellhound.

He opened his mouth, surely to let out some witty remark, when the smile faded from his face.

"Luka?"

I hadn't noticed the hand he was holding at his side until he removed it. Blood coated his palm.

Not black blood.

Red blood.

Luka's blood.

31

LENNOX

Panic consumed me at the sight of the blood coating Luka's hand. *His blood*. My chest tightened painfully as I rushed to him.

"Luka, what happened, are you okay?" My hand moved to where his had been. Blood soaked through his leathers.

Too much blood. He was losing too much blood.

"Luka?"

He grimaced as the color drained from his face. "I'm okay, I may have been nicked slightly."

"What do you mean *nicked?*" My mind flashed to the giant canines on the beasts. I quickly shook the thought from my head. Hopefully it had been its claws.

"You're bleeding. You need to lay down." I clutched onto his arms. He was losing blood. Lot's of it, and quickly. Quicker than he could heal from.

"I'm fine," he argued

I clenched my jaw. "You are *not* fine. I need you to lay down so I can take a look at it."

Declan, Nico, and Kara rushed over, and their faces paled at the sight of Luka. He remained standing, wobbling as he tried to stay upright.

"Please, Luka." My voice cracked. "Please Luka, let me help you."

He swung his head in my direction, his eyes had lost their gleam, no magic danced in them. I swallowed—he was already fading.

He closed his eyes and nodded. I let out a small sigh of relief. I didn't let go of his arms as Nico and Declan helped me lower him to the ground, a groan slipped from his lips as we laid him flat.

I pulled a blade from my side and cut the clothing around his wound. I peeled back the blood soaked fabric to reveal a giant gash in his side. We all sucked in a collective breath at the sight.

"That bad, huh?" Luka grumbled.

I stared at the wound, green puss oozed from the gash. It wasn't a claw, a fang had gotten him.

"Fuck," Declan mumbled.

Nico hissed. "Astria's tits. It got you with its fang didn't it?"

"I think so, mate." Luka grimaced.

"The fangs were poisonous. That's why he's deteriorating quickly." I looked to find Nico and Declan staring at me—worry written clearly on their faces. My own heart beat erratically in my chest.

"This is bad," Kara said, her voice thick with concern. "There is no way he can heal from this on his own with poison in his system."

I couldn't think straight as I held pressure to the gaping hole in Lukas' side. The wound was too severe, the poison already making its way through his body. His magic would never be able to heal it on its own. We needed a healer. He was losing too much blood and the gash was too deep to bandage without stitches. I could see the pain in his features. His hands clenched into fists at his sides as he took shallow breaths.

I held his fist in my hand, squeezing it between both of my

hands. Willing some of the pain to move from his body to mine. He tilted his head to look at me.

"It's okay, Lennox." His words came out strained, like every word hurt as it left his throat.

I felt tears pricking at the back of my eyes. "No, it's not." The words caught in my throat.

Think Lennox. Think. I cannot let Luka die. I will not lose another.

The others were talking around me, but I couldn't hear them. I couldn't focus on them when Luka was dying.

He was dying.

I couldn't let him die. He told me I had him, and he couldn't leave me like this. My magic hummed in my chest as I stared at Luka's face.

He might have accepted his fate, but I didn't.

I would not lose another person I cared about.

"I can heal him." The words left my mouth before I could stop them. Nico and Declan stared at me.

"What do you mean you can heal him?" Nico asked.

"I said, I can heal him."

Kara looked at me. "Are you sure you want to do this? There's no turning back if you do."

I nodded. "Yes, I have to. I can't let him die."

Kara nodded. "Let me know if you need my help."

"Do what?" Nico asked, fear had leaked into his voice, but I ignored him, placing my trembling hands on Luka's wound instead. His warm blood was sticking to them. I held back a gag as I took several deep breaths to calm myself. This wouldn't work if I wasn't calm. I focused as my mothers words filled my head.

Breath Sitara. Breathe. Become one with your surroundings.

"What is she doing?" Declan prodded and Kara shushed him.

I blocked them out. I needed to focus. I pictured Luka in my mind. I pictured his wound. I pictured his flesh stitching itself back together.

Sense the energy around you. Focus on the energy and pull from it. My heartbeat steadied. I closed my eyes as I focused on my mothers words again. I felt my magic tingling throughout my body— warmth flowing through me as my hair whipped across my blood-streaked face.

I felt my magic vibrate in my chest. It moved through my body. It pulsed like a drum through me, making its way down my arms and into my hands. I opened my eyes to find a bright light of magic flaring from my palms and projecting into Luka's body. I focused on the feeling of my magic moving through me and into him. His magic thrummed in response. It was a dull beat, but it was there. There was still a chance.

I continued to push my magic into him.

The thrum of his magic grew stronger with every breath I took until his magic was strong enough to accept mine. I gasped as our magic intertwined. I opened my eyes and watched Luka's skin glow before stitching itself back together the same way I had pictured it in my head. I didn't stop until there was nothing but smooth, fresh, pink skin beneath my palms.

But I still had to rid his body of the poison. I focused again, this time his entire body glowed with my magic. Someone swore behind me, but I continued. My magic flowed through Luka, ridding his body of every drop of poison. When it was gone my magic rushed back into me like a wave crashing on the beach. I panted as I removed my hands from his side—his blood now dried and flaked onto my skin. I sagged back on to my heels, exhaustion from what I had completed weighing on me.

I scanned Luka's body, watching the rise and fall of his chest. He was alive. Luka was alive.

"Holy shit. You healed him. You healed him with magic."

I ignored Nico's revelation, still too focused on Luka.

"Luka." I moved towards his face and cupped his cheek in my hand. "Luka, are you okay?"

He let out several more breaths before finally his eyes fluttered open and he placed his hand over mine.

I let out a shuddering breath as his hand left mine and moved towards his wound. His brows knitted together as he looked at the skin where his injury had been.

"Goddess above." He looked at me. "You healed me."

I nodded. "I did."

"How is that possible?"

I brushed my hair back from my face with a blood-crusted hand. "It's a long story."

"One she doesn't have time to tell right now." A voice smooth as velvet rang out from behind us. A voice I hadn't heard in a long time.

When I turned, Luciana was standing in the grove of trees behind us. Her hood fell low on her face, hiding her features, but I could make out her blood red lips as they curved into a smile.

"Hello, cousin. It's been a long time."

"It sure has," I replied as she moved towards us, her black cloak swishing in the grass as she walked. "I take it, you got my letter?"

She nodded. "I've been expecting you." She surveyed the scene around us, taking in the dead forms of the hounds. "Although, this is not the way I expected this reunion to play out."

Despite the circumstances I laughed. Goddess, I had missed Luciana.

Luciana's face turned serious again as she took in our state. "We will save the reunion for later, we need to get you out of here before any more Hellhounds find you." She looked at us and to the trees. "I'm surprised they haven't found you already with all the blood you've spilled here."

"Can you get up?" I asked Luka

"Yeah, I'm fine. Thanks to your super freaky secret healing powers."

I scoffed as I held out a hand to help him stand.

"You're welcome by the way." I didn't give time to respond

before I released his hand and turned to Luciana. "How did you know we were here?"

"I was tracking the Hellhounds. They've been a menace lately."

"You're a little bit late on the rescuing part," Nico chided.

Luciana turned toward the wolf. "Who said anything about rescuing, pup? Maybe I'll leave you here as bait."

Nico paled. I knew Luciana would gladly eat him alive and spit him back out if he continued to test her.

"I have so many questions," Luka remarked as he came to stand beside me, our shoulders brushing against one another. Luciana turned her attention from Nico back to the rest of the group.

"Ready?" she asked. Kara and I nodded.

"Ready for what?" Declan questioned.

"Don't get your wings in a bunch, bird boy, I need to get you out of here before anyone, or, anything discovers you."

A muscle ticked in his jaw, but he said nothing. I stifled a laugh, I doubted anyone had ever dared talk to Declan in such a way. Leave it to Luciana.

She held out a hand to me. "Everyone, hold hands," Luciana directed. "No matter what, don't let go, otherwise you'll be left behind."

Luka gave me a questioning look, but I shrugged and took his hand in mine. I felt Luciana's magic surround me as she spoke under her breath. Her lavender scent invaded my senses as my hair whipped around my face, the world around me blurring. Someone swore, but I couldn't stop a smile from appearing on my face.

Being surrounded by her magic felt like coming home. I closed my eyes and lost myself in the feeling. I opened my eyes once I felt my feet were on solid ground again. We were no longer in the woods, but standing outside a small village.

"What in Astria's tits was that?" Nico panted, clutching his stomach. "I'm going to be sick."

"You're a witch," Declan declared. Nico and Luka snapped their heads towards Luciana.

Her blood red lips curved into a deadly smile. She dropped the hood of her cloak as her glamor melted away, revealing her piercing silver eyes, pulsing and moving with magic.

"I am." She smiled and extended her arms on either side of her. "Welcome to the Mystic Court."

32

LUKA

I had so many questions.

I stared at the witch in front of me. *A witch*. Her silver eyes moved and pulsed with magic like nothing I'd never seen before. Her eyes were a living and moving show of power.

The witch, Luciana, Lennox had called her, turned and ushered us towards the small village.

"Can someone explain to me what the fuck is going on here?" Nico asked. The agitation was clear in his voice.

Declan stood beside him, assessing the area around us. Luciana ignored us as she continued walking, with Kara and Lennox at her heels—stopping only when she came to a small cottage.

"Let's get you all cleaned up first," Luciana said, scrunching her nose at our appearance.

I couldn't imagine what I looked like. I glanced over to Lennox, her body was coated in the black blood of the Hell-hounds. Red blood, *my blood*, stained her hands and clothes too.

"Once you are all cleaned up we can answer all the questions you have."

As much as I was bursting to know what in the Stars was going on, Luciana had a point, we all needed a bath.

"There are bathing rooms here. Everything you should need will be in there. I will send someone with some fresh clothes." Without another word, Luciana left.

I turned to Lennox, but she held up a hand. "You heard her. Shower first. Then questions."

☾

It took us a while to get cleaned up. The black blood from the Hellhounds clung to my skin and I scrubbed vigorously at the blood staining my body until my skin was raw.

My hand lingered over my healed wound. The skin was fresh and pink, but stitched together like I hadn't almost died from it an hour ago. How had Lennox been able to heal me? Healing wasn't a typical Fae power. Was it a side effect of her holding four elements? There were healers across Lethenia who could heal small wounds, but I had never heard of someone closing a gash that big and expelling poison from a body.

I exited the bath house to find Nico and Declan already outside dressed in clothing identical to mine, loose dark pants and a cotton long sleeved shirt.

"Awe look, we all match," Nico cooed as he slung his arms around Declan and I.

I laughed, wrapping my arm around Nico in return as Declan shrugged out of his grip.

"Did you ever think you'd find yourself in a witch colony?" I asked.

When Lennox had suggested coming here I imagined we'd end up in the capital city, Arcadia, not in a village. Both of them only shook their heads as we took in the village around us.

The village was formed in the shape of a circle, a village center of sorts sat in the center—a large fire surrounded by wooden benches. Several smaller fires surrounded the large fire. Dozens of tables of various sizes and shapes were littered around the center. Small wooden cabins surrounded the center.

Each of various sizes, but all made up of the same light wood with a dark steel roof. The homes continued behind the first circle, creating three or four rings of homes beyond the village center, disappearing into the trees beyond.

Several witches milled around the village center. None stopped to talk to us, but I could hear their whispers and felt their stares prickling at my back.

I didn't know much about witches, they kept to themselves, usually sticking to their court. My only knowledge came from stories and legends whispered throughout Lethenia.

Many Fae claimed witches stole their magic from the Goddess. They claimed the Goddess had cursed them during creation, making it so they could not claim magic and therefore they were unworthy—forcing them to use spells to steal magic from the land when they needed it. Other stories claimed witches were gifted their magic from the Goddess Astria herself. They claimed the witches were blessed, that they had more power than an average Fae so we should be wary of them. I guessed we'd soon learn which of those legends were true and which were shrouded in lies.

I turned at the sound of Kara and Lennox emerging from the bathing hut behind us. The sisters wore identical dresses, but in different colors. Kara's was a dark blue and Lennox's was a deep purple, the color brought out her deep tan. The dresses were loose fitting, cinching slightly at the waist with long sleeves and fell to the ground, vastly different from anything either of the females typically wore, but appeared to be the fashion in the village.

"Luciana said to help ourselves to some food and she will join us later." Lennox gestured to the village center where several witches were serving various different foods by one of the smaller fires. I nodded as we fell into line behind her.

We each filled our plates with food before sitting at one of the small circular tables. We ate in silence, enjoying a hot meal

.✦ 216 ✦.

for the first time in almost two weeks. It wasn't until Lennox finally finished her food that she addressed us.

"So I'm guessing you all have some questions."

"Goddess' tits, do we have questions?" Nico scoffed. "So you better start explaining, Your Majesty."

"Starting with how in the Stars you managed to heal Luka," Declan added.

The sisters exchanged a look, a silent conversation occurring between the two of them. Kara nodded before they both turned towards us again.

"The reason I was able to heal you is because I'm half witch."

I froze.

The fork Nico had been holding clamored on to the table as he muttered a curse under his breath.

"And so am I," Kara added.

"How is that possible?" I breathed.

"Our mother was a witch."

My head spun.

"Did anyone know she was a witch?" Declan asked. They sisters shook their heads in unison.

"You just learned the best kept secret of Lethenia."

No one knew. Holy Stars. The High King had married a witch in secret.

"Such blasphemy, a High King taking a witch consort," Nico remarked.

Kara smirked. "You don't know half of it."

"That's how you healed me."

Lennox blushed, the tips of her pointed ears turning pink. "Our mother thought it was important we embrace our heritage, taking it upon herself to teach us witch magic growing up. I only practice it when absolutely necessary, like today."

"How did your father manage to take a witch consort and not have anyone know about it?" Declan asked.

"It's a long story."

"Well, good thing we have plenty of time, Sweetheart."

33

LENNOX

I steeled myself to tell the story of my family's history. The story Kara and I would beg our mother to tell us every night growing up. I had it memorized by the time I was seven. But it was a story I had long since locked up in my mind in the box with all of the other memories I didn't let myself think about from *Before*.

But when Luka was dying I made the decision to use my witch magic to heal him. So now I owed him an explanation. I owed them *all* an explanation. While I was washing up I thought about what Luka had told me by the lake—how it's a shame to not share stories about the people we lost. That we should share their stories to keep their memory alive. So I would charge forward. I could, *I would*, tell them the story of how the Fae High King married a witch.

I would tell them the story of my parents.

The three males stared at me expectantly so I took a steading breath and began.

"My father, Bram, used to travel with his father, King Alessio, to other courts when he was younger. He didn't have any siblings and often got bored by himself back home. One summer, when he was thirteen, they traveled to the Mystic Court for the first time." I tucked a lock of hair behind my ear.

"It was on that trip he met my mother, Elena. They spent a majority of their time together and quickly became friends. After the first trip, they both looked forward to the next time they would see one another. Every time they were together they jumped right back in where they had left off. They even started sending one another letters while they were apart."

Letters Kara and I poured over the summer we found them in a box in our mother's closet. She had sealed it with a spell, but we had easily disabled it, exactly how she had taught us. She was upset when she first found us, equally angry and impressed at our skills.

Later that night, when she came to tuck us into bed she brought the box of letters with her. She reminisced over the letters with us, adding details that were not included in the letters, like the gifts our father would send her. The letters had started innocently, two friends keeping in touch. But as the years went on you could sense the change in the letters as their feelings for one another grew beyond friendship.

"The summer when my father was nineteen, and my mother seventeen, he told her he loved her. When she said it back, their mating bond snapped into place."

"Your parents were mates?" The shock was clear in Nico's voice.

Kara and I nodded. Mates were extremely rare in Lethenia —they were hand-selected by the Goddess to find one other. They were the perfect match, equals in every way. Paired to bring out the best in one another. Even their magic was rumored to sing to each other, magnifying both party's powers as they merged together as one after accepting the bond.

"My father promised her one day he would figure out how they could be together. He was the only heir, he couldn't abdicate his throne, and he didn't want to. He would have for my mother, but she wouldn't let him." That was my mother. She thought of others first—considering how her decisions would impact the others around her.

"When my father went back home he told his father everything. How he had been in love with my mother for years, that they were mates and he intended on marrying her but my grandfather denied his request. He claimed how important it was for the High King to have a pure, High Fae bloodline. He said if my father married my mother he would deny him the throne."

"For years they were together in secret. Only seeing each other when they could. They continued to write letters to each other while my father tried to find a way for them to be together. But my grandfather died unexpectedly." The death of the High King shocked everyone—it was rare for Fae to die young from an unexpected illness.

"My grandmother was in such immense grief she could no longer rule, forcing my father to become High King much quicker than he anticipated. But my father saw this as his opportunity. Since he was High King no one could stop him from marrying my mother."

"My mother came for his coronation and he told her of his plan. But my mother didn't like it. She didn't want to jeopardize his throne." My mother and her bleeding heart. Further proof her and Kara were one in the same.

"But my father wouldn't have it. He was tired of being together in secret. If he was going to be High King he wanted her next to him. He wanted his mate as his queen. He would either have her beside him, or abdicate the title."

What would it be like to be loved deeply like my father loved my mother? Willing to give up everything for the person you loved? That was the kind of love I hoped to find someday.

"My mother couldn't believe he'd give up his title for her. So she gave in, but under one condition, no one could know she was a witch. It would put both of them in danger." I looked at Kara, we both smiled softly.

"So she glamoured herself," Kara continued. "Made the magic in her eyes disappear, stifled her aura, and masked her scent. She brought two of her most trusted ladies maids with her and married our father. They told everyone she was a High Fae from a small village, who he had met and fell in love with."

It was partially true, after all. They just didn't specify where she was from. My mother never traveled much, she didn't want to risk someone catching on to her glamor. The only place she routinely visited was the Mystic Court, to see her mother, and sister. Which is why Kara, Nol, and I rarely traveled either. My parents were cautious of someone picking up on us being slightly different.

"But when they claimed they were mates no one questioned them," Kara added.

No matter how many times I had heard my parents' love story it was still hard to believe. Hard to believe two Fae could love one other so deeply they'd give up everything else in their lives for one another. It was because of their love story, and the way I had seen them be together when they were alive, that I still held out hope that perhaps one day I could find my mate. And if not my mate, at least someone who loved me the way my father loved my mother. I knew Kara felt the same. Which is why I needed to find a way to make sure neither of us ended up in an arranged marriage at the end of all of this. We had been through so much—lost so much. I refused to let us lose this one last link to our parents.

"Everyone loved my mother. Even my grandmother. Years later, they finally told her the truth. She was angry at first, but quickly got over it when she realized our mother came from royal blood."

Luka held out a hand to stop me. "Wait, your mother came from royal blood?"

I nodded. "My mother was heir to the Mystic Court throne."

They all sucked in a collective breath.

"Holy shit," Nico mumbled.

"You come from a double royal bloodline," Declan all but whispered, eyes wide.

"Wait." Luka turned his attention back to me. "That means—"

"Our aunt is Caterina Ambrose, Queen of the Mystic Court," I finished for him.

Nico swore under his breath. "That means Luciana is—"

"Heir to the Mystic Throne," Luciana interrupted as she sat next to Kara. Her blood-red lips curled in a mischievous smile.

"You're telling me we have four royals sitting here, unprotected, Goddess knows where in the Mystic Court," Declan mused, shaking his head. "This is a disaster waiting to happen." His wings twitched as he tucked them in close.

"Settle down, big bird." Luciana flicked a lock of coiled lilac hair behind her shoulder. "This is the Mystic Court. You are all safe here, I can guarantee it. Any guest of mine is a guest in this village." She looked at Kara and I. "Especially my cousins. They are technically heirs to the Mystic Court after all."

"Do the witches here know of your relationship?" Declan asked.

Luciana shook her head. "No, only a select few in my mothers coven know."

"Is Caterina here?" I asked, hope bloomed in my chest at the thought of seeing my aunt. I hadn't seen Caterina since shortly after my parents' funeral.

Luciana shook her head. "No, she remains in Arcadia with Endora, while I monitor the coven villages."

I nodded, reigning in my disappointment. I would have loved to have finally met my aunt's queen consort as well.

"We can talk more tomorrow about your plans, perhaps we

can find a way for you to see her while you're here," Luciana added.

I smiled softly at my cousin. We had always been similar, Luce and I. The rebellious rule breakers—although she made me look like a good youngling compared to her at times. Being the sole heir put a lot of pressure on her. When we were here to visit, Luce spent half of her time being the rebellious young witch, the other half being the doting heir with Nol. The way she grew up made her hard, but I knew who she was underneath her prickly exterior.

"I've had my sisters set up cabins for you." She gestured to the two cottages behind us. "Get some rest and we can talk more in the morning."

We all mumbled our thank you's before heading in our separate directions. Kara and I stopped to hug Luciana before we said goodnight and made our way to our cabin. Our cabin was small and made of slabs of wood with a small front porch with an overhang. There were no railings, but two chairs and a small table perched on the small porch. Inside, the entryway was small with room for only a wooden coat rack. Kara and I walked down the hall, finding two bedrooms, one on each side of the hallway. At the end of the hallway there was a small sitting room, containing only a small table with three chairs and a half empty bookshelf. At the other end of the hallway there was a small bathing chamber.

After wandering through the cabin, Kara and I retreated into our separate rooms. The room was small but functional. There was a decent-sized bed, a small armoire, and a mirror. A large window sat on the far side of the room, making the space appear larger. Luce had sent her sisters back to the clearing to get our horses and belongings. My bags sat at the bench at the end of the bed. I rummaged through my bag to find my nightgown, but I stopped myself as my fingers wrapped around the silk garment.

My body was exhausted, it had been a long day. Expelling

all the magic I did had taken a toll. But I knew if I tried to sleep now, it wouldn't come. There was something I needed to do first. I set my nightgown on the bed and tugged my boots back on before slipping out the door, quietly making my way to the cabin next door.

34

LUKA

The last person I expected to find on the other side of the door was Lennox. But there she was, standing in front of me.

"Hi." Her voice was quiet and hesitant. Like she was the one who was surprised to see me and not the other way around. "Can I come in?"

I nodded and opened the door further to allow her to step inside.

"What are you doing here, Lennox?"

She opened her mouth and closed it again. I waited as she considered her words. "Can we sit?"

I nodded before leading her down the narrow hallway. The moonlight shone through the windows in the small sitting room. I motioned for Lennox to sit in one of the chairs at the small circular table.

"Do you want a drink?" I motioned to the small collection of liquor on the table.

"Yes, please."

I poured us each a couple knuckles worth of the amber liquid before passing her a glass.

"Cheers to surviving today." I held my glass out to meet hers.

She rolled her eyes and shook her head before clinking her glass against mine. "To surviving today."

I brought the glass to my lips, relishing in the warm burn as it slid down my throat. Silence fell between us as we sipped at our drinks.

"So—" Lennox started. "You're still alive."

"I'm still alive." I let out a small chuckle. "Thanks to you."

She smiled slightly and took a drink.

"I plan on throwing a party in your honor when I get back to the Blood Court. All eyes on you for being such a hero," I teased.

She rolled her eyes, "I can't wait," she said, taking another sip. "I'll make sure you're right there on the dais with me, soaking in every minute."

I scoffed. "As long as I'm drunk it sounds like a fine idea to me." Lennox smirked before we fell into silence again. I ran my fingers around the smooth glass rim of my glass.

"Why are you here, Lennox?"

She stared at the liquid in her glass. "Would you believe me if I said I don't know?"

"Yes," I said. I studied her as she chewed on her bottom lip.

"How are you doing? Do you feel any lasting effects from the poison? Is your wound okay?" She gestured toward my side where the wound had been.

"Yeah, I feel fine. You did a pretty good job for a half-witch. I can't believe you kept that a secret from me."

She threw me an incredulous look. "Because we share secrets."

"Did you forget we're friends now, Sweetheart?"

She shook her head, trying and failing to hide her smile behind her glass. We fell into silence again. We had spent a lot of time over the past few months in comfortable silence—it was a place where we thrived. But this silence was different. Unsaid words hung in the air, threatening to suffocate us.

Lennox drained the last of her drink, her glass landing on the table with a thud. "Can I see your wound?"

I lifted my shift, exposing my side to Lennox. "Have at it, Sweetheart."

She rose from her chair and knelt next to me to examine the skin. Her fingers skimmed over the healed flesh and my skin tingled at the contact. She poked gently at the spot as she continued her examination. I watched with intensity as her hands roamed over my bare skin, her face fixed in concentration as she examined every inch of skin.

"Is Lennox Adair concerned about me?"

"No."

I stared at her as she continued to fix her eyes on my bare skin, her hands now fisted at her sides.

"Fine, maybe I am," she admitted as she tucked a stray hair behind her ear and stood, turning and stalking towards the window. "But, only a little!" She threw her arms out dramatically as she spoke. "You almost died for fucks sake, and I've never healed someone close to death so I think I have the right to be mildly concerned."

The concern was evident in her voice. *Her fear.* My mind flashed to the image of her kneeled ever me while I bled out. I had never seen her face filled with such fear.

It's okay. I had told her.

No it's not. Her words came back to me now.

I can't let him die.

I had accepted my death as I laid on the forest floor, but she didn't. I saw the moment her features changed from fear and panic to determination.

I can't let him die.

I hadn't comprehended her words while I was laying there. She didn't want to lose another person she cared about.

Had Lennox started to care about me? Did I manage to steal a piece of her heart, even if it was only a small part?

"I'm honored"—I placed a hand on my heart—"that High

Queen Lennox Adair decided, out of the goodness of her heart, to let me live to see another day."

She turned and glared at me. "Don't make me regret saving your life, Bloodsucker. I can undo it just as easily."

There she was.

"I only decided your life was worth saving because it would be an inconvenience to have to work with another vampire when we've come so far in tolerating each other."

"I'll let yourself think that if you want, Lennox." I walked until I was standing in front of her, she tilted her head back to meet my gaze. "But I think you more than tolerate me. I think you like me."

She rolled her eyes. "I'm leaving now."

She tried to push past me, but I blocked her path, not ready for her to leave yet.

The fire in her eyes dimmed when she noticed the expression on my face. Lennox watched with rapt attention as I brought her hand to my lips, placing a kiss on the inside of her palm.

"Thank you for saving my life, Lennox." I placed her hand against my chest, holding it to my heart with my own hand so she could feel the beat of my still very alive heart.

She said nothing as she looked at where our hands laid, where they rose and fell with my breath. My gaze dropped to her mouth as her tongue darted out across her bottom lip.

My magic swirled inside me as my heart beat faster in my chest. I wanted nothing more than to pull her into me, to place my lips on hers.

But I took a step back, putting space between us as I looked to the floor and I swallowed. "Goodnight, Lennox."

She took a step forward, but instead of moving toward the door, she stepped toward me. She placed her hands on my shoulders and reached on her tiptoes. I placed my hands on her hips to steady her as her warm breath skidded across my neck.

"I'm glad you didn't die today," she whispered in my ear

before she moved, placing a kiss at the corner of my mouth. "Goodnight, Luka."

Stars, I loved the way my name sounded on her lips, she didn't say it enough. She took a step back, untangling herself from me and moving towards the door. I stayed rooted in place —listening as she opened and closed the front door, making her way back to her own cabin. It wasn't until I heard the door click shut that I finally moved, making my way to my bedroom, the ghost of her touch still lingering on my body long into the night.

35

LENNOX

As soon as the sun rose I was up and getting ready, seeking out Luce before everyone else woke. I told myself it was because I needed information to get my plan underway. Not because I wanted to avoid a certain vampire.

I needed to put him out of my head.

So I went in search of Luce.

I found her talking to a group of witches in the village center. She dismissed her sisters as I approached, turning to me. "Good morning."

"Good morning."

Luce's dark, bronzed skin glowed in the morning light, her silver eyes gleaming. She wore black pants today, similar to the ones I wore, and a lightweight long-sleeve shirt in a deep plum color matching the shade of her hair.

"Are you hungry?" she asked.

I nodded, following her as she led me towards where an elder witch stood over a stove on the fire, her coiled hair bouncing as she walked.

When we reached the elder witch we each grabbed a bowl of porridge, both thanking the elder before sitting at a small wooden table. I had grown up learning about witch culture, but when we visited the Mystic Court we had remained in the capital city, Arcadia. I had only read about the villages, never visited them.

Every village was made up of witches from the same coven. When witches fully came into their power on their eighteenth birthday, they swore themselves to a coven. Most witches swore themselves to the same coven they were born into, but it was not uncommon to switch. Witches swore their fealty to their coven with a spelled tattoo of their covens signet. The magic linked them to their coven until they returned to the Stars. The Phoebus coven wears the sign of the sun; Hera, a six pointed star' and Selene, the royal coven, a signet of a crescent moon.

While we ate, Luciana explained to me that part of her job now was to travel around the Mystic Court and visit the different villages throughout the year, making sure everyone was doing well, and addressing any needs from the covens. I had noticed several witches this morning bearing the signet of the crescent moon which meant we were with Luciana's own coven, a Selene coven, it appeared.

Luce and I sent each other letters occasionally, but our communication had been lacking in the past few years. Most of the blame could be put on my end, not by lack of effort from Luce. So as we sat and ate our breakfast we took the opportunity to catch up with each other. I had missed my cousin.

"Won't that be a sight to see one day." She kicked me under the table as she pushed her empty bowl to the center. "The two of us as queens."

I scoffed. "I can't say I ever thought that would happen."

Luce noticed the falter in my smile, taking my hand and squeezing it, a sad smile on her face. I knew she missed them too, especially Nol.

While Luce and I had never bonded over our eminent titles growing up, she and Nol had. There were many times during our visits, as we got older, that Kara and I were left on our own while Nol and Luciana sat in on meetings, preparing for when they took on their titles. I may bear the crown now, but I never grew up bearing the weight of knowing someday I would be queen.

Luciana released my hand and sat up straight before saying, "So, tell me why you're here. You didn't come here for a visit because you missed me."

I spoke a silencing spell to keep our conversation between the two of us before I told Luce everything.

☪

"I've never heard of the Goddess having any kind of book of sorts," Luce said as she twirled a lock of hair in her fingers as she thought. "I've read about every book there is on Astria and I don't remember the mention of a spell book."

I sighed and took another bite of my breakfast. "Me either."

"You don't think they're looking for Hecate's spell book do you?"

I rested my chin in my hand. "I don't know. Luka said it was a book written by the Goddess, he didn't mention anything about Hecate." I doubted the Blood Court even knew of the original witch.

"Well, Hecate's spell book is the only ancient book I know about, and there's no mention of a cure for vampirism in it, but I will keep looking. I will send word to Arcadia this afternoon and ask them to send me any books from the palace library with information about Astria."

"Thank you."

"Of course." Luce smiled. "Anything to help you avoid an arranged marriage."

I scoffed. "Right." I shook my head, "Anyway, I don't suppose you'll be able to help me find a Seer, would you?"

Luce thought for a moment before speaking. "There are not any Seers in this village, and I don't know the location of any known Seers. Even here Seer's keep to themselves if they can."

Shit. I bit my lower lip, contemplating my options. There was one more thing I could try before we continued searching the Mystic Court blindly. "Can you show me where I can find some stones and bones?"

The smile that curved on Luce's face was pure mischief.

"I can do you one better."

☾

Twenty minutes later Luce and I found ourselves in the cabin the village used as a scrying location. Luce explained there were ancient spells placed on the hut to amplify summoning and scrying. The cabin was small. It had no windows, but a rectangle had been cut into the ceiling and was covered in glass, revealing the sky above, providing access to the Stars if needed.

The walls of the room were lined with shelves upon shelves of witch relics and materials. I scanned the labels of the jars lining the shelves, my finger making a line in the dust. Dragon scales, wolf hair, blood salt, Stardust—anything a witch's heart might desire I'm sure you would find on these shelves. In the middle of the room sat a small table with a dark purple cloth covering it. Luce moved past me and grabbed a rolled up map off of one of the shelves and set it on the table, using crystals as weights on each of the corners.

Scrying is an ancient witch practice often used to see things without a Seer. There are many different forms of scrying one can use, depending on what you are trying to see. The easiest way is to look into an enchanted mirror if you wish to speak with someone, but scrying isn't guaranteed to work. It takes a great deal of work of the mind, and if you are trying to contact someone—ultimately it is up to them if they want to answer your call.

Not only was I going to try and speak to a Seer, but I also wanted to find their location, hence the map. The stones and bones would be used as a conduit for my magic. When I felt the moment was right I would drop them on the map and hopefully they would show me the Seer's location. I took my time gathering two stones before we came to the cottage. I let my magic out, allowing it to guide me towards stones that called to me.

Luce said we could use a bone another witch had gathered, but I needed to gather the two stones myself. You could use any stones to scry, but it was said in witch legend if you picked stones that called to you, you had a better chance of scrying working. I wasn't taking any chances.

It took me ten minutes, but I finally found two rocks to satisfy me. I held them in my hand, their smooth exterior cold on my warm hand. Luce pulled a bone from a jar and waved it in dramatically before placing it in my open palm with the stones.

"The bone from a deceased witch at your service." Most witches allowed their bones to be used for magic after their deaths, claiming strong magic resided in their bones, even after their passing. No one knew if it was true or not, but half of witch practices were games of the mind in the first place. You had to believe in something for it to come to be.

Luce assembled the rest of the tools on the table in front of me, placing a piece of a fractured mirror in a stone bowl. The mirror would act as a portal for the Seer to communicate to us if they chose.

"You ready?"

I nodded, removing my dagger from its place at my side and handed it to Luce. She took it and I held out my palm to her, wincing as she drew the cool blade against the skin of my palm. I squeezed my hand together, forcing the blood to pool, before dropping three drops into the bowl on the table, the droplets splashed on the broken glass.

Luce sprinkled Stardust over my blood, whispering a spell under her breath that caused the contents of the bowl to hiss in reaction. I took my bloodied palm and squeezed more blood over my other hand, allowing it to coat the stones and bone.

Then I shut my eyes, closing both of my hands around the stones and bones. The blood was slick against my skin, but I blocked out the sensation, instead focusing only on what I wanted to see, the Seer. I held on to the objects in my hand as I pushed my magic outwards feeling for a connection.

I am Lennox Adair, High Queen of Lethenia. Daughter of Elena Ambrose. Answer my call.

Nothing.

I tried again. *I am Lennox Adair, High Queen of Lethenia. Daughter of Elena Ambrose. Answer my call. Reveal yourself to me.*

Still nothing. I gritted my teeth. My frustration building.

Take a breath. Anger will not help your cause, my dear.

My knees buckled as my mothers voice rang through my mind, clear as a bell.

Focus my dear, you can do this.

Was this real? Was she speaking to me or was I imagining her?

Lennox, focus. Breathe. This is important. You can do this. I believe in you. Breathe. Focus.

Breathe, I whispered to myself. I took several deep breaths in and back out. I felt myself center again. I could do this. I pictured my mother as I pushed my magic out again.

I am Lennox Adair, High Queen of Lethenia. Daughter of Elena Ambrose. Answer my call. I need your help. Please. Reveal yourself to me.

A chill ran through my body, goosebumps pebbled across my skin. Wind whipped my hair around my face inside the cabin. I repeated my words again. I was close, I could feel it, the thread was just out of reach, but it was there.

I am Lennox Adair, High Queen of Lethenia. Daughter of Elena Ambrose. Answer my call. I need your help. Please. Reveal yourself to me. Please.

The wind stopped as suddenly as it began and the hairs on the back of my neck rose.

Daughter of Elena.

The voice was a whisper in the wind.

Yes, I'm here, I answered.

Queen of Stardust. I have been waiting for you.

Waiting for me? What did she mean—

You travel with the King of Blood, I see. Interesting. Star crossed blood runs in your veins. Come to me. But you must bring the King of Blood with you. No one else.

Luka? You mean for me to bring Luka?

What? How did she know he was with me? What part did he play in this?

*Yes, the King of Blood and The Queen of Stardust. For you I have been waiting. Come to me. **Now.***

Her words were a sharp demand, sending pinpricks scattering across my skin. I released the artifacts in my hand with a gasp, my eyes flying open.

Luce stared at me wide eyed. My heart was beating like a drum in my chest.

"Did it work?" she breathed. I looked at the map in front of me. The stones and bones landed in a perfect circle at the far end of the Mystic Court. I nodded, swallowing the lump in my throat.

"There." I panted. "The Seer is there." I thought of the riddles whispered into my mind. None of them made sense.

The King of Blood and the Queen of Stardust. For you, have been waiting.

I had so many questions.

But one thing was clear. Luka and I would make this journey on our own.

☪

Luce and I cleaned up the hut and made our way back to the village center where we found Kara, Luka, Nico, and Declan sitting around a table, empty breakfast bowls before them.

I had no idea how long we had been in the hut, but they all stared at us expectantly.

Kara stood as we approached. "Where have you been?" she demanded. Luce shrugged.

"Your sister was scrying."

Kara's mouth fell open. "Without me?"

I let out a small laugh. "Sorry, I was impatient."

She narrowed her eyes, but dropped it, sitting back at the table as Luce and I joined her.

"So, scrying is real?" Luka asked. I nodded, but avoided his gaze. I wouldn't be able to do that for much longer if we were to set off on our own.

"Were you successful?" Kara asked with a gleam in her eye. She loved practicing witch magic.

I nodded. "I was able to connect with a Seer. She revealed her location to me, but she gave me specific instructions to follow, otherwise she won't see me." I paused, tucking a lock of hair behind my ear. Kara and Nico leaned in closer, Declan sat back in his chair, arms crossed over his chest, wings tucked in close behind him.

I finally let myself look at Luka. He was gazing at me expectantly, several pieces of his unruly hair falling across his face.

"The Seer was clear."

He tilted his head to the side.

"Only Luka and I can make the journey to see her."

36

LUKA

"What do you mean 'only Luka can come with you'?" There was a steely edge to. Declan's tone as he leaned forward in his chair, bracing his arms on the table, his wings rustling behind him. Lennox blinked at him, a crease forming between her brows.

"What did this Seer say, exactly?" Declan asked.

Luciana whipped her head towards Declan, glaring at him with those unnerving silver eyes.

"Are you implying you don't believe her?" The magic in Luciana's eyes swirled violently.

"A witch saying the heir to the Blood Court should travel without any guard sounds suspicious to me. Could be a trap," Declan said as he crossed his arms over his chest. Luciana narrowed her eyes at Declan. She opened her mouth, but before she could argue Lennox placed a hand on her arm, giving her a look.

Luciana leaned back, but continued to glare at Declan with her arms crossed over her chest.

"It's okay." It was Lennox who finally spoke. Her voice was calm, without a hint of ire. "I know not everyone is accustomed to the ways of the coven, but I assure you, Declan, this message came from a Seer."

She left no room for questions in the way she spoke. She was the High Queen, there would be no questioning her.

"Scrying is a sacred practice. There is no way for someone to interfere. I trust this Seer," Lennox stated.

Declan said nothing as he looked between Luciana and Lennox.

"This is our chance to finally get some answers. We have to go. I know how it appears to you, but this is a risk we need to take. I would not put Luka in danger." She glanced at me, the sincerity was evident in the way she spoke.

I believed her. But I needed Declan to believe her too.

"She's right, Dec. Whether this is real or not, we can't pass on this opportunity."

Declan sighed, a sure tell of his that he had lost and he was not happy about it. A rare occurrence when it came to the harpy.

"Tell me exactly what was said," Declan pressed.

I saw the tension release from Lennox's shoulders.

"She spoke in riddles of sorts. The first part I don't understand," she said as she looked at her hands.

"She called me the daughter of Elena, that's my mother. That was part of what I used in my calling," Lennox continued, reciting the next part of the Seer's message.

Queen of Stardust. I have been waiting for you.
You travel with the King of Blood I see. Interesting.
Star crossed blood runs in your veins.

I frowned, puzzling over the strange message.

"I'm assuming she's referring to my parents, being star crossed lovers of a sort," Lennox said as she looked at Kara who only shrugged.

"So, their blood runs in my veins, but why did she call me the Queen of Stardust?" Lennox worried her bottom lip between her teeth.

"Queen of Stardust?" Kara wondered out loud.

Lennox shrugged, releasing her lip. "I've never been called that before, I've never even heard of the title before."

"But, that's what we've always said to one another—I love you until the stars turn to dust. The phrase originated in the Mystic Court," Kara said as she looked at Lennox expectantly. "Do you think that has something to do with it?"

Nico leaned his forearms on the table. "I think you're reading way too much into this. Sounds like witch mumbo jumbo to me."

Lennox only shrugged her shoulders.

"There's more, right?" I asked. None of what Lennox had recalled so far had anything to do with me. Lennox nodded and recited the rest of the message.

Come to me. But you must bring the King of Blood with you. No one else.

The King of Blood and The Queen of Stardust. For you, I have been waiting.

"The King of Blood, that doesn't mean it's Luka," Declan declared. "He's not even king yet."

"I'm aware," Lennox snapped. "So, I asked her." She glared at Declan, her green eyes blazing. "I asked, 'does that mean I need to bring Luka' and she said yes, *the King of Blood*." She enunciated every word and cocked her head to the side when she was done.

I leaned back in my chair. More than content to let these two fight it out. I loved seeing Lennox riled up, but I rarely got to be a bystander. I don't know which role I enjoyed more.

"Luka isn't the King of Blood now, but he will be one day," Luciana added as she picked at her nails.

"So, Sweetheart, are you up for traveling all alone with me?"

"I don't have much of a choice in the matter, do I, Bloodsucker?"

I grinned at her.

"I can't believe I missed out on scrying, and now I don't

even get to go with to see the Seer." Kara stuck out her bottom lip dramatically.

"You and me both," Nico added. "But I bet I can come up with plenty of ways to keep you occupied while they're gone." He put his arm around Kara's shoulders.

Kara rolled her eyes and shrugged out of Nico's hold. "I'm flattered at the offer, wolf boy, but you're not my type."

She stood, patting Nico on the shoulder before walking towards her cabin, leaving Nico staring, mouth open, and speechless in her wake. Luciana and I doubled over in laughter and Lennox snickered into her hand.

I had never seen Kara resemble Lennox more.

37

LENNOX

The rest of the morning was spent preparing for Luka and I to leave the following morning. It didn't take long to prepare what we would need, since we hadn't even gotten a chance to unpack yet. And I spent the rest of the day with Luce and Kara before turning into bed early, hoping to get plenty of rest before heading out again.

I awoke early, as usual, dressed in my leathers, and packed up the rest of my belongings.

Before leaving I snuck into Kara's room and crawled into bed with her.

"What time is it?" Kara muttered, half asleep.

"Early." I snuggled in close to her, stealing any ounce of heat I could before heading out into the morning chill. "I wanted to say goodbye before I left, I didn't mean to wake you."

"It's okay." She yawned, eyes still closed. I squeezed her tight before placing a kiss to her cheek that she quickly wiped away with the back of her hand.

"I love you, Kar. Don't get into too much trouble while I'm gone."

I caught a glimpse of a small smile creeping up her face. "I'll try my best."

I stood reluctantly, sparing one last look at my sister before turning towards the door.

"Love you too," her sleep-filled voice mumbled from underneath the covers.

"Until the stars turn to dust."

"Until the stars turn to dust, Len."

☾

I wandered out past the third ring of homes to where Luce showed me the stables were yesterday, surprised to find her already waiting for me with one of her sisters.

"Good morning."

"Good morning." The witches echoed in unison.

"Is Luka here yet?" I asked, looking around as I greeted Odin with a scratch behind the ear.

Luce nodded. "He went to check on one last thing. He said he'd be back in a moment."

I stroked Odin's deep gray coat. The color, in combination with its silver iridescent specks, reminded me of the night sky.

"Where's Luka's horse?" I asked as I continued to stroke Odin. I hadn't spotted Luka's onyx-colored mare Zola anywhere.

"You will be sharing Odin." My hand stilled where it laid on my horse's neck.

"Excuse me? What do you mean we'll be sharing Odin?"

"It is safer you travel on one steed," Luce continued. "It makes less sound, less likely you will attract attention. It was Declan's condition if he was to let you two travel without him." Luce chuckled. "Bird boy didn't tell you, did he?"

No, he did not. I'm sure Declan knew damn well I wouldn't have agreed to it. I'd love nothing more than to pull him from sleep and give him an earful right now.

"You can't seriously expect us to share a horse?" I asked, crossing my arms as I looked between the two witches.

"Oh common, Sweetheart."

I turned at the sound of Luka's voice.

"I promise I won't bite." He smiled, exposing his fangs and swiping his tongue across them. "Unless you ask me to." He winked at me over his shoulder.

So much for getting some space from Luka. I rolled my eyes before turning my attention back to Luce.

"Thanks for everything," I spoke into her ear as we hugged each other tightly.

"Anytime. Be safe Lennox." I released Luce and made my way back to Odin, where Luka waited, holding the reins. I mounted my horse with a sigh. I was about to spend the next couple weeks with Luka, I couldn't let a little hiccup like this rattle me already. I gripped the pommel as Luka saddled up behind me. I sat up straight, limiting the areas where our bodies touched but I couldn't stop the small gasp from slipping from my lips as his hand splayed over my hip, holding me to him.

Without even looking at him I knew he was smirking. I tried to ignore the feel of his hand on my hip. This would all be so much easier if I hadn't gone to his cabin the other night.

Or if I had let him die in those woods.

We waved our final goodbyes and we were off. We had with us a smaller version of the map I had used to scry to guide us to the Seer. This one had been enchanted to ensure we were heading in the right direction. Our location was keyed into the magic of the map, showing us where we were on the map at any given time. The location of the Seer was on the far southern end of the Mystic Court. Luce estimated it would take us about a week to get there.

The sun was cresting the horizon as we departed. The orange light peaked through the trees as we headed deeper into the forest. I focused on the sunrise. On our task at hand. On trying to decipher the Seer's riddle. Anything to steer my mind from who was sitting behind me. I couldn't do anything about our thighs touching and I could have moved his hand off of my hip, but I also didn't want to deal with him potentially falling off the horse because I wouldn't let him hold onto me. He would never let me forget it if he did.

But I refused to let myself sink back into him; I had to maintain some kind of boundary. I already feared what might happen with us spending so much time alone together. It could go one of two ways: either I kill him or I end up fucking him. It was hard to picture an outcome where one, or both of those scenarios, didn't end up occurring. I should have found someone to bed last night, that might have helped cool the heat I felt coursing through my body with Luka at my back.

Several hours later, my back was already aching from how straight I was making myself sit. I arched my shoulders to try and relieve some of the growing tension. It was going to be a long few weeks.

"You can relax back into me if your back is bothering you."

"I'm fine, thank you."

Luka clicked his tongue. "Suit yourself, Sweetheart." We continued for a while longer, the ache in my back growing worse with every passing minute.

"Are you going to put yourself through this pain for the next two weeks just to spite me?" His breath was warm on my neck.

"I'm not doing it to spite you."

"Then why are you refusing to lean against me?"

I didn't respond. What was I supposed to say?

I don't want to lean back into you because I'm afraid it would further lead towards crossing a boundary between us that is already starting to blur since I saved you from almost dying.

No thank you. I'd rather have my back ache than admit that to Luka.

He grew frustrated with my silence and blew out a breath. "Honestly, Lennox, I'm surprised you lasted this long. You don't have anything to prove. It's me."

It's me.

Why did those words have an effect on me?

"It's a long journey. I'd rather you not be in pain the entire time. Relax. Please, Lennox." *Please, Lennox.* When he said my name like that . . . it threatened to crumble my semblance of resolve.

I sighed. "Fine."

He was right, although I wouldn't admit that to him.

Prick.

I sighed, relaxing my body into his, my back meeting the hard muscles of his torso. Luka's hand splayed on my waist gripped me tighter, his thumb brushing a path on the underside of my ribs. I let myself lean into the contact. *Lean into him.*

It's Luka.

☾

"Why does Declan despise me so much?"

The question had been plaguing my mind since we left this morning. It had been clear since he arrived in Alethens that he didn't like me. Not that I minded, but I don't know what I had done to make Declan act cold toward me.

"Declan doesn't hate you. He—that's just Declan. He likes you more than most people, when I think about it."

"Yeah, sure."

Nothing Declan did gave me any indication he liked me.

"Have you ever seen a half-shifted harpy before?"

I shook my head.

"That's because they don't exist. Declan is the only one. He was born half-shifted and he's paid the price for being the only of his kind."

My brows furrowed. "What do you mean?"

Luka hesitated before continuing. "Declan's story is not mine to tell. But what I can say is his life has not been easy. Nico and I got him out of the Twilight Court the minute he turned eighteen and could legally be out from under his fathers thumb. If I could have taken him with me the day I met him I would have." The pressure in my chest intensified at the words left unsaid.

"Declan has more demons than most, you have to give him time. He's the most loyal and trustworthy person I know."

"Okay."

"Okay?" Luka's tone was questioning.

"Okay, I'll give Declan another chance."

Luka said nothing, but the hand on my hip tightened, squeezing for a moment before releasing it.

☾

The sun was starting to set on the horizon when we came to the small town we had been planning to stay in for the night. The sisters had told us there would be a few on our way and we intended on making use of any we could find if it meant we could sleep in a bed for the night, bathe, and have a hot meal.

We had decided I would stay outside with Odin and get him settled while Luka went inside to get us a room. We wanted to raise as little suspicion of who we were as possible—including being seen together.

I had finished getting Odin food and water when Luka made his way back outside, swinging the key loop between his fingers. "You ready?"

I nodded and fell into step behind him as he led me into the Inn.

My body ached from the long day of riding. I couldn't wait to fall into bed and sleep. But any thoughts of restful sleep vanished from my head the moment Luka opened the door to our room revealing the single bed.

We both froze at the threshold.

Luka rubbed his hand over the back of his neck. "They said this was the only room available, I didn't realize it would only have one bed."

I swallowed the lump in my throat.

"It's not your fault." I managed to mumble out. "You didn't know."

"I can sleep on the floor," he offered as he walked into the room. The room itself was small. It contained a large bed with a bedside table on each side and a small dresser. Two small windows were cut into the wall on the right, and there was a door to the left, which I assumed led to a bathing chamber. There wasn't much space for him to even sleep on the floor.

When I looked back at Luka his face was etched with guilt. I knew he would sleep on the floor if it made me feel more comfortable. Even if it would make him less comfortable.

"You can't sleep on the floor. You'll be sore enough from the day of riding." I bit my bottom lip between my teeth. "I'm sure we can share a bed without killing one another." I tried to keep my tone light, hiding any hesitancy.

"Are you sure?"

"No, so don't keep asking me or I might change my mind."

☾

The warm water brought immediate relief to my sore back as I eased myself into the steaming bath. My hair fanned out around me as I sank deeper into the water. After it was decided Luka and I would be sharing a bed, he went and found us food, which we devoured quickly while sitting on the bed we would soon be sharing.

Exhaustion weighed at my bones as I soaked in the tub, I was tempted to close my eyes just for a minute, but I quickly washed myself before exiting the bath and wrapping myself in a towel instead. The last thing I needed was Luka barging in here because I had fallen asleep in the bath.

My wet hair dripped down my back as I riffled through my bag, my fingers stilling on the silk of my nightgown. I wasn't expecting to share a room on this trip, let alone a bed with Luka, and the only clothes I had were nightgowns. I considered sleeping in my leathers like I had in the forest before, but the heat of the summer was in full swing. I didn't want to sleep in those in this heat if I didn't have to.

Nightgown it was.

This particular nightgown was light blue, trimmed with white lace on the bottom and on the top where it curved to accentuate my breasts. The garment left little to the imagination.

I drew my magic to my fingertips, using my magic to pull the water from my wet hair, directing it back to the tub. I swept my hair over one shoulder and headed back out into the bedchamber.

Luka was sitting with his head between his legs when I opened the door. He looked up as I entered the room, his gaze darkening as he took in my appearance. A chill ran down my spine at his open perusal of my body.

I felt my nipples pebbling under the scrutiny of his gaze and a blush rushed to my cheeks at the realization he could see the effect he was having on me through the thin fabric. Heat spread over my skin everywhere his eyes roamed.

I took a deep breath before continuing into the bedchamber. "See something you like, Bloodsucker?"

Luka's smile turned feral as I brushed past him. Making sure to put a little extra sway into my hips as I did.

"Are you baiting me, Lennox Adair?"

I brushed my hair over my shoulder. "I would never dream of such a thing."

"You're not seriously telling me you sleep in such an item every night?"

I kept my back to him as I rifled through my bag. Allowing the hem of my nightgown to rise slightly. Luka cursed under his breath.

"Of course I do. You never know when someone might grace my bedchamber. It's best to be prepared."

Luka's gaze turned dangerous as he stood and prowled

towards me, nostrils flaring. I took a step back until my back hit the wall with a light thud. My chest heaved as Luka braced an arm on the wall on either side of my head, caging me in.

"Has someone else shared your bed since I've been in Alethens?" The words came out in a growl, sending goosebumps scattering down my spine.

I tipped my chin up. "Would it matter to you if they had?"

"Yes. No—I—" Luka tore his gaze away from me, placing his forehead against the wall beside me as he took several deep breaths.

"Why would it matter to you?" The words were a whisper as they left my lips. I shouldn't have asked, but I needed to know his answer.

But he remained silent. The only sounds in the room were our heaving breaths.

"Luka—" I fisted the bottom of his shirt, pulling him towards me in a silent plea to answer my question. He shuddered.

I closed my eyes, focusing on the sound of our breaths.

"Lennox—"

It was my turn to shudder as he spoke into my neck, his breath hot on my skin as he brushed his nose along the column of my neck.

"I . . ." he trailed off.

Heat flooded my body at the sound of his voice as his hand moved to my hip, his fingers brushing over the silken fabric.

"This nightgown. You—"

I opened my eyes as he pushed himself off the wall and turned from me. Running his hands through his hair as he made his way towards the bathing chamber, the door clambering shut behind him.

38

LENNOX

I was laying in a pool of blood, a knife protruding from my side. No matter how hard I tried, I couldn't move. All I could do was lay there and watch as the masked male sliced up my family. My voice was hoarse from begging and pleading for what felt like hours now. Days.

"Kill me instead, take me, and let them live. Please. I'll do anything to save them. Please."

My pleas were ignored as I lay there, hour after hour watching my family die, one by one—unable to save them.

"Please," I rasped. "Please. Take me instead." Tears rolled down my cheeks, mixing with the blood I was laying in. No longer only my blood, but my family's blood too. They were all dead. Mother, Father, Nol, Kara— they were gone. I was alone.

Please, kill me too, I tried to say, but my mouth felt like it was full of cotton, and the words remained lodged in my throat. The masked male, now done with my family, turned his attention to me.

"Now it's your turn." He sneered, his eyes, dark like black pits, glimmered. Good. He was finally going to kill me—put me out of my misery. Something on my face must have given away how I felt because the male smiled. A cold, cruel smile that sent shivers down my spine.

"You thought I was going to kill you too didn't you?" He barked a laugh. "No, I have a greater fate for you than death. You shall live."

No. No. No. *The male laughed at the panic crossing my features. Live. I was to live after I had watched everyone I love die.*

I thrashed as I tried to free my hands. If I could free my hands I could cast magic at the male to get myself free and end my life on my own. I couldn't live after everyone I loved died. I struggled against the bonds. A scream ripped from my raw throat.

"Kill me, please. Kill me."

"Lennox!" A faraway voice cried out.

"Kill me, please," I whimpered as the male walked away from me.

"Lennox, wake up!"

"Please." I was sobbing now, tears streaming down my face as my body shook.

"LENNOX!"

I awoke with a gasp, my eyes flying open. I tried to move, but my arms were pinned at my sides and something, no, *someone* was on top of me. My eyes adjusted in the darkness and I found Luka straddling me—his thighs on either side of me as he held my arms on the mattress. The moonlight illuminated his face, his eyes wild with panic.

"It was a dream," he whispered as he released my hands and moved off of me. I sat up as he knelt beside me, brushing the hair away from my face. His hand lingered on my face, trembling slightly as he ran his thumb across my cheek. "Are you okay?"

I sucked in air. Trying to catch my breath as my heart continued to beat erratically in my chest. "I think so."

"I'm sorry about restraining you." He winced as he ran his fingers through his hair. "You were screaming and thrashing violently and you started to cast magic in your sleep. I—I panicked."

I looked around the room and sure enough, several spots on the wall were covered in a layer of frost.

"Fuck, Lennox, you scared me." He scrubbed at his face with his hands.

"I'm sorry." I wrapped my arms around myself. "Thank you

—for stopping me before it got any worse." I wouldn't be able to live with myself if I had hurt someone while casting during a nightmare. I had a hard time controlling my magic when my emotions ran high, I needed to get myself under control. This was happening too frequently for comfort.

A blessing. My mother had told me. *It is a blessing that your heart has the capacity to feel so strongly. That your power reacts in response to your emotions.*

A curse was more like it.

"Do you have nightmares often?"

"Almost every night," I admitted as I stared at my bare feet. I couldn't bear to look at him. I didn't want his sympathy. I didn't want anyone's sympathy. Kara knew I had them occasionally. We talked about it shortly *After,* but she didn't know the extent of them, or how frequently they occurred. I doubted she even knew they still occurred. I had never wanted to worry her. Or let anyone know how much that night had affected me.

I steeled myself for Luka's interrogation. For his judgment.

"Lennox, it's okay." He placed a hand on my exposed thigh. "Can I ask what they are about?"

"My family." I took a deep breath. "It's usually different versions of the same dream. I watch my family be murdered and instead of killing me, he leaves me alive. Forces me to live after losing everyone I love."

"You ask him to kill you too, don't you."

"Yes." It felt shameful to admit. A tear slipped down my cheek, and I quickly wiped it away.

"You were screaming, 'kill me' right before I got to you to finally wake up."

I waited for him to say more—to pass judgment—but it never came. He remained silent, waiting for me to continue. Luka's hand moved on my thigh, he started brushing his thumb over my skin while he waited for me to continue.

"I don't want to die. But in those dreams I do. In those dreams, I don't only lose my parents and Nol. I lose Kara too.

I'd be lying if I said I wouldn't want to live in a world without Kara in it. I don't think I'd survive with no one left."

I focused on the soothing motion of Lukas thumb on my skin as he spoke.

"I used to think that sometimes too, after my parents died. I thought I had no one, but it wasn't true. I still had Nico and Declan. They saved me from myself. You have to remember you still have Kara. You can't think about a world without her. That's not living." I thought back to our similar conversation in the garden weeks ago. It sounded easy when he said it.

"If Kara were to ever leave you, you wouldn't be alone. Remember, you'd have me." Luka brushed my hair behind my ear. His hand lingering.

"Thank you." The air in the room suddenly felt too hot as our interaction before bed rushed back to my mind. Luka swallowed before looking away.

"Let's try and go back to sleep," he said as he moved and slipped back under the covers, holding them open for me. I ignored him, and instead slipped out of the bed and rifled through my bag.

"What are you doing?"

"Grabbing my book."

"You're going to read?"

I nodded as I returned to the bed, book in hand. "I can't sleep after a nightmare."

"Even at this time of night?"

I shook my head. "That's part of the reason why I train early in the morning. I'm usually up before sunrise."

A crease formed between his brows. "Lennox, you can't live that way."

I shrugged. I had been functioning on little sleep for years now.

"Come here and lay down. I'm going to help you fall back asleep," he said as he plucked the book from my hand and set it on his bedside table.

Prick.

"Fine," I relented, I didn't have the energy to argue with him right now. And as soon as he fell back asleep I could pick up my book again. I laid on my side and pulled the covers to my chest. I felt Luka move behind me before he hauled my body against his.

"What are you doing?" I protested.

"Helping you sleep," he murmured into my neck as he pressed his body flush with mine. His arm banded around my waist, holding me against him. His other arm rested by our heads. He drew my hair away from my face until I could feel his breath on my skin, sending goosebumps scattering over my body. I tensed as I tried to take in all of the places our bodies were touching.

"This will never work if you don't trust me," he sighed.

I didn't dare move, my body rigid against his. We were dangerously close to crossing a line.

"I promise I won't bite," he teased.

Him biting me was not what I was worried about.

I sighed and relaxed my body into his for the second time today. My skin heated every place we touched, and my nightgown offered little protection between the two of us.

"How is this supposed to help me sleep?" My mind was going haywire. I was in no way relaxed.

He shifted, and his arm wrapped underneath me and banded around my waist, while he freed his other arm to brush the skin of my thigh. Heat flared where he touched.

"Instead of thinking of your nightmare, I want you to focus on the movement of my fingers on your skin."

I sucked in a breath as I tried to focus on the pattern of his fingers as he brushed long, slow strokes on my thigh.

"If you continue to focus on my fingers you will eventually fall asleep, trust me," he urged.

I had nothing to lose, but sleep, so I closed my eyes and I let myself relax into Luka—focusing on the soothing strokes of those long, calloused fingers.

"Sleep, Lennox."

I continued to focus on the lazy strokes of his fingers at the hem of my nightdress, high on my thigh, down my leg. I was still focusing on the path of his thumb when sleep found me.

39

LUKA

I woke with a warm body pressed against mine, and our limbs intertwined as I held them to me. I pulled the body closer, nuzzling into their neck and taking in their sweet scent—floral with a hint of citrus.

Lennox, it was Lennox laying next to me. I opened my eyes, squinting at the sun leaking through the windows. Everything came back to me in a flash.

I panicked when I woke to her screaming and thrashing in bed. *Goddess above that nightmare.* I had never seen Lennox so rattled, so vulnerable. I would do anything to prevent her from going through that again. Holding her last night had seemed like a great idea at the time. Now, with my growing cock pressed against her ass, I wasn't sure.

I knew this would likely never happen again, so I took a moment to relish the feel of her smooth skin under my palms, stopping my hand before it could drift too high. I liked the feeling of her against me. Some parts of me liked the feel of her *too* much.

Fuck.

Reluctantly, I peeled myself away from her before she woke

up and knew exactly how I was feeling about her waking up next to me.

We were already walking a thin line.

My throat burned with the words I left unsaid last night. I couldn't explain the draw I felt towards Lennox. I couldn't seem to control myself when it came to her.

Something was brewing between us, but I don't think either of us knew what it was.

☾

The silence today was different. There were too many unspoken words floating in the space between us now. No matter how hard I tried to steer my thoughts in the opposite direction, they kept barraging me. Every touch reminded me of a touch last night—of skin against skin without the barrier of our leathers.

With only the fabric of her goddess-forsaken nightgown between us.

We didn't have a nearby town to stay in tonight, and we stopped when it grew dark, deciding a dense patch of trees would be the best place to set up camp for the night. Thank the Goddess we wouldn't have to share a bed again tonight. I didn't know if I'd be able to control myself sleeping close to her two nights in a row.

Lennox set up an air shield around us while I started a fire. We didn't mutter a single word to each other as we ate, and we kept our eyes fixed firmly on the flickering fire before us.

"I don't like this—" Lennox's voice cut through the silence as she waved her hand around as she searched for the right words. "All this . . . weirdness between us now." She wrinkled her nose in a way I had never seen her do before.

"Me either," I admitted.

"So, how do we fix it?" she asked.

I shrugged and turned my attention back to the fire.

"How about we put it all out in the open?" Lennox said as she stood, pacing back and forth as she continued. "Last night I had one of my nightmares and I am thankful to you for waking me before I encased the entire inn in ice. I am also thankful for you comforting me and not making a huge deal of it, and helping me get back to sleep. And as much as I hate to admit it, it was kind of nice, and I slept well with your fangs inches from my neck all night. And this morning I woke to your cock pressing into my ass and now everything is awkward between us and I just want to go back to how we were before."

I cringed. "You were awake?"

"Yup," she said, popping the *p*. "I faked being asleep to make it less awkward, but obviously that was the wrong thing to do. But can we focus on more important details than your cock?"

"It's a pretty important detail if you ask me."

She rolled her eyes. "Can we not do this male bullshit right now?"

I raised a brow. The sigh that left her lips was pure ire.

"Fine, from what I felt it appears you have a decent-sized cock," she said, giving me a placating smile. "Are you happy now? Can we move on?"

I smothered the laugh that threatened to slip out. Every day I discovered a new side to Lennox. This side might be my new favorite.

"For the record, my cock is more than decent-sized. But yes, you can continue."

She shook her head as she continued to pace. "What is with you lately? All this being nice to me—it's freaking me out. I like it better when you're a prick," she said.

"Was me talking about my massive cock *not* me being a prick?"

"You're infuriating."

I held my hands in surrender. "You said you liked it better when I was a prick, I was just trying to help you out."

Lennox rolled her eyes, collapsing back on the ground with a sigh, but not before flipping me a vulgar gesture.

"Do you feel better now?" I asked, thoroughly amused myself.

"Much."

"I will admit, I like this brutally honest version of Lennox. All this time I thought you were being honest with me, but you were holding back on me, Sweetheart."

"It's not proper for a queen to say the word 'cock' that much."

I couldn't stop the laugh that roared out this time. And when I looked at Lennox, a real smile was on her lips, lighting up her eyes in a way I rarely got to see.

"I used to always be like this, brutally honest. Sometimes— sometimes I feel like I not only lost parts of myself when my family died, but I lost parts of myself when I became queen. I had to mute certain parts of me that I loved. I couldn't just be me. I had to be *High Queen Lennox*."

I took her hand in mine and squeezed it. Growing up, knowing I would one day wear the crown, I knew I couldn't be myself in front of everyone. I learned what parts of me were appropriate to reveal in front of others from a young age. I had never known anything different, unlike Lennox.

"It gets exhausting holding it all in sometimes," she admitted.

I squeezed her hand again. "You don't ever need to hold anything back with me."

She nodded. "I know, but it's a lot easier said than done."

I stood and offered her my hand, pulling her to her feet. "Next time you want to talk about my cock, know you can tell me right away."

☾

I laid on my bedroll next to Lennox, staring at the starry sky as I tried to fall asleep, but I couldn't stop staring at the stars. I swear, the stars didn't look like this in the Blood Court. Their shine was muted. Here, they shined so bright I swear I could blind myself if I looked too long.

"Luka? Are you still awake?" Lennox's voice came quietly from beside me.

"Yeah." I turned on my side to face her, finding her already looking at me, her hands perched under her head like a pillow. The moonlight illuminated half of her face.

She closed her eyes and took a breath before saying, "I want to try something."

I shifted until I was resting my head in my hand.

"I'm listening."

"Last night with you holding me—that was the best sleep I've gotten in a long time. I don't go back to sleep after nightmares because I almost always have another one if I do manage to go back to sleep." She paused and I held my breath. "But I didn't last night. So I want to try something."

She hesitated. "Will you hold me tonight? I want to see if it will help me not to have a nightmare." Her voice was quiet, unsure, taking me by surprise.

She sat and scrubbed her hands on her face. "I know it sounds crazy, but I don't know—it's like your presence is calming or something." She put her hands down and stared at the fire.

"Did you just compliment me?"

"Don't get cocky on me now, Bloodsucker."

"I can't make any promises."

She sighed and laid back, covering her face with her hands before saying, "You're insufferable."

She moved to turn away from me, but I caught her, pulling her against me. She didn't resist as I banded my arm around her waist to keep her pinned to me.

"I'll do anything to help you," I reminded her.

She didn't say anything as I continued to hold her, pulling the blankets around us.

"Thank you," she whispered into the darkness.

I placed a soft kiss on her temple, her breath catching at the action.

"Goodnight, Lennox."

"Goodnight, Luka."

40

LENNOX

There was something strangely comforting about waking up in Luka's arms. Although, I suppose it would be comforting to wake up in anyone's arms.

My head rested in the space between Luka's head and shoulder, with every breath I took, I inhaled his cool, fresh scent. My arm was draped over his body, holding him to me with my hand fisted in the fabric of his shirt. His own arms were banded around my waist, with one hand resting on my back in a way that felt protective.

Too protective for someone who was just my friend.

I made a move to get up, only to be pulled back by the strong arm wrapped around my waist.

"Let me hold you for one more minute while I wake up," he mumbled, his eyes still closed, and his thick, dark lashes standing out against his tanned skin.

I stilled, an argument posed on my tongue. *I didn't have a nightmare last night.*

When was the last time I had slept without a nightmare?

I cozied back into my little crook and placed my arms across his torso again. Luka's eyes opened, he shifted, turning to look at me. I tilted my head to meet his gaze as he blinked at me.

"What?" I asked.

He opened his mouth and shut it again.

"What?" I persisted, poking him in the side. I stared at the half-smile formed on his face. The sun illuminating his face made his eyes bluer, and my fingers itched to brush the strands of dark hair out of his face so I could see them better.

"I didn't think you'd actually lay back down," he admitted.

I shrugged. "I didn't have a nightmare last night, I figured I owed you this much."

His arm tightened around me, his fingers bushing strokes on the small of my back. "When was the last time you slept without a nightmare?"

I considered his question. "I don't know."

He remained silent, the only sound the rise and fall of his chest.

"I can't remember the last time I slept that well," I admitted and Luka's arm tightened around me again, his fingers sweeping across my hip in a soothing motion.

"Well, I'm glad I could help you achieve that."

"You know this means I'm going to need you to do this every night now, right?" I teased.

Laughter rumbled through his chest—vibrating through my body all the way to my toes.

"There are far worse fate's I could imagine, Lennox."

His words sent warmth coursing through my body.

As I laid there, my head resting on Luka's chest, our limbs intertwined as he held me to him, I felt at peace, I felt comfortable.

Safe.

Emotions I didn't know I was capable of feeling anymore. All in the arms of a vampire, the same species of Fae who ripped those feelings from me in the first place. How could I feel safe in the arms of a vampire? The thought was enough to send me spiraling over the edge. I banished it, locking it up tight. I'd think about it later. For now, I was going to bask in the feeling for as long as I could.

Safe.

In Luka's arms, I felt *safe* for the first time in over two years.

☾

The summer sun was high in the sky, its warmth spreading throughout my entire body. I turned my face towards the light, basking in the warmth of it on my skin. I loved summer. The sun and the warmth—everything in full bloom.

We had been riding all day, and the tension of yesterday was gone. I leaned back into Luka as we rode, relishing in his strong torso supporting me from behind—steadied by his hands holding me to him.

"Will you tell me about witches?" Luka asked.

I turned so I could see his face. "What do you mean?"

"Tell me about them."

The crease in my brow deepened.

"Everything I've ever heard about the witches has been rumors and speculation. As a half-witch I imagine you know the truth. I'd like you to tell me about them."

I rolled his words over in my mind. He was right. Even in the Star Court little was known about witches. I couldn't count how many times I'd had to bite my tongue when I had over-heard conversations about witches spewing outrageous lies. They'd tell stories about how a witch lured a friend to a cottage and tried to eat them. How one had cut off someone's ear, or a finger, to use for a spell. But having to explain how I knew the truth about the subject was not something I was willing to reveal. Instead I'd walk away, grinding my teeth so hard they felt like they would turn to dust. The hardest part about being a half-witch was keeping the secret. If I wasn't High Queen it might not have been such a big deal, but there was a reason my parents decided to keep it a secret in the first place.

It was easy to place judgment, and spiel hate towards a group of people you had never met. It was the reason why witches kept to their court. If they did leave the Mystic Court they did it in secret. It was common for witches to be killed or tortured if they were caught. Not because they did anything wrong, but because Fae were afraid of them.

"What do you want to know?" I asked.

"Where do witches get their magic? Was it stolen? Or a gift from the Goddess? Or neither and something entirely different?" His question didn't surprise me. Every Fae had an opinion on the witches and it started here—are they blessed or cursed by the Goddess?

"They did not steal the magic, but it's not a gift either. Like every other Fae, witches claim their magic from the land. However, they have been blessed with the ability to call on elements they have not claimed."

Sometimes I wondered if that's how I was able to claim all four elements, because of my witch abilities. "According to our stories, after the Goddess Astria was scorned by her lover, and cursed them—creating vampires—she had no desire to stay on Lethina anymore. She sought out another Fae to help her figure out how to get back home to the sky. Our stories claim the Fae was Hecate, who would later become the first witch, after Astria blessed her for helping her get back home. She blessed Hecate's people with the ability to draw additional magic from the earth, therefore creating witches."

The witch interpretation of the story of the Goddess Astria and Hecate was one of my favorite's growing up. The year my mother told me it for the first time I made her recite it to me almost every night until she finally got me a copy of the story to read for myself.

"Unlike when you use an element you've claimed, witches have to have access to an additional element to call upon it. For instance, if I did not possess water magic, but I wanted to use it, I would have to have water near me to wield it. I cannot summon water out of nowhere like a Fae who has claimed the element can. Essentially, that's the biggest difference between other types of Fae and witches. Although I'm convinced any Fae could call upon additional elements if they knew how."

I think the biggest gift the Goddess gave the witches was information, a deeper insight on how to use our magic in different ways.

"You think I could summon water if you taught me?" he asked.

I shrugged. "I've never tried to teach a non-witch, but I'd be willing to try and test my theory."

Luka squeezed my hip. "I'm going to hold you to that," he stated, riling a scoff from me. "What about spells and other witch practices?"

"The other spells and rituals witches conduct are more of the same practice. They are calling upon the magic of the land. Relics and other objects help make the signal clearer—or better the chance of the call being heard or accepted. They are a conductor of magic."

Luka remained quiet behind me as he took in the information. "How did you know you had witch abilities?"

I considered his question, but witch magic had been a part of me my entire life, it was hard to recall when it started.

"Witches start displaying magic abilities from a younger age than other Fae. My mother started testing me when I was young to see if I had inherited any of her magic. I wasn't even aware she was doing it."

Mixed Fae are rare and their abilities have little documentation over the centuries.

"When it was clear I had inherited some of her abilities, she started teaching me about my witch heritage. She hadn't wanted to wait to burden me with the secret until she was sure I had the abilities. When Kara started demonstrating abilities when she was four, she joined in our lessons."

I thought back on our mornings while the three of us were

learning and practicing magic. About our mother telling us stories of her people, teaching us spells, and telling us about her life growing up. They were some of my favorite memories growing up.

"Witch magic never manifested in Nol. However, my mother wasn't at all surprised. Male witches are rare in the first place, it was even rarer if they exhibited any abilities." But once Kara and I started practicing witch magic, my parents told Nol about my mother's heritage too.

It never bothered him that he never developed witch magic, but he loved learning about our heritage. I almost felt like he loved it more than Kara and I did. Once Kara started exhibiting powers, we started traveling to the Mystic Court every year. My aunt and Luce had come to visit us occasionally, but we never knew they were witches until we knew of our own abilities. They came under glamor, keeping to my mother' story that she was from a small village in the Star Court. After we discovered our background, we'd spent chunks of time every year in the Mystic Court, learning witch magic from anyone who would teach us. Even though Nol didn't have witch magic, he still loved it there. He'd score texts and discover the most obscure spells and teach them to us.

"You mean not all witches were born with witch powers?" Luka's question disrupted my wandering thoughts of my brother from getting any farther.

I shook my head. "See what I mean about the potential of anyone being able to call additional elements? Witch magic works strangely. I think it depends on the Fae's mindset as they are trying to call upon elements."

I leaned back into Luka further as the sun continued to shine on my face. It felt freeing to talk openly with Luka about being a witch. It was easy to talk to him, it should have worried me, but it didn't.

In the back of my mind, I remembered I had much greater things to worry about.

We were on a quest to meet a Seer, in a forest with danger lurking at every turn.

I was facing the threat of war against my fragile kingdom.

There was a rebel group actively trying to kill me and my sister and take my crown.

But right now, at this moment, I couldn't find it in myself to care.

In this moment, sitting on Odin with the sun warming my face and Luka's strong hands holding me to him, I let those concerns stay in the back of my mind. There was nothing I could do about them at this exact moment.

It had been a long time, I wasn't sure if what I was feeling was true. But I thought at this moment, I might feel happy.

41

LUKA

As our travels continued Lennox and I fell into a routine. We spent our days riding in silence and getting to know each other, asking simple questions like what was our favorite food and color. Sometimes Lennox read to me from the books Luciana had given her before we left, hoping it might reveal new information on the book.

Each night we set up camp or stayed at an inn, on the occasion we came across one. When it was time for bed, Lennox settled in close to me, so I wrapped my arms around her and held her tight. Each morning I awoke with her beside me.

I was starting to look forward to those mornings and nights more than I should have.

This is all temporary, I reminded myself. This quiet intimacy that had settled between us would end the minute we returned back to our friends.

So I decided to take advantage of it while I could.

According to the enchanted map Lennox and Luciana had made, we should be arriving at the Seer today. What that would look like, we had no idea. Lennox and I had debated the topic over breakfast at the inn this morning. For all we know we could be looking for her in a town, in a cabin, or wandering out in the woods for fucks sake. There was so much unknown in front of us now, and it set us both on edge, popping our peaceful bubble. I could see it now in the way Lennox sat in front of me. Her body was rigid, wound tight like a bowstring. Any wrong move and she would snap.

I moved my hand from where it dangled at my side and placed it on her hip. She jumped slightly at the contact but settled. I started moving my thumb back and forth in slow motions on her side.

"Breathe, Lennox," I whispered into her ear.

She sucked in a breath as I coasted my lips across her neck and she tilted her head to the side.

I brushed her hair over her shoulder, baring her neck fully to me.

"You need to relax," I murmured against her skin.

Her eyes fluttered closed and she took in a deep breath, finally letting her body relax into mine.

I placed a soft kiss behind her ear and her hand grasped my thigh. I could hear her blood pumping through her, her heartbeat erratic. She shuddered as I grazed my fangs down her neck, my tongue darting out to lick the skin where my fangs had touched.

"Luka."

A twig snapped in the distance. I placed a hand over her mouth before she could finish her sentence. Though I wanted nothing more than to know what was about to come out of her mouth.

Her eyes popped open, immediately going wide at the intrusion. She moved to pry my hand from her mouth, but I held strong and leaned in, whispering in her ear, "I heard something, you need to be quiet."

Understanding flashed in her gaze and she nodded. I released my hand and looked around as Lennox reached for the dagger strapped to her thigh. Another twig snapped to our left and we both shifted our attention in the direction as the sound of rustling reached our ears.

If it was another hellhound I'd make sure to pay them back for the pain they caused me.

I leaned in close to whisper in Lennox's ear again. "We're being surrounded."

She nodded in agreement as she continued to scan the trees.

"When they show themselves, you take the right, I'll take the left," I instructed.

She nodded before taking my hand in hers and squeezing it. She looked over her shoulder at me as I squeezed back. Fire burned in her eyes that matched the trees surrounding us. We were being surrounded by an unknown creature and she was excited.

I shook my head to hide my growing smile.

Lennox Adair would be my undoing.

I slipped off Odin, landing quietly on the forest floor. Lennox's hands reached for my shoulders as she dismounted, and I placed my hands on her hips to steady her—letting my hands linger longer than they needed to as we stared at each other. The urge to pull her to me and claim her lips almost overtook me. But there was another rustling of the leaves and the haze lifted. The reminder that we were not alone washed over us like a bath of ice. We both removed our hands and took a step back from each other, turning towards the trees once again.

A small snake slithered across the ground, rustling the leaves as it moved. Its black scales shined in the light as it moved towards me. My magic swirled inside me, writhing its way towards the surface and I flexed my fingers. I had a feeling this wasn't a normal snake. The snake made it to me and started climbing up my leg. I tried to shake off the serpent, but it clung to my leathers. I summoned a vine instead and I watched as the vine closed around the snake, closing it in a firm grasp before I flung the vine away, the snake with it. Its hiss echoed through the forest as it moved through the air.

The snake hit the ground, erupting into a cloud of black smoke. The hiss rang out louder and then the smoke cleared, revealing a mountain cat the size of Odin.

"Shit," I mumbled. *Definitely not a normal snake.*

The creature stood on four legs—its yellow eyes burning as they looked at me. It let out another hiss, revealing rows of razor sharp teeth.

"Lennox, did you see that?" I didn't dare take my eyes off the creature as I waited for her response.

"Yes," she breathed.

The creature remained where it landed. Its head swung from side to side like a snake as it took me in. I had never heard of a creature who shifted from a snake to a mountain cat. But leave it to the Mystic Court to reveal yet another surprise to me.

"I think it's a Wampus Cat!" Lennox called from somewhere behind me.

I had no fucking clue what a Wampus Cat was and I really didn't want to find out.

"Are there any snakes over there?"

Lennox took several seconds before answering. "I don't see any yet."

The Wampus Cat was now prowling towards me—each step slow and calculated. I reached for the twin swords at my back. I had a feeling this magical being wouldn't go down easy.

"Fuck." I heard Lennox curse from behind me.

"What?" I turned to find Lennox backing away from a snake as it slithered at her feet. She reached out with her sword and severed the snake in two before it could reach her.

"I hate snakes," she revealed as she scowled at the creature before looking at me as a shutter racked her body. Her eyes widened as they met mine.

"Luka watch out!"

I turned as the Wampus Cat pounced. Its giant paws slammed into my shoulders, its razor-sharp claws piercing my skin as I landed on the ground with a thud. I hissed in pain as I rolled onto my back, trying to push the massive creature off of me. The thing was fucking heavy. Its weight held me down, rendering my swords useless as my arms laid pinned to the ground. I kicked with my legs with no luck. The cat only hissed at me, its slobber pelting my face.

"You fucker," I growled.

The cat hissed again, but this time it sounded more like a scream as it bounded off of me. I jumped to my feet. My shoulder screamed in pain, but I ignored it as I searched for Lennox.

The Wampus Cat now circled Lennox where she stood, her back to me, black blood staining the creature's white coat where one of her daggers was stuck.

I couldn't help but stand in awe at the sight.

"You hurt my friend." Lennox didn't take her eyes from the cat as she spoke, its blood dripping from her blade to the forest floor.

Friend.

"You won't leave this forest alive, kitty cat," she hissed.

I fell into place at Lennox's side, and her eyes roamed over my body before returning her gaze to the Wampus Cat. I heard the breath leave her lungs as she exhaled, her shoulders releasing.

I sheathed one sword and held the other firmly in my uninjured arm. I glanced at Lennox as I lifted my sword, a silent agreement passing through us.

Aim for the injured area.

We nodded and took off running towards the Wampus Cat.

My shoulder barked with pain as I put all my power into the blow. I prepared myself for the contact, but I met nothing.

The Wampus Cat was gone.

I met Lennox's gaze, finding her as perplexed as I was. I looked where the cat had been to find a snake instead. The fucker shifted back. Lennox moved closer, and she lifted her sword, ready to cut this sake in two as well.

"I'd put the sword down if I were you." A cracked voice came from the trees beside us.

Lennox froze, sword still in the air.

"Put your sword down, child."

I turned towards the voice as a figure emerged from the woods.

"You have no more use for that now."

The figure was small, their petite stature drowning in a well-worn brown cloak covered in patches made of a variety of fabrics. The hood fell over the Fae's face, keeping their features hidden in the shadows.

"I've been waiting for you two for a long time."

The figure removed its hood, revealing a well-aged Fae. Her dark, leathery skin was creased with deep wrinkles. She had to be well over two hundred years old to have aged so much. I had never seen a Fae appear this aged, but it wasn't just her age that was jarring, it was her eyes that I fixed on as they pinned me in place. Her eyes were sunken in, a light sheen of silver lining her iris with flecks of red swimming in the magic brimming there.

They were utterly terrifying.

Neither Lennox or I dared to move as we surveyed the female. Lennox still held her sword in the air, as if it was frozen in place.

The female sighed. "Come, children, I have been expecting you."

Lennox's sword fell to her side, her mouth falling open. "You're the Seer."

I whipped my head from Lennox back to the female as she nodded in confirmation.

"Holy shit," I mumbled.

The Seer wrinkled her nose. "You will not use such foul language here child."

"Sorry," I mumbled as Lennox held her hand to her mouth to stifle her laugh.

The Seer tipped her chin at us and turned. "Follow me."

Lennox and I sheathed our swords and followed after the Seer. Part of me couldn't believe we found her, that this was all real.

"Sorry about my pets."

I looked at Lennox and mouthed, *pets*, questioningly. She shrugged before turning her attention back forward.

"They are out here to protect my property from unwanted guests, they knew of your arrival, but clearly did not listen to my directions and one perished because of it."

"Those Wampus Cats were your pets?"

"Yes, I created them, I have many of them roaming these woods." She *created* the Wampus Cats. I let the information settle. The magnitude of power she must have if she was able to create life—I stopped in my tracks as I felt strange magic pushing against my skin, Lennox froze beside me.

"Do you feel that?"

I nodded.

The Seer raised her hands in front of her as she mumbled under her breath. When she lowered her hands the trees in front of us shifted. They fell away revealing a small clearing where a small cottage sat.

42

LENNOX

Luka and I followed behind the Seer as we approached the hidden cottage. Smoke billowed from the tumbling chimney. The cottage itself was small, the outside weathered, the dark wood splintered and sagging in areas and the roof was missing several shingles. Dark green vines, with pink budding flowers snaked up the pillars of the sagging porch attached to the front. A rocking chair and a small side table were the only furniture on the porch besides a few flower pots with over-grown plants.

We followed the Seer onto the porch, careful to avoid areas with missing or rotted boards. The two windows looking out the front of the cottage were coated in a thick layer of dust, preventing us from peaking inside.

The inside of the cottage was better maintained than the outside. A fire roared in the hearth at the back of the home. Two chairs and a small table were perched by the fire. The main room was small, but comfortable for one person. A small kitch-enette sat to the right of the room with a small circular table and the entire left side of the home was lined with shelves hosting rows and rows of witch materials. There may have been more witch relics here than in the scrying cottage back in the village. I couldn't imagine how one witch could have acquired this many relics on their own.

"Sit, children." The Seer gestured to the small table.

Luka and I sat while she scurried around the kitchen and until she finally sat across from us, handing us each a glass.

"Drink this," she requested.

I guess we were skipping the introductions and jumping right in.

"What is it?" Luka asked as he sniffed his cup cautiously.

I looked into my own mug. A thick dark green liquid sloshed in the glass. I raised the glass to my nose and took a sniff and immediately regretted it as the foul smell invaded my senses.

"You want me to See, yes?"

Luka and I looked at one other and nodded.

"Then drink." She threw her hands in the air when we still refused to drink. "Stubborn children, the Stars were right about you."

"The Stars spoke to you about us?" My magic swirled inside me.

"Yes, yes, so drink." She gestured to the cups again.

"I'm sorry, but we just met you. You invite us into your home and tell us to drink an unknown liquid. We don't even know who you are. Why should we trust you?" Luka asked as he stared at the Seer and set his mug back on the table. The Seer narrowed her eyes at Luka—the red flecks taking over her eyes.

Holy Stars.

"Your friend called upon me, seeking my gifts and you question *me*, King of Blood?"

I remained quiet, trying not to squirm in my seat as Luka and the Seer stared at one another.

I set my glass on the table and placed my hand on the Seer's arm. She whipped her head in my direction—her eyes were almost completely red now. I flinched under her gaze and quickly removed my hand.

"We don't mean to upset you. What Luka is trying to say is

can we slow down a bit? At least tell us your name before you offer us a strange substance." I smiled at her, but she ignored me as she looked between Luka and I.

"If you drink I will tell you my name."

"Can you at least tell us what the drink is first?" I asked.

The female sighed, looking at us as if we were nothing more than two petulant children, not a prince and a queen.

"My ability is great, but it is greater when I know the subjects whose lives I am looking into. I know little of the two of you, this drink is a spell of sorts. It will connect me to the two of you so my reading will be more accurate."

I smiled softly. "Thank you."

She tipped her chin at me and crossed her arms over her chest. "Now drink, we don't have all day."

Luka and I looked at one another one last time before bringing the glasses to our lips. The drink was bitter as I swallowed, residue from the magical substances grainy in my mouth. I tried my best to not think about what those substances might be as my eyes wandered towards the shelves of witch relics. The Seer looked between the two of us as we sat our empty glasses on the table.

Seemingly satisfied, she spoke again. "My name is Hecate."

I froze.

Hecate.

Holy Stars.

"Hecate, as in *the* Hecate?" I asked in disbelief.

There was no way.

"Yes, of course," she said as she gave me a quizzical look.

"But—but how?" My mouth was agape, I'm sure I looked ridiculous, but I didn't care. "You're supposed to be dead."

Luka whipped his head in my direction. "Wait, the Hecate from the story you told me?" he asked.

I nodded as I tried to steady my trembling hands. How was it possible I was sitting across the table from the original witch, blessed by the Goddess herself? According to the stories she was supposed to be dead. She died thousands of years ago, not long after the Goddess returned to the skies.

Hecate waved her hand dismissively. "What is dead but a word? Only few truly die in our realm. You should know this."

Luka and I continued to gape at her, words evading us both.

"When you were a child, the Goddess sent me back to this realm for this purpose."

"This purpose? You mean to meet with us?" Luka stammered.

Hecate shrugged. "The vision was never clear."

The vision? What vision? But Hecate continued before I could ask more.

"The Goddess and the Stars set everything in place." She nodded to me. "It was not a coincidence the heir to the Mystic Court and the Star Court were mates." Shock rolled through me. "When your parents fought against all odds and decided they would marry they set in motion a prophecy that has long been in place."

"What prophecy?"

"I'm afraid I cannot reveal that to you. You will learn it when the time is right."

I wanted to pry, to ask a million more questions, but it was not polite to pester an elder witch for information she could not give. Instead I bit my tongue until I tasted the metallic tang of blood. Luka's nostrils flared from where he sat beside me.

"Anyway"—she looked between Luka and I before continuing—"we knew a youngling born from your parents would be the key to everything. But we never knew who it would be."

The key to everything. What in the Stars was that supposed to mean?

"The key is you, Queen of Stardust." She pointed a long spindly finger at me.

"Me?"

"Yes, you, foolish child. Who else? Is one of your other siblings here? Did one of them call me?"

I stared at her, wide-eyed, not sure if she wanted me to answer her or not.

"It is you, Lennox Adair, High Queen of Lethenia, you are who I have been waiting for all these years."

"But what does this have to do with me? Why did she need to bring me?" Luka asked as he leaned forward, resting his elbows on the table.

"I cannot reveal that to you."

"Of course." Luka sat back in his chair, exacerbated.

"Have patience, child, everything will be revealed to you with time."

Luka opened his mouth, but Hecate held up a hand.

"I've had enough of this conversation," Hecate declared. "We need to let the spell take root for a few more minutes before we get started. I need to know more about what you want. What are you looking to find?"

My head was still spinning from what she had revealed. I wanted to question and push her for more information, but I knew she would never give more than she was willing. I should be grateful for what we had already received. So I pushed the thoughts of this so-called *prophecy* aside for later, for when Luka and I could discuss them in private.

Hecate rapped her long nails on the table, willing one of us to speak.

"Our courts have long been in conflict, especially since vampires murdered my family," I shared.

True remorse flashed over her features, the first sign of real emotion from her since we arrived.

"Yes, I was deeply sorry to hear of the passing of your parents."

I swallowed the lump in my throat. "To avoid my sister, or I, having to marry a vampire, Luka and I are trying to find a book King Arlo wants. Apparently it belonged to the Goddess Astria, and it contains a cure to vampirism in it. Arlo is threatening war if I can't find the book for him."

"On top of that, we believe the Vanir are after Lennox and her sister. I believe they want to kill them and take the crown," Luka added.

Hecate leaned back in her chair as she took in our information. Luka and I stared at her impatiently as she pressed her lips together in a thin line. "It is time we get started."

She wandered around the kitchen gathering various items before settling back at the table. I watched as she mixed ingredients in a stone bowl. Once satisfied she mumbled a spell under her breath before creating a small ball of fire and placing it in the bowl as well. The relics caught fire, a string of thick smoke rising from the bowl. Hecate closed her eyes and inhaled the smoke, only opening her eyes after letting out a breath. The red flecks had started to take over her iris again.

She stood, her chair scraping on the wooden floor as she pulled a knife from the kitchen drawer and gestured to Luka and I. "Give me your palms. You must be connected through blood for this to work."

Luka tensed beside me as I held out my palm to the witch. "Blood offerings are common in spells like this."

His nostrils flared as Hecate sliced through the center of my palm. She took my hand in hers and squeezed my fist over the smoldering bowl, I watched as three drops of my blood splashed in the blow, hissing at it met the heated stone.

She let go of my hand and gestured to Luka, reluctantly he unclenched his fist and offered it to Hecate and she repeated the process on his hand. The cut on my palm was already healing as she finished with Luka.

"Now, grab hands," she directed.

Luka took my hand in his, linking our fingers together as he arched a brow at me quizzically. I ignored him, focusing on Hecate instead.

She held out her hands to us. "Now give me your other hand."

We did as instructed and she closed her eyes and started chanting.

The words she spoke were of another language even *I* didn't recognize. It was not any spell I was familiar with either. She continued to speak for several minutes before finally stopping as the room became eerily still. The only sounds were our breaths. Every other noise seemed to have stopped.

Hecate remained still, eyes still closed, but began speaking again.

"I see two paths for you two young heirs. One of light and one of darkness. There are many paths leading to each. On the path of darkness I see blood, betrayal, destruction." Her face pinched, as if she was in pain herself. "So much destruction. Oppression. War. Nothing good comes from the path of darkness. Only pain. Kingdoms will be destroyed. Lethenia as we know it gone, turned to Stardust."

I felt like all of the air had been sucked out of the room, I couldn't breath at the idea of Lethenia being destroyed. Of seeing my beautiful city destroyed to nothing but Stardust. My stomach rolled as I squeezed my eyes shut. I could see it all too clearly. The once shiny streets of Alethens running red with blood, my people dead on the streets. Nothing but blood and ashes remaining. I felt Luka's hand squeeze mine, once, twice, three times, pulling me back from the darkness. I couldn't help but wonder if he was seeing the same thing as his thumb started moving back and forth on my wrist.

"On the path of light I see hope. I see peace between Fae. I see two kingdoms coming together as one, promising much to their people."

The darkness in my mind shifted with her words. The streets of Alethens were no longer bathed in blood. They were instead filled with Fae of all kinds smiling, laughing, dancing. Joyous celebrations took place as music filtered through the city. I felt a smile curve on my lips at the thought.

"How do we make sure we are on the right path?" Luka's

voice cut through the silence, echoing my own thoughts. "Can you tell us what we need to do?"

"I cannot tell you what you need to do to insure light."

My heart sank. This decision didn't only impact Luka and me, it was the future of all of Alethens we were talking about.

"What I can see is the path to the light depends on you two. I see you two standing hand in hand, together. People of every court surround you, supporting the two of you. The King and Queen of Blood and Stardust. Hope rests in your hands. You are the hope for the future. No one else, but your choices make the paths towards light or darkness."

"There are people close to you who will try to interfere with your choices. They will try to break you. Try to tempt you into the darkness as they try to repair what they believe is broken. There are far greater issues in play than the answers you seek now."

A light wind slipped around us, hairs coming loose from my braid and whipping around me. I opened my eyes, the bowl in front of us was now empty, the last of the smoke dissipating.

"Wait, that's it, that's all you can give us?" Luka asked, there was a slight edge to his voice.

"All? I gave you plenty, children. Be grateful." Hecate stood and started towards the door. I tried my best to stifle my irritation as Luka and I stood and followed Hecate.

"But what about the book? And the Vanir?" Luka demanded.

Hecate stilled. "Forget about the book, as you call it, it is not important. A cure for vampirism does not exist as you believe it does. Nothing good will come from that information coming to light."

"But—"

She held up a hand. "Trust me. The book needs to remain hidden. You will not like what you find in it. And if it ended up in the wrong hands . . ." She shuddered and took a deep breath. "As for the Vanir." Her expression darkened. "The Vanir are nothing the two of you cannot handle together if you keep on this path together. They are nothing but a group of disgruntled children."

"But if we are not to find the book, what can we give the Blood King to ensure I don't end up in an arranged marriage?" I asked, trying to keep my voice as even as possible.

Hecate was silent as she crossed her arms and looked at the ceiling, shaking her head before turning back to us. "I'm afraid I cannot offer you any insight on that."

"What do you mean you can't offer any insight?" Luka pressed.

She clenched her jaw. "I answer to the Goddess, not you *Prince*."

Luka opened his mouth to speak again, but I stopped him with a hand on his arm. "Thank you." I pressed my lips together as I stood. I was thankful she was willing to meet with us and give us what information she could, even if it did leave us with more questions than answers. Not that I had much experience with Seers, but I knew they had limitations as to what they could share as to not shift the future.

"Thank you, child." She took both of my hands in hers, the red flecks in her eyes were receding, but they still danced with magic as she stared at me with intent. "It was a great pleasure to be able to see you in the flesh."

She released my hands with a tight smile, the corners of her eyes creasing with the action. I nodded before turning towards the door where Luka waited for me.

I stopped as I made it to the threshold, turning to Hecate one more time, but she had already vanished.

43

LENNOX

Luka and I made our way out of Hecate's grove in silence, neither of us daring to speak. By some force of magic I'm sure, we found Odin in the trees where we had left him, grazing on the grass without a care in the world. I mounted him and Luka settled in behind me. His one hand gripped the reins and the other landed on my hip. I focused on his hand gripping my waist and the constant pattern of his thumb moving back and forth, instead of my spiraling thoughts. It should have been unsettling how much I had started to lean on his touch to ground me, but for the time being I couldn't find it in myself to care.

Neither of us spoke as we rode through the forests, back towards the inn where we had stayed the night before. My head swam as I turned over every bit of information Hecate had revealed to us. None of what she said made sense. We came seeking answers and I left feeling more defeated than before.

She had made it sound simple, there were only two paths. One would lead to the future I dreamed about. The other would leave my people in ruins. I wanted the path of the light, but how did I make sure I followed that path?

And the book. That Goddess-forsaken book. How was I

supposed to forget about the book when it was the only thing keeping me from an arranged marriage and the Blood Court from bringing war to my doorstep? War would lead down the path of darkness, wouldn't it? I needed to find a solution, *we* needed to find a solution. This was no longer only about me, it concerned Luka too. The future depended on the two of us, that much was clear.

When we arrived back at the inn we settled into our room, each of us bathing, wiping the day from our skin.

When Luka reentered the room after bathing he found me scribbling furiously on some blank pieces of parchment I had found in a drawer.

"What are you writing?" he asked as he sat on the edge of the desk.

"I'm writing everything Hecate said, so we don't forget."

"Good idea." He brushed his hand through his damp hair, picking up the paper with his other. Strands of damp hair stuck to his forehead, drops of water dripped down his face, over his sculpted jaw and down his neck. Luka looked up from the paper, a smirk playing on his lips as he found me staring at him.

I waved my hand and pulled the moisture from his hair and directed it back to the bathing chamber. Luka only smiled. "Thank you."

I dismissed him and moved back to my writing. "What do you think she meant by all this?" I doubted Luka had any more insight than I did, but maybe I was thinking too hard.

His smile faltered as he continued to run his hands through his now-dry hair, causing it to stick up in every direction in a way that should not have been as attractive as it was.

"Honestly, I don't know. I don't love riddles and prophecies and all that."

"Me either," I mumbled under my breath.

"But I do know one thing for sure."

I looked up to find him staring at me. His blue gaze threatened to burn a hole straight through me.

"You're stuck with me, Lennox Adair, whether you like it or not."

"What do you mean?" My voice came out an octave higher than normal.

"The only thing Hecate said that made sense was that we needed to stay together. All of the mention of the King and Queen of Blood and Stardust"—he gestured between the two of us—"that's us Lennox."

"You don't know that for sure." The lie slipped off my tongue easily. I wasn't ready to confront my future with Luka just yet. Whatever that might look like.

"Okay fine, I'll give you that. But she said the future depends on the two of us, and the decisions we make together. The hope of the future rests in our hands. Us. Together." His eyes didn't leave mine as he continued, "So even when I finally go back to the Blood Court, you will not be rid of me. We are friends for life now, Lennox." I let a laugh slip past my lips.

"You sure do have a way of seeing the bright side of things don't you, Bloodsucker."

Luka put his hand over his chest dramatically.

"Are you saying being friends forever is the bright side?" He beamed at me.

The laugh that slipped out this time was real as was the smile on my face.

I rolled my eyes. "It sure looks that way doesn't it."

Luka's face grew serious, he took my hand in his, linking our fingers together and placing our hands over his heart. "We're in this together Lennox, you and me—until the stars turn to dust."

My heart warmed at his use of mine and Kara's words, of my family's words. I liked the way they sounded coming from him.

"You and me, Luka. Until the stars turn to dust."

We stayed that way, our hands pressed together staring at one another, neither of us ready to break this moment. What he said was true. There were a lot worse things out there than having to work with Luka for the foreseeable future. A lot darker fates than having Luka in my life, as a friend or an ally, or—

A horse whinnied in the distance snapping me back to the present. I slid my hand out from underneath Luka's and turned back to the desk, my hand catching on its sharp edge.

"Fuck," I muttered as blood pooled instantly in my palm, a few drops splashing to the floor. I squeezed my hand into a fist to stifle the bleeding. I looked up and found Luka's hands squeezing the edge of the desk, his knuckles turning white from the pressure. His eyes were wide, the black of his eyes taking over the blue. Flecks of gold magic swirled in the black pits. His nostrils flared as he stared at my injured hand, his body tense.

"Luka? Are you okay?" I reached towards him only for him to take two steps back, moving out of my reach.

"Don't touch me," he snarled.

I flinched at his tone, recoiling as he turned his back to me and stalked towards the window. His hand fisted on the wood of the window frame, it groaned under the strain.

I stood there, unable to move as he faced out the window, breathing deeply, the muscles in his back contracting as they strained against the fabric of his shirt. What was going on with him? I had never seen Luka act this way, especially towards me. Did I do something wrong?

Finally his breathing slowed.

"I'm sorry," he ground out. "It just—it's been awhile since I've fed and—" He took a deep breath. "Your blood—"

My stomach dropped. I didn't know much about vampires, but I knew enough to know if a little bit of my blood was causing this reaction out of him I could assume Luka was nearing blood lust. I swallowed. "How long has it been since you've fed?"

He scrubbed a hand over his face. "I fed the morning we left, I knew it would be a stretch to make it until we returned, but being injured by the Wampus Cat this morning didn't help anything."

I flickered through what I knew about blood lust. It was said if vampires went too long without blood they would lose control and feed without abandon. They would crave blood so badly they would go to any lengths to take it, even killing. They had no idea what had come over them until it passed, all self-control overtaken by their need for blood.

I shivered at the thought of that happening to Luka. I know he wouldn't hurt me intentionally, but would he be able to stop himself if he was in blood lust? I didn't know enough about it to know for sure and I didn't want to find out. This was the side of vampires I had grown up hearing about—that I had grown up fearing. But here with Luka, there was only a small part of me that was scared. The larger part of me was concerned for him.

"How much longer can you go before you need to feed?"

He took a deep breath. "I don't want to put you, or anyone else at risk. I'll go downstairs and find someone to feed from later," he grit out.

He finally turned and faced me again, but kept his distance, remaining perched against the window. "I've got it under control now, the scent of your blood unnerved me."

I stared at him, unsure what more I could offer him right now.

His voice softened. "I would never hurt you, Lennox."

"I know." The words slipped from my lips. "I know you won't hurt me, Luka," I repeated.

His shoulders relaxed as he shrank back against the window frame. I took in the male in front of me. The male who had done so much to help me for little to nothing in return. I could do this for him. I could help him.

"Feed from me." The words were out of my mouth before I could stop them.

Luka's head shot up, his mouth falling open, but he didn't say anything. He stared at me, eyes wide, like he wasn't sure he heard me right. I moved until I was in front of him, and I placed my uninjured hand on his cheek, forcing him to look at me.

"Feed from me, Luka." I brushed my fingers over his jaw. It was now dusted in a thick layer of stubble after all of our travel.

"You don't understand what you're asking," he said as he removed my hand from his face and I tried not to flinch from the sting of his rejection as he brushed past me.

I spoke through the lump in my throat. "I do. You need to feed or you will continue to weaken. So, feed from me."

He let out a frustrated breath as he paced the room, running his hands through his hair. "Why would you offer to do this? You hate vampires. You said you'd never trust a vampire. You said you'd never let me, or any other vampire feed from you. What changed?"

"You . . . you changed. I mean, you changed me." I sighed —unsure how to explain all of the thoughts and feelings jumbled around in me. I wanted to help Luka because I cared about him. He had charmed his way into my life without me even noticing. So why would I let him suffer when I could easily help him?

"Despite how hard I've tried not to, I care about you. And I want to help you with this. Let me help you Luka."

He stopped pacing as I moved towards him, taking his hands in mine, unclenching his fists and intertwining our fingers.

"If we do this, there are a couple of things you need to understand."

My heart raced.

"First, you need to understand that it will hurt, but only for a few seconds, then you might start to feel—" he hesitated.

"Feel what?"

"Feel . . . aroused."

My eyes widened at his admission.

"It is a normal reaction to being fed from when feeding is consensual."

I couldn't help myself as a laugh slipped from my lips as I said, "There are worse things than being aroused by you, Luka."

His eyes darkened as tension radiated from his body, the force of it causing my magic to stir to my fingertips. He closed his eyes and took a deep breath before he continued.

"You need to promise me you will stop me, that you will not let me take too much."

I nodded. "Okay, permission to knee you in the groin if you won't stop drinking my blood. Got it."

"I'm serious, Lennox."

"So am I. Do you think I wouldn't take advantage of hitting you where it hurts?"

He shook his head. "Such a vicious creature."

I smirked. "Now c'mon, Bloodsucker, show me you can live up to the name."

I moved my hair to the side and bared my neck to him. His nostrils flared at the sight. I knew I could have offered him my wrist, or any other less intimate body part instead, but he'd scraped his fangs along the skin of my neck so many times I'd be lying if I wasn't curious to see what his bite would feel like there.

He leaned in, wrapping an arm around my waist and pulling my body flush to his, causing the air to whoosh out of my lungs.

"Are you sure?" His breath was warm on my skin as his nose brushed against my neck in a delicate motion. I placed my hand on the hard planes of his torso to steady myself as he pressed me against the desk.

"Yes, I'm sure." My voice was nothing more than a whisper against his cheek. The light graze of his fangs sent goosebumps scattering across my skin as his mouth traveled down the expanse of my neck. But still, he didn't bite. The anticipation made my entire body stand on alert.

"I trust you, Luka."

He struck.

Those three words snapped the remaining tether of his restraint. His hand gripped the back of my neck as his fangs pierced the skin of my neck. Hot, burning pain raced through my body. I let out a cry of pain as he took the first pull of my blood, but as quickly as the pain came, it left. By the third swallow of my blood, the pain was replaced by hot and burning desire.

I tugged Luka closer, fisting my hand in his shirt and the other in his hair—the strands soft between my fingers—like I had imagined. My hand in his hair urged him forward in silent encouragement as he drank. His grip on the back of my neck tightened as did the hand on the small of my back. He continued to drink from my neck, and each pull stoked the embers of desire burning hot inside me. I moaned at the feel of him against me and the effects of his bite. Desire pooled low in my stomach—between my thighs.

Our bodies were flush against each other, heat burned everywhere we were connected. My nipples pebbled as they scraped against his firm chest through the barrier of our clothes. But I wanted more. *I needed more.* I needed him. I ground myself against him, wrapping one leg around his to press myself closer. The hand on my back gripped me tighter in response, his hand on my neck moving to wrap in my hair, pulling my neck back farther as he continued to drink. I could feel him growing hard between us as I ground against him again, this time eliciting a groan from Luka, the sound vibrating against my heated skin and drawing a moan from my own lips.

I was the moth and he was the flame. I was ready to burn for him.

Too quickly Luka pulled away from my neck. I gasped as he licked the remaining drops of blood on my neck, shivering as the pad of his tongue lapped against my skin. I wondered what his tongue would feel like in other places.

He placed a kiss to the bite before pressing his forehead to mine. Our pants were the only sounds as we stared at one another. Desire still a burning flame inside me.

Luka swallowed, his breaths heavy. "How do you feel?"

How did I feel? The feeling from his bite was intoxicating. My entire body ached to be touched by him. "I feel—" My chest rose and fell. "I feel . . . fine." I licked my lips, Luka tracked the movement. "I feel . . . hot." *Unsatisfied.*

"Lennox—"

I used the hand still wrapped in his hair to pull him closer, urging him to continue—to finish what we had started. My other hand slipped beneath the bottom of his shirt. I reveled in the feeling of his hard flesh against the palm of my hands as I explored what remained hidden beneath his shirt.

"We can't." He gripped my wrists and took a step back. Letting my hands fall at my sides as he released them. I immediately missed the warmth of his body against mine.

"Why not?" I tried not to let the sting of rejection float to the surface as I took a step toward him and he took another step back.

"You're just feeling the effects of the blood, this will pass."

I huffed a breath. "I don't care if it's the effects of the blood or not. I want you, Luka."

I don't know what had come over me. Maybe it was the effects of the blood, or maybe I was finally ready to explore what had been stirring between Luka and I. But what I did know was I wanted Luka. I had never been more sure than I was at this moment.

"Touch me please, and let me touch you," I begged.

Luka looked away from me as his face pinched, his hands balling into fists at his sides.

"You have no idea how much I've wanted to hear those words from your lips."

My stomach dipped as he invaded my space once again. He leaned forward, his hot breath on my skin sending shivers skittering down my spine.

"But Lennox, when I finally fuck you, I want to know for sure you want me, not because my bite had its desired effect."

My body trembled at his words. He placed a ghost of a kiss

on my lips before pulling away. My heart shrank as he moved further and further away from me.

I needed more. I wanted more. I wanted *him*. But he didn't give me a chance to respond before he turned and left the room. Leaving me hot, bothered, rejected, and so fucking confused.

☾

Luka returned a while later, food in hand. There was no table in the room besides the small desk so we ate on the bed. Neither of us said anything while we ate, I avoided looking at him as shame over my actions started to work their way to the surface. I had practically thrown myself at him and he rejected me. Well, maybe not wholly rejected me.

Lennox, when I finally fuck you I want to know for sure you want me, not because my bite had its desired effect on you.

When I finally fuck you.

Every time my thoughts spiraled towards embarrassment I remembered those words.

When I finally fuck you.

Did that mean he had thought about fucking me? The tips of my ears turned pink at the thought. Heat pooled at my center.

"I'm sorry about earlier." Luka's voice brought me back from my rampant thoughts.

"There's nothing to be sorry about." My stomach knotted at the clear guilt and regret written in his features.

"Yes, there is. I shouldn't have fed from you."

I gritted my teeth. "Luka, I made that choice and I don't regret it." I moved until I was standing in front of him where he leaned against the desk. "You didn't force me to do anything I didn't want to do." I pressed a finger into his chest. "Now stop moping."

He stared at me. Mouth opening and shutting several times before closing again.

"For fucks sake, Luka. Make up your Stars damned mind. I can't take this anymore."

I turned and started gathering the items I needed to get ready for bed. I was so focused on trying to ignore him I didn't hear him approach. I didn't know he was near me until he grabbed my arm and turned me toward him. The breath whooshed from my chest at the sudden contact as he pulled me to him.

"Lennox, you have no idea how much it means to me, that you trusted me enough to let me feed from you." He dropped his hand from my arm, taking a step back as he ran his fingers through his hair. "Fuck, Lennox, you are so frustrating. I'm trying to be a good male here and you're making it fucking hard."

My chest was heaving as I closed the gap between us, letting my hands roam over his chest. My fingers traced the edges of the tattoos I so badly wanted to explore.

"What if I don't want you to be a good male right now?"

Desire sparked in his gaze. It seared clear through me, straight to my core.

"Lennox—" He stopped, tearing his gaze from mine and looking at the floor.

I schooled my features, tamping down my emotions so he couldn't see the hurt in my eyes. I removed my hands from his body, took a step back, and squared my shoulders.

"Let me know if you ever make up your mind, Luka."

I gathered the rest of my things and stormed off to the bathroom, slamming the door harder than I needed to.

☪

Once I was alone I created a barrier of air around me to block out any sounds before I let out a frustrated scream as I gripped the edge of the sink. Why did he have to be so Stars damned frustrating? Had I been reading this all wrong? Was it all in my head? I ran through my interactions with Luka. There were many that left me feeling wanted and desired by him. But maybe it was all an act. I wanted to be in control of this situation, and I thought I was. But he had all the power and it was driving me insane. I hated myself for letting him have this effect on me.

On top of everything, I had all of this desire built up inside me. Maybe that was why I kept offering myself to Luka. I needed something to quench the burning desire inside me. I debated taking care of it myself, but Luka would smell it on me the moment I reentered the bedchamber. The last thing I wanted was for him to know he had driven me to take care of myself. So I continued getting ready for bed as I stewed. By the time I slipped my silk nightgown on I had developed a plan.

I entered the bedchamber to find Luka sitting on the edge of the bed. I refused to cower under his gaze as his eyes roamed over every inch of my body. I smirked as he quickly stood and made his way to the bathing chamber.

I slipped beneath the covers and a few minutes later Luka crawled in next to me, curling beside me. It was comforting to know even after our arguments and the events of today he was still willing to cuddle next to me so I could sleep a dreamless sleep. I relished the way his strong back felt against me. How protected I felt with his arm banded around my waist. I breathed in the fresh scent of him.

After Luka got comfortable I made a point of squirming into him. Wiggling my ass against his front. He banded his arm around me tighter in an attempt to stop me, but I continued my wiggling.

"Lennox." Luka's voice was rough.

"Hmmm?" was the only response I gave as I continued to grind against him.

"What are you doing?"

"Just trying to get comfortable," I said as innocently as possible.

"You need to stop."

I did the opposite as I ground my ass against his length again and again, which was growing harder as my body continued to move against his.

"Lennox," he warned, "if you don't stop, I'm going to lose my restraint." His palm was flat against my stomach now as he tried to hold me still, but it did nothing to stop my movements.

"Would that be such a bad thing?"

"*Lennox*," he all but growled, the sound sending a shiver down my spine. I smiled as I ground into him again, feeling how hard he was behind me.

"Fine," I sighed, content with the results of my actions. "Goodnight, Luka."

The space between my thighs pulsed, but knowing how hard Luka was behind me, how hard *I* had made him, would have to be satisfaction enough for tonight.

He nipped at my ear. "You devious creature." His hand skated up my thigh, toying with the hem of my nightgown. I stopped his hand before he could go further, placing it on my stomach instead, patting my hand placatingly over his.

"Goodnight, Luka."

He sighed into my hair and shifted, placing a soft kiss on my temple, before laying back. "Goodnight Lennox."

44

LUKA

I fed from Lennox Adair last night.

The memory of her hands roaming over my body as I drank from her throat was the first thought that crossed my mind when I woke up with her tangled around me this morning. It was that same thought that kept running through my mind as I slipped out of the room before she woke. The feel of her body arching against mine, the sounds of her moans—*fuck*. I was completely and utterly fucked.

The High Queen of Lethenia let a vampire feed from her, let *me* feed from her.

I had massively fucked up yesterday in more than one way. Lennox letting me feed from had left me rattled. She had sworn time and time again she would never let a vampire feed from her. Yet, she willingly bore her neck to me. And Goddess above did she taste incredible.

Her blood.

Holy Stars.

I had never tasted blood as powerful and addictive as hers. It took everything in me not to drain every drop of blood from her body. It took even more will not to bend her over the desk and fuck her until she was screaming my name.

And she would have let me.

I should have taken the opportunity when she was pushing her ass against me last night. *Fuck*, if she would have ground her ass against me one more time I would have sank into her right then and there. She was purposely teasing me and it worked like a fucking charm. I fell asleep next to her with a rock-hard cock when I could have been fucking Lennox until she was hoarse.

The desire Lennox felt towards me last night was clear. And I wanted nothing more than to give into her, but I couldn't help but wonder how much of it was her, and how much of it was the effects of my bite. But the hurt that flashed across her features when I rejected her . . . maybe her feelings were her own after all. Tension had been building between us for months now, but I figured it was all on my end—that any signs she gave me were a result of her body's reaction to my provoking her, not actual feelings. But maybe I was wrong.

Not only did Lennox admit she cares about me, but despite all odds she trusts me.

Lennox Adair trusts me.

That's what I've wanted all these months. But now that I have it, I don't know what to do with it. Because the truth is I want more than her trust. It's not enough. I thought it would be, but it's not. I want more of her. I *needed* more. I want to collect all of the pieces of her, even the ones she thinks are too much for others. The pieces she thinks are too broken and damaged to let anyone near. I want them all. I want every shard of her until I've collected them all in a beautiful mosaic.

☾

Lennox was awake when I returned, already dressed in her leathers and sitting on the bed. She looked up from her book when I opened the door, a small smile gracing her face.

The sight of her smile made me stop dead in my tracks. I don't know what I expected from Lennox this morning. A denial? Anger towards what we did last night? But a smile? A smile was not what I expected.

"Good morning." Her words snapped me out of my haze.

"Good morning." I made my way towards her on the bed, holding up the coffee and pastry I held in my hands. "I brought you some breakfast."

"Thank you," she said, taking them from me. I couldn't take my eyes off her as she brought the steaming cup to her face and inhaled the scent. She moaned and my cock twitched in response.

Astria's tits, I was fucked.

"It's been ages since I've had a cup of coffee. Thank you." She took a sip of the steaming liquid, her tongue running over her full bottom lip to catch a spare drop.

"You're welcome," I said gruffly, shifting in my seat.

She raised a brow.

"I'm going to wash up and then we should head out," I stammered as I headed towards the bathing chamber, not giving her a chance to respond before I slammed the door. What in the fuck was happening to me? I felt like a teenager swooning over a crush. I scrubbed my hands over my face. I needed to get it together before I fucked things up even more than I already had.

Whatever this was between Lennox and me . . . I wanted it. I wanted *her*.

☾

My hand rested gently on Lennox's hip as we rode, drawing idle circles over her leathers. It took every ounce of restraint not to dip my fingers lower and see how she might react. The effects of my feeding from her were long gone. Would she let me tease her or would she brush my hand away?

My fingers moved lower, dancing along her inner thigh. Her

heartbeat quickened, but she didn't stop me. I kept brushing my fingers on her thigh, moving lower with every stroke as I skated my nose along the column of her neck. She leaned back into me, tilting her neck to give me better access. My fingers drifted closer to her center with every brush of my fingers, her legs widening in response.

I brushed my lips over her neck before letting my fangs scrape over the same spot where they had pierced her flesh hours ago. Her responding shiver sent blood rushing to my cock.

She leaned back further, resting her head against my neck.

"You drive me crazy," I whispered into her ear before placing a kiss below it as I brushed a knuckle over her center. Her grip on my thigh turned lethal, her fingernails digging into my leathers.

"Luka—"

Goddess I loved the sound of my name on her lips. I nipped at her ear as my fingers danced over her center. Even through her leathers, I could feel how much she was enjoying this.

"You want this don't you?" I asked as I placed a kiss on her collarbone.

Her body went tense as she sat up in the saddle. I stilled my hand and removed my lips from her neck. "Lennox?"

She brought Odin to a halt before climbing from the horse and taking off into the forest. Fuck, *I'd gone too far.*

"Lennox," I called after her. "Lennox, what are you doing?" I jumped from Odin and took off after her. "Lennox." I grabbed for her, trying to stop her, only for her to whirl on me, wrenching her arm from my grasp as my fingers brushed the sleeve of her leathers.

"Don't touch me."

Her eyes were blazing. Emotions swirling in their green depths.

"Lennox—"

"Whatever you have to say I don't want to hear it."

I watched silently as she paced back and forth, I could see her frustration rising with every step. I could *feel* it.

"I don't understand what your game is. Last night I all but threw myself at you and you rejected me. And now, today you want me? Now you want to touch me? Goddess, Luka! I need you to make up your fucking mind!"

"I—"

How could I explain to her what I didn't even know how to explain to myself? That ever since the day I laid eyes on her, I've felt a pull towards her. Like there was an invisible string tying me to Lennox Adair, but I've been too afraid to act on it. Afraid I'd scare her away if I did. Up until this morning I wasn't even sure if she felt anything toward me.

She threw up her hands in frustration and walked away. Was I going to let her walk away from me again? In a blur I was in front of her, she cursed as she bumped into my chest. She made a move to push me away, but before she could I gripped her neck and pressed my lips to hers.

Lennox hesitated for a moment before she kissed me back, but when she did, fire sparked between us. Her hands fisted my hair, pulling me closer as her lips sought out mine. I put all of my unsaid words, all of my pent-up emotions into kissing her. All of the tension building between us erupted as I devoured her mouth.

I gripped her hips, her legs wrapping around my waist as my hands found her ass and squeezed, causing her to moan against my lips. Stars above, she fit perfectly in my hands.

I moved us until her back hit a tree. Her hands fisted tighter in my hair as my tongue teased the seam of her lips, begging for entrance and she opened for me, a moan leaving her lips as the kiss deepened. One of her hands moved between us, finding its way under my leathers, her hand exploring the bare skin beneath—her nails scraping against my skin. Goddess I wanted this. I wanted more. I wanted every part of her.

But I removed my lips from hers before we could go any further. Lennox's brows furrowed, a protest posed on her lips, but I brushed a thumb over her swollen bottom lip before she could say it.

"When you said you trusted me last night—it felt like it unlocked something inside me that's been building since the moment I laid my eyes on you."

She swallowed. "What did it unlock?"

"Feelings—feelings for you I've been trying to deny."

She sucked in a breath.

"But I'm fucking tired of denying myself of you, Lennox. The way you make me feel is intoxicating. You have no idea what effect you have on me. Every argument, every scowl, every smile, every laugh that leaves your perfect lips stokes the fire burning inside me. The fire burning for *you*." I kissed up the column of her neck, speaking into her skin.

"And now. Now, Lennox, you make me feel like if I don't touch you . . . if I can't have you, I'll burn."

Lennox moaned as I tugged at her ear with my teeth.

"Luka." My name was a plea on her lips. "Kiss me."

I took her lips in mine again. She tasted so fucking good. Blood rushed to my cock as she ground against me. I groaned as she took my bottom lip between her lips and tugged.

"Violent creature," I mumbled into her mouth as she smiled against my lips.

"Tell me you're mine."

Her hand drifted under my leathers again.

"Tell me I can have you." I moved to her neck again. Licking and sucking at her skin as she writhed in my arms. Her back arching against the tree at her back. "Tell me I can have every piece of you."

Lennox stiffened, her hand underneath my leathers freezing.

"I can't," she breathed. My hands on her body stilled.

"What do you mean you can't?" I pulled back so I could see

her face, the desire in her eyes was waning, sadness creeping in instead, causing a pit to form in my stomach.

"You can't have me, Luka. I don't have anything to give."

Time slowed as she unwrapped her legs from my waist. Looking at the ground as she wrapped her arms around herself.

Her chin trembled. "Maybe in a different life, where I wasn't a broken shell of the person I used to be, I could give myself to you, but this isn't a different life. My reality is when my parents and Nol were killed it shattered my heart into a million pieces and I'll never be the person I was before that moment. I don't have a heart to give you, Luka." Her voice broke, but she continued, "My heart lies in shards, Luka."

I took her face in my hands, forcing her to look at me.

I instantly regretted it.

The sadness lining her eyes broke something deep inside me.

"The biggest pieces that survived the wreckage belong to my sister and my people—to my duty as High Queen. I've already given more to you than I have to give. There isn't anything else left. Everything else is purely ash and Stardust," she admitted and I watched as she sunk into herself. The sight felt like a dagger to the heart.

Lennox steeled herself—squaring her shoulders and blinking back the wetness in her eyes "I can give you my body, but that's all I can offer you."

Her words felt like pellets of ice hitting my skin as I absorbed them. Every word, another slice to my skin. I knew she wasn't trying to hurt me, but by trying to prevent the hurt she was making it worse. I knew I should say something, offer some comforting words about how it was okay and I understood. But I couldn't say that and I knew Lennox wouldn't want my bullshit right now. I understood what she was saying, but that didn't mean I agreed with it.

I took her hands in mine, intertwining our fingers. I needed to touch her, even if for one more moment. "This—this friendship between us. It's already more than I can give." She continued, "I can be your friend Luka, but I don't think I'll ever be able to give you more . . . even if I want to."

Her last words were barely a whisper, like she didn't want me to hear them.

"I wish you could see how I see you, Lennox." I brushed a strand of hair out of her face. "I know you think you're broken, beyond repair, but I don't think that. I think by admitting how broken you are you've started to heal. I didn't know you *Before*, but I know you now. I like you for who you are *now*, not the person you used to be Lennox. I care about you. If we're going to do this I need us both to be all in. I care about you too much for this to be just sex between us." I leaned my forehead against hers. "I will still be here for you. I'm not going anywhere. I'm going to be right alongside you, helping you repair what you believe is broken. I'll wait. For you, I'll wait. However long it takes."

She shook her head. "Luka—"

"No, you don't get to argue." I pulled her to me and she wrapped her arms around me without hesitation. "I'll take whatever scraps of you I can get, Lennox. Even if it's only being your friend right now."

She exhaled and I held her tighter before letting her go. Tears pooled in her eyes, but she wiped them away quickly. I wanted nothing more than to kiss those tears away as they fell.

She closed her eyes as I placed a kiss on her forehead instead. I took a step back, putting space between us. I already hated it, but I meant what I said, I'd take any scraps of her I could get. Even if being her friend got a lot fucking harder.

I held out my hand to her, one last time, I wanted to touch her one last time before we left this clearing and we became just friends. She eyed it for a moment before lacing her fingers with mine.

Lennox may believe she had nothing to give to me, but she was wrong. Without even realizing it she had already given me so much. Lennox Adair wasn't just any female. She was extraordinary.

She was worth waiting for.

I'd make her see that someday, that even if she was broken, it didn't make her unlovable, she didn't need to be fixed. Someday she'd realize every jagged piece of her was what made her irrevocably Lennox and that's what made her so alluring.

45

LUKA

We mounted Odin in silence. I hesitated as I took·my spot behind Lennox, my hand hovering over her hip. Lennox noticed my hesitation, she took my hand in hers and placed it on her hip, *where it belonged.* I thought selfishly.

We would move forward from this. It would just take some readjusting.

I drew circles with my fingers on her leg, her hip, her arm, as we rode. I focused on the motion of my fingers to keep my mind from drifting into more dangerous territory. Like where my hand had been earlier today.

"Well, well, if it isn't the High Queen and the vampire prince. What are you two doing out here together I wonder?"

Lennox and I both froze at the voices ringing out through the forest.

Fuck, fuck, *fuck.* The trees rustled before two figures appeared in a blur in front of us.

Vampires.

"Aren't you going to answer us, Your Majesties?" the taller of the two vampires asked. His black hair fell in a straight sheet past his shoulders. My grip on Lennox's hip tightened.

"I've been working in the Star Court with the High Queen, that is not a secret," I said carefully.

Lennox and I dismounted, approaching the vampires with caution. I wanted to step in front of Lennox, to protect her from these two males. But I knew she'd gut me if I tried to hide her behind me. Instead, I kept close to her, the backs of our hands brushing against one other as we stood and faced the vampires.

"I suppose you're right." The black-haired vampire glanced at his companion. "But that doesn't explain what you're doing out here in the Mystic Court, does it?"

"Care to enlighten us?" his companion asked, he was several feet shorter than his friend. His auburn hair gleamed in the sunlight as a wild grin spread on his face.

"We don't answer to you," Lennox said, her tone offering no room for debate. I glanced at her, standing tall beside me. Her hand rested on the pommel of her sword, but she had yet to unsheathe it. She had slipped back on her queen mask—the vulnerable Lennox now firmly tucked away.

"I suppose you're right."

A look passed between the two vampires causing uneasiness to settle in my stomach. Whatever they were doing out here, it wasn't good. They questioned why *we* were here, but why were *they* here? My grandfather didn't have any forces stationed in the Mystic Court, or the Court of Embers. There was no reason for them to be traveling this far south. Unless they didn't answer to a court, and they answered to the Vanir instead.

"What about you, *my prince*?" The tall one turned to me, glaring at me with his black angular eyes. "Do you answer to *her*?" He all but spat the word as he glared at Lennox. "Or do you answer to your people?" The question felt like a trap. Whatever answer I gave them they'd spin it in their favor.

"I answer to both." The dark-haired vampire sneered as the words left my mouth. The two of them prowling closer—the destain on their faces evident.

"So, you will protect a false queen over your own kind?"

I looked at Lennox out of the corner of my eye as the vampires moved in closer. There was no doubt in my mind now, they were part of the Vanir and they didn't intend for Lennox to leave these woods alive. Lennox squared her shoulders, tilting her chin up.

"I am no false queen. I could have you killed for saying as much."

The black-haired vampire opened his mouth to speak, only to be interrupted by his companion.

"Ahhh, I see, Your Highness." The red-haired male sneered. "You fucked her, that's why you're trying to protect her. I can smell you on her."

Lennox stiffened beside me, but neither of us said a word.

"How easy our prince switches sides to get his cock wet."

Lennox's grip on her sword tightened. "Don't you dare speak to your prince like that unless you want me to rip your throat out." The threat was clear in her voice, but the redhead ignored her, turning to me again as his partner spoke.

"Well, tell me this, was she at least a good fuck? I've wondered what royal cunt was like. Maybe I should have a go when you're done with her."

I struck before the last word left his mouth—my fist connecting with his jaw with a sickening crack.

A string of curses left his mouth as he stumbled backward before falling to the ground. I unsheathed my sword and raised it, intent on ending this right here and now. But the vampire was quicker, and the force of the impact reverberated through my body as our swords clashed.

Out of the corner of my eye, I caught Lennox as she fought against the other vampire, the clang of their swords rang out in the forest. I focused my attention back on the vampire in front of me, trusting Lennox could hold her own.

The male stood and charged towards me, and my sword nicked his arm as Lennox let out a cry of pain from behind me. I turned to see her gripping her side. I ran toward her but stumbled as a blade sliced into my leg. It wasn't deep, thanks to my leathers, but enough to elicit a curse from my lips.

I reminded myself Lennox could hold her own, I needed to focus on my own fight in front of me before I could help her, if she needed it. I raised my blade as I turned towards my opponent. The vampire rushed me—our blades met in a clash of steel.

He was sloppy, already losing stamina after a few blows. His defenses were weak—leaving openings for me to strike his undefended side. He hissed as my sword slid across his side, all his attention going to the injury.

I put all the strength I could into my next blow, and he saw my sword coming too late—lifting his sword only enough to avoid it driving into his chest. The vampire stumbled back, falling to the ground at my feet, his sword tumbling out of his hands. I used my earth magic to conjure vines to wrap around his feet, trapping him in place. The vampire tried to break through the vines, but I continued to strengthen them, wrapping them tighter and tighter around his legs. He reached for his fallen sword, but I kicked it out of his reach as my vines slithered their way up his body, trapping his arms to his sides.

I moved behind him and held my sword to his neck. Only then did I let myself look toward Lennox, finding her and the vampire encased in a ring of fire, making escape impossible for the vampire, but blocking my view of her. Panic squeezed my chest like a snake. *What if she was injured?* I quickly pushed the thought from my mind.

She was Lennox Adair. One of the greatest warriors in all of Lethina. She would be fine. I needed to believe she was fine.

I turned my attention back to the vampire under my siege. "Who sent you?" I growled, holding my sword tighter to his neck.

The vampire spit a mouth full of blood at our feet. "Like I'd ever tell you, fucking traitor."

His words churned something vile inside me.

Traitor.

Was that what I was? I was fighting against my own, in favor of a queen from another court.

Lennox was the High Queen, it was our duty to protect her.

Although I was protecting her at the cost of my own people.

Did that make me a traitor?

I shook the thoughts from my head and focused on the task at hand.

I pressed my blade deeper into the skin of his neck, forcing blood to trickle down his ivory skin. "Tell me who sent you," I gritted out.

"Must have been a good fucking cunt if that whore is worth slaughtering your people for, Your Highness." He sneered and my blade slid across his neck before I knew what I was doing. Blood splattered as I let him drop to the ground, the ice-encased vines shattering as he did. He laid on the grass, clutching his injured neck as blood pooled around him—the color already draining from his face.

"Don't you ever speak about your queen like that."

"That whore will never be my queen," he sputtered, blood dripping from his lips as he spoke.

I reached into the vampire's mouth and found his tongue, cleaving it off with my dagger before shoving the lump of muscle back into his mouth, silencing his screams.

"If only you would live to tell your *people* what happens when you speak ill of your queen," I growled. "Since you can no longer speak, there's no use in sparing your life, is there?" I patted his cheek before I reached again for my sword.

"You are a traitor and a coward and you will die that way." I drove my sword into his chest and I watched, chest heaving, as the light left his eyes.

When I finally looked up from the vampire's lifeless eyes, I found Lennox standing in front of me. She stared at me, eyes wide and panting. Blood speckled her cheeks and clothing.

Behind her the other vampire lay in a heap on the ground, his blood dripping from her sword.

"Are you okay?"

She nodded.

"Is he dead?" I asked, nodding toward the other vampire."

She nodded again.

I removed my sword from the male's chest—using his shirt to clean his blood off my blade before sheathing it. I gestured for Lennox to hand me her sword and I cleaned the blood off of it before standing and sheathing it at her side.

I let my hands linger on her as I surveyed her, looking for any injuries she may be hiding. Her gaze slid to the dead vampire behind me.

"You cut off his tongue."

I winced, I had hoped she hadn't witnessed my temper. I don't know what came over me.

"He deserved it. He spoke ill of you."

"So you cut off his tongue?" She raised an eyebrow.

"Yes."

A hint of a smile spread across her lips. "That must make us *really* good friends if you're willing to cut off someone's tongue for speaking ill of me."

I shook my head, pieces of my hair landing across my forehead as I stepped into Lennox's space. Even with blood speckling her hair and face she was still beautiful. She just killed a vampire, but still, those green eyes shone bright. I cupped her jaw with my hand, brushing my thumb across her cheek. My fingers left a trail of blood in their wake.

"You have no idea what I'd do for you, Lennox."

☾

Before we burned the bodies we searched both of the vampires for proof they were part of the Vanir.

We found the marking on both of them.

The auburn-haired vampire had the symbol tattooed on his chest, and the other, on his shoulder. We hoped to find something on them that would give us a clue as to where they were working out of, or how they found us, but we found nothing of use. So we burned the bodies, and mounted Odin again. It had only been a few hours since we left the inn this morning, but it felt like days.

As we rode through the afternoon Lennox kept gazing at me over her shoulder. Every time it looked like she was going to say something and decided against it, instead turning back around and focusing her gaze in front of us. When it started growing dark we stopped and made camp for the night. Once we were settled we shared a bag of nuts and dried fruit as we sat together next to the fire.

"You know, you're not a traitor." Lennox's voice pierced through the silence of the forest.

I stiffened. "You heard that?"

She nodded.

Truthfully, part of me wanted to believe I was a traitor. I had killed one of my own people, more than one. All for Lennox. I had killed my own people, without question, for *her*.

"Luka," Lennox said my name with authority, but there was a softness to it. She placed her hand on my thigh. Her gaze felt like it pierced through my soul. "You are not a traitor. Don't believe a single word he said. They are not true. *They* were the traitors." She continued to stare at me. But I couldn't take it anymore, her sympathy. I didn't want it.

I tore my gaze away from hers.

"They didn't intend for us to leave the forest alive."

"We don't know that for sure," I countered.

"Luka—"

"I struck first. Do you understand that?" Rage burned through my body. "I struck first because what he said about you made me want to kill him. One of my people spoke ill of you and I killed them without a second thought. What kind of male does that make me? It makes me a monster. A traitor."

"Despite what you think Luka, I think it makes you loyal, it makes you trustworthy. It makes you a good male."

"What have I ever done to prove to you I'm a good male?"

She let out an irritated breath. "You chose *me* over those vampires. Have you thought about what that means to me? What it makes *me* think of you? You could have easily fought against me. But you didn't. You fought *for* me, Luka. There was a split second when the vampires first arrived I worried you would turn against me because you're also a vampire. They were your people. But then I remembered you're more than a vampire. You're not a monster. You're *Luka*. I trusted you at that moment, that you would fight alongside me; that you would defend me, protect me. You cut the male's tongue out for fucks sake for what he said about me." She smiled, the kind of Lennox smile that made my heart clench.

She moved so she was sitting in my lap, straddling me, her legs wrapping around my waist. I placed my hands on her hips to steady her. One of her hands moved the hair out of my face, the other rested on my shoulder. With her sitting in front of me like this I had no other option but to look into her eyes as she spoke.

"You are a good male, Luka. Don't you ever dare to think otherwise." Her eyes told me so much about how she was feeling, but right now I couldn't discern anything. Too many emotions were dancing in the emerald pools.

"Those vampires were not your people. They were Vanir who did not see you as their future king, or me as their High Queen. *They* were the traitors. They had no intention of letting you, or me, leave those woods alive." Her fingers traced over the lines of my face, but her eyes never left mine. "I need you to believe me when I tell you, you are a good male, Luka."

I let her words wash over me as I held her tighter to me.

"I don't regret killing that male today," I admitted. "Just like

I don't regret killing the vampire that hurt you in the garden." *Or cutting off the fingers of the other bastard.* "When it comes to you Lennox, I . . . I lose all control. I lose all sense of reason. I want to be a good male for you so fucking badly, but you drive me crazy. Sometimes I wonder if there is anything I wouldn't do for you. I know I would kill anyone who dared to lay a finger on you, or speak any foul word towards you, without hesitation." I ran my thumb over her bottom lip. "I would kill for you, Lennox, so I'm sorry if I don't believe I'm a good male."

Her brows pinched together as she mulled over my words.

Part of me was scared, scared of the things I was willing to do for Lennox. This morning she told me she couldn't give me anything. But *this*, this felt like she was giving me something. What it was, I didn't know, but I was greedy, I wanted more of whatever *this* was.

"If you think protecting me makes you a bad male, so be it." She ran her fingers through my hair before resting her forehead against mine. "I like you just the way you are."

Our lips hovered inches from each other. It would be so easy to close the remaining gap, and claim her lips. My fingers twitched where they rested on her hips. I wanted more of her. I *needed* more of her. I could feel it in her body too, in the way her breath hitched, how her fingers trembled in my hair and on my neck. She wanted this as much as I did.

I swallowed.

Time. I needed to give her more time.

She placed a kiss on the corner of my mouth, her lips lingering on my cheek. "Thank you for protecting me, Luka."

"I thought you didn't need to be protected."

I felt her smirk against my skin. "I don't, but I've come to realize having someone willing to protect you isn't the worst thing in the world."

46

LENNOX

My body relaxed into Luka as the sun set through the trees, casting the forest in hues of yellow and orange. One of Luka's arms was banned around my waist, holding me in place against him. The other rested on my waist, where he drove maddening lines with his thumb across my leathers—the top of his finger dusting the underside of my ribcage. Even through the layers of clothing, his touch set my body aflame. Every maddening path of his thumb sent fire scorching through my veins and heat to my core.

I conjured up the feeling of his lips on mine. How I desperately wanted his mouth on other parts of my body.

"Is my touch distracting, Sweetheart?" Luka's breath was hot in my ear.

"What do you mean?" My voice came out breathy as I arched into his touch, his fingers skating lower. I felt the blush rise to my cheeks and the tips of my ears. It would be easy to let him slide his fingers inside my pants right now. To let him ease the ache that had been forming low in my stomach for days now. *Weeks.* An ache I worried only he would be able to ease.

But I couldn't do that.

Not right now when everything between us was such a mess. He wanted more. He didn't want just sex. He wanted *me*.

And that freaked me the fuck out.

It was true what I told him, I didn't have any more of my heart to give. Slowly, I'd been melding together the jagged remains, but it would never be the same. It would never have the capacity to love like it once did. The shattered rubble of my heart ached at that. I wanted to give into Luka. To let him have me. But he deserved more than fragments of me. He was so good. Better than me in every way, even if he thought he wasn't. He'd killed for me and he would do it again. I knew I was twisted to get butterflies at that thought, but it set my broken heart in a flutter.

I knew he wanted more, but he'd have to settle for being friends.

I'd have to settle with being friends.

We had been walking a dangerous line before I let him feed from me—*kiss me*. We were walking an even thinner line now. Both of us lacked the restraint to keep our hands off each other. Sleeping intertwined together at night, heated touches while we were riding; that's as far as this could go. The tension was palpable between us, a constant buzz surrounding us, but it would fade with time. Right? It had too. We would be okay. As okay as two people who wanted to fuck one another could be. Part of me thought we should do it, try and see if it eased the ache. But deep down I knew it would make it much much worse. We were both too emotionally invested in whatever this was to go down that road and it not end in disaster.

☪

We arrived back at the Mystic Court shortly after sunset, several days later. I had never been so happy to see my sister—this was the longest we had spent apart since we were children. I practically jumped off Odin at the sight of her.

"Len!" she yelled as she ran to greet me. I threw my arms around her the moment she reached me. "I'm glad you're back, I missed you."

"I missed you too."

We let go of one another and I glanced behind me to Luka, where he was reuniting with Declan and Nico before the three of them made their way over to Kara and I.

"Thanks for returning him in one piece," Nico said as he slung his arm around me.

"It wasn't easy, you could have warned me he wounded easily."

Declan looked between the two of us, his gaze far too serious for a reunion. "You were injured?"

Luka waved his hand dismissively. "Just a little scratch from a Wampus Cat, and the Vanir vampire only got one blow in."

Nico rocked back on his heels and howled, his eyes gleaming with delight. "Astria's tits, a Wampus Cat? Tell us everything."

☾

We all sat around the fire eating as Luka and I filled everyone in on what we had encountered. Kara, Luce, and Nico delighted in our stories, while Declan eyed the two of us disapprovingly.

"Damn Seers and their cryptic warnings," Luce mused as she sat back, crossing her arms.

"About that," Luka said as he glanced at me out of the corner of his eye. "I've been thinking about it. What if what Hecate was alluding to is the relationship between Lennox and I."

"I think that was the only clear thing she said," I countered.

Luka shook his head. "No, I mean, maybe this is the solution to all of our problems. Maybe we don't need some deal to present to my grandfather, but we can present our relationship instead. If we can show him, and everyone, that we are a united front . . . this might be your ticket out of an arranged marriage."

I mulled over his words. "You think King Arlo will go for that?"

He shrugged. "It's worth a shot. It's better than anything else we've come up with. I think if we talk up how well we get along, we could convince him. Problem solved."

"I doubt it will be that easy," Declan mused and I was inclined to agree with the harpy.

"I guess we won't know until we try." I sighed.

"You and me, Sweetheart." Luka winked. "We're going to change the world."

☾

"So," Kara said as she sat on the bed beside me back in our cottage. "Sounds like you and Luka got along well on your journey. You both came back in one piece."

I breathed out a laugh. "Can't say I didn't try."

"Oh c'mon, Len, you're telling me you spent almost two weeks together and you still don't like him?" She shoved at my shoulder lightly.

"I didn't say that, it's just . . . it's complicated." I folded my legs underneath me and fiddled with a loose thread on the blanket.

"It's complicated?" Her voice raised an octave. "What do you mean it's complicated?"

I sighed. Goddess. Where do I even start? "Well, he was injured and he needed to feed so I let him feed from me."

"You did what?" Kara's mouth fell open. "Tell me everything, what was it like?"

"You're not upset I let a vampire feed from me?" I thought for sure she would judge me for letting him feed from me.

"Why would I be? It was your choice. Clearly, you knew

Luka needed to feed and you trusted him enough to let him feed from you." The way Kara said it made it sound simple.

"Just because vampires killed our family, Lennox doesn't make Luka a monster too."

"I know, I guess I didn't know how you felt about him."

She shrugged. "He's a good male from what I know of him."

"He is, isn't he." I pulled my bottom lip between my teeth, wondering how much else I should tell Kara.

"There's something else you're not telling me." Kara nudged me again, this time with her foot. "Spit it out."

I shrugged and blew out a breath. "We kissed."

"YOU DID WHAT?" Kara's eyes lit up like the night sky as she grabbed my arms. I couldn't stop the smile from spreading on my face at her reaction. "Tell me *everything*."

So I did.

I told my sister everything, starting with the nightmare and ending with the words the Luka had spoken to me, *tell me I can have you*, and how utterly and hopelessly confused I was.

"Len." Kara took my hands in hers. "I understand the way you feel, you know I understand more than anyone. But you can't go on this way."

I furrowed my brows. "What do you mean?"

"I know you think your heart is too broken for love."

Love, who said anything about love?

"But that's not true. I have never known anyone who loves as deeply and fiercely as you. You're afraid of letting Luka in because you know what it feels like to lose the people you love and you're afraid of letting it happen again."

Her words hit me like a ton of bricks. Overwhelming grief crashing over me like a wave.

Kara took my hands in hers as she continued speaking. "Lennox, I'm begging you, please, don't cut yourself off from love, or happiness, or whatever you might have with Luka, or anyone else in your future because you're afraid of getting hurt."

I opened my mouth but no words came out.

"I know that's a lot to process, I'll let you sit with it." She moved towards the door, but stopped halfway there, turning back to me. "Lennox, I want you to be happy. You know that right?"

I nodded as I blinked back the tears that had started to form in my eyes. I closed my eyes and breathed deeply, trying and failing to stop the tears from falling.

Arms wrapped around me, enveloping me in a hug. I wrapped my arms around Kara and held her close. A sob choked from my throat.

"I love you so much, Len."

There was no stopping the tears now. They fell one after another.

"I love you, too."

I don't know how long Kara sat there and held me while I cried. Eventually, my sobs subsided, but Kara still held me. My little sister was so strong.

I pulled out of her embrace and wiped the remaining tears from my face. "What would I do without you, Kar?"

She took my hand and squeezed it tight. "You'd be the unemotional bitch some people make you out to be."

I laughed, still wiping the tears from my eyes. "I love you so much."

Kara smiled. "Until the stars turn to dust."

☾

Kara offered to stay in my bed with me, but I turned down her offer, needing time alone to process her words. I laid in my bed staring at the nocks in the wood ceiling as I turned over her words in her head. Was the reason I couldn't, or wouldn't let

Luka in because I was scared of getting hurt? Of losing someone I loved again? I thought I couldn't give any more of myself, but maybe I was trying to protect myself from getting hurt again.

No one would ever fill the void in my chest my family left, but maybe letting someone else in would help ease the ache. When I was with Luka I didn't think of them as much. And when I did, it didn't hurt as much. Luka encouraged me to talk about them—to move forward by shining a light on their memories instead of stifling them.

When I was with Luka I found myself focusing on him, on the things I had gained, instead of what I had lost. For once I was looking toward the future and what I might be able to have, instead of a future without the people I loved.

Is that what I wanted? A future with Luka? I had a lot to figure out, but he was at the forefront of my mind.

Finally, I drifted to sleep.

But I awoke before sunrise to a nightmare, the first one in over a week. I reached for Luka beside me only to remember I was alone.

☪

Luce found me as we were loading our horses the next morning, a mischievous glint in her silver eyes. She pulled me aside, placing a necklace in my hands.

"What is this?"

"I've been working on something while you were gone, a way we can communicate with each other."

"Really?" I examined the light purple amethyst stone connected to the delicate chain.

"The stone is enhanced with a spell, to activate it you'll need a drop of your blood on the stone then hold it in your hand and reach out to the person you're trying to contact." She pulled a matching necklace out from underneath her dress. "I'll feel the call through my necklace and will answer the same way. If we want to see one another we will have to place the stone near a mirror or a reflection pool, otherwise we will only hear our voices."

"Sounds simple enough." I ran my thumb over the smooth stone. "How come I haven't heard of magic like this before?"

"Don't ask questions you don't want to know the answer to, Lennox."

My stomach dropped. "I thought your mother told you to stop," I hissed.

"What she doesn't know won't kill her."

"Luciana! Ich—" I stopped not daring to say the words out loud. "*That* kind of magic is dangerous. It has consequences."

She scoffed. "Says who? Some old outdated legend? I've been practicing for years and have never suffered so much as a nosebleed."

I assessed my cousin. When Luciana made up her mind there was no swaying her. If she wanted to practice Ichor Magic, there was nothing I could do to stop her. Witch magic in its purest form doesn't steal magic from the earth, but Ichor Magic on the other hand—it was a forbidden form of magic. It used blood to amplify one's abilities, as well as siphon energy from the earth. All of the witch legends claimed it had consequences if not used in moderation. They just never said what those consequences were.

I gripped Luce's hands in my own, staring into her silver eyes. "Promise me you'll be careful, okay?"

Her gaze softened and she nodded. "I promise."

I smiled and pulled her into a hug. "I'll miss you."

"I'll miss you too. Be safe, Lennox."

47

LENNOX

Eleven days later we arrived back in Alethens.

Home. We were finally home.

The next few days passed in a blur. There was much for me to attend to and catch up on.. I had meeting after meeting with my Royal Council as they filled me in on everything that had occurred while I was gone. There was a never-ending list of duties I needed to attend to, and decisions I needed to make after being gone for over a month. I even took my dinner in my chambers as I worked through meals, and fell asleep late at night—the moment my head hit the pillow.

I had hardly seen my friends and Kara since we arrived back, only in passing conversations and quick waves as I went from meeting to meeting. I hadn't even had time to train. There was so much to do. We hadn't even had a chance to discuss what we were going to do about the Vanir now that we were back in Alethens. They had to have figured out we had killed two of their males by now. I'm sure they were planning their next move. We needed to be prepared for whatever that was.

By the evening of the third day back I had finally caught up on all of the immediate tasks that needed my attention. I flopped onto my bed, exhaustion weighing heavily on my limbs as I took advantage of this first moment to myself in days.

I thought about attempting to sleep, but I was wary of the nightmare that would plague me. After three years of my sleep being plagued by nightmares I wasn't afraid to go to sleep, but those weeks of peaceful sleep in Luka's arms had spoiled me.

As exhausted as I had been the last few days it hadn't stopped the dreams from reappearing. I missed sleeping in Luka's arms. I missed his comforting presence. Which led my thoughts down an even more dangerous path. Not only did I miss sleeping in Luka's arms, I missed Luka.

For weeks we spent the majority of our days together. Coming back to the palace I felt like I hardly saw him. I cared about Luka, more than I wanted to admit to anyone, let alone Luka, or myself. I thought about what Kara had told me, that I was choosing to not let Luka in because I was afraid of losing him, of getting hurt. I had thought about her words the majority of the journey back to Alethens and every spare minute since.

For the first time since my family had been killed, I had let someone in. And it wasn't just Luka. I had let Declan and Nico in too.

But it wasn't Nico and Declan who were sending me pacing around my room. Maybe being afraid was a good excuse before, but now, I wasn't so sure. When did I ever let fear stop me? Was I going to let fear prevent me from letting Luka in? From letting myself be happy for the first time in years? That's what I felt when I was with him, happy. I had felt more joy with him over the past few months than I had over the last two years. I know I would never be the person I was before my family died, but with Luka, I felt like I had gotten some part of her back. I was a different person now, but I could still be happy. And Luka . . . Luka liked the person I was now, every broken part of me.

Everyone else has been dancing around me for the past two years. Not willing to push me for the fear I might fully break.

But not Luka. Luka challenged me, he pushed me, he infuriated me, but it has made me a better person. It's made me stronger. Was I willing to give all of that up because I was afraid of getting hurt?

I am Lennox Adair, High Queen of Lethenia. I have been through fucking hell. I lost three of the most important people in my life, but I survived. I was thrust into a role I never imagined I'd have, but I'm good at it. I am a good queen. I lost so much, but I still have my wonderful sister.

I am strong.

I have endured.

I am a survivor.

When have I ever let fear dictate my actions?

Never.

And I was not about to start now. I felt the embers of the person I used to be rising inside me. Warming my spirit, urging me forward.

I needed to find Luka.

I wanted to see him. It was late. He was most likely already sleeping. Part of me wanted to slip into bed with him. I missed his warmth, his strong arm around me, pulling me close. I missed the fresh scent of him, the feel of his skin against mine. I paced back and forth across my room.

I should go and see if he's up.

I made my way to the door, convincing myself I needed to see him or I'd never sleep. I twisted the door handle as a knock sounded on the door. I pulled open the door to find Luka standing at the threshold.

"Hi," he said sheepishly. His eyes flicked to his still-raised fist before letting it fall to his side.

"Hi," I breathed. "I was coming to look for you," I told him. Part of me cringed at the admission, but the other part of me wanted him to know. I wanted him to know I was looking for him.

His eyes sparkled. "You were? Miss me already?"

"Clearly not as much as you missed me."

Luka laughed as he leaned against the door frame. Why was that attractive? Never in my life, before this moment, had I thought a male leaning on a door frame was sexy, but the way Luka was doing it . . . it made my mind wander into a dangerous place.

"I was wondering if you'd like to go for a walk."

I nodded. "Sure."

I followed Luka into the hallway, the door closing with a click behind us. I was keenly aware of how close he was as we made our way down the hallway.

My fingers itched to intertwine with his own as our hands brushed against one another as we walked. I balled my hands into fists as I peered at Luka out of the corner of my eye. His hair was wild and unruly—I loved it when it was like that. He hadn't shaved since we'd been back either, his dark stubble still shadowing his strong jaw, making him look even more rugged and unhinged.

"Were you truly coming to find me? Or were you just saying that to make me feel better about seeking you out?" he asked as he raked his hand through his hair as we continued walking.

"I was. I was debating crawling into bed with you so I could get a good night's sleep," I admitted as we exited the place and entered the garden.

"The nightmares came back?"

I nodded, gulping in the cool night air.

"So you wanted to get some decent sleep. That's why you wanted to see me."

I swallowed, my throat suddenly dry. "And I missed you."

Luka stopped dead in his tracks. "You missed me," he said the words slowly, like he was trying to understand what I meant. I huffed an irritated breath as I turned to face him.

"Yes, I missed you. What more do you need me to say?" I crossed my arms over my chest.

Should I have kept my thought to myself?

Maybe he'd lost interest in me since we'd been back.

Maybe he'd found another to set his attention on.

The thought alone made my stomach roll.

"Nothing," Luka said as he stepped into my space. He was so close now I had to tip my head to meet his gaze. His blue eyes were staring intently into mine as he brushed a stray hair out of my face and tucked it behind my ear. I shivered at the ghost of his fingers lingering on my face.

"I missed you too, Lennox."

My breath caught in my throat as I continued to meet his gaze. *He missed me too.*

But what if he was only saying that because I had? I tore my gaze away from his and I stared at my feet instead—his hand fell from my face as I did. I wrung my shaking hands as I went over my options. If I didn't tell him how I felt right now, I'd regret it. That much I knew. I didn't care if he didn't feel the same. I need to get it out.

I've never been good at expressing my feelings, but I guess I need to start somewhere. What better place to start than jumping off the deep end and confessing my feelings to a vampire who's been a pain in my ass for months now?

48

LUKA

"Lennox, talk to me," I whispered, taking her chin in my hand and tilting her face to meet my own. I could see the cogs turning in her brain, but I had no idea what she was thinking. All I knew was she missed me.

Lennox missed me.

I clung to those words as I clung to anything Lennox gave me. She gave away so little of herself I considered anything she gave to me a treasure.

"I am so incredibly broken." Her voice wobbled. "I have been ever since I lost my parents and Nol. I swore after they died I'd never wanted to feel that way again. So I started shutting people out. If I didn't get attached, I couldn't be hurt if they left. Kara was the only person I let myself care about. I didn't even realize what I was doing until Kara pointed it out to me the other week. All these years I let the fear of getting hurt get in the way of my happiness. Anytime I started to get close to someone I pushed them away." Her hands reached for me, but she hesitated, opting to fist her hands in the bottom of my shirt instead.

"Until you." Her words were a caress against my skin. "I tried hard to keep you out. But you managed to sneak your way into my life. I didn't even notice at first. You've started to help me put back together the broken pieces of myself. These past few years I feel like I've been living behind frosted glass. Everything has been muted and gray within this wall I surrounded myself with. Until you."

Until you. My heart beat in sync with those words.

Until you.

Until you.

Until you.

"You, Luka. You shattered that glass and broke me free. You brought color and light back into my life. I didn't realize how much of my life I'd been living in the dark until you started to pull me out of it." A tear slipped down her cheek, and I brushed it away with my thumb.

"I'm still broken, and I can't offer you much, but what I do know is I care about you. I know that I don't want to push you away. I don't know what this is between us, but I want to try and figure this out. And I know I want you, Luka. I want you. I'll give all of the broken, shattered pieces of my heart to you if you'll have them. I . . . I want to be yours, if you'll still have me."

The words I spoke to her in the forest echoed back into my mind. *Tell me I can have you.* My mind spun as I tried to process what she was telling me. There were so many things I wanted to say to her.

"Tell me I can have you," I echoed back to her.

Her hands fisted tighter in my shirt, pulling me closer. "You can have me." Her eyes felt like they were baring into the deepest depths of my soul. "You can have all of me, Luka. Every broken and damaged part."

That invisible string tying me to her all these months solidified into something real and tangible between us. I leaned forward and touched my lips to hers in a featherlight kiss before pulling back to look at her.

"I want you too, Lennox." I kissed her like I had been

wanting to kiss her since that day in the forest. She smiled against my lips as I grasped the back of her neck, pulling her closer to me, my other hand finding the small of her back. She molded her body to mine as she kissed me back, eagerly, wrapping her fingers in my hair. Stars, I loved it when she did that.

She pulled back, straining her head to look at me as I continued to hold her to me.

"You want me?" she asked, her smile hesitant, like she wanted to believe she had heard me right, but didn't, couldn't believe it.

"I want you, Lennox," I said before sealing my lips over hers again.

She gasped, allowing space for my tongue to sweep in. Goddess I loved the taste of her. She tasted sweet like honey, despite the steely exterior she put on. I forced myself to pull back, needing a moment to look at her again. Her face was flushed, lips swollen, and her eyes glimmered like emeralds— *fucking perfect.*

"I want you, Lennox," I repeated to her. "I will take all of you. Even the parts you think are too damaged. I will take whatever scraps of you you're willing to give me."

She smiled at me, and Goddess I wanted to make her smile like that every minute of every day.

"You're mine, Lennox."

She stood on her tiptoes and pressed another kiss to my lips. "C'mon," she said, taking my hand. She pulled me through the garden and back upstairs towards her chambers. She opened the door and pulled me inside, locking the door behind her.

"Lennox Adair, are you trying to seduce me?" She smirked as she prowled towards me.

"Maybe." She pulled her dress over her head, leaving her in nothing but her undergarments, which were nothing but scraps of black lace.

Stars above, she was breathtaking. I couldn't wait to take my time and explore every inch of her perfect body.

"Is it working?" she drawled.

I groaned as she made her way to me, slowly, her hips swaying as a coy smile spread on her perfect pink swollen lips. Her chest heaved under my gaze, her breasts rising and falling with every breath. Her peaked nipples were visible through the thin lace of her undergarment.

When she reached me she wrapped her arms around my neck before leaning in to kiss me, causing the chest I had been ogling a second ago to brush against my own.

Lennox Adair would be the death of me.

49

LENNOX

Luka's hands roamed over my body as he devoured my mouth. His calloused palms against my bare skin sent shivers down my spine. I moved my hands under his shirt, my fingers pressing against the firm ridges of his abdomen. I worked his shirt up his chest, removing my lips from his so I could remove his shirt the rest of the way before tossing it aside.

I took a step back, allowing myself a moment to look at him. I reached out and ran my fingers over the toned expanse of his stomach—tracing my fingers over every ridge before moving to his shoulders, tracking the dark lines of his tattoo that peaked over his shoulders and up his neck.

Luka's patience waned, he gripped the back of my neck, claiming my lips again in a searing kiss and stopping my slow exploration.

Later.

Later I could take in every inch of him.

I moaned as his hands moved down my back, his fingers slipping under the band of my undergarment. I wrapped my legs around his waist as his hands moved further before squeezing my ass in his palms, earning another moan from my lips. I ground against him. The feeling of his growing cock against the thin fabric of my undergarment . . . *more*. I needed more. There was still too much fabric between us.

My lips didn't leave his as he moved us towards the bed, seeming to have read my mind. I clung to him as he laid me down, my legs still locked around his waist—I wasn't ready to let him go. I tangled my fingers in his hair as he moved from my lips, kissing and sucking at the skin on my neck. I arched into him as his fangs scraped at my neck, and a moan slipped from my lips at the sensation.

"If you like the feeling of my fangs on your neck, imagine what they would feel like on other parts of your body," he murmured against my skin.

I shuttered.

Would he bite me in other places?

Did I want him to?

His fangs scraped against my neck again.

Yes. Goddess yes, I wanted that.

He teased one of my nipples through the thin silk of my undergarment with his thumb before taking it in his mouth through the fabric. My back bowed off the bed at the sensation.

"What if I bit you here?"

I whimpered as his mouth moved to my other breast. He licked and sucked at the tight bud through the fabric. As he removed his mouth from my chest, I looked at him, finding him staring at me with a wicked smile before removing the garment.

Words died on my tongue as he took my breast in his mouth again. He licked and sucked and—

"Fuck!" I screamed. The scrape of his fangs on my nipple was enough to end me over the edge alone.

"So responsive." He chuckled into my skin.

"You prick." I tightened my hold on his hair as he continued his exploration of my body with his mouth, moving his way down my stomach until he reached my thighs. I sat on my elbows to look at him as I heard his knees hit the floor.

His fingers hooked in the fabric of my undergarments before pulling them down my legs and discarding them. He placed his hands on my thighs and spread them open, baring me to him. His eyes darkened as he took me in.

He looked at me like he wanted to devour me.

He placed a kiss on the inside of my thigh. "So fucking beautiful," he said as he continued to tease the sensitive skin of my inner thighs—his tongue and fangs touched everywhere except where I wanted him.

"Luka, please," I begged, bucking my hips to try to get his mouth where I wanted it. He planted a hand on my stomach to keep me in place.

"Tell me where you want my mouth, Lennox."

Of course, he wasn't going to make this easy. I wanted to lash out at him for playing me like this, for torturing me, keeping me on edge. But I wanted him more.

"I want your mouth on me," I panted.

A wicked grin spread over his lips as he nipped at my inner thigh with his fangs, his stubble rough against my sensitive skin.

"I need you to be more specific, Sweetheart."

"Fucking prick," I swore, falling back onto the mattress as he continued to tease me until I couldn't take it anymore and I was a whimpering mess.

"I want you to fuck me with your fingers and mouth." The second the words left my mouth he did just that. His tongue licked up the center of me, a moan leaving my mouth at the sensation of his tongue finally where I wanted it.

"So fucking wet, is all of this for me, Sweetheart?"

My back arched off the bed as he plunged two fingers inside me, his tongue lapping and sucking at the bundle of nerves at the apex of my thighs.

My pleasure built with every wicked stroke of his tongue and pump of his fingers. My fingers found his hair and I pulled him closer. I could already feel my release building in my spine.

"Luka."

"That's it, Lennox."

I moaned as he thrust another finger inside me, his fingers and tongue now working in tandem.

"Come for me," he growled from between my thighs.

I screamed as my release rocked through me. My legs locked around his head as I clenched around his fingers. He continued to lick and suck at me as I writhed beneath him until the waves of my climax subsided. As the aftershocks waned, he removed his fingers from me, bringing them to his mouth. I watched with hooded eyes as he sucked every last drop of my arousal from his fingers.

"You taste so fucking good, Lennox."

He moved back up my body and claimed my lips. I could taste myself on his tongue. My hand reached for him, stroking him through his pants. He groaned against my lips as I continued to stroke him. Reaching for his belt as he nipped at my neck. I couldn't wait any longer. I needed him inside me.

I moved to sit on my knees as Luka stood. I fixed my eyes on him as he slid off his pants and undershorts, kicking them to the side. I licked my lips at the sight of him standing naked before me, my mouth dry at the sheer size of him. I reached for him, not able to wait another second.

"I take a weekly contraceptive tonic," I told him as I placed another kiss on his lips.

"So do I," he said into my lips.

My hand moved to take him in my hand, earning a rough groan from his lips. "Lennox, " he warned.

I stroked him again. "Then why are you not inside me yet?" I panted. That was all the encouragement he needed before he pounced.

Luka laid me on the bed and kissed me, his length slipping over my center, teasing me. I reached down to guide him inside me, but Luka caught my hand and pinned it above my head.

"So impatient," he chided before grabbing my other wrist, holding both of them in his hand above my head.

I bucked my hips in response and a snarl formed on my lips. I'd had enough of his games. I had no patience left. He continued to tease me, grinding himself against me as I laid helpless beneath him.

"Please, Luka."

He positioned himself so the tip of his cock slipped into me. I lifted my hips in an attempt to get him in farther, but Luka placed his other hand on my hips, keeping me still.

"Please, what?"

I scoffed. I was irritated, but I needed him inside me right now more than I needed to fight with him. He stared at me with lust-filled eyes as he waited for my answer.

"Fuck me, Luka."

He slammed into me and my breath caught in my lungs at the sheer size of him filling me. My walls stretched to accommodate the size of him.

"I love the sound of you begging for my cock." He pulled out only to slam back into again.

He let go of my hands to grip my hips as he fucked me. His pace was rough and hard, every thrust hitting that spot deep inside me, making stars dance at the edges of my vision. He slung one of my legs over his shoulder, hitting even deeper and my eyes rolled back in my head as incoherent curses slipped from my lips.

"Such a good girl. Look how well you take my cock."

Luka's grip on my hip was sure to leave bruises, but I reveled in the idea of being marked by him. I felt my release coming closer and closer with every thrust of his hips.

"Luka." I reached for him, tanging my fingers in his hair as I pulled his lips to mine. His fangs scraped at my bottom lip as he pulled away.

"Bite me." The words slipped from my lips before I could comprehend them. His thrusts slowed as he looked at me, sweat lined his brows and his hair fell across his face. Stars above, he was handsome.

"Luka, bite me, please." I wanted to feel like I did the first time he bit me.

"Are you sure?" His eyes bore into mine.

"Stars, yes, please," I whimpered.

He pulled out of me and I was about to protest before he spoke. "Turn over, on all fours."

In any other situation, I would have protested at Luka giving me orders, but not tonight. Tonight I would do anything he asked. He watched me with a predatory gaze as I moved to all fours. I looked over my shoulders at him as he fisted his cock, his eyes drinking me in. He moved behind me, rubbing his cock up and down the center of me, coating himself with my desire.

"You look good like this. Ready and waiting on all fours to me to fuck you."

He ran his hand down my spine and over my ass before slapping it lightly. I yelped at the sudden sting as wetness pooled at my core.

"So fucking beautiful," he praised as he lined his cock up with my center and thrust back in with a groan as a scream tore from my throat. His fingers dug into my hips as he thrust into me at a punishing pace. His hand left my hips and found my throat, pulling me until I was flush against him. His thrusts slowed as he took my lips with his. Kissing me long and slow.

He removed his mouth from mine and stared into my eyes. "Are you sure?"

I nodded. "Yes, please Luka, bite me."

I screamed as his fangs pierced my throat, but the pain was quickly swept away by an avalanche of pleasure like I'd never felt before. He continued to drink from me, his thrusts becoming slow and languished as desire coursed through my body like a flood. I thought I had felt desire the first time he bit me, but that was a fraction of what I was feeling now. I moaned as he continued to drink from me. My hands tangled in his hair to bring him closer. Luka groaned as he finally pulled away, placing a kiss on where he had bitten. I stared at him as he licked my blood from his lips, a wicked smile on his lips.

"Fuck Lennox, I don't know what tastes better, your blood or your cum."

My body clenched at his words, so filthy and dirty, I could have come simply from those words falling from his lips. Luka smirked as he thrust inside me again, harder this time, stealing the breath from my lungs.

"I want to come on your cock," I moaned.

Luka's thrusts quickened, and I found purchase on the headboard as one of his hands found my breast and the other the bundle of nerves at the apex of my thighs.

"Fuck, Luka."

"Whose are you?" He thrust again.

My head swam, I was drunk on desire, his words not computing in my mind.

He wrapped his hand around my neck, pushing me against him as he nipped at my ear. "Whose are you, Lennox?"

"Yours," I panted. "I'm yours, Luka."

He growled at my admission, his fingers pinching the bundle of nerves and I combusted. I screamed as I came, my release crashing over me. A second later, I felt Luka twitch inside me as he came with a groan.

We stayed like that, him holding me as I kissed him as we both came back down.

When he finally pulled out of me he gently laid me back on the bed. Moving my hair from my face before kissing my forehead. Our limbs tangled together as he pulled me to him, I cuddled into the space between his neck.

"I can't say this is what I expected to happen when I knocked on your door tonight."

"You're saying you didn't expect me to fuck me?"

"I mean I'm always hoping that's how things will end up when it comes to you, but—"

I swatted at him playfully.

"Prick."

He pulled me closer, placing a kiss on my hair. "That's why you like me."

50

LUKA

I want to be yours if you'll still have me.

Lennox's words filtered through my mind. I should have been exhausted after our endless activities last night, instead, I was invigorated.

Hearing Lennox say she was mine while I was inside her wasn't something I'd forget anytime soon. I peered over at where she slept beside me. Her hair was a mess, it lay in a tangle of golden waves on the pillow and over her face. I reached over and moved the hair from her face—letting my fingers linger on her soft skin.

There was still a part of me that wondered if she'd regret it all when she woke up. When I knocked on her door last night, this wasn't what I was expecting to happen. Did it cross my mind? Of course. Sex with Lennox was constantly on my mind. But now that I had her, I wanted to be inside her all the time. We had only fallen asleep a few hours ago, having spent the rest of the night worshiping each other's bodies.

The sight of her riding my cock while I sat back and watched would be one I'd replay often.

Last night, when I'd knocked on Lennox's door I didn't come to seduce her. I came because I had missed her. We had hardly seen one another since we had arrived back in Alethens and I found myself wondering where she was, what she was doing, and wondering if she was missing me like I was missing her. I never expected her to confess her feelings for me. But now that she had—I wouldn't let her take them back. I was holding her to them.

Holding on to *her*.

Lennox Adair was *mine*.

I studied her features while she continued to sleep—her full lips, her soft jaw, and her long delicate neck. I wanted to memorize every valley and plain of her body with my hands, with my lips, teeth, and tongue.

Lennox rustled, stretching an arm above her head as her eyes fluttered open. She turned toward me, squinting as she rubbed the sleep from her eyes. Her face broke into a smile when she looked at me. Her smile had been rare, until recently.

"Good morning." Her voice was still rough with sleep. She leaned forward and placed a kiss on my jaw, wrapping her arms around my neck.

"Good morning."

Neither of us made a move to get out of bed. Instead, we lay tangled in one another. I traced circles on her arm, trying to calm myself while my thoughts ran rampant. Was she here to stay? Was she mine? Or would she change her mind once she walked out the door? We had woken up like this many times before. What made this time different? Besides that we'd fucked. She could still change her mind.

"Lennox."

"Hmmm," she murmured, not moving her head from where it laid in the crook of my neck.

"Last night—"

I felt her stiffen in my arms.

Fuck. I knew this was too good to be true. "Do you regret anything?" I asked.

My chest tightened as I braced myself for the answer I

didn't want to hear. Part of me wanted to live in this morning bliss, but I needed to know where we stood. She sat up, moving out of my embrace to look at me fully. I propped myself on my elbow as she studied my face, searching for something.

"No, I don't." She pulled her bottom lip between her teeth. "Do you?" she asked quietly.

"Of course not," I stammered.

Fuck.

This was not how I intended this to go. I could see it in her face she was debating running. I reached for her, cupping her face and swiping my thumb over her cheek.

"I don't regret a single thing when it comes to you, but I want to make sure you didn't change your mind."

Her eyes softened and she leaned into my touch. She moved and placed a kiss on the inside of my palm.

"I don't regret a thing when it comes to you either, Luka." She moved until she was straddling me. Her hair cascading over her naked body as the sun casted her in a glow. I leaned back and took her in.

"I meant what I said last night, I'm yours."

I grew hard beneath her as she leaned forward and took my lips in hers in a searing kiss.

"I'm yours," she whispered into my mouth.

I ran my hands down her spine and she moaned as I moved my hands to her breasts, running my fingers over the sensitive buds. I cursed as she ground against me before sliding onto my cock.

☾

"Do you want to train with me today?" Lennox asked as she drew lines across my chest.

"If you still have the energy to train I must not have worn you out enough." I rolled on top of her as she giggled, peppering kisses down her neck. She swatted at me as she bucked her hips against me.

"I'm serious, Luka. I haven't held a sword in days. I'm itching to have one in my hands."

I continued to kiss my way down her body. "I have a sword right here you can wield."

She laughed again, the sound loud and bright. "You are vile."

I made my way to the apex of her thighs, placing a kiss directly above her center.

"And that's why you like me."

"Prick," she muttered.

☾

Several hours later we still hadn't made it out of Lennox's bed. We hadn't even been able to bathe without keeping our hands off of each other. Lennox had given up on trying to persuade me we needed to leave, so we spent the day in bed. When we weren't fucking, we were talking. Getting to know one another. But the whole time, we never stopped touching each other.

"My uncle will be here in a couple of days," I told her as we sat on the balcony in a chaise lounge. Lennox sat between my legs, my arms wrapped around her. An empty bottle of wine sat on the side table next to us as we stared at the night sky. She remained silent as I continued to glide my fingers up and down her bare arm. "He's coming to check in on the progress we've made."

She blew out a breath. "And what are we going to tell him exactly? That we think our relationship is enough to quell the unrest between our people?"

I could hear the irritation in her voice along with a hint of fear. I knew the threat of war, of an arranged marriage, weighed heavily on her mind, they did on mine too. My uncle's visit would do little to soothe it. I brushed her hair to the side, placing a kiss on her neck.

"Don't think too much about it."

Her grip tightened on my arm wrapped around her waist.

"I'm sure my grandfather is sending him to give him something to do. This visit doesn't mean anything. My grandfather and Lorenzo have a tumultuous relationship. I can't imagine what it's been like without me there as a buffer. I'm certain half of the reason behind this visit is to give my grandfather some space away from Lorenzo."

"What if he wants you to go back?" she asked.

My hand stilled on Lennox's arm and my heart with it. I hadn't even considered that he might ask me to come back with him. I knew I would have to go back to the Blood Court eventually, but I didn't think it would be anytime soon. Honestly, the timeline didn't matter much until recently. I missed the Blood Court, but I loved being here in Alethens, with Lennox.

I just got her, I wasn't ready to leave her yet.

She shifted in my arms, leaning back to look at my face. Uncertainty glowed in those emerald eyes. Uncertainty that I wished I could take away, but the truth was I couldn't. Neither one of us knew what this was between us yet. We had no idea what the future held for us. Hecate said our futures were linked, but what did that mean in reality? I doubted my grandfather would let me stay here because a Seer said Lennox and I needed to continue to work together.

I sighed and cupped her face, brushing my thumb over her cheek. "Then I'll tell him I can't go back yet. That we're still working on strengthening our relationship."

The corner of her mouth lifted a fraction of an inch. I held rank over my uncle, so unless he came with a direct order from my grandfather, he couldn't make me leave with him. But we would cross that bridge if we came to it.

"I'm not ready to leave you yet." I brushed my thumb over her bottom lip, and her mouth parted in response.

"I'm not ready for you to leave yet either."

Sincerity shone in those grassy eyes so I leaned forward and brushed my lips against hers in a soft kiss. The truth of our words transcending in the action. I pulled away, brushing a strand of hair from her face.

She smiled before turning back around, clutching the blanket to her chest as she reached for another bottle of wine.

I drew her hair over her shoulder, exposing her bare back to me. She shivered as I placed a kiss on the back of her neck as my fingers ran down her spine. I placed another kiss to her shoulder as she filled her glass. Then I started kissing my way down her back, pausing when I came to her left shoulder, my eyes scanning over the pale ink of a tattoo I had failed to notice before.

"Was this here before?" I asked as I brushed my fingers over the delicate markings. A sun with rays of differing lengths sat in the center of the tattoo. Nestled next to it was a crescent moon to the right, stars and Stardust littered the right side of the tattoo and melded throughout.

Lennox glanced at me over her shoulder as she nodded.

"How come I never noticed it before?"

"Because it's been fully glamoured every time you've seen it before."

"What do you mean—"

I sensed Lennox's magic before I saw it washing over her tattoo—the pale ink shifting into full color. The tattoo was no longer in white ink, but black. I continued to run my fingers over the ink. The stars were made of different shades of black, gray, silver, and white ink. The entire tattoo now held an incandescent glow, like I was truly looking at the night sky and the glowing sun.

"It's technically an illegal tattoo."

My fingers stilled. "What do you mean an illegal tattoo?"

Her shoulder rose and fell as she took a deep breath. "When a witch turns eighteen and they come fully into their power they have to pledge themselves to one of the three covens. Once they pledge themselves to a coven they get a tattoo to mark their devotion. If you pledge to Selene, you get the symbol of the moon."

I ran my fingers over the lines of the moon on her shoulder.

"Pheobus you get a the sun."

My fingers traced the rays of the sun.

"Hera the stars."

My fingers dusted over the scattering of stars.

"Then why do you have all three?" I asked.

"I wasn't allowed to pledge myself to a coven since I wasn't a full witch, but I did it anyway. I symbolically pledged myself to all three covens, taking a piece of them wherever I go."

"Why does that not surprise me one bit, Lennox Adair."

She laughed and shrugged her shoulders. "I was the rule breaker. Luciana and I did it together. I was visiting her for her eighteenth birthday; it also happened to fall on the second night of the Star Eclipse."

"What's the Star Eclipse?"

"It's a celebration the witches hold twice a year. It's a celebration of life and death. For three days and nights we honor those who have passed in the last six months. By some act of magic—an ancient spell the stories say—during those three days souls are released back into the universe in an explosion of Stardust. Their ending of this life and turning into Stardust marks the beginning of new life built from the ashes of their Stardust," she finished as she leaned back into me, looking at the night sky.

"Is that why your family says 'until the stars turn to dust'?"

She nodded against my chest. "It's a promise to love one another until our souls find rest."

What would it be like to love someone that way? My family had never been like that. My father maybe, but he was never one to openly give affection with his words.

"What about your tattoos? Do they have any meaning?"

I chuckled, thinking about the various markings covering my

back. "Not really. I got the first one when I was drunk and lost a bet."

"Let me guess, you lost a bet to Nico and that's why you have a wolf that looks oddly like him on your back."

"You guess correctly, Sweetheart. And that was a compromise. He originally wanted me to get his face." Her laughter rumbled through my body. "The rest I've added over the years. Some have meaning, some don't."

"Will you tell me about them all someday?"

I placed a kiss on the top of her head. "If you want me to, yes, I'll tell you the origin of every tattoo."

Everything. I wanted to tell her everything.

_____

51

LENNOX

For the first time in three years, I was happy. Truly happy. The feeling was unusual in my chest at first; like one of the missing pieces of myself that had been ripped from me the night I lost my parents and Nol had been returned to my fractured soul. I was still not yet whole, but I felt like I was slowly melding myself back together. The pieces didn't fit right yet, but someday, they might.

I had friends, I had my sister, and I had Luka. The future was no longer a dark cloud looming over my life. I no longer wanted to live day by day, I was ready to look forward to the future.

Luka's uncle, Lorenzo, had arrived this afternoon and Luka and I welcomed him together in the ballroom.

Lorenzo Rossi looked nothing like his nephew. His onyx hair fell past his shoulders, it was a stark contrast to his ivory skin. But what set me on edge were his eyes. They were leached of all color, the dark pools had not even a glimmer of magic lurking in them.

Luka and I didn't reveal the nature of our relationship to him. We presented ourselves as friends—allies. It took everything in me not to reach for Luka under his uncle's unnerving gaze.

There was a dinner celebrating Lorenzo's arrival tonight. The royal counsel would be in attendance along with several of the lords and ladies of the court.

Dressing for dinner I donned a proper gown for the first time since before we had departed to the Mystic Court. The dress was a simple, off-the-shoulder gown made of dark green chiffon that glittered like the night sky. It was cinched at the waist and tapered out in a ballgown-like fashion, much more feminine than what I typically chose.

My hair fell in waves down my back with sparking clips pinning it back from my face, accentuating the lips I had painted a dark maroon. A simple crown made of silver and black gems sat upon my head.

A knock sounded at my door, and I opened it to find Luka leaning against the doorway.

He was a vision in all black—a Dark Prince. Over his black button-up shirt, he wore a black jacket embroidered with gold thread. His hair was styled away from his face, and I itched to run my fingers through it and mess it up in the way I liked it so much. His stubble, that I loved feeling against my thighs, was now gone, his face cleanly shaven.

I hadn't seen Luka dressed up since the ball months ago. Back when I was too stubborn to admit how good he looked. Now, I let my eyes wander over his body shamelessly.

He prowled into my room, shutting the door behind him as his eyes raked over my body.

"You look . . ." His eyes darkened as they locked with mine. "Breathtaking."

A blush creeped into my cheeks. This male had seen every inch of my body, but the way he was looking at me right now stripped me bare.

"Thank you." The words came out in a whisper as Luka's eyes flicked to my lips and back up to meet my eyes.

"I mean it, that dress looks incredible on you." He ran his fingers up and down my bare arm, causing goosebumps to pebble over my skin. "But I'd love nothing more than to peel it off of you right now."

"We can't be late." I put a hand on his chest, but it did nothing to stop his advances.

"Didn't you tell me something once about how you can never be late because you're the queen?" He asked as his fangs scraped against my neck, my body bowing to his touch.

"Luka." I fisted his jacket, pulling him closer.

His lips hovered over mine in the lightest of kisses while his hand traced up the skin of my thigh through the slit in my dress. How he managed to find it among the layers of tule—

"Do you have any idea how crazy these slits in your dresses drive me? Especially knowing you have daggers sheathed here." His hand skated higher, resting on the daggers for a second before continuing its exploration. "As much as I loved seeing you in your tight as fuck leathers while we were traveling, I missed these infuriating slits in your dresses. Always teasing and taunting me."

I pulled his lips to mine, meeting him in a hungry kiss as his hand slipped into my undergarments. I moaned as his fingers slid through the center of me.

"Fuck," he hissed. "You're already wet for me, Sweetheart."

I gasped as he plunged two fingers inside of me without warning. I ground against him, desperate for more as he thrust his fingers in and out.

"Luka, I need more."

"Tell me exactly what you want, Lennox."

"I need you inside me. Now."

I fisted his shirt as his fingers continued to pump in and out of me as he licked and sucked at my neck. I moaned as his thumb brushed the bundle of nerves at the apex of my thighs. I moved for the buttons of his trousers, desperate to feel him.

Before I could get any further he removed his fingers and spun me around, pinning me to the wall.

His fangs scraped against my neck as he grasped my hands in his and placed them above my head on the wall in front of me.

"Keep them there," he ordered.

I looked over my shoulder at him as he removed his cock from his trousers. I licked my lips as he pumped himself. "Look at you, my beautiful queen, eager and ready to take my cock."

He gathered my skirt around my waist, moving my undergarments to the side before rubbing himself along my center.

"Luka," I whimpered.

I yelped as he delivered a sharp smack to my ass. The pain sent desire straight to my core

"Tell me exactly what you want," he growled.

"I want you to fuck me."

He smacked my ass again before plunging inside me in one thrust. I screamed at the sensation of him filling me before he pulled out and thrust back in again.

"That's it, take it. Take my cock, Sweetheart."

He continued to thrust into me rapidly—my release already building along my spine. Luka reached in front of me and freed one of my breasts, pinching my nipple in his fingers. The action sent another wave of desire through me.

"Look at how well you take me. Fuck, you feel good, Lennox."

Moans of pleasure left my mouth. It was too much, *he* was too much. His hand on my breast moved until it found the bundle of nerves at my center.

"Come for me Lennox," he growled, his fangs scraping the shell of my ear. He delivered another smack to my ass and I combusted. Stars blurred my vision, my knees threatened to come out from under me as pleasure rolled through me wave after wave.

"Good girl." Luka thrust inside me again as he came with a groan.

We both stood, panting as we came down from our release. Luka pulled out from me and gathered me in his arms, depositing me on the bed.

"Stay there," he commanded and I nodded and watched as he fetched a washcloth from the bathing chamber and cleaned me up.

"What did I do to deserve you?" he asked, kissing the inside of my knee.

I didn't have the words. I often asked myself the same thing. So I pulled him to me and kissed him instead. Hoping my kiss would convey everything I didn't have the words to express.

52

LENNOX

Luka and I made our way to the ballroom hand in hand, only separating before we reached the doors. He·squeezed my hand before releasing it and gesturing for me to enter first.

·The dining room was filled with Fae; several dignitaries from the Star Court had made the trip to Alethens to celebrate Lorenzo's arrival.

Luka handed me a flute of champagne off a passing tray. I swallowed half the glass in one gulp.

"Careful, Sweetheart," Luka whispered into my ear as he placed his hand on the small of my back. "Getting drunk before dinner might not be appropriate tonight."

He had a point, I needed to stay sharp to dodge questions from his uncle and steer the conversation in the way we wanted it to go. But that was also why I felt the need to drink, to help quell the nerves in my stomach.

Although the knots twisting in my stomach had nothing to do with Lorenzo and had everything to do with the fear that Luka might have to return to the Blood Court. Luka had tried ·his best to reassure me it wouldn't happen, that his uncle didn't have that power over him, but it did little to staunch my nerves.

What I told him several nights ago was true—I wasn't ready to let him go yet.

And that scared me more than anything because him leaving was inevitable—whether it was tomorrow, or two months from now.

Lorenzo's arrival was the first bit of air to be released from the perfect bubble Luka and I had been living in. The first reminder that we couldn't live like this forever. He was the heir to the Blood Court, he needed to go back and claim his throne.

But then what would happen between us?

There were too many unknowns in our future. All I knew was that I cared for Luka. He was the light in the darkness I've been surviving in.

"There they are." Nico's voice snapped me back to attention. His silver hair glowed in the light of the chandelier as he approached us, arms spread and a wild grin lighting up his bronzed face. "What kept you two held up for so long?" he asked as he draped an arm around my shoulder.

"Nothing." I brought my glass to my lips to hide my smile.

"Nothing, huh? I expected more from you Luka."

A laugh bubbled from my lips as Nico nudged Luka, who only glared at him.

"Maybe he was tired. You have been keeping him up awfully late every night," Nico whispered in my ear, loud enough I knew Luka heard. "The walls are thin, you know."

I felt a blush creeping up my cheeks. Goddess I didn't want to know if that was true to not.

"You're an ass, you know that, Nico?" Luka remarked.

"I do have a great ass, don't I?" He turned, admiring his own behind before bumping me with it lightly.

Luka and I both stifled a laugh. I couldn't help myself in Nico's presence. His charisma was infectious.

"I'll let you in on a secret," I whispered, leaning in close to Nico. "Luka has no problem keeping me satisfied. That vampire stamina sure comes in handy."

Nico winked at the two of us. "Way to go Lennox."

Luka looked between the two of us, brows raised in question.

"Now, if you don't mind me, I'm going to go and see if there is anyone interested in giving me a proper farewell before I leave tomorrow."

I shook my head at him as he wandered farther into the dining room, winking at me over his shoulder. I was going to miss him when he left.

"Do I even want to know what you said to him?" Luka asked as he held out his arm for me. I looped my arm through his and let him lead me further into the room.

"I was telling him the perks of sharing a bed with a vampire."

Luka chuckled. "Don't encourage him, haven't you learned? It only makes him more intolerable."

☪

After everyone had their fill of champagne we all sat down to dinner. Conversation flowed freely as we ate. It wasn't until after the main course had been served that Luka finally asked the question I'd been waiting for.

"So, Uncle, to what do we owe the pleasure of your visit?"

"We?" Lorenzo looked between the two of us. "Are you insinuating you're a part of this court now, boy?"

Luka bristled. "You know what I mean."

Lorenzo took a sip of his wine before speaking again. "Your grandfather is growing tired of waiting."

Luka stiffened beside me, but before he could speak he was interrupted by a boom that echoed through the palace.

My ears rang from the noise as the room rumbled. I stood, reaching for my daggers as the room tilted beneath me. I stumbled as the dining room continued to move. I reached for the chair to steady myself, only to be caught by Luka instead. His wide-eyed gaze moved to mine as he pulled me to him, shielding me as the chandelier swayed violently above us. The sound of glass shattering pierced the air.

I looked around for Kara, finding her shielded by Declan as the room continued to tremble. Seconds passed before the room, once again, stilled. The room was mostly intact, although the glasses on the table had been knocked over and shattered, and decorations had fallen from the walls and now littered the ground, but everything else appeared to be intact.

"What was what?" Declan's voice was sharp over our collective mumbles as he released Kara, who fell into step beside Nico. Declan's wings were wide as he surveyed the room, his hand on his daggers at his side. Alethens didn't have any active volcanoes, it had never experienced a land tremor.

I swallowed the lump in my throat.

An explosion, it had to have been an explosion.

I closed my eyes and took a deep breath before opening them again and seeking out Luka's gaze. His eyes told me enough, he had come to the same conclusion I had.

Declan was already moving towards the double doors leading to the dining room as Enric rushed inside. Sweat slicked the young guard's brow as he tried and failed to catch his breath.

"Enric, what is it?" I asked.

Voices trailed behind him—people were shouting, their voices intertwined with the clang of steel.

"Everyone stay here," Declan demanded as he drew his sword from his back. "I'm going to go see what's going on."

"I'm coming with you," Nico added. Declan didn't protest and the two took off without a backward glance.

Luka followed me as I met Enric at the door. "There's . . . there was . . ." His chestnut hair was plastered to his dust covered forehead—his dark eyes wide with fear.

"Enric, breathe. You need to take a breath so we can understand you," I encouraged.

His eyes were wide as he stared at me, but he nodded, taking several breaths before trying to speak again. "An explosion, there was an explosion."

My legs wobbled beneath me. Luka noticed and wrapped an arm around my waist to keep me from falling. I squeezed my eyes shut. I needed to follow my own instructions and breathe.

"Where." My heart beat pounded in my ears.

"The front gate. They blew up the front gate." Enric trembled as he braced an arm on the doorway. "They're coming. I was sent to warn you, Your Majesty—"

Enric gasped, his eyes going wide as he stood frozen in the doorway, an arrow protruding from his chest.

53

LUKA

I watched as the young guard fell—his hands going to his chest as he tumbled to the floor with a gasp. Lennox's scream pierced the air as she reached for Enric, calling out his name. Declan was barking orders from the hallway as I fell to Lennox's side as she cradled the youngling's head in her arms.

Her hands trembled as she reached for the arrow, her fingers brushing the iron shaft before she pulled it from his body.

His heart. It had gone straight through his heart.

Several more arrows whizzed through the air as shouts rang out in the distance. I covered Lennox as much as I could as she continued to hold the boy's body in her arms, the blood coated arrow fell to the ground beside us, as she covered his body with her own.

The enemy was here. We needed to move.

"Lennox, we have to go," I urged her.

"I can save him," she whispered as a tear rolled down her cheek. I watched as she pressed her hands to the boy's body like she had to mine all those weeks ago in the woods, a glow illumi-nating from her palm. I moved so I was still protecting Lennox, but reached for Enric's neck, pressing two fingers there.

Nothing. There was nothing there.

He was dead.

I didn't know how Lennox's healing magic worked, but I doubted bringing someone back to life would be an easy feat, or one that wouldn't have a cost. There was a balance that must be maintained between life and death. Even I knew that.

"Lennox." I leaned into her, wrapping my arm around her. "It's too late. He's gone."

She pressed her hand to the back of her mouth to stifle a sob.

"I'm sorry," I said, as I held her to me.

I looked around the room. The lords and ladies that had been invited to the dinner were crowded in the corner where Kara stood addressing them as the sound of battle rang out in the distance. The fighting might not be to us yet, but they had to be looking for Lennox and Kara. They'd realize soon enough the sisters weren't in the fray and come looking for them.

"Lennox, we have to go."

She didn't move, her gaze fixed on Enric's lifeless eyes. I took a deep breath before taking Lennox's face in my hands, forcing her to look at me. My heart clenched at the sight of the sorrow lining her beautiful face.

Death. She had witnessed too much death in her life.

"Lennox, I'm sorry, Sweetheart, but we have to go." I brushed a stray tear away with my thumb before I continued, "We couldn't save Enric, but we can go and save others, but we need to go now. You are their queen, they need you."

She nodded, taking a deep breath as she did. She closed her eyes and straightened her shoulders.

I watched as she became High Queen Lennox Adair in front of my eyes.

"Okay." Her voice was rough as she spoke. "Okay." Her voice was stronger this time. She stood, reaching inside of her layers of tulle and palming a dagger in each hand. She let out a deep breath as she stood up straight, her eyes no longer rimmed in tears, but steely fire.

"Let's go make them bleed."

54

LENNOX

I followed the sound of steel on steel as I ran from the dining room, Luka and Kara at my heels. The sight of Enric's lifeless eyes threatened to slip back to the forefront of my mind, but I banished it.

Battle did not allow time for grief.

I did not allow time for grief.

I ignored the feel of his dried blood flaking on my hands as I gripped the handles of my daggers and continued towards the sounds of fighting.

Hallway after hallway we ran, the sounds getting louder and louder with each step I took towards the grand hall. My stomach hollowed at the sight of the foyer when we arrived. Bodies littered the ground. Some wore the white and gold of the Star Court, others wore all-black ensembles, complete with black masks covering the lower halves of their faces. On the chest of their jackets, embroidered in golden thread, was the sign of the Vanir.

The Vanir were here. In my *home.*

My boots splashed in the puddles of blood pooling on the floor as the three of us made our way towards where Nico and

Declan stood fending off a group of five Vanir dressed in all black.

Where were the rest of the Star Courts Royal Guard? Where was Captain Kahle? By the looks of it, there were only five Royal Guard bodies on the ground, so where were the rest of the forces? I whirled at the sound of approaching boots, ducking in time to avoid the arc of a sword. I slid across the floor on my knees, my gown soaking up blood in the process.

I stood as the Vanir turned, landing a blow to his jaw before he could raise his sword. I felt his jaw shatter beneath my fist as his blood splattered across my face. His sword fell to the ground as he swore and grasped his broken jaw.

I wiped his blood from my face with the back of my arm as I reached for his fallen sword only for him to jerk me back by my hair. I screamed as he pulled me back, my crown falling at my feet as his grip turned tighter on my hair. He held me far enough from him that every attempted punch only met air. My scalp burned as I kicked, landing a soft blow to his leg as I tried to get him to loosen his grip on my hair. He landed a punch to my stomach in retaliation, sending me keeling over, grasping for breath.

That would leave a nasty bruise.

The male finally let go of my hair as he laughed—the sound cold and oily against my skin.

I remained bent over as I looked at him out of the corner of my eye. He wasn't even paying me any attention anymore, his gaze fell elsewhere. *Arrogant fool.*

I swept my leg out, knocking him off his feet. He landed on his back, and his head smacked against the marble. I wasted no time climbing on top of him, digging my knees into his sides, and using my vines to secure his arms. With his arms restrained I landed blow after blow to his face. Blood sprayed and bones cracked, but I continued my assault. My knuckles screamed in pain from the blows, but my heart sang a song of vengeance. My soul was thirsty for blood.

My head snapped up at the sound of my sister's scream.

"Nico watch out!" Kara cried as an arrow whistled through the air toward the wolf. Nico's silver hair glimmered as he ducked, narrowly avoiding the arrow before it shattered into pelts of ice at Kara's will. My sister whirled, her ice dagger finding itself in the female's chest. She fell to the ground with a gasp as Nico turned towards Kara,

"Thanks, princess," he breathed, still smiling despite the chaos surrounding us.

Kara only nodded before advancing on another Vanir. Only four Vanir soldiers remained. My magic twitched at my fingertips.

Four Vanir I could easily handle.

I turned back to my opponent. Bloodthirst could wait, I needed to end this fight now. I reached for a discarded sword and sliced it across the male's neck without a second thought.

With the male now dead I stood and closed my hands into fists and watched as the remaining soldiers ceased their fighting. Their weapons crashed to the ground as their hands reached for their throats as they struggled to get air to their lungs. My friends turned to me as I held the soldier's life in my hands.

"Leave one of them alive so we can question them, the rest can die." I closed my fist tighter, further cutting off the soldier's air, they gasped, their lips starting to turn blue as the veins pulsed in their necks. I heard, more than saw, Nico's blade cutting through the two bodies in front of him, Luka did the same, cutting off the head of the Vanir with his twin swords. I heard the squelch of blood and the sound of bone cracking as Declan's blade snapped through the male's neck before the head rolled across the golden floor with a sickening thud.

I released my magic on the last male. He gasped as the air rushed back into his lungs. My vines were wrapping around his hands before he could breathe one full gulp.

"Nico, bring him to the dungeon."

The silver-haired wolf nodded as he pushed his hair back from his face. "Of course, Your Majesty." He took the Vanir soldiers' makeshift handcuffs in his hands before ushering him out of the foyer.

"What the fuck happened?" I asked Declan. The harpy's massive wings twitched in time with a muscle in his jaw. "Where are the rest of the Guard?"

"Your guess is as good as mine. You know their procedures. At least some of them should have been here. Instead, only six showed, and they didn't arrive until after Nico and I. They should have been here minutes, *seconds* after the blast erupted."

My stomach hollowed. Not good, this was not good. Where are the rest of them?

Dead, they were dead somewhere. I hoped it wasn't true, but if they were, I hoped Captain Kahle was among them. The bastard deserved death for letting something like this happen under his watch.

I shook my head. "Even with the blast destroying the gate, those soldiers should have never made it inside the palace. Our forces should have easily outnumbered them before they even got to the front doors."

Declan nodded, his solemn expression doing nothing to quelch my worries.

"I know——" I fell into Luka beside me, who grabbed me with solid arms. The room continued to rumble, but nowhere near as violently as the first blast. Even the sound was diluted like it was coming from far away——

I pushed out of Luka's hold as I rushed towards the doors leading to the garden, stopping only to pick up a sword from a deceased guard. Luka called after me, but I continued running until I was on the far side of the garden that looked out at the city beneath. I froze when I reached the edge and Alethens came into view. Time slowed as I watched the dark smoke billowing from the center of my city.

I broke into a run, my feet taking me toward the stables. I jumped on Odin, winding my hands through his mane as I kicked him into a run and headed toward my people.

55

LUKA

I continued after Lennox, pausing only when I saw what she did, Alethens bathed in destruction. Dark smoke rose from the city, turning the blue sky dark. I ran with her towards the stables as we both mounted our horses and took off towards the city center. Lennox's golden hair whipped behind her as we bounded toward the heart of Alethens.

The smoke grew thicker the closer we got to the city, causing my eyes to burn and a cough to rise in my throat, but Lennox continued through the smoke, only slowly slightly when the smoke started to mar our vision. As we got closer I expected there to be sounds of destruction, of fighting, of devastated people, *of screams*, but there was none. The city blocks were eerily quiet. The pit in my stomach deepened.

Eventually, we reached a point where we could no longer travel through with our horses—the rubble of the ruined city was stacked too high in front of us. Lennox said nothing as she lept from Odin and started climbing over the the piles of debris.

"Lennox, wait!" I called as I followed behind her. Her gown snagged on the jagged rocks, but it didn't slow her as we climbed. She only ripped at the fabric until it tore, using her dagger to cut through the fabric if needed. Once we cleared the pile of rubble Lennox took off again, running toward the city center.

The *remains* of the city center.

The buildings that once stood tall were nothing but crumbled bricks around the once-bustling courtyard. There were, not only businesses in these buildings, there were homes here.

I took my place next to Lennox as she stared with hollow eyes toward the remains of her city. Silent tears made tracks down her ash-streaked face.

"Homes, these were people's homes. And now they're all dead," she whispered. If anyone had managed to survive the explosion, they wouldn't have survived being crushed by the rubble.

I took her hand in mind and urged her forward. "C'mon, let's see if anyone can tell us what happened."

We stepped over the rubble, keeping our eyes forward as we made our way towards where Declan was talking with civilians, and several members of the Royal Guard.

"Any idea what happened?" I asked the Harpy.

Declan's wings were tucked in tight as he shook his head. "The civilians said everything was as normal until the blasts rang out. They told us the buildings went down instantly."

"It must have been pre-planned. Whatever they used was planted." I noted.

Declan nodded. "I suspect there was multiple of whatever was used to ensure the whole block came down at once." Declan surveyed the rubble. "Whoever did it wanted to make sure no one survived."

I squeezed Lennox's hand as she remained silent beside me.

"But why, *who* would do such a thing to innocent people?" I said as I shook my head.

"The Vanir," Lennox spoke as she nodded her head towards the neighboring block. "It was the Vanir."

I looked to where she nodded. Written across the bricks of

the only remaining building in thick red lines were three interlocking circles and an intersecting triangle, the sign of the Vanir.

Fuck.

"The attack at the palace was a distraction. They meant to
keep us occupied while my people remained unguarded." Her
words were cold, devoid of all emotion. Dread settled in my
stomach like a rock.

"We killed their people, so they killed mine."

"Lennox—this isn't your fault."

She whirled on me, wrenching her hand out of mine, her
eyes wide and swirling with magic. "But isn't it? This is their
payback for killing their members that day in the forest, the ones
in the garden. This is my fault."

I gripped her arms. "Lennox this is not your fault. They—"

I stumbled, scraping my hands on the rubble as Lennox
forced me down as a dagger flew over our heads. Her hair
whipped across her face as she turned towards the source of the
weapon. I couldn't see anything as I surveyed the few remaining
buildings. Another dagger flew, missing us by a few feet this
time. Its black pommel clanged to the ground beside us.
Lennox's eyes gleamed dangerously as she reached for the
discarded dagger, a snarl poised on her lips as she stood.

I had no choice but to follow my queen as she ran towards
the building where the daggers had flown from. I needed a fight
as much as she did.

56

LENNOX

I took the stairs two at a time as I reached the stairwell of the building. Pictures were hanging haphazardly on the walls from the explosion. Any merchandise once in the store was now destroyed and covered in a thick layer of ash. I coughed into my arm as my lungs burned and my eyes stung from the smoke inhalation. I sheathed the Vanir's dagger at my side next to my borrowed sword as I continued, Luka at my heels as we climbed. I planned on killing the bastard who was cowardly enough to throw a dagger and hide with his own goddess-forsaken blade.

I strained my ears for any sounds as we continued up the stairs, keeping my steps as quiet as possible. The rustling of the tulle of my dress was another story—the fabric swished with every step, causing me to wince. Luka pressed a hand to the small of my back, motioning for me to stop.

"I'll create a barrier of air," he whispered.

Why hadn't I thought of that? I shook my head as I felt his magic surrounding me as he created the pocket around us to stifle our sounds.

"Thank you," I whispered, offering him a weak smile. He rose to the step I was on and pressed a kiss to my forehead.

"You're welcome." He took my hand in his and squeezed,

his eyes searching mine. "Lennox, take a deep breath. We will find them and we will make them pay for what they did. But we can't do that if your mind is somewhere else. I won't risk you."

I breathed in deeply. He was right. I needed to pull myself together. "I can do this."

I have to do this.

"Okay. If you're ready, let's go get 'em, Sweetheart." He flashed me one of his smirks that drove me crazy.

We were both covered in blood, our clothes dirty and ripped, bearing weapons that were not our own. My city lay in ruins around me. My people were dead on the streets But this male, *Luka*, managed to calm my raging emotions and bring me back to myself.

Goddess I—

There was a crash above us as something fell. Luka gripped my arm as we both turned towards the sound, pressing our back against the stairwell as we strained to hear anything else.

Voices.

They were up there. We shared a look before continuing our ascent.

The voices were clearer now, two, maybe three, Fae as we reached the top of the stairs. Luka and I crouched near the top, carefully peaking through the spools of the dark, wooden banister. The room appeared to be an attic of some sort. Boxes were stacked high throughout the room and discarded furniture, covered with worn and dusty clothes were littered throughout the crowded space. Through the stacks of items I couldn't see any of the Vanir in the room, only heard their whispered conversation.

"We need to get out of here before they decide to come looking for us," a female voice said. Her voice was muffled, I assumed, from the mask she wore like the Vanir in the palace.

"The queen will long be occupied with the carnage. I'd like to watch and see it play out," a male voice responded. "I do like watching my prey squirm."

My blood boiled. My people were dead, *dead*, and he was looking forward to watching my reaction. A monster, he was a true monster. I removed the Vanir dagger from my side and gripped it tight. I'd delight in watching them bleed.

"Master said we're not to linger after the attack," the female responded.

Master.

So there was someone leading them.

"I'm going to move in closer, see if I can get a shot at them without them noticing us," Luka whispered as he drew a bow from his back. "You stay here and keep listening, see if you can hear anything else of importance." I nodded in approval and he was off, silently climbing through the piles of items.

"We're supposed to meet him at the rendezvous at dusk. We're already going to be late. I don't want to risk angering Master any further."

One of the males chuckled, the sound sending pinpricks down my spine. "Anger him? He's going to be delighted when he hears about how things transpired on our end."

On our end.

Did that mean their Master was somewhere here in Alethens? Had the head of the Vanir come to my doorstep without me even knowing? My fingers gripped the wooden ledge, it groaned under my lethal grip. I needed to get out of here. We needed to find out where their Master was hiding and end this once and for all.

I looked toward Luka, he was still silently creeping toward the voices. I could hardly see him through the items. We—

My eyes went wide as a hand clamped over my mouth. I made a move to elbow my assailant, but he was already two steps ahead of me. His other arm clamped around my body, pinning my arms to my sides as he hauled me up, pressing my back against his chest. He pressed into the pressure point on my wrist, causing my dagger to fall to the ground. I thrashed against him, screaming through his makeshift gag as he stood.

"If you scream, I'll slit your throat," he whispered as he removed his hand from my mouth and pressed a knife to my throat. I swallowed at the sting of the cold steel against my heated skin. He shifted his hold until my hands were pressed together in front of me, held together in his other hand, rendering my magic useless. *Fuck. How did I fail to notice his arrival?*

"It appears we have a spy on our hands," my assailant boomed as he climbed the remaining three stairs, announcing our arrival to the rest of the room.

"You've got to be shitting me," the female remarked as I came into view. Her chestnut eyes gleamed as she took me in, a cat-like smile forming on her lips. "The queen herself decided to pay us a visit?"

The other two males in the attic looked between one another at their companions' realization. "Are you serious? This is the queen we've heard so much about?"

"The one and only," I gritted out before I lurched forward as my assailant forced his knee into my back. My throat pressed further against the blade with the movement.

"I told you not to speak," he hissed. There was a roaring in my head as my blood dripped down my neck. I'd make the bastard paid for making me bleed.

"One of you find something to bind her with. She won't remain compliant for long." The female directed as she looked towards the males with wide eyes.

"We need something to keep her hands secured. I've heard her magic is powerful, I don't want to be on the receiving end," the female continued.

I couldn't help the smirk that fell on my lips. At least she was smart. Too bad she'd still have to die. My eyes flicked to where Luka remained hidden amongst the boxes as the other two males scrambled to find something to secure me with. Luka's eyes locked with mine, his arrow was nocked and ready, aimed right towards me. I dipped my chin lightly and his arrow flew.

The sound of the arrow moving through the air was the

only warning before Luka's arrow embedded itself in the shoulder of my assailant. The male screamed in pain, his grip on me coming loose. I caught myself in a crouch as he dropped me, palming a dagger in each hand as the other vampires readied their weapons, searching for the source of the arrow.

My daggers found purchase in the two males before they realized I had thrown them. They both cursed and hissed in pain and they bounded towards me. I looked around the room trying to find the female, but she was nowhere to be found.

I unsheathed the borrowed sword at my side as I stood. My magic recoiled at the unfamiliar weapon.

It will have to do for now.

Three more of Luka's arrows flew from where he remained hidden. The first two missed, but the last one found itself in my assailant's chest. A fourth arrow sliced through his throat. I turned before I could watch the first drop of blood pool and ran toward the remaining males.

I blocked the long-haired male's first blow, the impact pushing him back as I turned towards his friend as he attempted a move to my side with his blade. I stepped back, narrowly avoiding his sword as it nicked the side of my dress at my hip, a strip of tulle falling to the ground. His onyx eyes gleamed as he came towards me again.

This time I was prepared. I blocked his blow, our swords coming together in a violent clash of steel that reverberated through my body. I gritted my teeth as I tried to push him backward, but he didn't relent. I kicked out with my leg, hitting his knee and causing him to stumble as the other male bounded towards me again. Our blades clashed for several beats before we both took a step back, chests heaving as we assessed one another as the other male came and stood by his companions side.

"Look who else decided to make an appearance." The female's voice came from behind me. The blood in my veins turned to ice at the sight of her holding a blade to Luka's neck.

"We have the Blood Prince in our midst too, what a delightful surprise," she crooned.

I gritted my teeth. I'd kill her for touching him. I gripped my sword harder, the groves of the pommel now digging into my palm.

"Put the sword down, Your Highness and I'll let the prince go. It's you we want, not him."

My chest heaved. Whoever had provided intel to her on me didn't do their job very well if she thought I'd go without a fight.

"If you value your life at all, release Prince Luka, now," I demanded.

"You don't make the rules here, Queenie. We do." The long-haired male sneered. I narrowed my gaze on the male, still keeping my gaze on Luka out of the corner of my eye.

"Do you forget who you're talking to?" I arched a brow. "I am Lennox Adair, High Queen of Lethenia. I make the rules."

I struck. My blade sliced across the male's stomach before he had time to move. Luka used my distraction to get himself out of the female's hold, her blade clambering to the ground as he slammed his elbow into her neck.

As much as I wanted to see these Vanir bleed, we didn't have the time. I blocked the males next blow as a plan formed in my mind.

"Luka, shield yourself. *Now*," I called out as I summoned water to my fingertips. As soon as I sensed his magic I cast my own outwards towards the remaining three vampires in a wave. They coughed and sputtered as the water crested over them, soaking them from head to toe. As soon as my fist closed shut they froze, every drop of water coating their skin turning to solid ice. I took in their faces frozen in panic and ignored them.

It only takes one songbird to sing. My fingers danced before I closed my hands into fists tight enough that my nails bit into my palms. The two males encased in ice shattered into thousands of pieces. Several of the shards nicked me in the violent burst. I focused on the small sting of pain instead of what I had done.

"That's new," Luka commented as he moved around the frozen statue of the female. His boots crunching on the frozen remains of the males.

"I thought I'd switch it up a bit."

Had I actually done that?

"She should still be alive." I pushed my magic out, feeling for a life bond from her. "We only needed one of them to get the information we needed. I thought this would be the cleanest, and quickest way to get what we need." And she deserved a slow and painful death for thinking she could lay a hand on Luka.

Luka smiled, tucking a strand of hair behind my ear. "Smart thinking, Sweetheart."

I finally met his gaze, surprised not to find a hint of fear or horror in them. "You don't think it was too much?" I swallowed.

He shook his head, causing a dark lock of hair to fall across his face. "You're never too much, Lennox. You did what needed to be done." He brushed a thumb across my cheek. "I'm proud of you."

I laughed. "You're proud of me for smashing two males into a million pieces?"

"Yes." His voice was serious. "You exercised a lot of control towards people who had a hand in killing your people. You could have made their deaths much more painful, but you knew this wasn't the time for a long and painful revenge. So yes, Lennox, I'm proud of you."

Words evaded me. I didn't deserve him. *Too good. He was too good for me.* I leaned forward and placed a light kiss on his lips. "Thank you for saying that."

He nodded as he smiled. "Anytime, Sweetheart." He draped an arm around my shoulder as he led me towards the stairs.

"Let's go find Declan and tell him what we found. I'm sure he can find someone to transport her to the palace for us so we can have some fun."

I rolled my eyes. "You're calling torturing fun?"

"That's not the kind of fun I was thinking about."

I huffed a laugh as I swatted his chest. "You're terrible."

He held his hands in surrender. "Hey, I thought you might be in need of a distraction after all this." He winked as he continued guiding me towards the stairs. "I'm at your service for whatever you need me for, My Queen."

We found Declan outside immediately and filled him in on what had transpired in the building. He sent a small group of men right away to bring the female to the palace. I swore he almost smiled at the news of me turning the Vanir into living ice sculptures.

"Did you find any more information?" I asked Delcan after he had finished giving the order. He only shook his head, a lock of his long dark hair coming loose from its knot at the nape of his neck.

"It's strange. From what I can gather there are gaps in the guards schedule. Several guards who were supposed to be patrolling the city have been unaccounted for all day."

Where were all the guards? They were most likely missing at the gates too.

"Lennox! Luka!" I turned towards Nicos's voice as it rang out over the rubble, he appeared on his horse, making his way toward us. He quickly dismounted and made his way through the destroyed street.

"What is it?" Luka prodded.

Nico winced slightly. "Lorenzo is demanding you both come back to the palace."

"You've got to be fucking kidding me. If he thinks he can demand an audience with us at a time like this . . ." Luka snapped.

"He claims it's too dangerous for you to be here, and for him to remain in the Star Court. He wants to leave but he wants a word with you and Lennox before he does."

"I am not leaving my people to appease him right now." I planted my hands firmly on my hips.

Luka took a deep breath beside me. "Lennox, let's just go."

I whirled on him. "What? Are you seriously asking me to leave right now?"

He scrubbed a hand over his ash-streaked face. "I know it's not ideal, but it will only take a minute to talk to him and he will leave. He'll be out of our way and we won't have to worry about him anymore."

Fire raged in me at the gall of Lorenzo Rossi for making a demand of me like this. But Luka had a point, having him gone would be one less thing to worry about.

"I've got everything under control, Lennox," Declan said, placing his hand on my arm lightly. "There's not much more you can do here anyways, go deal with Lorenzo and take a bath and get some rest. I'll send word if we need you." Delcan's eyes were sincere as he spoke—sincere and *caring?* That was new.

"Fine," I conceded. He gets five minutes and that's it. I'm only doing it because I want him gone." And a bath did sound nice right now.

Luka nodded towards his friend. "Thank you."

Declan nodded, his eyes still soft as he took in the two of us with the most emotion I had never seen him emit in the months since I had met him.

"Yes, thank you, Declan."

His wings twitched in response to the small smile I gave him before I let Luka lead me back towards where we had left our horses.

I spared one last glance towards my city before turning back to the palace to face another form of destruction.

57

LENNOX

"Ahh, you're back."

We found Lorenzo in the ruined dining room. He was relaxed in a chair, legs propped on the table when we arrived. The gall of this male. My city had been attacked and he was acting like it was an inconvenience to him. The smell of burning flesh clung to my nostrils, and he was relaxing without a care in the world.

"Won't you sit and join me?" He gestured to the seats across from him at the destroyed table.

Luka and I sat. I only did so for fear my legs might give out from under me if I didn't.

"I do wish you would have bathed before joining me," Lorenzo said, wrinkling his nose at the two of us. I shook with anger, my jaw clenched as Luka placed a hand on my thigh.

"You have five minutes of my time before I leave and go back to my people," I gritted.

He drained the rest of his glass before sitting upright in his chair. Most of the glasses lay in shards on the table and floor, but he had managed to find one that had survived.

"Fine, I'll cut to the chase. You have failed to provide us with what we want."

"Then maybe you should be more specific with what you are looking for." I tried my best to keep my voice devoid of emotion and keep my stewing anger at bay.

Lorenzo narrowed his eyes towards Luka. "You told her."

Luka stiffened beside me.

"Your grandfather will be disappointed to hear that, boy." He shook his head, his inky hair swishing around his face with the movement. "But clearly, you failed." He looked between the two of us. "Unless you *did* manage to find the book?"

A solid hand landed on my thigh, squeezing lightly. I peered at Luka out of the corner of my eye, he still faced forward as his thumb started brushing a path on my thigh.

"We haven't found the book, but we have come up with an alternative."

Lorenzo clicked his tongue. "Care to enlighten me, boy?"

I moved my hand underneath the table, linking my fingers with Luka's. I glanced at him, *I'm not going anywhere*, his eyes said as he squeezed my hand. I squeezed back before turning my attention back to Lorenzo.

"We have come up with an alternative to the book." Luka's voice was steady and sure. "Lennox and I have developed a strong relationship during my time here. We believe that if we demonstrate to the rest of Lethenia that a relationship between the Star Court and Blood Court is flourishing it will start to heal the unrest that has been festering across the continent when it comes to the vampires."

Lorenzo speared a piece of meat and brought it to his mouth as he mulled over our proposal. How he managed to find food in these circumstances . . .

"That has potential," he said, and I felt the weight pressing on my chest lighten. "But we need more than just a *friendship* between our courts. A marriage would seal the deal entirely. Unexpected that you, Your Majesty, would come to this conclusion of your own."

My blood froze. *A marriage would seal the deal.*

No. No. *No.* This wasn't happening.

Everything I had done to prevent this from happening was all for nothing. My head swam. How had I been so naive? Offering a *friendship* when a marriage was on the table in the first place . . . I had walked myself right into his trap.

"It appears you were successful after all, boy."

My head snapped in Lorenzo's direction. "What do you mean?" I asked.

Lorenzo smiled. "My nephew was always good at turning on the charm, although I didn't expect you to fall so quickly for it, Your Majesty. He will make an excellent High King, don't you think?"

The ground slid out from underneath me as his words registered in my mind.

Luka threw Lorenzo a look. "That's not how we arrived here." He looked to me. "Lennox, let me explain."

Something inside me cracked at those words.

Silently, I slid my hand from his. "I don't want to hear it. Not here. Not now," I muttered under my breath.

I let him in. I trusted him. Was everything between us a lie? A ploy to get me to like him so I'd easily agree to marry him when the opportunity arose? I slipped my shaking hands under my thighs. My emotions, my magic, *everything* was bubbling to the surface, ready to explode. This, this on top of everything else today . . . *too much* it was all too much.

But I was Lennox Adair, High Queen of Lethenia and I would not show these males weakness. I forced my emotions back down as I took several deep breaths. *A few more minutes.* I needed to hold on for a few more minutes before I could explode. But right now I couldn't be the naive girl who fell for Luka's charms. Who fell for a *vampire's* charm? *Goddess, how could I have been so senseless?*

Every fiber of my being wanted to argue against this fate for myself, but as the conversation wore on Luka's gaze bore into the side of my face. Begging me to look at him. I couldn't. I wouldn't. I feared what would happen if I looked into those piercing blue eyes.

"It doesn't have to be you, you could offer your sister instead."

"No." Kara would have no part in this. "I will marry your nephew." The words felt like sandpaper in my throat. *Your nephew.* I didn't dare mutter his name or I might fully crack.

"Lennox."

I ignored Luka's whisper. He reached for my hand again, but I moved it out of his reach.

"Perfect. We will keep in touch, the Blood Court will throw an engagement party of sorts to celebrate the happy couple."

I nodded, the words hardly registering. My brain swam with the consequences of what I had agreed to. I had agreed to an arranged marriage—walked myself into a trap of my own making. The only way out would end in war—that was the only alternative now. I felt tears threatening to spill down my cheeks. I took a deep breath, hoping my voice would come out steadier than I felt.

"If you will excuse me, I need to return to my people."

Lorenzo only nodded and I refused to meet Luka's gaze as I stood from my chair.

"Safe travels."

"Lennox," Luka whispered. Every fiber in my being wanted to meet his gaze. To let him support me. He had become that person to me. The person who I looked to during times of need. How could I need the person that caused me this pain in the first place? I turned and left the dining room without looking back.

The second the doors closed behind me I took off running towards the training center. I couldn't turn to Luka anymore, so I reverted to my only other coping mechanism. Fighting.

Tears slew from my eyes and I ran towards the training center. My dress tangled in my legs as I ran through the woods, the blood-soaked skirt snagging on fallen branches.

I grabbed a handful of daggers and headed for the target before the door could shut behind me.

The first blade hit the target with a thump. *How could he?*

The second blade flew from my hand. *I trusted him.*

Another blade. *I'm having an arranged marriage.*

A sob tore from my chest as my dagger hit the center target. *My city. My people.*

My vision blurred as tears fell down my face splattering on the floor beneath my feet. The sound reminded me of the sound of Enric's blood dripping on the marble floor.

People were dead because of me. *Enric* was dead because of me. I was distracted. I should have been better prepared. I should have known they'd come after me, but I was too distracted. *Goddess.* Too distracted fucking Luka to worry about my people. How could I do this? How did I let this happen?

I had given Luka everything I had. Every broken part of me and . . . my fractured heart that had started to piece itself back together was back in pieces. The pain was unbearable as the broken shards pieced my flesh. The blade that had found the center of the target felt like it had embedded itself in my heart instead.

58

LUKA

I excused myself from the dining room as quickly as I could. My uncle tried to insist. I stay and celebrate my new future, *my engagement*, with him before he left, but I needed to find Lennox. I saw the look on her face when she realized what I had kept from her. I knew it had broken her. *I* had broken her.

It was never supposed to come to this.

I knew how Lennox felt about an arranged marriage, but I still went along with everything. I chose to keep this from her, and I hated myself for it. *Find the book.* My grandfather had instructed. *Charm her in the process. Perhaps she will fall for you and agree to marry you without us having to force her hand.* I had abandoned any hope of charming her upon first meeting Lennox and banished any thought of it in the weeks following as I got to know her.

The moment she realized I kept information from her I saw her building her walls back up. The walls I had spent months slowly and steadily trying to break down, brick by brick, until she finally let me in.

She put her mask back on and played the role of queen and that was the only thing keeping me from running after her the second she left the room. She didn't want my uncle to see her weakness. That *I* was her weakness. And I wouldn't let him see it either.

Once I finally escaped I took off running towards the training facility. I knew with certainty that's where she'd be.

I found her there, sweat beading on her ash-covered forehead, swinging her sword with intensity. She was so focused she didn't even notice me arriving.

"Lennox."

She swiveled towards me at the sound of her name. Sword still raised. The ferocity in her red-rimmed eyes softened as she met mine. Her shoulders relaxed, but then she remembered. Her gaze turned icy as it pinned me in place.

"What are you doing here?" she spat. The tone in her voice was one I hadn't heard in months. Not since I first arrived.

"Lennox, please let me explain." I reached for her, only for her to recoil, taking two steps back. The knot in my stomach tightened.

"There's nothing for you to explain, Your Highness."

I had never heard her speak with such disdain.

"You lied to me," she hissed.

"I didn't lie."

She cocked her head to the side. "Fine, you willingly withheld information from me, but I don't see a difference."

I winced as her words hit me. "Yes, I knew it was a possibility we would have to get married, but I never thought it would come to this. I was confident that we would find the book and avoid all this."

"You withheld information, *important* information I had every right to know." She placed her sword back on the rack and picked up a handful of daggers.

"You're right. I'm sorry." She threw a dagger. Hitting the center of the target.

"The thing is—" she paused, still facing the target, not so much as glancing in my direction. "I understand why you didn't tell me at first. It would have done nothing to thaw the relationship between us." She threw another dagger, brushing back loose hair from her face with the back of her arm. "But . . . when things started to change between us." She released a shuddering breath. "You should have told me. You had every opportunity to tell me."

She paused before throwing the next dagger. "I trusted you."

My heart splintered at the wobble in her voice.

"I let you in and I trusted you and you broke my trust."

I could hear the anger building with every word. The sadness faded with every dagger she threw.

"Not only was I blindsided in there by your uncle, but I was blindsided by *you*." She finally turned to me, tears rimmed her eyes as she pushed a finger forcefully into my chest. "You're supposed to be on my side. I thought I was *yours*."

I thought I was yours.

Was.

My chest constricted. I had truly fucked up.

"How am I supposed to trust that what happened between us was real?" The words came out a whisper. "How am I supposed to believe anything between us was real and not you playing me with the hope I'd agree to marry you without a fight? How do I know this wasn't your plan all along? Offer our relationship as a solution knowing it would end in an arranged marriage anyway."

"Lennox——" I reached for her, but she brushed out of my grasp. "It was real. All of it was real. Every second of it. You know how deeply I care about you. Lennox, I'm yours."

"You knew." Her green eyes softened. "You knew what it meant to me, to have this one thing I could choose in my life. You knew and you didn't tell me. You took away the one choice I had for myself. Like every other choice in my life, this has been taken away too."

I had thought about telling her about my grandfather's plans the night of the ball, while we were laying under the stars, but I didn't want to ruin our fragile alliance at the time. Why I didn't tell her any of the times after that—I don't know. I hoped it would never come to this. That I'd never have to tell her because I clung to the hope she might pick me for herself, without an arranged marriage hanging over our heads.

"I'll do whatever I can to earn back your trust. Fuck, Lennox, I'm sorry. What can I do to get you to trust me again?" I ran my fingers through my hair. It was taking everything in me not to reach for her. To grab her. To pull her into my arms. Anything to ease the pain in her eyes. The pain I had caused her.

She closed her eyes, taking a deep breath before she spoke. "I don't think there's anything you can do that will ever make me trust you again." She was closing herself off again. Letting anger and sadness take over. Leaning back into the darkness. I wouldn't allow it.

Another dagger flew towards the target. I didn't see where it landed, I was too focused on Lennox. I needed her to look at me. To see on my face how truly sorry I was.

"We should have anticipated the Vanir attack tonight."

Goddess the Vanir, I had forgotten about the attack after the events in the ballroom.

"My people died because I was too distracted by you. I was too busy *fucking you* instead of protecting my people and doing my job."

I winced. Lennox has a bigger heart than anyone, I knew those losses would weigh heavily on her. But guilt—she had no reason to feel guilty.

"Lennox, you know that's not true. Even if we had anticipated their attack there is no way we would have been able to anticipate that explosion. You know that," I argued.

"It doesn't matter now. It's too late. I can't go back and save them now." A tear slipped loose, she brushed it away with the back of her hand.

I reached for her, lightly grasping her wrist and she turned towards me. She stared at the floor, not meeting my eyes.

"Don't shut me out, Lennox." I took her chin in my hands.

She let me tip her head up to meet my eyes. Where there was hard steel minutes earlier, there was now sadness in her tear-lined eyes.

"I know you care about me," I rasped. A tear slipped from her eye, and I wiped it away with my thumb as her lower lip trembled.

"Maybe I did but not anymore."

My heart cracked fully now, but I refused to let her shut me out so quickly. I would do anything to make this up to her. To earn her trust again. However long it took—I needed her to know how much I cared about her. What lengths I would go to to make this right. I couldn't lose her.

"Lennox, I lov—" The words died in my throat as Lennox knocked my arm from her chin and shoved me against the wall. She pushed her body against mine, pinning me in place as her arm banded across my chest, her dagger pressed to my throat.

"Don't you dare say those words," she growled out.

"Just because you won't let me say them doesn't mean they're not true."

I felt the tip of her dagger pierce my skin. A trail of warm blood running down my neck. Part of me thought she might slit my neck. Let me die for the pain I caused her, and I would let her. Time and time again I would bleed for her if it meant it took away even an ounce of the pain I caused her.

Lennox released me and took two steps back. She didn't meet my gaze as she tilted her gaze above my head instead.

"Lennox—"

Her eyes flicked up to meet mine and for a split second, I saw a glimpse of the person I had fallen in love with. But in a second she was gone and instead, I found the cold gaze of my High Queen.

"You need to leave."

"I'm not leaving until we figure this out." I reached for her and she shrugged out of my grasp.

"I need you to go home, Luka." My name was nothing but a whisper on her lips. A plea, not a demand.

"I'm not going anywhere without you, Lennox." She crossed her arms over her chest. "I meant what I said. I'm not ready to leave you."

"Well, I'm ready for you to leave me, now." Her words were devoid of all emotion. She was back to the queen I had met all those months ago who refused to let others in. "As your queen, I command you to leave and return to your court."

I shook my head. "For fucks sake, Lennox. Don't do this."

She set her shoulders, tipping her chin up—appearing as the queen everyone knew her as. Not the female I had come to love.

"Failure to follow my order will be considered treason."

59

LENNOX

Luka's face crumpled as the words left my lips. It broke yet another shattered piece of me. I couldn't look at him anymore. I knew his broken expression would haunt my dreams.

If he failed to follow a direct order from the queen I could have him sent to the dungeon. Or killed.

I was starting to think I'd never be able to repair myself after this. Part of me didn't want to. I wanted to embrace this pain to prevent myself from ever letting anyone in again.

I looked down slightly to glance at Luka, defeat was written across his features along with an expression I had never seen before.

It was cruel to order him to leave, but I needed him gone. I needed space. I needed time.

Because I was going to have to marry him.

I was afraid if he stayed he'd be able to convince me to let him back in. And I couldn't do that.

Luka turned to leave, but he stopped halfway to the door, turning to face me again.

"You might not want to fight for us Lennox, but I will. And I will never stop fighting for you. I will fight for you, for *us*, Lennox Adair."

I sucked in a breath.

"I meant it when I told you, it's you and me until the stars turn to dust, Sweetheart."

What was left of my fractured heart crumpled. The moment the door shut behind him I let the sob building in my chest out and I fell to the floor.

I cried until no more tears were left to fall.

I don't know how much time had passed when Kara found me on the training center floor. My eyes felt swollen, my dress was stained with tears, blood, and ash. There was now a hollow hole in my chest where my heart had once been. I was certain now there were only two small slivers of it left. One for Kara and one for my people. Every other part was now gone, never to be recovered.

Kara didn't say a word as she picked me up off the floor. She slung an arm around me and led me back towards the palace. The world around me felt fuzzy. Nothing seemed real. I didn't even remember making it to my bedchamber. Or Kara helping me out of my dress and into the tub.

Nothing felt real. Today felt like a dream.

A nightmare.

A nightmare I would never wake up from.

Kara turned off the lights and crawled into the bed behind me, wrapping her arms around me as he pulled the blankets over us.

"Go to sleep, Len," she whispered into the darkness. "I love you."

She didn't offer me platitudes. She was simply there. Somehow Kara always knew what I needed. Her and Luka, they both knew how to take care of me. But now it was only Kara and I again. The thought gave me a sense of deja vu.

The tears started falling again. This time they were silent as they tracked down my cheeks and soaked the sheets. I don't know if I was crying because I missed my parents, or because I missed Luka. Or maybe it was both. I told myself I was never going to let this happen again. I never wanted to feel like this again.

Eventually sleep found me. Only to wake a while later, a scream lodged in my throat from a nightmare.

60

LUKA

I looked over my shoulder as Alethens faded behind me. I had left the palace as Lennox had commanded me to.

If she hadn't used her power as queen to make me leave I wouldn't have left. I felt like I was leaving a piece of me behind. I was leaving a piece of me behind. I was leaving Lennox behind.

I loved her.

I knew that now. I had been slowly falling in love with her since the moment she first insulted me. I meant what I said when I left her in the training facility. I would never stop fighting for her. Fighting for us.

But I caught her sobs when I left—the sound of her body crashing to the floor. It took everything in me not to rush back in and gather her in my arms. To kiss away her tears.

But she didn't want me there.

So I sat outside. Listening to her sobs until Kara arrived. Only then did I leave.

I wanted nothing more than to right what I had wronged with Lennox, but after hearing her break down, because of me —I was starting to wonder if it was the right thing to do. Lennox's heart was fragile to begin with, and I broke it. She trusted me with the fragile parts of herself and I broke them further. I worried she'd never be able to repair what I broke.

What I shattered.

Maybe it was best if I stayed away. The thought of hurting her again was unbearable. I'd find the book myself. I'd find us a way out of this arranged marriage. I had already broken her enough, I could do her this one good thing.

I might not be able to have Lennox Adair, but I knew I would never stop loving her. She was woven into the threads of my being. She could never love me after what I did to her.

But I would make Lennox Adair happy again, even if it meant I wasn't there to see it.

END BOOK 1

ACKNOWLEDGMENTS

I'm going to be upfront—this is probably going to be long and emotional because I have so many amazing people to thank. After all, I would not be here without them.

First and foremost, thank you to my parents. You have loved and supported me in every aspect of my life, including when I decided to do something crazy like write and publish a book. I am so incredibly grateful for you both.

Mom, you showed me what it looked like to love reading from a young age and encouraged my love of books and you still do today. From that love of books sprung a love of writing, which led me here. Dad, I truly believe that you saw me as a writer before I ever did. Every time you asked me to help you write or edit something for the fire department it fed my little writer's heart, even back then. It may seem insignificant, but when I'm doubting myself as a writer those are some of the moments I think back on to remind myself that I am a writer. And that I have been for a long time.

To my siblings, Josiah, Jaden, and Ellie, my relationship with the three of you is what inspired the sibling relationships in this book (the good parts, not the traumatic parts of course). I love you three with my whole heart.

To the rest of my friends and family who have been nothing but supportive to me since I told you I wrote a book—I cannot express how much your support of my dream means to me.

To my gurls, Emily and Hannah. Where would I be without your friendship keeping me sane? Thank you for calling me out on my bullshit, holding me accountable, telling me when I'm being too mean, and just putting up with me in general. I love you both to the moon and Saturn. And Emily, you were one of the first people I told I was writing a book, thank you for not laughing in my face and telling me I was crazy.

To Emily and Abby, my besties for the resties, who knows how many hours you've spent on Marco Polo listening to me drag on and on about this book? Thank you for never telling me to stop (at least to my face) and being so excited and supportive of me along this journey. How'd I get so lucky to have you two by my side?

To Elise, my best friend of over twenty years. When I told you I was writing a book you said, "I always knew you would," you have no idea what those words meant to me.

To my beta readers, this book would not be possible without your feedback and support. Thank you so much for investing in me and this story. You truly helped me make this book what it is today.

To my editor, Caitlin, thank you for helping me make this book the best version of itself, I couldn't have done this without you. To my cover designer Bianca and map artist, Lindsey, thank you both so much for helping me bring this story to life.

To my ARC readers, thank you so much for taking a chance on me. I am continually overwhelmed by your excitement over wanting to read my book baby. Your support means the world to me.

To the book community, I would not be here, writing this, if it were not for you all. You gave me the hope and inspiration that I could do this and then blew me away with your support when I told you I did. When I joined the book community I never thought I'd make friends, but I did. I'm so incredibly thankful for all of my book besties.

Thank you to Taylor Swift, your music was in the background more times than not while writing Lennox's story. It drove me, inspired me, and gave me the dance party breaks I needed while writing and editing.

To my dog Leia, who cannot read, but still deserves acknowledgment. She gave up a lot of cuddles while I was writing, but she stayed curled up by my side the entire time. She still needs to learn that when there's a laptop on my lap she can't lay on me, but there are plenty more books to come for her to learn that lesson.

Lastly, thank you, reader. Thank you for taking a chance on me, my book, and my characters. It means more than you will ever know.

AUTHORS NOTE

Writing a book has always been a dream of mine. Even so, while writing Queen of Blood and Stardust I doubted myself constantly. I felt like I didn't have the right to write a book even though my love of writing had always been woven into who I was. Even when the words were pouring onto the pages day after day and nothing had ever felt so right—I still doubted myself. It took me a lot of months of spiraling to realize that this was something I could do. That I had a right to write and publish a book.

Part of it probably had to do with that when I dreamed of writing a book I never imagined it would be in the form of a fantasy romance novel that I would write in my twenties. I always told myself I wasn't creative enough to write fantasy romance. That my brain didn't work that way.

But on November 15, 2022, I sat to jot down the idea for a fantasy romance book that had come to me the night before while I was trying to fall asleep. It didn't stop with that one sentence. The ideas started flowing and I never stopped writing. Still haven't.

That idea was the catalyst that changed my life.

When I imagined writing a fantasy book (right before I told

myself I didn't have the mind for that) I always thought it would be a modern fantasy and the male MC would be the morally grey asshole that I was always drawn to in other books.

Queen of Blood and Stardust is not that book. I truly believe that Lennox's story has been waiting inside me, waiting for me to write it for so long. How else do I explain how this story just started pouring out of me? Lennox's story didn't fit into the book I thought I wanted to write. Just like the male main character I had dreamt up wasn't who Lennox needed. So I created Luka instead and let the story unfold from there. I ended up writing a story that I am so incredibly proud of.

When I got the idea idea for Queen of Blood and Stardust it was centered around a girl who had suffered a lot. She had already come into her immense power, but she had recently stepped into a new role. She was very lonely, but she was strong. The very first scene I visualized was her welcoming someone new into her court.

That scene made it into the final draft.

ABOUT THE AUTHOR

Kaitlyn has always loved writing. Writing a book has been a dream of hers forever, she just never imagined that dream would come true in her twenties in the form of a fantasy romance novel. Queen of Blood and Stardust is Kaitlyn's debut novel.

When Kaitlyn isn't writing she enjoys relaxing by one of Minnesota's Great Lakes with her golden retriever Leia by her side and Taylor Swift playing in the background.

Follow along with what she's doing next
kaitlynswansonbooks.com